Faster Pastor

Sharyn McCrumb's

other novels include

Once Around the Track

St. Dale

The Ballad Series

Devil Amongst the Lawyers

Ghost Riders

The Songcatcher

The Ballad of Frankie Silver

The Rosewood Casket

She Walks These Hills

The Hangman's Beautiful Daughter

If Ever I Return, Pretty Peggy-O

Foggy Mountain Breakdown and Other Stories

Faster Pastor

a novel

Sharyn McCrumb
Adam Edwards

Ingalls Publishing Group, Inc
PO Box 2500
Banner Elk, NC 28694
www.ingallspublishinggroup.com

This book is a work of fiction.
Names, characters, places and incidents are either the product of the authors' imaginations or are used fictitiously, and any resemblence to any person, living or dead, business establishments, events or locales is entirely coincidental.

Front cover image from a photo by
Norbert Van Grondelle

Book design by
Judith Foster Geary

Library of Congress Cataloging-in-Publication Data

McCrumb, Sharyn -
Faster pastor : a novel / Sharyn McCrumb, Adam Edwards.
p. cm.
ISBN 978-1-932158-88-5 (hardcover : alk. paper)
1. Stock car drivers--Fiction. 2. Clergy--Fiction. 3. Stock car racing--Fiction. 4. Tennessee--Fiction. 5. Inheritance and succession--Fiction. I. Edwards, Adam, 1980- II. Title.
PS3563.C3527F37 2010
813'.54--dc22
2009047560

Manufactured in the USA
First printing April 1, 2010

Acknowledgments

The authors would like to thank Bob and Barbara Ingalls of Ingalls Publishing Group, who believed in this book and understood its premise, and our editor Judith Geary, whose grace and enthusiasm transformed the project into an adventure. We are also grateful to all the experts who were generous with their time and expertise, enabling us to craft a story with so many disparate parts, from rock guitars to Mexican slang to police procedure to serpent handling.

Our special thanks to: Lt. J.A. Nieuhaus-Kettering, OH P.D.; Oregon Deputy Sheriff Spencer Arrowood; Watauga County Asst. DA Gail Fannon; Professor Carmen Tesser and Sr. Uriel Paras Hernandez, who were the godparents of the character Jèsus Segovia; musician Richard Cunningham who was our director of church music; and Father Paul D. Williams, Jr., who drag races GTO's, and who was both kind and informative in our interview. The late Appalachian scholar and folklorist Dr. John D. Richards helped in the creation of Travis Prichard and his congregation, and we mourn his passing.

Adam Edwards: I would like to thank my coauthor Sharyn for her wonderful guidance and collaboration in this journey of writing a novel, without her patience and vision for the story I most certainly would have been lost. My older sister Hanna deserves credit for helping me learn how to read when I was little. It didn't come naturally for me, so thank you, and I really wish we'd had time for you to teach me how to spell. I would also like to thank my Mother for constantly making me think this was a worthwhile project. I think she would encourage me in anything that I didn't have to travel at 200 mph to do.

I would like to thank Brennan Shepard, for years of support as Crew Chief in my racing endeavors in the Pure Stock, Late Model and Truck divisions. Without the fun we had in those first years of racing, I wouldn't have been foolish enough to continue pursuing such a lofty dream.

Sharyn McCrumb: Thanks to Adam for the adventure of writing this book, including the ridealong he gave me at Lowe's Motor Speedway at 170 mph, but especially thanks for having the discipline and perseverance to finish what we started—a rare trait in a novice author. He was a joy to work with. The enthusiasm and support of my circle of NASCAR friends—both the fans and the famous—was invaluable to me in the completion of this project, and I thank them all for their friendship and their faith in this endeavor.

Faster Pastor

Chapter One
Pushing up Daisies

The *black car was still behind him, right on his tail, just where it had been for the last fifteen minutes. He didn't know what would be worse – speeding up on this winding Tennessee mountain road or letting the black car catch up with him, although now that he thought about it, the end result would probably be the same either way.*

He speeded up.

Pajan Mosby clutched the scrap of poem in her hand, and tried to concentrate on Reverend Bartlett's eulogy, so that she wouldn't miss her cue. She had been a bit surprised that in his carefully outlined funeral instructions, old Jimmy Powell had requested that she read a poem, but she didn't mind. He had been a nice old fellow, already elderly when she was a child. She remembered him as a great favorite with the neighborhood kids, always up for sandlot baseball or a fishing expedition to the river. He had outlived his family before his heart finally gave out in his ninetieth year, but he certainly didn't lack for mourners. Most of the town had turned out for the graveside service, and the pallbearers, Jimmy's old cronies, all wore caps emblazoned with "3" or "24" or "8," a nod to Jimmy's love of NASCAR. Someone had remarked that it was good that he'd be buried facing the highway so that he could watch the cars go by.

It was a pretty spot to spend eternity in, she thought. A rolling meadow dotted with wild daisies and shade trees, all visible from the road above, which skirted the valley on a little ridge cut into the side of the mountain. And a few hundred yards off to the right was the river, where one long ago summer Jimmy had taught her to skip stones across the surface of the water.

She blinked, feeling the sting of tears. No, she mustn't get all maudlin at poor old Jimmy's funeral. He'd expect her to read his poem in a loud clear voice with no sissy blubbering to spoil his send-off. She could almost hear his voice admonishing her: *Anybody what totes a gun to work didn't ought to be crying at the funeral of someone who went when he was good and ready.* She would do him proud.

Everyone was looking at her, and she suddenly realized that Rev. Bartlett had stopped speaking, and was making faces at her. Obviously, she had missed her cue. Pajan nodded to show that she understood, and stepped up in front of the row of wreaths that flanked the coffin.

"Jimmy asked me to read this," she told the assembled mourners, as she unfolded the paper. "It's a poem. I think he wrote it himself." Surely. She cleared her throat and began in a clear, stilted voice,

When the Angel drops the checkered flag
And says my race is run…

He was a much better driver than the guy in the black car. Indeed, that fact had long been one of the central tenets of his self-esteem, but now, despite a good five minutes' head start about twenty miles back, he was being overtaken by his nemesis, on a steep, winding road where pulling over was not an option. That hardly mattered, though. He had a pretty good idea that the driver of the black car was in no mood for a civilized resolution. He dipped the right side wheels off the road on the inside of the turn and then swung wide with the left wheels onto the yellow line to block the black car in case he was crazy enough to try to pass on this two-lane corkscrew. Another tap on his bumper impelled him to speed up again – doing eighty now, which, according to that triangular yellow sign, was about twice the speed recommended by the Tennessee Department of Highways …

Almost finished now, thought Pajan.
And when I see the finish line
Before the Pearly Gate,
I'll take my place in Victory Lane
Where Dale and Davy wait …

The assembled mourners started to scream and run, and Pajan looked up from her typescript, thinking that the poem hadn't been all that bad. And then she saw it, too: a white car had left the road at the curve and was sailing through the air – straight for them. The shrieking crowd scattered, heading for the shelter of the nearest grove of trees, well away from the trajectory of the airborne car, and from there they watched what happened next.

The soaring car seemed to hang in the air for a long moment, and then it thumped to the ground, uprooting a swath of daisies a few yards from the casket, skidding forward, scattering metal folding chairs, until the nose of the car touched the row of wreaths a foot away from the coffin itself.

In the silence that followed, one of the pallbearers called out, "That Jimmy Powell damn sure knew how to stage a funeral!"

Chapter Two
Unavoidably Detained

The moonfaced policeman peered anxiously through the bars. "You're sure you're not hurt?"

"Hurt," said Cameron Berkley, "is a relative term."

The cop, whose name badge read *Westcott*, grinned. "'Course I reckon you're used to spectacular wrecks."

Also a relative term, thought Camber, leaning back on the thin mattress covering the metal shelf that his jailer laughingly called a bed. It was true that he had experienced his share of automotive acrobatics. Once at Talladega he had gone airborne at 200 mph, and the car had spiraled through the air like a football before it settled upside-down in the infield grass. But as dramatic as those NASCAR wrecks had looked on slow-motion replay, they probably weren't as dangerous as the header he'd taken this afternoon off that Tennessee mountain road. In racing, he wore a fire resistant suit and a complex array of seat belts and harnesses. He sat in a custom-made seat that fit his body like a glove, and the seat itself was encased in a steel roll cage, all designed to protect the driver from just such deadly contingencies as aerial ballet. Today, though, all he'd had between him and eternity was a seat belt. The fact that he landed in a cemetery was probably a cosmic joke—just to underscore the warning about race car drivers who treat two-lane mountain roads as if they were super speedways. Point taken.

He was too proud to admit it to the inquisitive officer, but in truth, he was somewhat the worse for wear after his unscheduled crash landing. The seat belt had done its job well enough, but he still had sore shoulder muscles and a headache that felt suspiciously like a concussion.

"It sure was providential you crashing old Jimmy Powell's funeral," said Westcott. "A race car driver, you say. Imagine that."

Resolutely ignoring the throbbing at his temples, Camber tried to make small talk with the officer who was, after all, the person who would bring his dinner and should be encouraged not to spit in it. "The deceased was a NASCAR fan, was he?"

"Sure was. You should see the collection of racing memorabilia he left behind. Dates all the way back to the 'Forties. Why, he's got stuff there signed by Roy Hall."

Camber, who did not even date back to the 'Seventies, thought he might have heard of Roy Hall, but through the pounding of the headache he couldn't quite place him. "That's nice," he murmured.

"I expect you'd know all about that old stuff Jimmy had in his collection, bein' a race car driver yourself."

Camber closed his eyes, because he knew what was coming next. When people found out that he was a driver, they invariably asked three questions. *How fast can you go?* (Depended on the track and the car; roughly 200 mph.) *How much does it cost to race a car?* (If you have to ask, you definitely cannot afford it.) And *How do you get started in racing?* Which wasn't a short answer question. He had never managed to condense his entire life story into a sound bite.

Besides, since he was sitting there in a jail cell, shouldn't they be talking about his one allotted phone call or the availability of a lawyer, or bail or something?

Officer Westcott cleared his throat, "Say, fella, How fast can—"

* * *

Camber stretched out on the metal bunk, thinking that it was good thing he was used to being uncomfortable, because this cell was as spartan as they came. Like a really big roll cage, he told himself. The town jail was a two-cell affair tucked away behind a solid steel door in a corridor inside the police department. A small rectangular window in the steel door allowed an officer to peer in at the prisoners without actually having to go into the cell block. There was a metal toilet attached to the wall of his cell, but no privacy and no sink. Good thing he was a race car driver. He was used to not having to pee for hours at a time. Of course, it helped that the temperature in a stock car was around a hundred and twenty degrees, so that you sweated instead of peeing. The cell was uncomfortably warm, but nowhere near hot enough to alleviate the problem. He decided that his best option was to try to sleep until they let him out for a hearing, or for whatever was going to come next. It wasn't easy to sleep with this possible concussion doing a drum solo in his head, but even the semblance of a nap would be better than having to conduct a NASCAR seminar for a bored cop.

"Where is that redneck moron who ruined Jimmy's funeral?"

Even Westcott, with a gun in his holster, looked a little shaken at the sound of that imperious voice. In the doorway stood a small dark-haired young woman whose expression suggested that it would take tranquilizer darts to subdue her.

Camber didn't remember seeing the woman before, but since she was definitely dressed for a funeral, he had a pretty good idea who the "redneck moron" was. He waggled his fingers at her through the bars.

"You!" Ignoring Westcott, she marched up to the cell door and peered in at him. "Have you sobered up yet?"

"I was not inebriated," said Camber truthfully.

"Ha! That's a crock. You came sailing off the highway like—*inebriated?"*

"Well, intoxicated if you prefer," said Camber, belatedly wondering if there were some legal distinction between the two terms. "Anyhow, I wasn't."

Seeing the look of astonishment on Pajan Mosby's face, Westcott chuckled and jerked his thumb in Camber's direction. "Talks just like *NPR*, don't he?"

Distracted from her rage, she nodded slowly. It wasn't just the five-syllable word, certainly non-standard vocabulary for jailhouse drunks. It was also the accent—or the lack of one, and the prisoner's urbane assurance that he was equal to anything he would encounter in a small-town lock-up. Her eyes narrowed. "I thought you claimed to be a race car driver."

"Now I *am* guilty of that," said Camber affably.

She glanced back at Westcott. "What's his name?"

"Cameron Berkley. Says so on his Virginia driver's license, too."

She gave him a wry smile. "So he's *not* claiming to be Jeff Gordon, then?"

Camber patted his cheeks in mock alarm. "I don't look that old, do I?" he said. "Gordon's got ten years on me, at least! Although, this *has* been a rough day." She obviously didn't know much about racing, he thought. Jeff Gordon was a good eight inches shorter than Camber, and much lighter in coloring. Camber liked to think of himself as a younger, thinner, better-looking version of Tony Stewart, but this hardly seemed like the time to play image consultant.

Her suspicious glare returned as she peered at him through the bars. "Who *are* you?"

"Ca-me-ron Berkley," The prisoner's frown suggested concern for his interrogator's short-term memory. "My friends call me Camber. But if you won't believe this nice policeman or the DMV of the Commonwealth of Virginia on the subject of my identity, I'm sure it's no use *my* telling you."

The angry young woman regarded him thoughtfully, and wrinkled her nose as if—metaphorically, anyhow—she smelled a rat. "You *do* talk funny," she announced.

Camber raised his eyebrows. "I beg your pardon?"

"Exactly!" She nodded triumphantly. "Most of the race car drivers we have around here would've said '*Whut?*' So would most of the NASCAR Cup drivers, for that matter. But *you* talk like a TV anchorman. Big words. Broadcast accent. And yet you came off the highway at a hundred miles an hour and managed to control the car well enough to avoid a whole field full of people, and you claim you're a race car driver, which I almost believe, because I know what *Camber* means."

He perked up. She knew what *camber* meant? Was she a racing fan? His momentary elation subsided, though, because her forbidding expression told him that even if Dale Earnhardt, Jr. showed up to bail him out in person, *which was not happening*, this woman would still think he was pond scum.

Her scowl deepened. "So, what gives?"

Camber sighed. Here it came. The story of his life. "With all due respect, ma'am," he said, "That is a two-aspirin question, and besides, I think I really should be talking to a lawyer, or, at the very least, to a bail bondsman."

Through the clanging of his headache, he heard them laughing.

The story of his life in a sound bite? That was easy.

I was the Falls Church redneck.

Most people just blinked at him in total incomprehension when he said that, but nonetheless it was fundamentally true. Cameron Berkley—in those days, years away from being known as "Camber"—had been born within a Metro ride of D.C., the only child of an ordinary suburban Beltway couple—two nice college-educated people with dull, respectable government jobs, who did *not* watch NASCAR, or listen to country music, or eat possum. They had gotten divorced, of course, when Cameron was seven, but that only made him all the more average in Beltway society. Nobody expected anything else these days.

Cameron had been raised by his mom in an ordinary brick house in a genteel Falls Church neighborhood, where he attended the local public schools with the usual complement of preppies and jocks. On weekends with his dad he had been carted to youth soccer league games, enrolled in the neighborhood Scout troop, and encouraged to thrive in the mainstream culture of elitist Northern Virginia, where one was expected to dress well, go to a good college, and, in due time, marry a cheerleader, settle into a sedate white-collar job in a cubicle somewhere, and take up golf.

But Cameron Berkley was a changeling.

The way he figured it, on July 26, 1980 there must have been some nice country-fried couple from somewhere near the Tennessee line—a strapping young dude who was maybe a jackleg mechanic and his pregnant wife, with big hair and a name like Wanda Jean, who had been passing through Fairfax County on their way to the NASCAR race that weekend at Pocono, PA. He pictured them passing through Fairfax in an old Chevy plastered with NASCAR decals, when Wanda Jean or Sally Jo, or whoever she was, had gone into labor and been rushed to the county hospital, where just after midnight on the 27th she had proceeded to give birth to a baby boy, while her husband, watching TV in the maternity ward waiting room, was cheering for Neil Bonnet to take the checkered flag at Pocono. Camber wasn't sure they even televised NASCAR races back in 1980, but the scene fit nicely in the movie-in-his-head.

That down-home couple was so real in Camber's mind that he could almost see them. He imagined them with a strong family resemblance to himself. He figured that when they checked out of the county hospital, the nice blue collar couple from the hills had been given Baby Boy Berkley, while their real child—who was no doubt intended to be named Bobby Cale or Darrell Dale—had been christened Cameron Berkley and sent home to a Winnie-the-Pooh themed nursery with the two genteel suburbanites from Falls Church. "Blood will tell." Somehow despite all his parents' suburban propriety, little Cameron Berkley had grown up with an instinctive love for country music, fields and woods, and stock car racing.

He figured that somewhere in far southwest Virginia, there was probably a skinny, bespectacled kid in khakis and a Brooks Brothers shirt, trying to get his friends to drink Merlot and to watch the World Cup soccer tournament with him.

Yep, a changeling.

It had been obvious even before he could talk.

Almost as soon as he could walk far enough to reach the sandbox, he had traded all his plastic dinosaurs for Match Box cars and Hot Wheels gear. He hadn't just played with the toy cars, either. He had devised elaborate chase scenes, complete with intricate jumps and horrific, shattering crashes. The box of tiny cars had been his miniature empire, in which he was driver, car owner, track manager, and crew chief, all rolled into one.

After the Match Box era had come Big Wheels and then bicycles. This entailed more elaborate jumps and a few unfortunate crashes, which had put his mom on a first-name basis with the staff of the local emergency room, but eventually—the hard way—he had learned motor skills, coordination, reaction time, and, best of all, judgment. That last attribute wasn't infallible, obviously, or he wouldn't be sitting in a jail cell in the middle of nowhere, but at least on a race track, he seldom made stupid mistakes.

Of course, the changeling story was simply Camber's own private mythology to explain why he had felt so out-of-place in Beltway suburbia. He shared the same blood type as his parents, after all, and people always said that he resembled his dad. But sometimes he wished the switched-baby story were true, because, for one thing, that would mean that he and Tracy Berkley-Brown were not related in any way. But, alas, he very much feared that they were.

"He's right about the lawyer, you know," said Pajan Mosby, who was somewhat calmer now, but no less exasperated.

Further attempts to question the young man in the cell had not yielded much information. He'd kept holding his head and groaning, and finally he lay back on the bunk with his eyes shut and refused to talk any more at all.

Pajan and the officer had finally given up and left the cell block. Now they were talking softly on the office side of the reinforced steel door. Stoney Westcott glanced back through the small glass panel. The figure in the cell was not moving. Stoney shook his head. "I gotta tell you, Pajan, he must have taken a pretty hard hit in that wreck. If he's not faking that headache, I think we'd be better off seeing about a doctor."

"Have you noticed any symptoms other than the headache

he claims to have? Any strange behavior?"

Stoney hesitated. "Well, I asked him did he want anything to drink, and he asked for a Ramune Hello Kitty Soda. You reckon he's hallucinating?"

"No, I think it means he really *is* an asshole from northern Virginia."

"Yeah, but he could still have a head injury."

"He told you: it's just a mild concussion," said Pajan. "He said there's nothing they can do about it. Just wait for the brain swelling to go down. And if he's a race car driver, he certainly ought to know about head injuries. Besides, we don't exactly have a state of the art medical center handy. If he makes bail, he can go to the Mayo Clinic for all I care, but he can pay for his own treatment. I doubt he'd bother, though. He seems more inclined to want to sleep it off."

"That sure was some header he took off the highway," said Stoney. "I reckon you'd have to be a race car driver to survive that, and not hurt anybody when you landed. Cameron Berkley. Have you ever heard of him?"

Pajan shook her head. "No. He's not a Cup driver, obviously. We'd have heard of him. Maybe he drives CART or ARCA or something. But his nickname is a racing term. *Camber.*"

"Yeah? What's it mean?" Stoney Westcott's hobby was fishing.

Old Jimmy Powell had taught her that, in one of his many discourses on racing. "Camber is the angle between the vertical axis of the wheel and—" Noting the glazed look on the officer's face, Pajan stopped the lecture with a shrug. "Basically, Stoney, it's a factor in a car's steering and suspension." She was still thinking about the wreck, though. Another thought occurred to her. "You gave him a breathalyzer test, of course?"

Stoney Westcott nodded. "First thing we did, Pajan. He passed it. Like he told you. He wasn't drunk."

"Well, that's too bad," said Pajan. "Because drunks sober up, but *stupid* just goes on forever."

* * *

Some time later Camber Berkley woke up with that momentary lurch of disorientation in which you wonder where you are and why, before memory floods back with full consciousness, making you wish you hadn't bothered to remember.

Jail.

Small town in the back of beyond. He wondered how much time had passed since his race with the black car had ended in a nose dive off the ridge. Well, it didn't matter. He had certainly lost that competition, and thus his big career chance for the weekend.

Sooner or later somebody here—probably a local magistrate—was going to ask him why he had been driving that corkscrew highway like a bat out of hell. Should he tell them the truth, he wondered. He couldn't see any percentage in it. If the truth would make anyone feel sorry for him, or cause them to admire his bravery, or if it would have justified his wreck, then he would have trotted out the explanation in a heartbeat, but even to himself he had to admit that an unvarnished account of the circumstances did not cast him in a favorable light. In fact, even if he put the most positive, self-serving spin he could think of on the sequence of events, telling anything approaching the truth would not help his case one bit. He tried out an explanation in his mind, to see if he could concoct a version of the facts that would make himself sound worthy or sympathetic.

Not a chance.

"Well, sir, you see, it's like this ... My cousin Tracy is an arrogant, spoiled little jerk, and I'm a better race car driver than he is."

"In which case, why didn't Cousin Tracy land in the field below the highway, Smart Ass? How come you wrecked and he didn't?"

For about two seconds, Camber found himself wondering where Tracy was. Surely he had seen Camber's car go off the road. And he hadn't stopped to make sure that Camber wasn't hurt?

Of course he hadn't.

Camber's concussion would have to be a lot worse than it

was before he'd start believing that Tracy Berkley had an unselfish bone anywhere in his body, or that he would let any circumstance whatsoever deter him from his mission, which was to reach Lowe's Motor Speedway near Charlotte before dark.

If Camber were being completely honest, which he had no intention of being, he'd have to admit that had the situation been reversed, he wouldn't have stopped, either.

Strictly speaking, Camber had no business being en route to Charlotte at all, just as he'd had no business answering his cousin's cell phone, which is what started it all. But Tracy had insisted on going upstairs to find some wonderfully expensive new publicity photos of himself in his firesuit for Camber to admire, and Camber had been sitting there wondering how he could express his sincere admiration for those photos without Dramamine, when Tracy's cell phone had rung, and without thinking, Camber had answered it.

The caller I.D. indicated that the person phoning was "Flash," the self-awarded nickname of a rookie Cup driver who wasn't as good as he thought he was. Camber always mentally added "in the pan" whenever he saw the word "Flash" in connection with that driver's name. That was interesting. The racing web-site, which he had checked that morning, said that "Flash" had wrecked his car at practice for the upcoming weekend race at Lowe's.

"Hey, how ya doin', Buddy?" said Camber, who didn't much care.

"Aw, the docs claim I got a concussion, Trace."

Several thoughts ran neck and neck in Camber's mind: the first being that if Flash in his current mental state could mistake Camber for his cousin Tracy, then the head injury was beyond dispute. His second thought was that a diagnosed concussion would surely put a driver out of the car for the Sunday race, which was when he realized that what he had intercepted was not merely a social call. If he could successfully impersonate his cousin for a few more minutes, long enough to extract the pertinent information before Tracy came back downstairs with his infernal photo album, Camber figured he would be the front-runner for whatever offer was being made.

Don't talk too much, he told himself. Flash might spot the difference in voices. Besides, he couldn't sound too sympathetic. Tracy had never spared a thought for anyone other than himself in his whole life. "That's rough, man."

"Yeah," said the driver.

"Guess you tore up the car, huh?"

"Like I care. It's only a race car. They can make more. It wasn't my fault. They shouldn't spilt rookies like me going in the corner, Trace. I ran my line. That was all I could do, right?"

"You just need more seat time," said Camber warily.

"That's what my dad says. I just need time on these super speedways, and a little luck. We can't buy luck."

Several cynical replies hovered on Camber's lips, such as a remark about Flash's rich daddy who was supposedly bankrolling his ride, but he thought better of mentioning it. "Right."

"So we're going to have to put someone in the car till I get 100 percent. And they asked me to recommend somebody."

Camber's heart leaped. "And you said Trace—er—*me?*"

"Well, naw, man. I said Chad Chaffin. I've seen him bounce between rides lately, or Tina Gordon. Woman behind the wheel: that could get us some press."

Then why are you calling Tracy? thought Camber. But he knew. "Your team wants someone they wouldn't have to pay to drive, right? Someone who could just fill in for a week or two until you get better." Without the money his father was securing for the team, they just needed to get the car in the race. The points would help them keep their provisional; after all, Flash wasn't the best qualifier. Qualifying is half the car and half driver nerves. Flash lacked the latter.

"Well, yeah. I figured you might like a shot at a ride, just to show people what you can do. You interested?"

"Sure," said Camber, thinking fast. "When do they need me?"

"Look, I gotta go in a minute. They want me to take an MRI. Look, where are you, man?"

"Home," said Camber. "I mean, my folks' place. Close to

Knoxville." He had almost said "my uncle's place in Knoxville" but at the last moment he'd remembered that he was impersonating Tracy. He hoped he sounded dumb enough.

"Can you get down to Charlotte by tonight. Start in the morning?"

"Sure," said Camber. "Count on it."

He heard footsteps on the stairs and broke off the connection just as Tracy came lurching down the stairs with a stack of albums and photo boxes balanced precariously in both hands, and steadied with his chin.

Narrow escape, thought Camber, thinking that he'd have been willing to gnaw off his own foot to escape sitting through a Show & Tell session of that magnitude with Tracy holding forth. He was glad to have an excuse to leave, although he couldn't exactly be truthful about what that excuse was.

Camber was at the front door before his cousin reached the bottom step. "I'm sorry, man," he said. "I just got an urgent call. Gotta go."

"A call?" said Tracy, offloading the photo boxes onto the sofa.

"Um, yeah. Mom. Dad's away on business and the car is acting up."

"Can't she just call a garage?" asked Tracy. "I mean, you're at least eight hours away."

"Well, you know mom," said Camber, forcing a laugh. "She panics. Anyhow, give me a rain check on the photos. See ya!"

He was through the door, into his car, and gone before Tracy had time to make any more perfectly sensible observations about his spur-of-the-moment excuse. Once he reached the road, Camber streaked out as if he'd just seen a green flag drop. He figured he could make it to Charlotte in four hours, tops, and he settled back in the seat, doing the speed limit, because he didn't want to spoil a sure thing by taking unnecessary chances.

It was maybe fifteen minutes later that he saw Tracy's black car in his rear view mirror. It was just a speck on the horizon at first, so that he couldn't be entirely sure that's who it was, but in less than a minute the car had narrowed the gap considerably, and by then Camber knew not only who was following him, but why.

"Flash must have called back."

The injured driver had forgotten to tell something to his prospective relief driver, or he'd had a question, and so he had called Tracy's cell phone again, only this time the call was answered by *Tracy.* Who had no idea what flash was talking about. *What previous conversation? What driving job?*

Unfortunately, Tracy had been able to figure out what had happened in less than a minute, and he had been on his way in a heartbeat, burning asphalt to catch his cousin the ride-napper.

That's when the movie-style car chase began in earnest. At first Camber had thought he could outrun the competition, but "money buys speed" does not apply only to stock car racing: it also meant that Tracy's new BMW had a considerable advantage of the elderly Detroit rust bucket that Camber was driving. Still, for a couple of white-knuckle miles along corkscrew mountain roads, Camber had managed to give Tracy a run for his money. There were moments when he had thought he might actually pull it off from sheer bravado, leaving his more cautious cousin behind in a spray of gravel, but then a quick succession of sharp curves had allowed Tracy to close the gap between them and to execute a few bump-and-run maneuvers, finally sending Camber over the edge and into the cemetery in the field beside the river.

Now here he was in a poky county jail with a throbbing headache and an immediate future full of lawyers, while Tracy was barreling into Charlotte, ready to head out to Lowe's Motor Speedway for his shot at the big-time. The one consolation was that there was no television, telephone or access to email available in the cellblock, so at least for the foreseeable future he would be spared all news of Tracy's NASCAR debut. Cold comfort, but he would take what he could get.

* * *

Later that evening when Deputy Westcott brought him a plate of mystery meat in gravy and boiled potatoes, Camber decided to postpone this gastronomic form of Russian roulette with an attempt at conversation.

"How come your lady friend there is so mad at me?" he asked, trying to sound concerned rather than hostile.

Westcott shrugged. "She thought the world of that fellow they were burying when you crash landed in the grave yard. She figured it was disrespectful of you to spoil the services like that. Now, I don't think old Jimmy would'a minded, but you can't tell Pajan that."

"So was he a relative?"

"Nope. He was ninety-something, so he'd outlived what family he had, but he was everybody's favorite around here. Never saw him mad at a soul. I think he'd have got a kick out of you wrecking his funeral, because he was crazy about NASCAR."

"I wish he was still around," said Camber, who felt that his popularity locally could use a boost.

"You should see the stuff old Jimmy collected over the years. Folks used to come for miles to see his NASCAR stuff. One time we had Cale Yarborough's gas man right here in this town."

Camber tried to look suitably impressed. "So, what did the old boy have? Die-cast cars? NASCAR autograph cards?"

"Some of that," Westcott admitted. "But he had been a fan since the 'Forties, and he didn't mind keeping a lot of things that most people would have considered junk. He was a widower, of course, so he was lucky not having a little woman to make him get rid of that stuff."

Camber took a bite of the mystery meat and wished he hadn't. "What stuff?"

"There's a list of it somewhere. On account of the will. Let's see ... Jimmy had a lug nut from every single car that ever won the Daytona 500—from Lee Petty all the way up to Kevin Harvick. Every one of them signed, too, by the driver. And Daytona 500 race programs signed by all the drivers who raced. I think he had near 'bout every year. He had car parts from wrecks—also signed—by Earnhardt, David Pearson, Bobby Allison, Richard Petty—everybody who was anybody, I reckon. And one of Curtis Turner's old firesuits. A helmet of Davey Allison's. I got a copy of the list around somewhere."

"I'd like to see it," said Camber softly. He was feeling chills along the back of his neck. He had begun to shovel forkfuls of stringy beef and boiled potatoes into his mouth with absolutely no sensation of having done so.

Stoney Westcott, who seemed to have nothing better to do, since the current jail population consisted of Camber himself, hurried out into the office, and returned a few minutes later with a ten-page list of items. He passed the paper through the bars, and Camber set down the tray with trembling hands, and began to read the list.

"Pretty good, huh?" said Westcott with a smirk of civic pride.

Camber looked up. "Look, he really had all this stuff? I mean, it's not fakes or reproductions or anything?"

"Oh, it's real. I remember seeing a lot of this stuff when I was a kid, and NASCAR souvenirs weren't big business back then. Why, you could walk off with a car part after a race just for the asking. But not many people bothered. When I look at the prices some of that junk goes for on eBay, I'd have to say that old Jimmy Powell was just ahead of his time."

Camber barely heard him, because he was captivated by the list. It was like the Holy Grail of NASCAR collectibles. There were things on the list that Camber didn't even know existed, by people who were not famous by ordinary standards, but within the sport ... oh, baby.

A tire signed by Lloyd Seay. *Lloyd Seay?* One of the pioneers of racing, a bootlegger turned pro. Seay had won a race at Daytona when they still ran the cars on the beach. He had been dead eight years before NASCAR had even existed as an organization ... Killed in a moonshining dispute at the age of twenty-one, but he had been the first awesome driver from Dawsonville, Georgia, well before "Awesome" Bill Elliott was even born. Camber had never heard of anybody having a Lloyd Seay racing souvenir.

He let out a low whistle. *What else was on here?*

The list read like a Who's Who of Motorsports. Everybody who was anybody had contributed something to Jimmy Powell's collection. Camber supposed that the most valuable items were the ones from the Forties and Fifties, the signed tires and helmets from the likes of Tim Flock, Red Byron, and Roy Hall. He saw Ralph Earnhardt's name on the list, too. The autographs alone were worth a fortune.

"This stuff ought to be in a NASCAR museum somewhere like Charlotte," he murmured, still scanning the items.

"Yeah, I wonder why Jimmy didn't think to donate it to some place like that," said Westcott. "But as it is, he left instructions for the whole shebang to be sold, and the proceeds given to charity, I guess you could say. Some of the folks at the funeral were thinking about having a Saturday night auction at the Moose Lodge, but I think it's worth more than that. What do you reckon, being in the sport and all?"

Camber looked up, still reeling from the thought of undiscovered treasure, and in his confusion he blurted out the truth before he thought better of it. "What do I think? I think this stuff is worth about two million dollars. Easily that. Maybe more."

In hindsight, he probably shouldn't have said that, but he found the urge to show off irresistible, especially when it came to matters concerning motor sports. Modesty was never one of Cameron Berkley's more conspicuous virtues, anyhow.

Chapter Three
Full Court Press

Maybe it was the head injury, but when Cameron Berkley looked back on the events of what could laughingly be called his trial, he always remembered it as a montage of court room movies ranging from *My Cousin Vinny* to *Inherit the Wind.* In Camber's previous imaginings he had always pictured the film version of his life as an action-adventure epic starring any James Bond actor at the age of 26, but in his current role as The Defendant in this small county courtroom, he was very much afraid that the part was more suited to whoever-played-the-Werewolf in the horror movie of your choice. At least, that's how everyone else there seemed to view him: as an unkempt, alien creature in shabby clothes who might go berserk at any time. The deputy had not handcuffed him, but his expression suggested that tasers and pepper spray were not entirely out of the question, should he make one false move. Nobody bothered to talk to him, either. Not even his lawyer, who would remind no one of Gregory Peck in *To Kill A Mockingbird.*

Camber's hastily-appointed legal representative—*the first guy in the phone book who was not otherwise busy that morning*—was a slight, flustered man in a rumpled brown suit and a skinny tie, whose horn-rimmed glasses dwarfed the rest of his face. His yellowing business card, which read "Edwin Peebles," had obviously spent many months in the lawyer's wallet. Nothing about the man inspired confidence, but Camber didn't see that he had many other options, and after all this was only a traffic case, in a Podunk town, so what did it matter?

Mr. Peebles had looked distinctly wary of his newly-acquired client. "Do you have any questions?"

Camber hesitated. "Well, this isn't my primary concern, but just so I can stop wondering about it, could you tell me the name of this town? I think I must have mis-read the sign."

Mr. Peebles allowed himself a taut smile. "People often think that," he said. "In fact the town's name is indeed *Judas Grove.*"

"You guys actually named a town for Judas?"

"Well, therein lies a tale," said the lawyer, and, with all the patient serenity of one who charges by the hour, he settled back to tell it.

When the little east Tennessee town was founded in 1865, its residents had intended to name it Judah Grove, in honor of the Confederate Secretary of State, Judah P. Benjamin. After Appomattox, Judah Benjamin had escaped capture, and fled to England, with—according to rumors—most of the Confederate gold stashed away in his luggage. The townspeople did not hold that against him. In fact, they admired his enterprising spirit. The dissenting opinion in the community turned out to be the only one that counted: the newly-appointed postmaster, a carpetbagger who got the job because of his Union connections. He had no intention of allowing these Tennessee turncoats to name a town after a Rebel, and, as a rebuke to them for siding against the Union, he christened the town Judas Grove, after the most famous traitor of all.

When the postmaster finally left office in 1876, there was some talk of changing the name back, but by then Judah Benjamin was a fading memory to the residents, and there was no consensus on a new name for the town. At the community meeting, the mayor, who was a book-keeper, pointed out that, since Judas Iscariot was the treasurer among the disciples, he could be honored for his fiscal competence as God's Bookkeeper. No one was swayed by this argument, and there was some talk of renaming the town "Elijah," but since several residents actually were named "Elijah," the idea was shelved.

Before further suggestions could be put forth, Mrs. Liberty Powell, the judge's wife and an avid gardener, stood up and said, "It's the name of a tree, mind you. The judas tree is the other name for the flowering redbud, which we have in abundance all through the woods hereabouts. It seems to me that we could keep the town name Judas Grove in honor of the tree."

The mayor nodded. "It's already on all the maps," he said. "It would take years to get it changed. And if we keep the name, we won't have to reprint our stationery."

The motion was carried, and Judas Grove sailed on past two more century marks, feeling few effects from its odd name, except perhaps that its residents got more than their share of traveling missionaries, who probably reasoned that anyone living in a town named Judas was in greater than average need of salvation.

"I'll bet you tell that story a lot," said Camber.

"Well, people are naturally curious," said Mr. Peebles. "Now about your little legal difficulty—"

"You'd think that a town named after Judas would be tolerant of the sins of others."

"You—er—you crashed old Mr. Powell's funeral ... Literally. Crashed into it."

"Yes, but I didn't mean to," said Camber. "My car went off the road on that sharp curve, and that's where I landed. You know: momentum, inertia. I certainly obeyed the laws of physics, anyhow."

The lawyer, blinked at him, apparently disinclined to consider a physics defense. "Ah umm."

"I see myself as an injured party here, really," Camber went on. "The victim of a tragic road accident. In fact, I am thinking of suing the state highway department for the condition of that road. I might have been killed."

The attorney peered at the paperwork and intoned: "Speed in excess of ninety miles per hour."

It was Camber's turn to blink. "How would they know that?"

Mr. Peebles smirked. "Physics."

The pre-trial consultation was not encouraging. Camber was all for pleading not guilty, and banking on his appeal as a dashing young race car driver to charm the jury into an acquittal, but his attorney thought otherwise.

"Well, you could go that way," Peebles said, in tones suggesting that he was humoring a maniac. "I expect the case would drag on for months, though, and with legal fees running $200 an hour, it might be expensive. Of course, I guess you race car drivers don't have to worry about money."

Camber hesitated, hating to distance himself from the likes of Dale Earnhardt and Jeff Gordon by admitting that practically all he ever did was worry about money. He wasn't a Cup driver, which meant that he didn't have a corporate giant for a sponsor, or even a team out there trying to keep him in tires. He drove when he could, trying to impress somebody enough to take him on as their permanent driver, and he worked at whatever jobs didn't interfere with his racing schedule. Money was a sore subject. He had enough to make it from one month to the next, more or less, but certainly not enough to keep lawyers as pets.

"Race car drivers can't afford the negative publicity of a lengthy trial," he said. "It would make the sponsors nervous." Which was basically true, except that he didn't actually have any sponsors.

Edwin Peebles was giving him the appraising look of a mind reader who doesn't care for the fine print. But he was a courteous man who saw no point in embarrassing people just to prove that you had figured out their shabby little secrets. So he coughed discreetly and said, "Or you could just stand up in front of Judge Mosby right now, plead guilty, and take what's coming to you."

A fine, probably, Camber figured, and he did see the sense in saving large amounts of money that he did not, in fact, possess. "Does the court take credit cards, Mr. Peebles?"

The lawyer ventured a faint smile. "I believe so, these days," he said. "One must move with the times."

Having thus decided on a guilty plea with no back-chat, Camber's attorney-client conference lasted less than half an hour. Camber was a little disappointed to be shortchanged in his first court-room drama. This was always happening to him. When he did drive in the rare televised race, he was always having to call his friends to tell them where to pause the TIVO so that they wouldn't miss the one nano-second that his car had appeared onscreen during the race. The perennial also-ran, that was Camber. You'd think that when he was the defendant in the case, he get a little more attention, but apparently not.

What a shame. He had envisioned dazzling a jury with a parade of expert witnesses, *"Tell us, Mr. Harvick: if you had gone off that curve at ninety miles per hour in the defendant's car, do you think you could have steered the car in order to avoid the funeral area? You do not? Thank you. Next witness: Tony Stewart …" Yeah, right.* Unfortunately, since Camber's acquaintance with Cup drivers hardly extended past an occasional "How ya doin'," he didn't think any of them would actually remember him, much less show up to help a lower-echelon colleague with a minor traffic case, even if he had tried to summon them. Even imagining the conversations made him wince. *"Hello, Mr. Gordon, this is Camber Berkley. You said hello to me at a race once, and I was wondering if you could take time out of your busy schedule to come to a town in Tennessee that is only on the map two days a week to testify for me in a minor traffic case. Hello? Hello?"*

After all, he thought, why not just pay the $200 fine, or whatever it was, and save all the money on attorney's fees and other expenses that he'd otherwise spend trying to fight it. Not to mention the time factor. Okay, he had lost the chance to drive this weekend at Lowe's Motor Speedway, but surely some other opportunities would arise, and he needed a clear schedule to allow for any opportunities that might be forthcoming.

Thus, although he had no overwhelming faith in Mr. Peeble's legal expertise, Camber decided to take his advice, and thus the course of least resistance, mostly because the $238 he had in the bank and his $1200 credit card limit wouldn't allow him to decide otherwise. Besides, by requesting an immediate hearing, he wouldn't have to worry about bail, or coming back to town, or any of the other messy eventualities that would accompany a lengthy jury trial.

So there he was in the sleepy county courtroom, the day after his automotive sky-dive, hoping to be done by noon, so that he could tackle his next problem: getting his car back into drivable condition. Camber had left the scene of the accident in the back of a sheriff's department car, while his Detroit rust-bucket had been towed to some local garage, where it was no doubt disintegrating peacefully while awaiting its owner's release from jail. If its captors wanted more than two hundred bucks to release it from impoundment, Camber planned to hop a Greyhound out of town and write off the car as a total loss. He was a good enough jackleg mechanic to buy another junker at some handy auto graveyard, and restore it to working order without expending too much time and expense. While all these thoughts bump-drafted each other in his head, Cameron settled himself at the defendant's table in the tidy little courtroom, and tried to look like an earnest pillar of the racing community. It was unfortunate that he didn't have any dress clothes with him. It was hard to look important in jeans and a Talladega tee shirt, and somehow orange prison jumpsuits did not confer the same air of excitement and glamour as the superficially similar firesuit, but he would make the best of it. He'd smile a lot. That ought to help.

It wasn't exactly a trial—not by cinematic standards, anyhow. There was no press; no gallery packed with avid spectators; no jury, even. Just a few very bored-looking "officers of the court" standing around waiting for the judge to drop by. Occasionally one of them would make a friendly remark to one of the others, and then they would all glance uneasily at the only stranger in the room—which was Camber himself—as if to reproach him for putting a damper on the occasion, which Camber considered most unfair, considering that he was the guest of honor. He tried giving them a grin and a little wave, as if to say *"Don't mind me,"* but these efforts at cordiality only made them stiffen and turn away. Even Mr. Peebles, who was supposed to be on his side, had left the table to socialize with his colleagues. Camber felt like the corpse at a funeral—a necessary encumbrance, of course, but not one that is encouraged to participate in the festivities. He sighed and settled back in the uncomfortable wooden chair to wait for show-time.

Boredom and anxiety: He recognized the combination as the pre-race set of feelings. He supposed that he could pretend he was about to be interviewed on *NASCAR Inside* after having his car disqualified for mechanical infractions, or trying to explain a $10,000 fine for getting into a shoving match with a fellow driver after a race. Since Camber's driving experience in competition was regrettably minimal, neither of those things had ever happened to him, but he had seen Michael Waltrip and Matt Kenseth being interviewed in just such situations, and he tried to remember how they had handled it. As far as he could recall, their approach had been quiet contrition, topped with judicious measures of earnest integrity. *Okee-dokee.* Cameron tried to look earnest and humble. A Jeff Gordon imitation. Or maybe Carl Edwards. Got it.

Just before the proceedings began, another person joined what Camber was beginning to think of as the courthouse office party. The irate young woman, who had been the only visitor to his jail cell, swept in and took a seat behind the railing in the spectators' section of the courtroom. He tried the smile again, since they were, after all, speaking acquaintances, but she gave him a look that could have frozen motor oil, which he took to mean that she remembered him all too well.

He wondered what she was doing in court. She looked quite severe in a navy skirt and blazer, with her dark hair was pinned up in a no-nonsense bun at the back of her neck. Witness for the prosecution? Surely they weren't going to bother to call witnesses to testify that he had wrecked his car in the midst of Jimmy Powell's funeral. Mr. Peebles wouldn't dream of letting him deny that fact, anyhow. He obviously had no imagination, and his manner suggested that if anyone had attempted to give him an original idea, he would have tried to exchange it for breath mints.

The young woman had turned away from him as much as possible. Now she was consulting some paperwork in a folder on her lap. Maybe she was just there as an observer, he thought, here to see that the disrupter of her friend's funeral was duly punished. He hoped she wasn't a newspaper reporter, because publicity about this incident would be a bad thing. NASCAR took a dim view of reckless driving on public thoroughfares.

It was a pity that they'd met under such unfortunate circumstances, Camber thought. Reasonably attractive women who knew something about racing weren't all that easy to find. In fact, if she would stop looking at him as if he were a cockroach, she'd be downright interesting. She looked up just then, caught him looking at her, and gave him another withering look. Oh well, it was a thought.

Cameron felt an irrational stab of optimism when the judge turned out to be a ringer for the 80's Daytona 500 winner Benny Parsons. In his present state of gloom, he decided that he would take good omens wherever he found them, and surely having a judge who looked like a NASCAR legend was a hopeful sign. Unfortunately, the resemblance between his honor and the genial, hard-driving Mr. Parsons was only skin-deep. Certainly it did not extend to a fondness for motorsports, if his malignant expression was any indication. He listened carefully to Mr. Peeble's perfunctory explanations. It soon became obvious that Isaac Newton's First Law of Motion would not be one of the laws governing the disposition of his case today. At Camber's insistence, his attorney offered it up as a mitigating factor, to which the judge replied, "Nice try."

Almost before one could say "foregone conclusion," the prosecution and defense attorneys ran out of things to say. Camber had spent most of the time trying to decide what he was going to say when the court asked him for a statement, and he was ready to launch into his Jeff Gordon imitation, but he never got the chance.

When the judge finally did turn his attention away from the two attorneys to take notice of the prisoner, he merely remarked, "Well, Mr. Berkley, what are we to do with you?"

Camber opened his mouth to offer some helpful and eminently merciful suggestions, but the judge held up his hand, ordering him in no uncertain terms to remain silent.

The prosecuting attorney murmured, "There is the matter of the will, your honor."

"I was just thinking of that," nodded the judge. He looked again at Camber, this time with the thoughtful expression one gets when one looks at a chicken while thinking up recipes. He looked down at the paperwork on his desk, smiled, and said, "The nice thing about being a local judge is that I have some leeway in your sentencing procedures, which enables me to be merciful in cases where circumstances warrant it."

Camber began to feel hopeful, but then the judge continued, "It also allows me in exceptional circumstances to be creative."

He didn't like the sound of that. What did creative mean in back-of-beyond Tennessee? Tar and feathers? Being shackled to the local ax murderer on a chain gang?

"Now, you broke quite a few laws with that flying car stunt, young man. Speeding. Reckless driving. Reckless endangerment, considering all the people you could have killed at the funeral. Why, I expect if we gave our learned counsel here time to consult his law books, he could have you so hamstrung with felonies that you wouldn't see the light of day for quite a spell. Especially since I could take it upon myself to see that the sentences ran *consecutively*, like cars run in qualifying, rather than *concurrently*, like they do in an actual race. I take it you follow me?"

Camber, struck dumb by this unexpected reference to motorsports, managed to nod. *Consecutively*. One after the other. Who knew how many months that could end up being if they really did get creative? He wondered if anybody in NASCAR liked him enough to pay his legal fees, because nobody else he knew would be able to afford it.

"Well, I'm glad you understand the gravity of the situation, because *gravity* is what got you in this mess in the first place, wouldn't you say?"

Camber nodded again, wondering if prisoners were supposed to laugh when judges made wisecracks. On the whole, he thought not.

"So taking gravity into account as a mitigating factor, and also considering that the deceased whose funeral you *crashed* was a racing fan, I am, as I said, inclined to exercise my discretion in the disposition of this case. In short, young man, I am going to offer you a deal."

"Yes, sir?"

"I take it that you are an actual professional race car driver? Experienced and all?"

Camber was puzzled. Why did they want to know? "Yes, sir," he said. He wasn't anything as exalted as a NASCAR Cup driver, but that was just a question of luck and money. He had certainly driven those tracks, sometimes with those guys, and he figured that in a well-funded car he could hold his own against any of them. He decided not to go into detail about his difficulties in finding a ride in the upper echelons of racing. The question, as he understood it, was could he race, and the answer to that was a definite yes. He wondered what the Benny Parsons look-alike had in mind. Not moonshine running, surely, in this day and age?

"It's a choice, really. You can do a substantial amount of jail time for all these vehicular infractions of which you are indisputably guilty—or—" The judge held up a forefinger for emphasis. "Here's where the choice comes in. In lieu of doing a lengthy stretch in our local jail, you can teach a little driver instruction here in the county for two weeks, while you stay in the lock-up. Of course, you owe us a fine and court costs of $1,000, so if you're ready to pay that, you'll be free to go. Go to a motel, that is, and pay your own room and board while you do your two weeks of driver instruction."

"Driver instruction?" Cameron blinked, wondering if this was the big finale of the judge's comedy routine, after which all present would laugh uproariously and adjourn for lunch, while he would be bundled off to the slammer for decades. But no one was laughing. They were all looking at him with expectant interest. Well, except for the stern young woman, who still seemed to think he was a new species of cockroach.

"You want me to teach drivers ed? After I went airborne off a country road at ninety miles per hour and plowed through a crowded funeral, you want me to teach high school kids how to drive?"

Now everybody *really* laughed. When the snickering subsided, the judge took a deep breath, wiped away tears of mirth, and said, "Well, no, Mr. Berkley, we do not propose to have you teaching our local young people the finer points of reckless driving, thank you all the same. But, as it happens, we find ourselves in need of someone with exactly your skills.

You would be required to go to our county speedway every day for the next two weeks, beginning at eight o'clock in the morning, and there you will teach the art of stock car racing to an assortment of willing, mature pupils."

"You want me to teach people how to race?" Camber took a deep breath, but before he could exhale arguments, he remembered that the alternative was a stint in the county lock-up, and, while he couldn't imagine why a backwoods place like this would need a stock car racing instructor, he was quite willing to oblige them if it meant staying out of the slammer. "I'd be glad to, your honor," he said. "Could I ask why?"

The judge waved away the question. "Oh, somebody will get around to explaining that to you. Will you be paying your fine now?"

Camber winced. "No, sir. I think the county's accommodations best fit within my budget."

Judge Mosby didn't look surprised. "I suppose we'd have to see to it that you don't skip town while you're working off your sentence, though." He looked at the prosecuting attorney. "This would be similar to work release, wouldn't you say, George?"

The attorney nodded. "Electronic ankle bracelet? I think so."

"Can you calibrate the thing to encompass the area of the local track?"

"I think so. I'll have to check, Your Honor."

The stern young woman stood up. "But, Da—er, Your Honor ... what's to prevent the prisoner from cutting off the electronic restraint and leaving the jurisdiction?"

The judge tried not to smile as he considered this. "Well, Pajan, we do have the fellow's car impounded, but I suppose he could go bounding off through the woods if he took a notion. What concerns me more is seeing that he does a good job on this assignment of his. I suppose he ought to have some supervision, but I don't think the sheriff will want to assign a deputy to a baby-sitting detail."

"I'll do it," said Pajan. "This was Jimmy Powell's last wish, and I'd like to see that it is properly carried out."

He hesitated. Camber could see the family resemblance now between the judge and the stern young woman, and he suspected that a silent battle of wills was taking place. Finally his honor said, "In a supervisory capacity, I suppose? You will accompany the prisoner to the track and oversee the instruction process. No weapon, no handcuffs."

"Of course."

The judge turned to Camber. "You have no prior record, barring a few old traffic incidents, young man. If it were otherwise, I would not even consider letting you be supervised by an unarmed officer of the court, but I want your word that you will uphold your end of this bargain with honor and diligence."

Camber nodded. "I will, sir."

"Good. Because if you don't, we will put you *under* the jail."

And that was it, really. There were some forms to fill out, and various other court-related formalities, but basically Camber's day in court was over. Mr. Peebles shook his hand, and wished him luck, murmuring something about charging his fee to Camber's credit card.

"Are you going to tell me what I just let myself in for?"

His lawyer hesitated, glancing at his watch. "Well, I'm running a bit late. Tee time at the country club waits for no man. I'm sure Pajan will explain, but of course if you need me ..." He glanced at his watch again for emphasis, and Camber shook his head. Peebles nodded, and hurried away to catch up with the prosecutor.

Camber was just congratulating himself on his newly-restored freedom when his court-appointed baby-sitter approached with a scowl suggesting that in his case a firing squad would have been a lenient sentence. He quickly rearranged his features to convey contrition and earnestness, but Pajan Mosby did not seem unduly impressed by his efforts.

"So," he said, "Why don't you tell me about this community service business over lunch?"

She smiled. "Love to."

Twenty minutes later he was back in his cell balancing a plastic tray of soup beans and cornbread on his lap, while the stern young woman sat in a folding chair on the other side of the bars, watching him with interest. She was obviously trying to look official and intimidating in her new blue suit and her sensible lady-lawyer high heels, but she was too young and cute to pull it off. Cameron decided to humor her, though. She had friends in high places.

"You know," he said, "when I suggested lunch, I was thinking more in terms of a restaurant or even some local fast food joint."

"I don't think so," said Pajan. "As far as I am concerned you are still a felon and a thug. I'd rather eat with a pack of wild dogs."

"I'm sure you'd fit right in," murmured Camber, but he was careful not to say it too loudly.

"So enjoy your—whatever that is—and consider this a business meeting."

Camber set down the spoon. "Look," he said, "who are you, anyway?"

She gave him a frosty smile. "I am the person who can keep you out of jail. Aside from that, I am an officer of the court. They told you that. Bail bondsman. Law student."

"Judge's daughter?"

She reddened a little. "That, too. But don't think I'm not capable of doing my job. My father's brains will take me a lot farther than his influence."

Camber nodded and went back to his lunch, because chewing seemed more diplomatic than arguing with his court-appointed baby-sitter.

"I'm licensed to carry a gun, too."

"You won't need one," said Camber. "I do my rough-housing with a front bumper."

"You won't get the chance. Your driving skills will be utilized in a strictly advisory capacity."

He sighed. "Do you always talk like a high school civics textbook?"

Pajan favored him with a saccharine smile. "Would you like me to simplify my language for you?"

"Oh, I *understood* you," said Camber. "I went to college, too, you know. I just think you need to stop showing off. What exactly do you mean by an *advisory capacity?*"

"Well, it's your own fault, really," Pajan said. "You told us that Jimmy Powell's collection of NASCAR was worth a fortune. In his will he stipulated that the collection should be sold, with the proceeds going to a local church. But in order to decide which church would get the money, he ordered them to have a race at the local speedway. The money will go to the church of the winning pastor."

Camber almost swallowed his fork. "The *pastor?* You mean clergymen are going to *race?*" When she nodded, he said, "Well, do any of them have any experience driving a race car?"

"No. That's where you come in. Your community service assignment is to tutor all the local ministers in how to drive a stock car, so that they can all compete in the race."

Camber started to laugh. "Teach a bunch of middle-aged out-of-shape duffers how to race? You have got to be kidding. What you want is a nanny, not a race car driver."

Pajan Mosby stood up. "Well, perhaps you'd prefer to spend the next couple of weeks in a jail cell, instead of out at the county speedway. It would give you a chance to catch up on your reading, I'm sure. I believe there's quite a nice selection of decorator magazines and romance novels in the jail library. It's stocked by donations, you see, so they have to take what they can get. I'm sure you'd enjoy *House Beautiful.*" When he hesitated, she added sweetly, "And I could arrange to have an article sent to one of the stock car racing magazines. I'll bet they'd love a nice photo of you behind bars reading Barbara Cartland."

Camber shuddered. "All right. But I'm pretty sure this would come under the heading of cruel and unusual punishment. Listen, stock car racing is a dangerous sport, you know. It's not like baseball. People do get killed out there."

"Well, if you're worrying about liability, you're covered on that. Each participant will sign a waiver, agreeing not to sue you, the county, or the person who lends him the race car."

"Wait—I'd forgotten that all the ministers were borrowing cars from the local racers. Why can't one of them—"

"Because they all have day jobs," said Pajan. "Besides, you're the expert, aren't you? They might as well learn from the best."

Before Camber could preen himself on the unexpected praise, she added, "At least the best driver currently incarcerated in our jail. In a town that doesn't even have a stoplight."

Camber sighed. "It's a dangerous sport," he said again.

"Yes, but they'll only be competing against each other. It's not as if there'll be any really dangerous professional drivers out there being reckless."

"In my experience, it's the amateurs you have to watch out for."

"There's a lot of money at stake. And no one is forcing them to do this. Jimmy Powell meant a lot to me, and he wanted a stock car race as his memorial, so I intend to see that he gets one. Your job is to make that race as safe and professional as you possibly can."

Camber sighed. "Well," he said, "ordinarily, I would say that those guys haven't got a prayer, but obviously … they do."

Chapter Four
Penance

"Gather around everyone. My name is Camber Berkley, and I'll be your instructor for the forthcoming race." *God help us all,* Camber thought to himself looking over his charges. The assortment of middle-aged men grouped around him seemed to be dressed for a volleyball tournament—sneakers, sweatpants, tee shirts—and, in one case, a lanky man, whose hair was a tribute to Elvis, was wearing a shabby black suit jacket over gray work pants ... He'd barely trust this bunch to ride in an elevator, much less a stock car.

Time to begin his community service.

* * *

A scowling Pajan Mosby had checked him out of jail an hour earlier, after first making sure that he'd already been served his breakfast swill, so that she wouldn't have to appear with him in a public restaurant. Camber was wearing the electronic ankle bracelet, but at least the device didn't show under the leg of his jeans. He didn't think this tangible reminder of his incarceration would inspire confidence in his new students, who presumably did not consort with the criminal classes, except in their professional capacity of visiting ... shut-ins. He thought of making that remark aloud, but present company did not seem to appreciate his sparkling wit, so he decided to go with earnest silence, in hopes that she would give him points for that.

Pajan had very little to say to him as they left the jail, but he did manage to talk her out of handcuffing him to the armrest on the passenger seat by reminding her that her father had forbidden her to use handcuffs. She shrugged. "I guess I can trust you."

"Well, of course you—"

"I have *Mace* in my purse."

She eased the car out of the courthouse parking lot. Her radio was tuned to the local classical music station. "I hope you don't mind," she said, in tones suggesting that she hoped he did.

Camber stifled a yawn. "I don't mind," he said. "It won't keep me awake. They tell me that I have execrable taste in classical music, by the way. I like all the jingle boys: Sibelius, Carl Nielsen, Elgar, Rimsky the K., Tchaikovsky ..."

Pajan smirked. "Throw in Wagner and Stravinsky, and you'll have the whole orchestral Luftwaffe."

"True. I'm a philistine. I cannot hear the opening strains of *Swan Lake* without picturing Bela Lugosi in a cape."

"I thought being from the Beltway, this would be your kind of music."

"I'm not a representative sample of that culture," said the Falls Church Redneck. "But I can tell you, you wouldn't do 180 mph to Pachelbel's Canon. My driving music has to be louder than the engine."

"Too bad Attila the Hun wasn't a composer," said Pajan.

Camber had a wide collection of music, mostly centered in two areas: Classic Rock, and Modern Top 40 Pop and Rock. Sometimes he felt that he could get in sync with some of the NASCAR greats like Dale Earnhardt, Davey Allison, and Rusty Wallace by listening to the music that might have been on the radio when they were working on their first race cars in dusty little garages around the South. His musical time machine consisted of Credence Clearwater Revival, Bob Dylan, The Doors, Skynyrd, and Bob Seger.

When Camber was working on his own cars, he played the classic rock radio station that came in clearest, and since his first races cars were indeed relics from nearly thirty years ago, he often felt like someone in a time warp until he saw something that would snap him of his trance: the price of gas, for instance, or a computer screen.

Socializing with the other up-and-coming drivers in the sport, which sometimes felt more like baby sitting, required him to listen to modern country and rock. He found it a little harder to draw inspiration from most of this music, but listening to it did spare him the confusion of turning and expecting to see a 70's-haired Rusty Wallace sipping a beer instead of the much less exalted sight of preppy Cousin Tracy holding a cold Smirnoff Ice. Justin Timberlake, the Dixie Chicks, 3 Doors Down, Camber enjoyed listening to all this music, but he knew it didn't quite define him. He often felt like someone caught between generations, and that Metallica and Alabama characterized him best.

Pajan's classical music station didn't define him at all, but at least it was soothing, And considering the probable driving level of his reverend pupils, 1790 was probably the right musical year for him today, anyhow.

With very little further conversation and absolutely no stops for coffee, Pajan had taken the two-lane blacktop highway out of town, past a huge metal structure that he thought must be a warehouse, and farther on past a little suburban neighborhood of brick ranch and white-frame houses with green shutters and manicured lawns. These simple houses gave way to sprawling farms, where red and white Hereford cows and, here and there, a few quarter horses grazed in rolling pastures. After another mile or so of pine and poplar forest, they arrived at a battered metal sign that marked the entrance to the county speedway, a half-mile asphalt oval, ringed by metal bleachers, and encircled by green fields and steep wooded hills. As they turned onto the speedway road, two deer grazing at the far end of the meadow looked up as the car went past them, but they could not be bothered to run.

On that quiet summer morning, the speedway reminded Camber of a photo he had once seen in a travel magazine: a small Roman coliseum that had been excavated in the ruins of Pompeii. Like that ancient arena, this empty speedway seemed like a perfectly-preserved artifact from a vanished civilization. Camber always had that same eerie "lost civilization" feeling at Talladega—except on race days, that is. Then the place reminded him of Mardi Gras.

Pajan drove through the open gate and onto the grassy infield of the speedway itself. She pulled the car up beside the assortment of sedate-looking vehicles already parked there. The ministers had arrived early. Camber wondered if they had driven out to the speedway in convoy, because he'd be willing to bet that most of them had never been here before. Camber could see a gaggle of casually dressed men, talking and taking pictures of each other against the backdrop of the speedway.

When Pajan turned to her passenger, her stern expression had been replaced by a look of anxiety. "You are going to behave yourself, right?"

"A deal's a deal," said Camber. "I said I'd teach these guys to drive, and I will."

"And you'll be careful with them, so that nobody gets hurt?"

He nodded. "If you people are going to allow them to race, I guess somebody has to see that they don't kill themselves. Are you going to stick around for the lesson?"

Pajan hesitated. "No," she said. "I probably should, to make sure you don't try to escape, but I have work to do. And you do have your ankle bracelet, so I suppose there's no danger of your getting very far. I'll come back for you later."

"Your faith in me is touching," said Camber with a mocking grin.

Pajan nodded toward the ministers. "Faith is *their* job."

He waved as she gunned the engine and took off without a backward glance. So much for the irresistible charm of a race car driver. Maybe he'd be more popular with his new pupils.

He motioned for them to gather around. "You guys are the preachers here to learn to race, right?"

Solemnly, they nodded. "You're our instructor?" one of them said.

"Right. Name's Camber Berkley. I just wanted to welcome you all, and wish you luck." This prompted a round of hand-shaking and introductions.

He surveyed the collection of attentive faces, which ranged from anxious to confident, while a couple of the more optimistic souls beamed with professional benevolence. Camber repressed a sigh. Rank amateurs. And their lives depended on his skills as an instructor. *Oh, boy.*

"Maybe we should get acquainted before we start," he said. "I don't promise I'll remember all your names right off the bat, but I'll do my best."

He did a silent head count. There were ten of them, but the only name he managed to retain after the first flurry of introductions was that of Fr. Francis Spillane *"Call me Frankie"*, a wisp of a fellow in jeans, with an impish face and a shock of graying auburn hair. He was a good five inches shorter than any of the others, and his lilting accent was definitely not a product of Tennessee,

"You could be a stunt double for NASCAR driver Mark Martin, Father" Camber told him. "He's about your size."

Fr. Frankie nodded. "Back in Ireland, they said I was missing a good chance to be a jockey. I guess I've come round to it at last, in a way, haven't I?"

"Well, you'll have one advantage over your colleagues, anyhow," Camber told the diminutive priest. "You know, drivers get in and out of a stock car through the window, and it will be easier for you than it will be for some people." He tried not to glance at the portly gentleman to his right, who looked as if he would have trouble walking up the ramp into a horse trailer.

The wiry, dark-haired man, who had reminded Camber of an early Elvis, said ponderously, *"Well, the Scripture speaks to that, doesn't it? It is easier for a camel to pass through the eye of a needle ..."*

"*...Than it is for a fat guy to crawl in the window of a stock car,*" said Camber. "I'll go with that. Tell me your name again, sir?"

The man stuck out a calloused hand. "Travis Prichard. I'm pastor of the Sanctified Holiness Church of God. Now, I don't have a fancy degree in theology like some my esteemed brethren here, but I have raced a car a time or two, back in the day."

"What level?" asked Camber, hoping to have found a capable assistant.

Prichard looked embarrassed. "Oh, nothing to brag about," he said. "It was a sin of pride to even mention it. Just back roads and a little dirt track. Long time ago."

"Well, some things you don't forget," said Camber. "Let's hope you'll find the experience useful now."

"This will really help me connect with my flock," said another of the ministers. He was wearing a red velour track suit with a gold chain at the neck, and his toothy smile put Camber in mind of a used car lot rather than a house of worship.

"And you are—?"

"Romney Marsh. Church of the Crystal Path. Everyone is welcome. We're a fairly ordinary middle class bunch—homeowners, soccer moms, a few professional people. You wouldn't think there'd be any stock car racing fans among them, would you?"

"Yeah," said Camber evenly. "I would."

"Well, you probably saw our church on the way out here. Big metal structure ..."

Camber nodded. "Looks like an airplane hangar? Yes, I noticed it." And shuddered, he finished silently. "What denomination are you?"

"Oh, we are an interfaith worship community. Everyone is welcome."

"No belief necessary," muttered Rev. Scarberry.

Marsh responded with a tight smile. "On the contrary, Andrew, we believe in fellowship and promoting a feeling of peace and well-being in our worshippers—"

While the sparring continued, Camber turned to the closest

minister, Rev. Richard Cunningham, and murmured, "What exactly is the Crystal Path?"

Rick Cunningham whispered back, "As far as we can tell, it's sort of a cross between the Unitarians and a Vegas lounge act. They sing hymns that sound like greeting card commercials, and during the service they show nature scenes on a big-screen TV above the pulpit. Oh, and they have a worship service dance troupe."

Camber tried to picture The Rockettes in a spiritual context. He failed. "Well, what do they believe in?"

Cunningham shrugged. "Networking."

"Yeah, but, I mean … Jesus? Buddha? Big Bird?"

"They don't seem to care."

"Well, me, either," said Camber. "I'm here to teach you guys to drive, not to worry about doctrine. May the best man win."

A distinguished silvery-haired gentleman, who could have starred in a vitamin commercial for active senior citizens, held up his hand for attention, distracting Scarberry and Marsh from their theological debate. "Would it help you if we wore name tags?"

Camber shrugged. "I'll catch on soon enough," he said. "You're the Episcopalian, right?"

The silver head inclined in a regal nod. "I am, indeed," he said. "Well remembered. Paul Whitcomb."

Camber smiled. No reason to tell the fellow that he hadn't remembered him. Because Paul Whitcomb just looked like the person that central casting would assign to play an Episcopal minister, he made a lucky guess. There were nine prospective drivers—too many to keep straight on such short acquaintance. Fr. Frankie was easy to spot, being the smallest of the bunch, and just now he had committed to memory the distinguished Episcopalian and the "racing redneck Elvis" Pentecostal guy. The heavy-set, russet-faced man was Andrew Scarberry, representing the First Baptist Church. Camber made a mental note to have him bring a doctor's certificate to the next practice. He didn't want to have to deal with a novice having a coronary at the speedway.

One of the other ministers was a Fundamentalist Baptist, who seemed quite a different sort of Protestant from Rev. Scarberry. There was Rev. Cunningham: he was the Presbyterian, and the last two, a youngish blond guy and a frail, birdlike old fellow identified themselves as a Quaker and a Lutheran, respectively. Camber took a long look at the frail Lutheran pastor, and amended his previous mental note: he would ask them *all* to bring a medical release form. Stock car racing was not for the faint-hearted. Aside from that, he didn't really care who represented which faith. It was their driving ability that concerned him, but, since he was a native of the culturally-diverse Washington Beltway, it did occur to him that the list seemed rather skewed.

Camber went down the list again. "What, no rabbi?"

"Well, we don't have a synagogue," said Fr. Frankie. "The nearest one is in Knoxville, I think. Anyhow, we emailed them to ask if they wanted to participate in a stock car race, and they declined with thanks."

Rev. Scarberry smiled. "Well, they did use the word *meshuggah.* But anyhow we did ask them."

Rick Cunningham nodded. "We are a small, rural county, you know. There are several faiths that are not represented locally, and we contacted some of them, but they all chose not to participate, either because the racing idea did not appeal to them or because the distance involved was too great for them to come all the way out here to practice several times before the race."

"So we're it," said Fr. Frankie cheerfully. "The only clergymen in the area mad, bad, and desperate enough to compete for the prize money."

"Well, from what I hear about Jimmy Powell's NASCAR collection, it should bring quite a lot at an auction," said Camber. "A couple of million, maybe, if the right people are bidding. But racing is a risky business. I hope it's worth it to you."

The frail-looking Lutheran pastor, Stephen Albright (whose name Camber had just located on the class roll) smiled. "It isn't easy to come by a couple of million dollars in a small rural parish. We all have pet projects that need funding," he said. "*Di immortales virtutem approbare, non adhibere debent.*" Seeing Camber's blank look, he coughed apologetically. "I'm a classical scholar. It's a passion of mine. Sorry."

Fr. Frankie grinned, "D'you want a translation of that, son?"

Camber shook his head. "Not really, but I'd be interested to hear what causes would make you risk your life in a race car. So—what do you want the money for?" He looked around, making this a general question.

Paul Whitcomb said, "Well, my church—St. David's Episcopal—has a tiny meeting hall and an antiquated kitchen, which makes it difficult for us to host meetings and wedding receptions. A million dollars or so would add a nice wing to the facility and a professional kitchen."

"Outreach," said Romney Marsh, he of the velour track suit and the big metal Barn of God. "Definitely *Outreach.* That's what churches need. Ways to attract new members."

Camber blinked. "Missionaries?"

"No. Billboards. Advertising. The Crystal Path could use a completely revamped professional-quality web-site, and maybe some TV ads on the Bristol station. We have to move with the times, and media saturation doesn't come cheap."

"I guess not," said Camber.

Romney Marsh warmed to his theme. "Plus we'd like to bring him some guest speakers to attract visitors to the worship service."

In his mind Camber tried to cross reference the concepts of *church* and *guest speaker*, and all he could come up with was, "The Dalai Lama?"

Marsh shook his head. "I'm thinking NFL players," he said. "Maybe a race car driver. Say, do you happen to know Dale Earnhardt, Jr.?" Seeing Camber's stricken look, he went on, "Well, we can talk about that later. But, you know, I was thinking we need to book some secular celebrities that people would want to meet. Of course, they'd have to testify to some spiritual experience, but we need big names. People flock to events like that. Mostly they come to meet the celebrity, but then they see how friendly and comfortable we are as a fellowship, and maybe they come back. It's a form of recruiting. Beats knocking on doors. Somebody from one of those *Star Trek* shows would be a real blessing. We could get a mob of folks out to meet one of them. Costs money, though, to get folks like that."

It was a moment before Camber could trust himself to speak. Grasping at straws he turned to the diminutive priest and blurted out, "Um ... Father Frankie, what's your project?"

"Nothing so glamorous as all that, I'm afraid," said Fr. Frankie solemnly. "What I had in mind was a day care center. We get a fair number of migrant workers coming through the area these days, and mostly they're Catholic, so we've felt the need to provide child care, so that these people will have some place to leave their little ones while they work. And then in the evening, wouldn't it be grand if we could offer classes for the GED, and also to teach English as a Second Language?"

"It sounds like a lot of work," said Camber, but he was smiling.

"We'd like to improve the church," said the portly Rev. Scarberry, unasked. "The First Baptist Church is the oldest one in the county. Dates back to 1839. It needs some preservation work, though."

Travis Prichard raised his eyebrows. "Preservation work, Brother Scarberry? You've been talking about copper-plating that steeple of yours."

"Well, yes, but copper-plating would be an effective way to preserve the wood—"

"We don't even *have* a church," said Prichard. "We meet in the old laundromat building out near the trailer park, and the congregation sits on metal folding chairs."

Camber found himself thinking about the Spanish Inquisition. "Okay," he said. "Thanks for sharing all that with me about those good uses you all have planned for the prize money, but we're here to worry about how to make this race as safe and exciting as we can. So let's get to it."

"Did you all forget to invite me?" The inquiring voice was sweet and feminine, but sheathed in razor wire. Camber spun around, wondering how he had overlooked the newcomer. She must have been crouched behind the van listening, he thought.

"Welcome aboard," he said. "Are you one of the local clergymen—er, clergy persons?"

If he had to sum up the woman in one word, that word would be *wiry.* She was forty-something, small and sinewy of build, and her mouse gray hair was a tortured mass of crinkly curls that may have been contrived by a hairdresser, but, if so, he thought she'd have been better off using the money for lipstick. The woman's personality struck him as wiry, as well, because she was standing there knotting and unknotting her fists, and her posture would have been appropriate for facing a firing squad. *And this bundle of nerves wants to drive a race car?* Camber thought. *Heaven help us.*

Paul Whitcomb spoke up. "Hello, Agnes. I guess each of us thought one of the others must have told you. I'm glad you could come. Camber, meet Agnes Hill-Radnor, who runs a local center for—er—spirituality."

Camber nodded to the stern-looking woman. "Welcome, ma'am," he said. "You're the pastor of a church?"

"I am not," she said. "My work is more philosophical in nature. I am founder and director of the Institute of Angels."

"Really? Have you caught one yet?"

Agnes Hill-Radnor's only response was a frosty glare, so Camber said, "So, it's a charity, then? I mean, you don't actually study angels?" He chuckled at his little joke.

"Oh, but she does," murmured Rev. Cunningham.

Old Rev. Albright cleared his throat, to signal that another load of Latin was on the way. "*Parturient montes, nascetur ridiculus mus,*" he intoned.

This time Camber did look to Fr. Frankie for a translation, but the priest's expression plainly said, "I'm not touching this one."

Ms. Hill-Radnor responded to Camber's question with a tight little smile, bearing no resemblance to good humor or amusement. "Indeed I do study angels," she said. "You would think that a group of clergymen, who profess to believe in such celestial matters, would be the foremost supporters of my work, wouldn't you?"

"Probably not," said Camber, who was thinking of the Spanish Inquisition again. "But what exactly do you do?"

"I should think that would be evident," she sniffed. "We study angels. I—well, for personal reasons—I became interested in the spiritual presence of celestial beings, and I used a legacy from my father to fund the center. Scholars and spiritualists from six countries have come to my institute. It's quite renowned."

"Yeah, but have any *angels* showed up yet?"

She sighed, with the weariness of one who has had this discussion far too often to be civil. "Throughout history there have been many recorded accounts of human encounters with the messengers of God. Not just prophets and people in the Bible, but ordinary souls all over the world, who have in times of crisis reported the presence of angels."

"Mons," murmured Rev. Albright.

"Exactly. *Mons,*" said Agnes Hill-Radnor, flashing him a grateful smile.

Camber looked blank, but he noticed that Travis Prichard and several of the other ministers seemed equally bewildered by the comment.

"Mons was a battle in World War One," said Stephen Albright, with the air of someone hoping to forestall a longer explanation.

"August, 1914," said Agnes Hill-Radnor, who was not to be denied her opportunity to show off. "It was the first battle between the British and German armies on the Western Front. The British, under the command of General Sir John French, were proceeding through Belgium, hoping to meet up with the French forces at Charleroi. But before they got there, they encountered the Germans, and General French decided to attack, apparently not realizing the strength of the opposition."

"Aye, there was a lot the British didn't realize in that benighted war," muttered Fr. Frankie.

"And the angels?" said Camber. "Did they help the British win the battle?"

"Total victory for the Germans," said Fr. Frankie cheerfully. "The British always think they're on the side of the angels, but apparently the feeling isn't mutual."

"But where did the angels come into it?" asked Travis Prichard, to whom this tale was also news.

"They appeared to the retreating troops, as a sign of encouragement," said Ms. Hill-Radnor.

Camber blinked. "They were taking *sides?*"

"That's not important," she snapped. Her expression suggested that the conversation had become a runaway train that she was anxious to derail. "The point is that angels are a universal source of spiritual comfort—"

"Have you asked the Germans about that?" Fr. Frankie contrived to look innocent as he asked.

She plowed on, ignoring him. "—Spiritual comfort to millions. Proof of the existence of angels is our assurance that there is a heaven. Angels are all we know of heaven—"

"*And all we need of hell,*" said Paul Whitcomb with a gentle smile. "Sorry. I thought you were paraphrasing Emily Dickinson, and I couldn't help finishing the quote. I love Emily Dickinson, don't you? Such profound simplicity."

The director of the Angel Institute was not amused. "I never got the hang of simplicity," she said.

"Well, I hope you can get the hang of driving at a hundred and fifty miles an hour," said Camber, who felt that it was time to bring the discussion back down to earth. "You do understand that this competition is a stock car race?"

She nodded. "Ridiculous, of course, but they tell me that the money involved is substantial. It would be useful."

"A million or two always is," Camber agreed, resisting the temptation to ask her if angels weren't above sordid matters like cash flow. "I just want to make sure that you understand the risks involved. Cars wreck. They turn over. Sometimes they catch fire. You will all have helmets and safety equipment, of course, but nothing is foolproof." He wouldn't tell them yet about the tragedies in the sport—not just the drivers who had been killed, but the ones who ended up with pins in their spines, or, worst of all in his opinion, the ones who suffered brain damage. He didn't want this bunch of amateurs to think it was easy, though. Too many people thought that.

Agnes Hill-Radnor's gave him a condescending smile. "I'm sure I'll be under someone's protection out there."

Camber gave up. "Well, if you've got a guardian angel, lady, I hope he's Dale Earnhardt."

"There is one thing to be thankful for," said Paul Whitcomb. "It's just going to be us in the race. We won't be competing against any professional drivers."

"And the more you can teach us, the safer we'll be." Andrew Scarberry made a show of looking at his watch, indicating that as far as he was concerned the chitchat was over, and it was time to get down to the business of learning to drive a stock car.

"Yes, let's get on with it, if you don't mind," said Travis Prichard. "I have a day job to get to after this." Seeing Camber's look of surprise, he added, "I told you my church was poor."

Chapter Five
A Wing and a Prayer

"Okay, drivers," Camber took the hint; race car drivers aren't big on boredom. "Let me deliver a brief sermon here, and then we'll get right to the physical part of the lesson."

In an instant they were all polite attention, so he launched into his customary student-driver speech.

"Okay, first of all, I have been racing for seven years now; professionally for three, and, I have to tell you, this pastor race is just about the craziest thing I have ever heard of." That was a bit of an exaggeration, because Camber had witnessed many bizarre spectacles in racing. At little local tracks like this one, he had been present when they had hosted figure-eight races in which the competitors drove old school buses through a tight and intricate series of turns. He had seen and occasionally joined bumper-to-bumper rush hour races, and he had participated in roll-over contests, but the thought of putting a bunch of untrained preachers behind the wheel of 3400-pound weapons and sending them out at top speed trumped every weird racing practice he had ever seen. He took a deep breath. "It's crazy."

The ministers exchanged uneasy glances.

"But it's just *us,*" said Bill Bartlett. "We won't be doing any cut-throat driving amongst ourselves."

"And it is a lot of money," Travis Prichard said. "You've heard some of the things on our wish lists. Most of our churches could really use the contribution."

Camber nodded. "So I gathered, but even if you all try to be as careful as possible, race cars are dangerous. Even in the hands of experts, they can wreck"

Romney Marsh tapped Ms. Hill-Radnor playfully on the arm. "You mustn't drive faster than your guardian angel can fly, Agnes."

Camber sighed. Great. A bunch of people who thought they were under divine protection, and who thought danger in racing was a joke.

"I know all of you believe you have Someone watching over you," he said. "I hope you're right about that, but just in case He plays favorites, it will be my job out here to keep all of you safe. We are going to go over safety equipment and check out the demo car, so that you'll all be familiar with what you're going to drive. Before we're through today, we will even study which line on the track to take, but first I need to start you off with the basics. Give me a second here to check out this stock car they've provided for the lesson."

The stock car, left by one of the local race car drivers for instruction purposes, was a pale blue mid-eighties Monte Carlo with a red car number painted on its side panels. In his days at a local track Camber had raced against a fair number of these, and this one was a fair example of its type. The car's interior was almost bare, and its exterior color of pale blue continued inside the car, covering the floor boards, roll bars, and firewalls. All it contained was the small black dashboard with three gauges, the gear shifter sticking up from a crudely-cut hole in the transmission hump, and an archaic racing seat.

The only thing this car's racing seat had in common with those on modern day race cars was its brand name. This flimsy aluminum bucket seat lacked all the rigid bracing and massive head-and-shoulder restraints that are standard in modern racing: the innovations that have contributed so much to improved driver safety. The seat's padding had worn thin from years of service at the local track, and its covering was studded with bits of rubber and track debris, now permanently fossilized into the fabric.

This rig was surely the work of shade tree mechanics, Camber thought, but he knew that on the track you could not judge the prowess of a race car by its appearance. If looks equaled performance he would not have won any of the trophies currently gathering dust on the top of his bookshelf. The cars he was accustomed to racing were often considerably the worse for wear, because a new paint job and panels were luxuries to be thought of after you got the car running and to the track. For Camber there was never enough time or money left over to attend to his race car's cosmetic needs. He didn't mind the beat-up look of the race car. What mattered was its performance.

After he had finished inspecting the loaner stock car, Camber demonstrated the way to enter and exit the vehicle through the driver's side window. Several times he executed the entry-exit maneuver in one practiced, fluid motion that made the procedure look much easier than it actually was. His pupils, all of them older and most of them heavier than he was, would soon find out that the move was harder than it looked.

Inspection and demonstration completed, he turned back to the class. "Okay, gentlemen—and lady—lesson one ..." He reached back inside the car and pulled off the steering wheel, brandishing it in the faces of the startled pupils. "This is a steering wheel. It is exactly the same as the steering wheel on the car you drove here in, with the exception that this one *comes off*."

There was some head-turning among the group. Some of them were checking to see if anyone had already known that fact about a race car. Only the Pentecostal pastor, Travis Prichard, with his prior racing experience, had remained expressionless and calm.

"They make race car steering wheels detachable so that you can get in and out quickly and safely," Camber told them.

"Be sure that you always double check to see that the steering wheel is attached properly and snapped into place. It is awfully hard to make it though Turn Three if you're trying to steer with the little knob that would be left if this steering wheel came off." He could tell by the looks of dismay on some of their faces that they understood the potential calamity in this. *Good,* he thought. *Frightened students do not showboat.*

"Any questions yet, drivers?"

The heavyset guy in the navy blue jogging suit raised his hand. He was frowning. "Andrew Scarberry. First Baptist," he said, by way of reminder. "'Preciate all your help here, young man. Now my question is—can't they afford a better set of tires for this car?"

Camber glanced at the tires and winced. "Don't even get me started on tires," he said, rolling his eyes. "It is true that Tracy, er—my cousin—needs a set of stickers every time he puts a race car in first gear, but I swear that is just wasting his parents' good money. Anybody who can't squeeze an extra twenty laps out of a set of scuffs doesn't need to be a race car driver."

Camber rattled on, oblivious to the looks of bewilderment on the faces of his pupils. "I have been in several races where I had to make it through the whole weekend on one set of tires; practice, qualifying and the race. *On the same set of tires.*

"I would go from pit to pit just before the race and beg teams for a set of used-up tires, just in case I ran over something and got a flat. It is true that new tires make you go faster, for a while, but really they are just a band-aid for *handling* problems. Your money would be better spent testing with different car set-ups, trying to get rid of the problem."

All ten of them were now staring silently at the smooth, treadless tires on the race car, as Camber warmed to his theme.

"Look here." He motioned them over for a closer look at the right front tire. "Most teams mark the sidewall with how many laps there are on a set of tires. You can see that this tire has only one 50-lap race on it. For as fast as you guys will be going, we could run these tires from now until Christmas. Now, does that answer the question?"

Rev. Scarberry, who had first posed the question, looked

confused, as did everyone else. Meekly, he pointed to the perfectly smooth tires. "But these tires ... they don't have any *tread* left on them."

That question jerked Camber back to square one. "Oh," he said. "*Tread.*" He had forgotten what beginners these people were. Now, trying to hide his embarrassment over that emotional outburst, he took a deep breath and reverted to tour guide mode. "Well, no, they don't have any tread at all, but, see, that's normal for a racing tire, guys."

"It is?"

"Yeah. See, race tires' grip comes from the composition of the rubber, also known as the *compound.* When the tire heats up from the friction, the rubber becomes tacky like bubble gum, which makes it grip the track."

"What about when it rains?" asked Fr. Frankie.

"We don't race in the rain, so we don't need grooves in the tires to get rid of water. Not having grooves gives the tire a greater surface area, thus producing even more grip." The group nodded sagely, and after several of them bent down to feel the texture of the tire, Camber decided to change the subject.

"Who has another question?"

The silver-haired man in the Brooks Brothers polo shirt—that was Paul Whitcomb, the Episcopalian—was leaning in the driver's side window and examining the simple cockpit. "Minimalist," he said. "Did they give you the keys to the car? I don't see one in the ignition. In fact, I don't see an ignition, either." he asked. "Where do you put the key in?"

Camber smiled. He had been expecting that one. "See those two switches, one labeled *Ignition* and the other *Start?* That's what starts the car. No key required. Flipping on *Ignition* is like turning the key on your street car. One click. You know where all the lights turn on? The Start switch is a momentary switch that engages the starter motor to spin the engine. Just like turning your key all the way to the start position."

Agnes Hill-Radnor was studying the instrument panel. "Is there no speedometer? How do you tell how fast you are going?"

To Camber this question was as inevitable as the sun coming up tomorrow. "No speedometer," he said. "Too much trouble. We change gears in the rear end so often that the reading would always be off, anyway. In racing we use a stopwatch to get our average speeds, and we use our tachometer to gauge the speed of the car when we're going down pit road."

Camber thought this spiel was proceeding much like the standard speech he would give at any sponsor event, but every question from this group reminded him that they were the rankest amateurs he was ever likely to meet, and that this whole charade of a race was not only unusual, but also dangerous. Thanks to his highway duel with Cousin Tracy and the sentence handed down by that backwoods court, he had no alternative but to push on, though, and to try to make sure that he taught them enough to keep them from getting killed out there.

He forged ahead. "Now, one more time I want to show you the proper way of getting in and out of the car, and then I want each of you to try it. I have been in racing long enough to see just about every way of getting in and out of one these cars. Head first, feet first, backwards, forwards."

"We know it isn't easy," said Rick Cunningham. "When we first arrived, Romney Marsh tried to climb into the car to pose for some pictures. They have a big screen TV over the pulpit in his church, and he wanted a shot to share with his folks on Sunday morning. But halfway into the car he realized that getting in through the window wasn't as easy as Bo and Luke Duke had made it seem."

"Especially if you're bigger than a mailbox," nodded Scarberry, patting his well-padded stomach.

Getting in and out of a race car in one fluid motion was by now such second nature to Camber that he had to stop and think out the process step-by-step. "The best approach is to stand at the rear of the driver's window, and place your right leg into the car." After he demonstrated this, he stopped to explain the next move. "See, I'm sitting on the window now. While you are sitting on the window and holding onto the roll bars, lift your left leg in. Now you have both legs inside the car. Then you walk your feet from the seat down toward the pedals while lowering your body off the window and down into the seat, while your arms are still holding the roll bars above the window."

Suiting the action to his description, he slid gracefully into position behind the steering wheel. He looked out apologetically at the portly Rev. Scarberry. "Of course, being the size of a horse jockey never hurt the situation, either. Okay, I'm going to come out now, and let each of you take a crack at it."

The entering-the-race-car exercise had not been an unqualified success, although Fr. Frankie, whose size was reminiscent of a cast iron lawn jocky, mastered the moves almost immediately. Travis Prichard was too big to be graceful, but since he had prior racing experience, and he knew what he was doing, he made a fair job of it.

Camber had to assist several of the others who had managed to get themselves stuck in some very uncomfortable-looking positions. *This is the real photo op,* Camber thought, as he helped Rev. Albright slowly reverse the maneuver that had positioned his head next to the pedals while the lower third of his stick-insect legs dangled out the window. He was a good sport about it, though, laughing at his own awkwardness.

Eventually, in varying stages of grace, they all managed to get into position with minimal assistance. Agnes Hill-Radnor had tensed up immediately when she tried to crawl through the narrow window opening, and when she finally did manage to get herself into the car in an upright position, she was shaking. She would have kicked out the passenger side window, if there had been one.

"It takes practice," Camber told her. "You'll get the hang of it before too long. Now, does anyone have any questions on buckling these five-point belts? Great, next..."

Although he moved along quickly from point to point, he was careful to stress that this information was not to be taken lightly. In racing almost everything is a matter of life and death. He was glad to see that some of his pupils were taking notes. After he had discussed gauges, shift patterns, clutches, and fire systems, he felt that he had covered almost everything about the operation of a stock car. They wouldn't be able to absorb this mass of new information all at once, but at least he had laid the groundwork for future sessions.

When he had finished the lecture, he motioned for them to follow him over to the end of pit road. "Okay, guys, now we are going to take a lap around the track. This will be the most informative lap that you will ever take around this place. It will also be the slowest." He smiled, as he saw them glance back at the car. "People, we will be *walking.*"

Camber always tried to pace out an unfamiliar track before practice in order to get a feel for the track's braking points, apexes, acceleration points, best places to pass, and its alternative grooves, because familiarity with those features would serve him well during the race. This time he would have to walk a few paces and then stop, in order to explain to the group what a driver should be doing at this part of the track, and where the car should be positioned. After each short commentary, he would walk another few feet, stop again, and repeat the process.

"Okay, everybody. Raise your right hand and wave."

After a moment of bewilderment, they all obediently waved back at him.

"Feels like *Sesame Street,*" muttered Rev. Scarberry, lowering his hand.

Camber grinned. "Reason I asked you to do that—if something goes wrong, or if you are coming in the pits, you had better get your hand up and waving,"

An instant later he had turned serious again, once more demonstrating the hand waving back and forth in the air. "In my first ever race, some dipsh—" Eying the clergymen, he shifted to a milder epithet. "—some *moron's* ignition cut out, and he made a dive for the pits without that warning wave, and without letting anyone else know what he was doing. Problem was, I was coming off Turn Two low, setting him up for the pass. And—*WHAM!!!*" Camber crushed his hands together for dramatic effect as his listeners staggered back a pace from the force of the dramatization.

"I hit him square in the left quarter panel, sent him spinning into the pits, and that left me heading straight for the start of the inside wall." He pointed to the low white-painted wall encircling the infield.

"Now in the big leagues, the speedways use water barrels along the wall to cushion the impact, you see, but at little short tracks like this, the best they have is an old tractor tire. That collision tore my front end all to he—" Camber stopped short again, "—*heck.* Let's just say it was bad."

"You don't have to downshift on our account, you know," said Fr. Frankie.

"I'm sorry?"

"Your adjectives, man. Sometimes letting fly with a good swear word offers a relief denied even to prayer."

Travis Prichard cleared his throat. "Within reason," he said. "And remembering that there's a lady present."

"Thanks," said Camber. "I'll keep both those things in mind."

By this time Camber and his flock were standing midway between turns three and four, nearing the end of their walking lap. Camber pointed. "See this spot on the track right here?"

They nodded.

"If you're going to make it into the pits safely, you had better be slowed down and off the brakes by *here.* The banking drops away and the apron can get real dusty and dirty, making it slick. The first time I ever spotted in a Busch race, it was for this new kid. Man, was he in over his head! Anyway, we were in practice, and, when he was coming into the pits, he lost it and backed into the water barrels. Wrecked the car, and shut down practice, because they had to clean up all the water. That got us all a trip to the trailer, and I had to avoid eye contact with all the other spotters as we walked down."

Their expressions told him that he'd lost them again.

"The trailer. In racing it's like the principal's office. A place where you sit on a couch and get belittled by the people who control whether or not you'll ever be allowed around a race track again. When they give you hell, your reaction had better be that of a school boy getting scolded—whether it was your fault or not—or else they will come at your hard card with a pair of scissors faster than a sucker punch in the school yard."

"Hard Card?" Another new word. He decided to skip it for now. NASCAR's disciplinary system would not be an issue in this little local race.

The group had finished walking the track, and they were standing again at the middle of pit road. Camber thought that by now he had given them a personal anecdote for every instruction or warning he could think of. They were close to the saturation point on new information. Any further lecturing would be more than they could absorb in one session. But since Pajan had not yet returned to collect him, he wasn't finished yet.

"Well I guess I'm rambling now," he said, wondering what he ought to do next. They seemed to have run out of questions, probably because they were overwhelmed with too many new words and concepts. Now what?

Scanning the possible teaching tools available at the track, Camber spotted a church van in which several of the pastors had ridden to the track. His eyes lit up. "Whose van is that?"

A burly fellow in an orange University of Tennessee tee-shirt raised his hand. "Belongs to the church."

"And you are—?"

"Oh. I thought you might remember me from before. I'm the Methodist minister. William Bartlett. Bill. I was conducting the funeral the other day when you—uh …"

"Oh, right. I'm sorry for the interruption."

Bill Bartlett smiled. "Well, nobody got hurt, and to tell you the truth, I think Jimmy Powell would have loved it."

"I hope so," said Camber. "Okay, then, I guess you've seen me drive, so you'll have to have a little faith here. Would you mind if we take the van out for a spin, sir?"

"The *van?* On—on the track?"

"Yes, sir. I'll be driving it. It'll be great for a demonstration." Camber ambled over to the van and peered inside. "Oh, good. A fifteen-passenger job. There'll be plenty of room." He tugged at the door. "Everybody in! I hope there's enough seat belts, guys."

"Should we pray first?" asked Romney Marsh with a chuckle.

"I was thinking of Last Rites," said Fr. Frankie. "Especially if this thing tips over and one of you big fellas lands on me."

Camber held open the passenger door, and waited while his charges clambered inside and buckled themselves into place. Agnes Hill-Radnor was careful to claim a window seat, to minimize the squashing from her fellow passengers.

"Everybody ready?" called Camber. "Seat belts fastened? It may be a bumpy ride!"

As Camber started accelerating down pit road, he glanced in the rear view mirror, noting that his charges were all leaning toward the middle of the van in so that they could peer through the space between the front seats. He grinned, knowing what was coming next.

"Okay, guys, I know this is just a van, not a race car, but the principle is the same. First thing ... You want to ease the car up on the banking at the end of pit road. You'll do the same thing coming off. Remember to try to be off the gas and off the brake. I don't want anyone spinning while they're trying to get on or off the track."

The top-heavy van leaned hard to the left as it slowly traversed the banking in turns one and two. When it reached the back straight, the occupants were able to recover from their gravitationally-mandated lean to the left, and to return briefly to an upright position in their seats. Camber was circling the track at a sedate 30 miles per hour, which to the passengers seemed to be the fastest possible safe speed in this van.

As they slowly circled the track, Camber, glancing in the rear view mirror, could tell from their body language that they were becoming accustomed to the exercise, and they were thinking that it wasn't so bad, after all. They would soon learn differently.

Camber continued the lesson, calling back over his shoulder: "You should break the maneuvers down into segments when you're out here on the track. The routine for a single lap is: GAS, BRAKE, TURN, GAS, BRAKE, TURN, GAS. All together now."

"*Gas, Brake, Turn, Gas, Brake, Turn, Gas!*" They chanted happily as they leaned forward to watch Camber's feet. He was suiting his actions to the chant.

"Can we do *The Wheels on the Bus* next?" asked Paul Whitcomb.

Camber smiled. Let them laugh. "Remember to stay in the groove," he said, "but if you do get out of the groove, don't panic. Just let off the gas, and slowly get back on the right part of the track. Be smooth. Smooth is fast!"

"*Smooth is fast,*" Bill Bartlett repeated. "I keep hearing sermon ideas in everything."

"Occupational hazard," said Scarberry, who had been seated by himself in the seat farthest to the rear.

Slowly Camber began to accelerate, so that he actually did need to brake going into the turns. As they picked up speed, the front of the van sank down, causing the passengers to lurch forward every time Camber applied the brakes.

"These are big heavy cars you'll be driving. You need to keep that in mind. Get your braking done in a straight line. Not in the turn! *Brake, Turn, Gas!*" Camber was still not pushing any limits. In fact, he had noticed that the van handled about as well as the rust bucket that got him into this whole mess. *Pushing like a dump truck,* he lamented to himself. Well, so much for the warm-up.

"Let's see how it feels in real time, shall we?" Camber called out, as he pushed the accelerator to the floor.

The van's engine screamed as it picked up speed. A glance in the rear-view mirror showed him a scene of white-knuckled panic. The passengers had tightened their grips on the door handles, seat backs and even on the shoulders of whoever was in the next seat. Nobody yelled, but that was probably only because they had temporarily forgotten how to breathe. A few seconds later Camber applied the brakes as hard as he could, knowing that it was going to take everything the poor van had to slow itself down.

He heard a few strangled cries from the back as he released

the brakes and steered the van down the track into the turn. At least nobody had lunged for the door and tried to bail out. This time as they entered the turn, there was no leaning to left. Now they were thrown to the right as the force of the corner came close to tipping the van. The van did not launch itself off the corner with much élan, but it wasn't from lack of effort. Camber had the gas pedal imbedded in the gray nap floor mat. *Brake, Turn, Gas.* Seconds later they were at the end of the straightaway, which meant that he was going to do the hard braking all over again.

As the van careened around the half-mile track, the tires screamed; the engine squealed and groaned like a creature in pain. Each time Camber tugged on the steering wheel, the van's differential responded with a tortured whine. Ignoring these mechanical protests, Camber kept up the breakneck pace until he was sure the van had given him everything it had.

After only a few blurry, harrowing minutes, which to the passengers in back had probably seemed longer than a senate term, he eased off on the throttle and steered them smoothly off the track and back down pit lane.

As Camber brought the steaming van to rest in the infield, he glanced back at his charges to see how they had fared during the ride. Nobody was throwing up. That was good. But all their faces were the color of chalk, and their expressions suggested that they had just been hang-gliding over hell. That was good, too. He wanted them to fully understand that racing was neither easy nor safe. Not for people, and not for vehicles.

Camber hopped out, slid open the passenger door, and took a few steps back to avoid the stampede. The wannabe race car drivers tumbled out en masse. Agnes Hill-Radnor was the last to exit. She seemed so wobbly that Camber put his hand under her elbow to steady her as he helped her out of the vehicle. She was too dazed by the experience to remember to thank him. Or perhaps, since he had engineered the whole ordeal, she did not feel that any thanks were in order.

They staggered around on the grass, trying to readjust their bodies to a lower gear. The brakes on the van were smoking and the hood was too hot to touch.

Stephen Albright pointed a skinny finger at the column of white steam snaking up out of the grill. He nudged Fr. Frankie. "Oh, look," he said. "You've been elected Pope."

The priest managed a wan smile. "I figure I'm halfway to sainthood by now. Surviving that infernal van ride counts as me first miracle."

Camber gave them another couple of minutes to catch their breath. When they had all calmed down and were ready to listen again, he said, "Now do you have a better idea of what this is all about?"

Solemnly they nodded.

"It's a dangerous business," murmured Bill Bartlett.

"But at least all we have to worry about out there is each other," said Fr. Frankie.

"Some consolation that is!" said Agnes Hill-Radnor. "Most men think they're invincible anyhow. And a man who thinks that God is his co-pilot is just about my worst nightmare."

"Well," said Romney Marsh, shaking Camber's hand, "speaking of worst nightmares, that was quite a ride. Somebody ought to put you in charge of recruiting converts, my friend. I believe that van ride would bring anybody to Jesus. I'd like to tell my congregation about the adventure. Will you come to my church this Sunday— that is, tomorrow?"

Camber hesitated. "Well, thank you, Mr. Marsh," he said. "Since you're the first one to ask me, I guess I can't plead a prior engagement. Thanks for the invitation. But I didn't bring a suit with me. Are there any rules for your church?"

Romney Marsh laughed and patted his shoulder. "Just turn off your cell phone, son."

Travis Prichard, who looked considerably less affected by the van ride than his colleagues, wiped his hand on his dusty gray work pants in order to shake hands with Camber. "I appreciate the lesson, Mr. Berkley," he said. "It sure brought back some fond memories of my youth. I'd like to invite you to come to my church for services as well."

"I'll do my best to work it in," said Camber, who thought it would be discourteous to mention how eager he was to leave town. "It's nice of you to ask me."

Rev. Scarberry smirked. "You know, I think Brother Prichard's invitation to his church might count more as retribution than kindness. His people are snake-handlers."

Chapter Six
Past Praying For

"**Are** you out of your mind?" hissed Pajan Mosby. She had arrived just in time to witness Camber's virtuoso performance with the battered church van, and judging by her look of outrage she had barely managed to keep from shooting out its tires in order to stop him. Shortly after her arrival, the ministers managed to regain their composure, and, after another round of hand-shaking, they had gone their separate ways, promising to return the next day for further instruction. Pajan and Camber were on their way back to the jail now, and even though the ministers had assured her repeatedly that no harm had been done, she was still horrified by what she had seen of lesson one.

"You could have killed them all!" she said, for perhaps the third time in as many miles.

Camber sighed. Sooner or later all women started to sound like his mother. "Look, he said, "I know you want this race to take place, on account of your dead friend and his NASCAR collection, and if you want my help to make it happen, you'd better stop trying to micromanage the instruction process. I do know what I'm doing. My methods may look risky to you, but I need to make sure that those guys understand that racing is a dangerous sport."

Pajan nodded. "Especially on a public highway," she said sweetly.

Camber sighed. "Point taken. But at least I'm a professional race car driver. That bunch of amateurs would be dangerous in Wal-Mart with well-oiled shopping carts. And that reminds me, where's my car?"

"We had it towed to Farley's Garage. When you finish here and pay them for storage, you can have it back. Of course, if you want them to fix it, that will cost extra."

"I can fix it," said Camber, whose mechanical skills were definitely worth more than his bank balance. "And, since you mention car repair and my getting out of here and all, I need to make a phone call. I forgot to ask Stoney to return my cell phone this morning. I told him that he ought to allow me to keep it with me in the lock-up, since it is a *cell* phone, but he was not amused."

Pajan wasn't laughing, either. She kept both hands on the wheel and her eyes on the road, acting as if he were simply an extraneous and irritating car noise.

"Well, anyway," said Camber, "I can't just drop off the face of the earth without letting anybody know where I am. Keeping me here without notifying anyone of my whereabouts borders on kidnapping. It's probably illegal. I could sue the town and find out. Anyhow, there are people who care what happens to me, you know."

Pajan sighed. "I hope this isn't a trick to entice one of your low-life friends into coming and spiriting you away from here."

"Of course it isn't," said Camber. "I thought you knew about law. You could always issue a warrant and haul me back from anywhere I went. You think I want a traffic conviction in a one-horse town hanging over my head for the rest of my life?"

She shrugged. "There is a statute of limitations."

"What, about seven years? I plan to be famous a lot sooner than that, Lady, and I want to put this behind me. But I do need to check in with somebody."

Pajan took her eyes off the road long enough to smirk at

him. "Is Talladega Barbie waiting for you?"

Camber sighed. "No. More like the Igor of Mooresville."

* * *

In the Bren-mor Machine Shop in Mooresville, North Carolina, Brennan Morgan was scowling at the perfectly good carburetor that he had just spent an hour rebuilding. It made a nice change from scowling at his cell phone, lying there on the workbench, plugged into its charger so that it would have absolutely no excuse for not ringing. For good measure he glanced at the clock and even at the calendar, where a picture of Jimmie Johnson in Victory Lane *Was he ever anywhere else?* grinned out at him. Idly he took his Sharpie and darkened the concentric circles already drawn around the Cup champion's head.

No, he was not mistaken about today's date. Camber was supposed to have been here yesterday, and he hadn't shown up. Yesterday Brennan had been annoyed that his best friend had disappeared without checking in, but today he was seething. Things had been going fairly well for months now, and to find that once again Camber was being cavalier about his commitments annoyed him. *So what else was new?* It hadn't been so bad when they were back at college. Camber had been a reasonably considerate house-mate back then, and he had even managed to make good grades while still keeping up the social life of a ferret on crack, but now that they were supposed to be adults and business associates as well as friends, Brennan thought it was time for Camber to show some maturity. He needed Camber's help, and he had a business to run. Not much of a business yet, granted, but at least he was trying to make a go of it like a responsible adult.

After graduation Brennan Morgan had sunk his life-savings and all he could borrow from relatives into the leasing and outfitting of his machine shop, which was located in an old building in the industrial area of town.

The machine shop was a concrete structure with an arched spanned roof, like an airplane hanger. The side of the building that faced the street had a large roll-up door for vehicles, and two walk-through doors: one that opened to the shop floor, and one that opened to a stairwell up to the second floor, which covered half the length of the building. The back of the building, facing an alley, had loading dock doors, almost obscured behind a slew of engine blocks and other scrap metal piled up on the loading dock. Inside, the shop floor was full of lines of complex machines, some new and shiny with computer screen controls, and some left over from a much older era. Rows of fluorescent lights cast a purplish glow on the machines, but did little to illuminate the dark concrete floors.

Brennan had planned to use the second floor as a suite of offices when the company grew, but ever since he signed the lease, he had been operating the business end of things from the shop floor, at an old wooden desk pushed up against the wall in between the lathe and the hot tank. The location of the desk was determined by the fact that the telephone line came through the wall from the outside at exactly that spot.

Camber saw the vacant second floor of Brennan's new business as an opportunity for himself. He needed a cheap place to live in order to pursue his dream of a racing career without the annoyance of a regular job. When he asked Brennan if he could live upstairs, provided that he cleaned up the space, Brennan said that he could have half the space if he would work fifteen hours a week in the machine shop. In order to economize on rent payments, Brennan intended to occupy the other half himself. He also pointed out that the success of the machine shop might eventually benefit Camber, too, because once the business became profitable, Brennan might be able to afford to sponsor a race car. So they had a deal.

Brennan scowled at the silent phone. *Now, where the hell was Camber?* At first the thought of a serious accident or an illness had not crossed Brennan's mind. Camber always seemed to have far more luck than he deserved. What he did not have was the diligence to work day in and day out at a regular job regardless of the tedium involved. Oh, Camber wasn't lazy. He could spend fourteen hour straight tinkering with the engine of a race car, just to get an extra hundredth of a second of speed. It was the monotony of regular employment that defeated him.

Brennan was the steady one. They probably made a good team with their complementary strengths, but since Brennan's forte was practicality and discipline, he found that the partnership worked best if he could keep Camber close enough to be shouted at.

Now, though, the irresponsible, charming half of the team seemed to have slipped his leash. He hadn't been answering his cell phone, either. Brennan had started calling Camber's number at 9:10 a.m., when he realized that the upstairs quarters were empty, and he hadn't shown up downstairs at the shop for work. The only response he got when he phoned was Camber's jaunty voicemail message, which would have been a perfectly normal request to leave a name and number and the call would be returned, except for the fact that *Born to Be Wild* was playing in the background as he said it. Brennan had not bothered to leave a message after the first try, and then he had only said, "It's me. Where the hell are you?" So far, despite the recorded assurances, his call had not been promptly returned.

This was serious. Brennan had an engine modification to test, and he could have used some help. Although the shop did all sorts of engine repairs and modifications for race cars, the eventual aim of the business was to make Brennan's mark in racing mechanics with the manufacture of one small engine part: 605-R Chevy heads. To Brennan those cylinder heads were the family legacy and fortune, or the magic beans from the fairy tale— just add a ton of luck and hard work.

Back in the late 'Sixties and early 'Seventies, Brennan's great-uncle Dewey, who had been an engineer for General Motors, had developed those cylinder heads.

Most of Brennan's infrequent dates began—and ended—with his companion of the evening asking tentatively, "But what is a cylinder head?"

And Brennan would wade into an explanation. "Um … well … they're metal pieces bolted on top of the engine block to house intake and exhaust ports, the valve assemblies that control the air flow through those ports, and the holes for the spark plugs to screw into, and the combustion chamber."

"The what?"

"Combustion chamber. You know, where the compressed fuel and the air mixture ignite."

At this point, his female companion was usually looking at him as if he had started speaking in tongues, and Brennan would plunge ahead, attempting to clarify his story, when perhaps he should have been working on making it interesting instead. "These cylinder heads are heavy chunks of metal," he would concede, "But anyone who thinks that no care and love went into the design of these metal mazes would be sadly mistaken." Said, while waving his fork for emphasis.

"Sadly mistaken," echoed his date solemnly, but irony was lost on Brennan.

"Cylinder heads are exposed to the most extreme temperatures in an engine, and they have some of the fastest moving parts. In addition to their functional duties, they must also have channels to funnel lubricating oil to all of the engine's moving parts, and essential coolant to keep the engine from melting into a giant paperweight."

The best response to this declaration came from an auburn-haired pediatric nurse, who said, "I made a sewage treatment plant out of Legos once."

Camber Berkley, Brennan's college room-mate at Virginia Tech, was the first person who actually listened to Brennan's cylinder heads story in its entirety without either snickering or nodding off. That counted for a lot.

The rest of the story was this:

Back when Brennan's great-uncle Dewey had worked at GM, the company had made a few 605-R Chevy cylinder heads. But after only a few dozen of them had been turned out, a major malfunction in the hydraulic machine that breaks open the mold to reveal the finished cylinder head completely destroyed the original casting molds. The few usable ones that survived the breakdow n were slapped on nondescript Chevelles in order to keep the production line moving, and after that the casting was changed back to a previous inferior design.

But Great-Uncle Dewey, who had designed those cylinder heads, managed to salvage a set, which he stashed away in his garage as a memento of his invention, which, according to him, could have changed high-performance engine building forever. Brennan grew up listening to the old man's stories of his fabled invention, and the fame and fortune that had eluded him in that terrible moment when the hydraulic line burst.

After Great Uncle Dewey died, Brennan was helping the family clean out the garage, when he found the cylinder heads under a work bench. Then and there Brennan decided to see if his uncle was telling tales or if his family really was destined to make engineering history. The original design plans at GM had been destroyed a long time ago, and the few surviving cylinder heads, fitted onto Chevelle motors on the production line, had been scrapped and melted down along with the rest of the engine, when those cars reached the end of their street life. The owners of those cars probably never realized the potential horse power under their hoods.

Brennan's goal in life was to duplicate his great-uncle's lost innovation. In order to do that, he would have to reverse-engineer the original design, using the production prototypes that he had found in Dewey's garage. His dream of reproducing those fabled cylinder heads led him to study automotive engineering at Virginia Tech, and then to scrimp, save and borrow in order to open his machine shop.

"So," he had asked Camber, when he first confided his plans back at the university. "Do you think this sounds stupid?"

"No way," said Camber. "I think it's brilliant. But what about GM? Your uncle worked for the company when he designed the 605-R heads. So can you manufacture them without paying a royalty to GM? Technically, don't they still own the design?"

"I checked on that," said Brennan. "Under current U.S. patent law, for patents filed prior to June 8, 1995, the term of patent is either twenty years from the earliest claimed filing date or seventeen years from the issue date, whichever is longer. It has been more than twenty years, and GM did not renew the patent."

Camber nodded. "Makes sense. Cars have changed, and they wouldn't be using that design anymore."

Brennan leaned forward, eyes dancing, thrilled to find someone who shared his obsession. "But GM did put those cylinder heads in a few factory-made cars. Do you know what that means?"

"Sure. Since those heads were originally a GM design, and since they were placed on production vehicles in the factory, then according to the rules of racing, *they'll be considered stock,* which means that they will be legal in every stock class of local and regional racing. You can market those heads to racing teams in asphalt, dirt, and drag racing. If they're as good as your uncle said they are, you'll make a fortune."

Brennan nodded. "I figure if I can perfect this design, I could easily sell 10,000 in the first year."

"It's brilliant," said Camber. "Like inheriting a gold mine."

So the friendship had been forged, and a couple of years later, after graduation, Brennan had opened Bren-mor, doing all types of engine work in order to pay the bills, but in his spare time, with Camber's help, he worked on the design for those cylinder heads.

So where was his trusty sidekick when he needed him?

He knew that Camber had spent the weekend at his uncle's place at the lake in Tennessee, and that his cousin Tracy had also been there. That alone should have guaranteed that he would be back from the weekend on time. Even a routine day job was preferable to spending too much time in the company of the spoiled and boastful Tracy.

Tracy. Since Camber was not answering his cell phone, Brennan supposed that he could ask Tracy where Camber was. He flipped through the pile of business cards in an ashtray on his desk until he found the gold-embossed one with Tracy Berkley-Brown's number printed beneath crossed checkered flags. ("So much money, so little class," Camber had said when he saw it.) Camber would be quite annoyed if Brennan called

Tracy to check up on him.

Good.

He smiled as he punched in the numbers. A couple of seconds later there was a click and a voice said, "Yo, this is Trace."

"Yeah. Hi, Tracy. This is Brennan Morgan, down at the machine shop. I'm looking for Camber."

"Why?"

"Because he was supposed to work here today, and he hasn't shown up. He's not answering his cell phone, either, I know he spent the weekend at your place, so I thought you might know where he was."

Tracy Berkley-Brown laughed. "The last time I saw him was in my rear view mirror, doing a nose-dive off the highway."

"He had a wreck?"

Tracy laughed even louder. "Well, more like a short flight."

"Was he hurt?"

"Dude, I didn't stop to find out. Served him right. Do you know what stunt that weasel tried to pull?" Tracy launched into a scurrilous (although fairly accurate) account of his cousin's cell-phone impersonation of himself in an attempt to hijack Tracy's chance to sub for the injured Cup driver.

Brennan listened patiently (or, at least, without interrupting) through this recital of Camber's crimes, but his mind was running through a list of possible next moves. The Tennessee Highway Patrol? Hospitals along Highway 23? A call to Camber's parents to see if funeral arrangements were under way? No to that last one. He was talking to Tracy. If his first cousin had been killed, surely he would know about it. Not that he seemed overly concerned. Camber always said that he and Tracy had a biblical relationship: "Like Cain and Abel."

A wreck, though. Brennan hadn't seen that coming. He thanked Tracy with more civility than he felt was strictly warranted, and hung up, trying to picture Camber swathed in bandages, and hovering near death. This image was somewhat marred by a vision of leggy blonde nurses grouped around the hospital bed, having their pictures made with Camber and clamoring for his autograph, while a TV crew stood by to film the last moments of the beloved driver.

A wreck? When you really considered the matter, it wasn't all that unbelievable. It wasn't as if Camber were a steady, conscientious driver or that he lived a prudent and cautious life. No, he pushed his luck every chance he got. The thing was: he always seemed to get away with it.—Until now, perhaps.

Mentally, Brennan qualified his opinion of Camber's luck. Physically he led a charmed life all right, walking away from wrecks and passing calculus exams that he'd barely studied for, but there were other dimensions to good fortune, and in those areas Camber had not been so blessed. He didn't come from a wealthy family, or a family with long-term connections to stock car racing: A fatal flaw indeed for someone who wanted to become a Cup driver, because no matter how talented or handsome or determined you were, your chances of breaking into racing were almost non-existent unless you had large infusions of cash to help you get started.

Since tons of money were not an option in Camber's case, he was trying to compensate for his impecuniousness with experience, hard work, networking, and everything else he could think of. So far this had not been a success.

To get a Cup ride, a driver had to prove himself first in one of the lower echelons of racing, like ARCA. Most of the kids who started out there were bankrolled by their parents to the tune of a million dollars or more. Lacking that initial investment meant that Camber had to scurry around on the fringes of the sport, acting as a back-up driver, a racing instructor, or a member of the pit crew, always hoping that a last-minute opportunity would give him a chance to race.

Brennan wanted to be a driver, too, or at least he wanted to take a crack at it, maybe for the wrong reasons—although he would not have admitted that, even to himself. Camber was a great guy: smart, tall, handsome, outgoing, hardworking. In fact, that was exactly the problem. If you are a short, shy, gnome-like nerd, it's hard to play perennial second banana to the golden boy. Oh, Camber was never a jerk about it, but, then, he didn't have to be. In Brennan's experience Camber went through life with permanent Extra Credit, just for looking like the movie good guy, while Brennan worked for everything he got, because nobody ever decided to be nice to him just by looking at him. And Camber wanted to be a race car driver, which would add fame and fortune to the other aces he already held. Brennan didn't know if he could stand it, although, of course, he never let on that he minded, because Camber had always been totally supportive of his own ambitions.

Brennan thought he probably could drive a race car, but he didn't want the job for the thrill of the ride, like Camber did. Brennan wanted the adulation—the way even scrawny, ordinary-looking guys got treated like rock stars just because they drove a Cup car. He figured it was as close as he could come to finding out what it would feel like to be Camber Berkley.

He did not share this dream with many of his acquaintances, because he seldom shared his feelings with anyone, and, besides, he was afraid that people might understand all too well why he wanted to be a race car driver. In terms of racing, Brennan differed from Camber in ways other than his motives. He didn't see any sense in scurrying around trying to get discovered, the way Camber did. Brennan figured that he would make his fortune with Uncle Dewey's cylinder heads, and that would give him the financial security to finance his own racing ventures.

So far, neither he nor Camber was making much progress toward their goal, so it remained to be seen whose strategy would work best.

One thing was certain: Camber's absence wasn't helping Brennan's plans or his business. He gritted his teeth and glared at the silent telephone. Brennan dismissed the thought of serious injury. It was much easier to picture Camber off somewhere enjoying himself so much that he had conveniently forgotten his promise to help with the engine modification. But if Camber stayed incommunicado for much longer, then he had better be in a hospital somewhere. If not, Brennan would be happy to arrange it.

* * *

"How did it go, Father?" Mrs. Mancini, the church secretary, set a steaming mug of coffee on the kitchen table, and went back to unloading the dishwasher.

Strictly speaking, housework was not in Mrs. Mancini's job description, but since the parish could not afford a housekeeper, she liked to keep an eye on the priest, to make sure that he wasn't trying to subsist on Vienna sausages and bottled water. Fr. Francis insisted that his dietary habits weren't a question of poverty or a lack of cooking ability; it was just that he would get too involved with other matters to bother about preparing a meal. Nevertheless, Mrs. Mancini, who was raised to believe that a man in the kitchen was like a chimp with a hand grenade, considered it her duty to oversee his efforts, so that he wouldn't poison himself or starve to death. She also encouraged the ladies of the church to make an occasional microwavable casserole to leave in the refrigerator, and when things were slow in the church office, she would slip over to the rectory and tidy up the kitchen, removing from the refrigerator any item that looked as if it might walk away on its own.

Mrs. Mancini was fond of saying that since she had not only grandsons, but sweaters, older than Father Francis, and a cat that probably outweighed him, she felt perfectly capable of looking after him now and again. And, clearly, somebody had to. He might know theology and thoroughbred horses like the back of his hand, but his domestic skills were past praying for.

Fr. Francis referred to her as St. Rita, because, in common with the saint, she had the given name of Marguerite and a late husband named Mancini. Mrs. Mancini considered it a great compliment to be compared to Rita of Cascia, the patron saint of impossible tasks. It never occurred to her that the good father might be hinting that it was she who was impossible. Self-doubt was not one of Mrs. Mancini's vices; just as self-awareness was not one of her virtues.

She had been brewing coffee to fortify herself before she gave the kitchen floor a quick once-over with the sponge mop. It was a fortunate coincidence that Fr. Francis had walked in just as the coffee was ready. By the time he had seated himself at the table, she had convinced herself that she had known he was coming, and that the coffee had been made for him.

Now whatever was the matter with him? She eyed him critically. Fr. Francis had walked in the back door, looking a paler shade than usual under his shock of graying red hair. With barely a nod to acknowledge her presence, he had gone straight to the kitchen cabinet for the aspirin. He shook out a couple of tablets, and when he filled a glass with tap water, his hand trembled. From the looks of Himself, he could use a bit of a stimulant, and no wonder, she thought, out there messing around with race cars. Bad enough when he had insisted on show-jumping one of the Henderson's horses at the Chattanooga horse show last spring. It was a mercy he hadn't broken his neck doing that. And now—race cars. At least horses didn't go two hundred miles an hour.

She thought that if Fr. Francis had lived back in Roman times, he'd have tried to get himself thrown into the coliseum just so that he could go one-on-one with the lions. Idly, she wondered if martyrdom could be considered blessed if the martyr in question was simply a thrill seeker with an exaggerated opinion of his own invincibility.

Mrs. Mancini began to unload the dishwasher, making more noise with the clatter of plates than was strictly necessary. Father Frankie winced. He ladled sugar into the china mug, and for once she did not comment on the folly of this unhealthy practice. If he was learning to drive a race car, he might need something a good deal stronger than caffeine and sugar by the end of it. Mrs. Mancini did not approve of stock car racing, million dollars or no million dollars, but she reckoned it was just like a man to think he was being brave and gallant when he was just being a foolhardy dolt.

Father Frankie, happily unaware of this assessment of his character, took a long fortifying sip of over-sweetened coffee and closed his eyes. "Well, it was certainly an enlightening morning."

"Did you actually drive the race car then, Father?"

"Not yet. We still have quite a bit to learn before he turns us loose with expensive machinery. But the instructor put the whole lot of us into Bill Bartlett's van, and he hurtled around that track full-tilt, with us rattling around in the back of the thing, praying for deliverance, or, failing that, for engine failure." He smiled at the memory of it.

Mrs. Mancini sniffed. "Served you right, messing with race cars and such."

"It's quite a change from the horses, that's for sure. I do believe we were going faster than I can think. That young driver fella made it look easy enough, though."

"Well, I suppose you'll have an advantage over the others," Mrs. Mancini conceded.

"From the horses, you mean? Well, I don't know about that. Mr. Prichard from Sanctified Holiness has actually driven stock cars in his time, so he told us this morning. I'd say he has the initial advantage."

"Oh, that laundromat church!" Mrs. Mancini sniffed at the whole idea of Sanctified Holiness, which, in her opinion, was barely a notch above biting the heads off chickens. "I meant that you would win because God will want you to have the money for His Church."

"Well now, I wouldn't be asking for any special favors," said Fr. Frankie. "I'd be grateful if He'd just keep me from breaking my neck out there."

* * *

Meanwhile, Brother Travis Prichard, whose church did not hold with exalted terms like "Father" or "Reverend," had gone straight from the speedway to his day job as an auto repairman at Farley's Garage, the old tin-roofed building beside the gas station.

"Sorry I'm late," he called out to owner Darrell Farley, who was bent over the innards of a car, oblivious to anything else in the garage. "I had to go to the speedway for the first meeting for the pastors' race. I'm just going to put on my coveralls. Do you need any help?"

"Naw!" Without emerging from the depths of the car's engine, Darrell Farley waved a wrench in Prichard's general direction, a gesture that he correctly interpreted as a greeting.

Prichard nodded, and kept walking. After he changed clothes and got to work, Darrell would take a break from his current repair job and pepper him with questions about his adventures at the speedway. He just didn't want to look too eager right off the bat. It was a guy thing. The same unwritten rule kept Travis from volunteering too much information unprompted. You had to be casual about these things, and the bigger a deal it was, the more offhand you had to be about it.

They weren't too busy today. That was good. Just a couple of cars around, mostly newish ones that probably just needed a new inspection sticker or maybe some new brake pads. Prichard could do those jobs in his sleep. What he really enjoyed were the problems that took skill to diagnose. He liked to think of himself as a car doctor, healing the sick.

"Hey, Travis, you can help me with the air conditioning on this one!" Danny Simpkins, the youngest employee, a recent graduate of the auto mechanics program at the local community college, was a stocky, redheaded kid who drank too many sodas and needed somebody standing over him most of the time to make sure he didn't mess up a simple repair job. That framed diploma on the office wall did not impress Travis Prichard one bit.

Danny was frantically waving for him to come over and inspect the car, but Travis shook his head and kept walking. "I reckon you can do just fine without me, Danny," he said, still heading to the storage room for his coveralls. An air conditioner problem. Danny had probably been joking about wanting his help, anyhow. They all knew that Travis Prichard did not approve of the fancy and expensive luxuries with which prosperous people tarted up their cars. He came from a simple sect of hard-working people, who generally didn't have much and who'd worked hard to get that. He didn't approve of waste or showy possessions.

He only managed to be tolerant of air conditioning, because, after all, Tennessee did get hot in the summertime, and babies and old people could be stricken by the heat, but don't get him started on the subject of fancy gizmos like seat warmers.

His other bone of contention was Danny himself, a nice enough kid, but inclined to give himself airs about that fancy college degree of his. As if a piece of paper was any guarantee that he was any good at fixing cars. His performance certainly didn't live up to his pedigree. Why, Danny hadn't even been born in the era before automatic transmissions and fuel-injected engines. If you asked Prichard, Danny had never been around a real car engine: one that you could fix with a tool box on a country road, if you had to. Travis had grown up back in that golden age of mechanics, when taking a car apart had been considered an evening's entertainment among the men in his family. There hadn't been any computer diagnostics around back then. Nowadays, most repair shops were like health clinics for rich people—a bunch of guys in white coats, looking at rows of machinery.

The Prichards had learned to fix cars, because they couldn't afford to pay somebody else to do it. All the recreational activities the Prichard men had enjoyed were ultimately practical. They didn't fritter away days chasing a golf ball across a manicured lawn. Their hunting and fishing trips provided fresh meat for the family at no real cost, and their tinkering with machines not only saved them from repair bills, but also provided the Prichard boys with a practical education that eventually led to a steady job with decent wages. Even the family pets had to earn their keep: hunting dogs and barn cats that kept down the mouse population, and chickens that supplied the eggs for the family's breakfast. Travis didn't have any use for impractical things. And if Danny was any example, then a college degree was an impractical thing.

Travis missed the old days. He had gone no farther than high school, and he saw no reason to go to college in order to learn how to fix cars. That's what your driveway was for. The fancy computer diagnostics did not impress him, either. He figured that any mechanic worth his salt could figure out what was wrong with a motor without having to ask some machine for help with the problem.

He was polite enough to keep his opinions to himself, but it galled him when the baby-faced Certified Mechanic asked for his help to repair an engine.

Unaware of his colleague's antagonism, Danny stood up, and wiped the sweat from his forehead with a grubby forearm. His face crumpled with weariness and chagrin. "Oh, come off it, man," he said. "I have tried everything. This guy's air conditioner is just not working. There is no air blowing out. I thought it might be the fan motor, but the input voltage is good. And, before you ask, we did a resistance check. The switch is fine, too."

Momentarily distracted by the problem, Travis Prichard thought for a moment. "Did you check the cabin air filter?

"Sure did."

Prichard nodded. He had assumed that Danny would have tried all the easy answers, the ones recommended by the car repair manuals. What he didn't do very often was think for himself. But if Prichard had a genius, it was thinking in unconventional ways. Now he said, "What's the make and model?

"It's a 2006 Toyota Tacoma," said Danny. "Why?"

Prichard's response was a satisfied smile. A Tacoma. He'd figured as much. "Tell you what, Danny," he said, savoring the triumph. "I got some good news and some bad news for you. The good news is that your problem is just a little piece of duct tape that has been sucked across the blower housing inlet."

Danny blinked. Prichard hadn't come within ten feet of the vehicle. "Uh… what's the bad news then?"

Prichard grinned. "The bad news is you are going to have to take the whole dashboard apart to get to it."

Danny stared at him. Relief mingled with doubt on his face. "Well, you sound sure about it, but you never even looked under the hood, Travis, so how can you be so sure what's wrong with the car?"

Travis Prichard was sorely tempted to refuse him an explanation, so that he could savor his reputation for omniscience, but pride was a sin. He gave Danny a patient smile. "The duct tape would have been left over from production," he said. "It's a piece that is common to all cars on the line. That bit of tape can come unraveled and be sucked across the inlet. That's why I asked what the make and model the car was. I think I saw a TSB about that, but anyhow I've come across that problem a few times myself here in the shop. It's just experience, Danny. It'll come."

* * *

"So, Pajan, I hear you're baby-sitting a jailbird."

"So I am," said Pajan, holding up her coffee cup for a refill. She was having her usual lunch of chicken salad in her usual booth in the Canterbury Café downtown, and, as usual, Dinah Forrester was the waitress who kept her supplied with coffee. Dinah, a silvery blonde with a Dolly Parton figure, looked and dressed about twenty years younger than she was, which was good for the café's business. She was a great favorite with all the local civic leaders and businessmen, who made the Canterbury their informal meeting place. As a result of their patronage, Dinah always knew everything. The word around town was that she only read the local newspaper to find out who had been caught.

"So the race car driver taught racing lessons to the preachers out at the speedway this morning?"

Pajan nodded. "I just dropped him back at the lock-up."

"Well, why didn't you bring him to lunch with you so that I could have a look at him? They say he's twenty-something with big brown eyes and wavy black hair—and that he's over six feet tall—not a scrawny little runt like most race car drivers. I hear that this boy is drop-dead gorgeous."

"Well, I don't know about gorgeous, but he can certainly drop dead for all I care," said Pajan.

Dinah set down the coffee pot and regarded her thoughtfully. "Is he as handsome as all that, Pajan?"

"I don't know what you mean," muttered Pajan, assiduously stirring her coffee.

"Oh, I think you do, Miss Lady. This guy is not Jack the Ripper now, is he? He didn't kill anybody, or rob a bank, or do any damage at all except to wreck his own fool car. So I ask myself: *why are you so dead set against him?*"

"He ruined Jimmy's funeral, Dinah. Have you forgotten that?"

"Are you forgetting that I knew Jimmy Powell, too? And if you'd be honest about it, you know as well as I do that Jimmy the diehard NASCAR fan would have flat out loved having a race car driver crash his funeral in a flying car stunt. I just hope he was looking down from heaven yelling 'Boogity' when it happened, because he would have plain flat loved it."

Pajan's frown deepened. "It was disrespectful. Irreverent."

"Well, Hon, so was Jimmy," said Dinah with a sigh of exasperation. "He had to die before he'd get to a church service. This isn't about Jimmy. This is about somebody else, and I don't mean that cute little trick keeping Stoney company in the hoosegow. This is about you, Pajan. And, in a manner of speaking, you're seeing ghosts, aren't you?"

Pajan made a show of looking at her watch. "I don't know what you're talking about, Dinah. But I have to be getting back to work. I'll see you tomorrow."

Dinah sighed. "Well, I usually say 'don't do anything I wouldn't do,' but for once I sure do wish you would."

* * *

Brennan finally gave up on waiting for Camber's call, and went upstairs to rinse out the coffee pot. When he came back, the answering machine light was blinking. With a scowl of annoyance, he set the coffee pot down on his desk, and played back the message.

"Hey, Brennan. How ya doin', Buddy? This is Camber. I'm on a borrowed cell phone, because mine is—well, I don't have it with me right now. So I guess there's no point in me asking you to call me back. Anyhow, I guess you're probably wondering why I didn't show up this morning, like I'd promised., but believe me I have a really good reason, and I need your help, because I have something coming up that—*Beep!*"

Brennan sighed. That was a lot of help. And he didn't even know where Camber was. Well, all he could do was wait. Sooner or later he was bound to call back. Probably.

Chapter Seven
Lion Among the Christians

"Hey, Stoney, thanks for the room service. But you forgot the mint under my pillow. Oh, and you also forgot the pillow."

After a long day at the county speedway, Camber was back in his jail cell, passing the time with the deputy while he ate what he called "the evening swill." He took a fork full of meat and gravy, and examined it without favor. "I think I've figured out what happens to your road kill around here."

The deputy smiled politely at the joke, but then he said, "If you don't like what we serve, you can always order in from the diner. We had some rich woman from the lake in here for a weekend once on a drunk driving charge, and that's what she did."

Camber brightened. "That's an option?"

"Sure. You can either give me the money or phone a credit card number over to the diner and they'll run you a tab. Want me to get you a menu?"

"You mean I'd have to pay for it? Out of my own pocket?"

Stoney shrugged. "Well, they do take Visa."

Camber shook his head. "Thanks, anyway, Stoney, but I'll pass. Your cooking may not suit my palate, but it is definitely within my price range."

"I thought all y'all race car drivers were rich."

"It's like baseball, Stoney. If you make it to the majors—which in racing is the Cup series—then you've got it made, but down where I am in the minor leagues, the pickings are slim."

The deputy considered this. "How long does it take to make it?"

Camber sighed. "As long as you've got," he said. He didn't want to go into the long explanation of stock car racing replacing polo as the sport for kids with millionaire parents. A jail cell was no place to dwell on depressing realities. Besides, he had other worries besides his diet. *What did they make the gravy out of around here? Chalk dust?* He looked over at Stoney, who was leafing through a copy of *Sports Illustrated,* while he waited for the prisoner to finish eating. "Hey, did I tell you I've been invited to church tomorrow? I can go, can't I? I mean, it's not technically work-release, but it's certainly a blameless destination."

Stoney shrugged. "I'll have to run it by the sheriff, but it sounds okay to me. It's not like you're a dangerous felon or anything. You know you could pay your fine and get yourself a motel room if you wanted to."

"I'd miss your company, Stoney," said Camber.

The deputy smiled. "To tell you the truth, we're all hoping you'll get real famous and come back here someday to do a fund-raiser."

"Consider it a promise. I'll have to get famous so as not to disappoint you. But about this invitation to church ... there's a problem. I'm running out of clean clothes. I only had enough for the weekend I was spending at my uncle's place at the lake. And don't suggest a local dry cleaner, because, even if I could afford it, the service is only twelve hours from now, so they couldn't have them ready in time. I don't suppose your dry cleaners stay open past five on Saturday?"

"They close at noon," said Stoney.

"Well, I need clean clothes by tomorrow morning." Camber brushed some not-at-all-imaginary dirt from the knees of his jeans. "Racing can be hard on the wardrobe, you know."

"So I see." Stoney nodded sympathetically. "But if your

uncle lives at the lake, he must be pretty well-off. Why don't you ask him to lend you some money?"

"I wouldn't give him the satisfaction," said Camber. "He already thinks I'm the black sheep of the family, especially compared to his own blue-eyed boy. I hope my family never finds out about any of this."

Stoney nodded sympathetically. "So which church have you been invited to?"

"Romney Marsh's. What's it called? The Glass Way or something?"

"Church of the Crystal Path," said Stoney, in a carefully neutral voice. "I went one time, back when I was dating a girl who was selling those products where you give parties at people's homes to get them and their friends to buy stuff. She told me she made a lot of her contacts through the church, and I went along with her a time or two."

Something in Stoney's tone of voice made Camber look up from the last few bites of his dinner to study the deputy's bland expression. "So you've been to this church, have you? How was it?"

Stoney hesitated. "It was all right," he said. "Interesting."

"Why do I picture myself tied to a stone altar next to a dead goat?"

"No, they're just fine," said the deputy. "It just wasn't what I was used to, that's all. But they're nice folks. They'll make you welcome."

"But they'll expect me to look presentable, I suppose."

Stoney nodded. He took a long look at Camber's dust-coated jeans and the tee shirt streaked with smudges of what was possibly engine grease. Definitely not church attire in the Bible belt. "Well, it's not as if you wanted to go to a beer joint or something," he said at last. "I guess you could even argue that a trip to church constituted rehabilitation."

"You could," said Camber, returning his attention to the watery mashed potatoes, which he suspected were instant. Or possibly library paste. "Do they serve refreshments after the service?"

"Juice and cookies in the vestibule, as I recall," said Stoney.

"Look here, I'll tell you what ... We have a washer-dryer downstairs so that we can clean up in emergencies. Towels and emergency blankets, you know, or in case some drunk throws up on somebody's uniform. There's a couple of towels in the basket that could use a wash, and I reckon it wouldn't hurt anything if I added your clothes to the load."

"I'd really appreciate it, Stoney."

The deputy smiled. "Oh, well, when you make it big in NASCAR, get me a hot pass to Bristol. Go on and finish eating, while I go look for one of those orange jumpsuits that we put on prisoners when they go out on work crew. You can put that on, and then pass me all the clothes you need washed. We might as well do them all while we're at it." He surveyed the prisoner with a critical eye. "Don't you have anything fancier than that to wear?"

"Yeah, but I was wearing it when I wrecked the car."

They were silent for a moment, picturing Camber's car sailing off the highway and into the middle of Jimmy Powell's funeral service.

"Well, then, that outfit is past praying for," said Stoney, "We ruined those clothes trying to haul you out of the car. I think the rescue squad boys actually threw them away after they finished checking you over. And you're too tall and skinny to borrow anything from me, so I guess you'll be going casual tomorrow."

"Well, I guess I have a good excuse," said Camber. "I think clean will matter more than fashionable, don't you?"

"Oh, yeah," said Stoney. "You'll give them a good chance to practice tolerance and Christian charity towards an unfortunate felon. Say, how are you getting there tomorrow? – Not that I'm offering, mind you."

"No, I'm good," said Camber. "Rev. Marsh said he'd have one of the staff members pick me up. So I'll have clean clothes. I have a ride. Can you think of anything else I might need?"

Stoney took the armful of dirty clothes and shrugged. "Business cards."

* * *

Since he was sleeping on a surface that had more in common with a railroad track than it did with a decent bed, Camber was glad that he had spent a tiring day at the speedway. You'd have to be exhausted to fall asleep on the metal shelf that they had the nerve to call a "bed." At least, he didn't have to spend the next day locked up in here. The prospect of a church outing and non-jail food had cheered him up considerably. He folded his newly-laundered clothes, read a couple of pages of an ancient *National Geographic* that Stoney had found in a drawer, and fell asleep. His last thought before he drifted off was that he still hadn't gotten in touch with Brennan.

By nine the next morning Camber, dressed in his newest tee shirt and his least-faded pair of jeans, was on his second cup of coffee when Stoney appeared waving the key to the cell. "Your ride is here," he announced. "I had her wait in the office. I figured that would be less embarrassing all the way around."

"Yeah, thanks, Stoney," said Camber. "That was good thinking.—Did you say *her?*"

With an enigmatic smile, the deputy unlocked the cell door. "Whenever you're ready."

As they walked down the corridor from the cells to the office part of the sheriff's department, Camber imagined every possible permutation of the "she" waiting to collect him. His theory of preparing for the unknown was to imagine something so impossibly terrible that nothing that actually happened would disappoint him. In picturing the waiting woman, he had started with images of a grandmotherly church secretary and fast forwarded through increasingly forbidding images to prison matrons and Latin teachers, until at last he had arrived at the leering green face of the Wicked Witch from the *Wizard of Oz*.

This technique served him well, because the young woman waiting for him in the sheriff's swivel chair came as a pleasant alternative to his dark imaginings. She was a petite blonde about his own age, and she was wearing a low-cut white sundress under a raspberry-colored bolero jacket, and white stiletto heels. So they weren't Puritans, obviously, at this church. On second look, he decided that she was the human equivalent of a Legos building project: her hair was a carefully and professionally dyed ash blonde; her skin was dermabrasioned and possibly bo-toxed to the smooth consistency of plastic, and then carefully made-up to look "natural;" and her body-by-Bowflex had been toned to a perfection nearing that of Barbie's body-by-Mattel. Camber had no particular objection to this artificial elegance—but he wasn't overly impressed by it, either.

However, the fact that she was smiling at him as if he had just come out of the Oval Office instead of the county lock-up, made a nice change from Pajan, who usually looked at him as if he had just crawled out from under a leaf in her salad.

"Hi," he said, coming over to shake the woman's hand. "Camber Berkley. Thanks for picking me up.'

"I'm Julia Ryeland," she said, with an even bigger smile. "So you're the race car driver. Oh, my!" She was checking him out, but trying not to be too obvious about it.

"And what do you do?" asked Camber.

"Oh, this and that. I help Rev. Marsh out at the church, organizing the refreshment committees, doing the computer work—just whatever needs doing, really. But, of course that's in addition to my real job, which is ..." she paused for dramatic effect. "Selling used cars! Isn't that amazing—both of us in the car business, you might say."

"Quite a coincidence," said Camber, who didn't think it was anything of the kind. He wished he had time for a last-minute bet with Stoney on how long it would take her to offer him a deal on a replacement vehicle for his wrecked car.

She looked at her watch. "Goodness, it's getting late. We've got to get to the service now. We'll talk on the way. Bye, Stoney!" And with that, Julia Ryeland swept him away to her car, a red Mustang convertible with white leather upholstery. He bet it didn't come from the used car lot.

"Now, I've heard about your little accident, so I'm not going to let you drive!" she said, giggling as she slid behind the wheel. She took out a white silk headscarf and tied it over her carefully-styled hair. Camber wondered why women bought convertibles. After a few miles at highway speed, unless they remembered to wear scarves, they usually ended up with a hairstyle like Bart Simpson's mom.

Camber was hardly buckled into the passenger seat before Julia Ryeland roared off down main street, which was fortunately deserted on a sleepy Sunday morning. Camber stifled a yawn, and settled back to enjoy the ride, thinking what a relief it was to be traveling with someone whose driving he did not have to critique. At least, not professionally. His private opinion, which he would keep to himself, out of courtesy and self-preservation, was that she wasn't the hotshot she evidently thought she was.

"It must be very exciting being a race car driver!" said Julia, speeding up as the town limits sign flashed past them.

"The racing part certainly is," said Camber. "But like any other job, it has its tedious moments, too."

She glanced at him and shook her head in disbelief. "I think it looks like fun," she said. "I'd give it a try in a heartbeat. Besides, it sure pays well!"

Camber nodded. There didn't seem to be a right response to this remark. If he agreed that racing was a lucrative career, he would either be bragging or lying, because he certainly wasn't earning much of anything in the lower echelons of the sport. On the other hand, admitting that he was broke and unimportant would disappoint her and take away her fantasy of chauffeuring a NASCAR celebrity. So he just smiled.

He recognized a couple of the little brick houses along the side of the road, and then the pasture with some black and white cows lounging beside a pond. They had turned onto the road that led out to the speedway. Then he remembered that Romney Marsh had said that his church was on the same road. He tried to remember how much farther it was to the big metal barn-like structure.

"So do you know Jeff Gordon?" called Julia, raising her voice above the noise of the wind.

Another tricky question. How do you describe the acquaintance of a four-time NASCAR Cup champion and an unknown guy who was still trying to snag a full-time ride? At various tracks over the years, Camber had indeed said hello to Jeff

Gordon, passed the time of day with him, while they were waiting around for something-or-other, but they weren't exactly pals. Gordon would probably know him on sight, but he'd never be able to come up with Camber's name.

Camber opted for the diplomatic response, "Jeff is a great guy."

"Well, he sure is adorable. But then, you're not so bad yourself." She glanced away from the road and looked at him, this time with concern. "Are you doing okay? By all accounts, that sure was some wreck you had the other day."

"I'm fine," said Camber. "A little more bruised than I would have been in a race car, but I was lucky."

"Well, they say the Lord takes care of drunks and fools."

Camber opened his mouth to protest that he hadn't been drunk, but then, considering the second option he decided not to say anything. Fortunately, Julia was not the sort of person who noticed awkward pauses, because they only meant that her turn to talk again was coming around even sooner. They hadn't gone more than half a mile before she started up again. "Well, I'm glad you weren't hurt, but I hear that the crash just totaled your car."

"Well, I'm a pretty good mechanic," said Camber evenly, thinking here it comes.

"Yeah, but I can't imagine a hot shot race car driver driving a patched-up old car. Maybe you should come by the lot, and see if we have anything you like."

"Maybe I'll do that," said Camber, who made a point of never arguing with juggernauts. "After I've had a chance to assess the damages on my own car, of course. Now tell me about your church. How did you come to join?"

"See for yourself. We're here!" She pulled into the parking lot on the side of an enormous warehouse-like structure that seemed to be made of scrap aluminum. The Barn of God. Camber supposed that if you were a new congregation, somewhat lacking in millionaires, and you wanted to build a large imposing, structure on a church mouse budget, then this big metal monstrosity is probably what you would end up with. Practical? Yes. But no one would ever mistake it for the Cathedral of Notre Dame.

From force of habit he took note of the cars in the parking lot: a lot of SUVs, and an assortment of economy cars—Saturns, Tauruses, Chevy Cavaliers. No, definitely no rich tycoons in this bunch. Maybe he wouldn't look too out-of-place in his shabby jeans.

As soon as he got out of the car, Julia took his arm and steered him up the path toward the sanctuary.

"Concrete," he said.

"What?"

"Well, the sign says *The Church of the Crystal Path,* but ..." He pointed to the sidewalk which was definitely concrete.

She sighed. "Everybody says that. The *crystal path* is a spiritual reference, of course. But it wouldn't be practical to actually build one. We did think about acrylic, though."

Camber willed himself not to shudder. He wondered what sort of car Julia would have recommended for a *hot shot race car driver,* as she'd called him. Hot shot race car driver. Oh, boy. He hoped word hadn't gotten around about that, because he didn't relish the thought of spending the entire day telling people just how unimportant he was in the grand scheme of NASCAR. He'd have to, though, if people asked him about it, because he didn't want to misrepresent himself either, because getting caught exaggerating would be a nightmare.

Julia, still clutching him by the arm, was waving with her other hand, calling out cheerful greetings to the other church members hurrying into the building. Camber had expected to see lots of older people and families with young children, but so far the people he'd noticed were mostly well-dressed thirty-somethings who had come alone. Some of them smiled at him and said good morning, but since the service was starting soon, nobody lingered to get acquainted, so Camber had a few moments to study the building. Despite the industrial-looking tin exterior, the vestibule of the sanctuary looked like an ordinary suburban church. A red carpet covered the concrete floor, and the cinderblock walls were painted a soft ivory.

On a hall table under a big mirror they had set an open guest book topped by a computer-printed sign that read, "Please sign in!" Beside the book was a large glass bowl full of business cards.

"You don't want me to sign in, do you?" Camber asked Julia Ryeland.

"Well, of course, we do. We have the biggest mailing list of any church in the county. How could we keep track of you if we didn't know where to find you?"

Camber hunched over the open book, trying to decide what address to give them, the Mooresville Big Star grocery store or *Dale Earnhardt Incorporated.* He had no connection to either place, which was the whole point. He was pretty sure he didn't want the likes of Julia Ryeland being able to find him, and if he gave them the address of Brennan's shop, he was afraid that somebody might turn up on his doorstep one day—or , in the case of Julia, track him through the swamps of Lake Norman, baying.

"Well," said Julia, "I guess we'd better go in if we want to get good seats." She took his arm again and steered him toward the large double doors that led to the sanctuary.

Camber had grown up attending a church in Virginia that dated back to the Civil War, and after the relatively traditional vestibule, he had expected a traditional place of worship: a stained glass window, rows of wooden pews, a choir loft facing the congregation, and perhaps velvet curtains and brass candlesticks to underscore the pomp and majesty of the building.

What he saw was: none of the above. The sanctuary was certainly vast. A forty-foot vaulted ceiling soared up to the rafters of the metal structure, and the room was large enough to hold five hundred people, but in décor the place reminded him more of a high school cafeteria than a house of worship. Or possibly a college lecture hall in which required freshman classes were taught to several hundred students at once. It was obviously designed to appeal to young professionals.

Several hundred plain metal folding chairs were arranged in raised tiers, just like a lecture hall, and most of them were already occupied by murmuring groups of people, who were both younger and more casually dressed than Camber would have expected in a church setting. He was relieved about that, because it made him feel less out of place in his clean, but casual clothes.

The room was decorated in a plain, modern style—white walls, white ceiling, light oak table and pulpit—but the carpet was dark, probably in order to save on cleaning costs. Camber stared up at the big screen television mounted high on the wall above a small platform to the left of the pulpit. Something told him that the church service wouldn't be much like the ones he was used to.

He was right about that. Things started off sedately enough with a genial welcome from Romney Marsh, who looked sleek in his shiny black suit. With reading glasses perched on the end of his nose, he read out a list of announcements about forthcoming meetings, collection drives, and calls for volunteers to help with various community projects. Then, scanning the audience, Marsh said, "We have a very special guest worshipping with us today. I guess most of y'all have heard about the race car driver who had a little road mishap around here last week. Well, I'm here to tell you that he's a better driver than that incident would lead you to believe. You can take my word for that, because I was his pupil in a class of race-car driving for yesterday. Anyhow, Camber is staying here in town and sharing his driving skills with all of us ministers in Jimmy Powell's memorial race for the proceeds of his NASCAR memorabilia auction. I hope you'll all wish him well after the service— and when we get to the silent prayer portion of the proceedings, I sure could use one, folks."

This drew a good-natured laugh from the congregation, most of whom had turned around to look at Camber. He smiled and gave them a little wave, but he had never been so embarrassed in his life.

Fortunately he wasn't famous enough to take up any more time in the church service. Rev. Marsh suggested that the church members take the opportunity to meet Camber, "maybe get his autograph," in the reception following the church service, and then he moved on to introduce the opening hymn, whose lyrics scrolled across the big screen TV, while on the platform below a musical group had assembled and was accompanying the singing.

Camber studied the musicians with interest, because he had been expecting to see an elderly lady organist, and perhaps a college student playing along on guitar on one of the hymns, but he had underestimated the Crystal Path's musical versatility. They had a five-man band, consisting of a keyboard player, two guitarists, a saxophonist, and, encased in a plexiglass cubicle so he wouldn't blow out the microphones, was a pony-tailed-drummer, whose equipment included everything but the jawbone of an ass.

Camber had a love of gadgetry and a knowledge of music that stemmed from third-grade piano lessons and membership in a short-lived group he'd belonged to in high school *The Back Stretch Boys.* In a matter of months he had abandoned his role as suburban rock star to return to the steering wheel of a Late Model Stock car, but he still remembered his musical escapades well enough to know what he was seeing. He just hadn't expected to see it in a church.

He was certain that the keyboard player, a gaunt balding man with a mournful expression, was playing a Kurzweil, the F-16 of the keyboard world. Already in the course of the prelude and one hymn he had changed its sound from classical guitar to pipe organ to Gregorian chant. Camber was waiting with interest to see what he would do when he really felt like showing off. A napalm strike of bagpipe sounds, perhaps.

In addition to a standard drum set with cymbals, the drummer was also well-equipped with an assortment of musical bells and whistles, which in terms of percussion meant multicultural doodads from Africa and the Caribbean: mariachis, chimes, and all sorts of odd little feathered noisemakers. The guy even had a conga drum leaning against the plexiglass, in case a musical selection called for more than the usual rhythm and soul.

There were two guitarists: one with an acoustic guitar, a pudgy high school kid playing rhythm, and an aging John Lennon in jeans and tinted granny glasses, whose electric guitar had probably played a lot more rock than *Rock of Ages.*

Since there was a microphone directly in front of the rock star wannabe, Camber guessed that somebody thought he was the better player.

As if Providence had echoed his thoughts, the Jumbotron flashed up a photo labeled "The Praise Team," showing the Lennon guitar player; a blonde woman singer in a long dress and dangly diamond earrings; the drummer; the keyboard player; and the saxophonist, a pale little guy whose gray suit was so loose and baggy on his skinny frame that he looked like a baby elephant.

He went back to thinking about his own experiences in a band. Because he was good with all things mechanical, Camber had been a sound and lighting technician for his school's auditorium. When four of his friends organized a band in order to play in one of the schools variety shows, the teacher in charge of the show stopped their rehearsal to tell them they couldn't be in the show unless they had a singer.

They were attempting to do death metal music, and in desperation they looked at Camber, who was running sound board, and said, "Can you be our vocalist?"

Camber, who was already attending some of the band practices to manage the sound equipment, said, "Sure." With a digital effects processor, he dropped his voice by a few octaves, sounded like the devil, and the band's problem was solved. Looking back on it now, he decided that middle school and early high school bands have a lot in common with aspiring race car drivers. If the desire to be in a band or to drive a race car is rooted, not in the job itself, but more in the glamour of the job, then the result is sure to be a disaster.

Camber's rock band buddies weren't very good. The band argued more about what their name was going to be more than they ever practiced. "Fire Escape" was a close second, but finally the guys agreed on "The Back Stretch Boys," as a nod to Camber's racing interests, and also in the hope that some hot but dyslexic girls might see them perform and mistake them for the genuinely famous "Back Street Boys." This gambit did not succeed, and neither did the band. In the course of a year, they lasted long enough to do two variety shows, one cover song and one original. Camber wrote the words to the original song, the rest of the band wrote the music. He supposed it was a rite of passage for adolescent boys to want to be rock stars—TV made it look easy, but of course it wasn't. It wasn't long before he decided that if he was going to toil endless hours on a long shot that might never pay off, he'd rather do it in racing. At least he was good at that.

He turned his attention back to the Vaguely Vegas music from the Crystal Path praise band. He didn't try to sing along with the congregation, even though the words to the hymn were now scrolling along the screen against a rainforest waterfall backdrop, alternating with more close-up shots of the minister and the performers themselves. It was all very show biz.

Six Flags Over Jesus, thought Camber.

He scanned the lyrics, noting a conspicuous absence of the words "God" and "Jesus." Idly, he began to wonder if the words could be used for, say, a political campaign or a sports car advertisement. He thought that they could. *"You are the wonder of the world. You bring us hope and happiness. Your presence lights up the each day."* Pretty generic.

Church lite, he thought.

Since he was in a small town in east Tennessee, he supposed that he had been expecting traditional gospel tunes, with a slight country and western flavor, but he would have been off by a country mile in that respect. The young professionals who made up the membership roll of this church were of the MTV generation, and their musical tastes seemed more akin to a Vegas lounge act than the Grand Ol' Opry. Camber tried to picture the deity to whom these hymns were directed, but all he could come up with was a mental image of Marlon Brando in *The Godfather.*

Julia Ryeland touched his arm. "Isn't it an inspiring service?" she whispered. "And you'll love the reception afterward."

"An offer I can't refuse," murmured Camber.

He began trying to think up ways to refuse, though, when, a few more minutes into the service, Romney Marsh introduced the "Crystal Path Dance Troupe," and a gaggle of nine year old girls in white dresses sashayed up to the open space in front of the band platform. With winsome smiles, they lurched about in unison, as if their only exposure to ballet had been watching the tutu-ed hippos in *Fantasia.*

Camber slouched lower in his folding chair, and wondered if Fr. Frankie could perform an exorcism on him that would wipe out the entire memory of this experience. Probably not. He spent the rest of the hour trying to decide how he would describe this service to Brennan in a sound bite. Finally, he settled on, "The rejected acts from American Idol, accompanied by Hallmark greeting cards set to Muzak." The thought of that conversation kept him smiling through the remainder of the service.

And when Romney Marsh thundered out, "What if Jay-sus was your neighbor?" Camber tried to picture the mournful, bearded face on a traditional stained glass window as his neighbor behind bars across the corridor from his cell. "Now that would be a miracle," he thought to himself, trying hard to keep from laughing out loud at the absurdity of it.

* * *

Meanwhile, across town in a more traditional house of worship, a silent, but heartfelt prayer was being directed to the Deity by a troubled worshipper who was probably unaware of the irony of the supplication.

Okay, Lord, the prayer went. I need some help here. I am in deep fiscal trouble, through no fault of my own, and I beseech thee for justice – okay, and mercy, too – but mostly for justice to rectify this awkward situation. I am having a little cash flow problem, Lord, which expect you already know about, since you are all-knowing and all-seeing. I wish I was. But, no, I am an imperfect vessel, and I did not foresee that which has come to pass. Lord.

When I took that bank loan to build those houses at the lake, everything seemed so simple and straightforward, but then misfortune set in. It wasn't my fault at all, Lord. Just the economy, bad timing, and my usual streak of rotten luck. Not that I am blaming You for that, Lord, although it would be nice if You would make a little effort on my behalf every now and again.

I could really use Your help now, Lord. I'd like to think that Jimmy Powell's two million dollar legacy is Your answer to my prayers. It sure will be– if the right church wins the race. So if You meant for me to benefit from that money, I guess You won't object to my taking steps to see that the right folks win. They say "Heaven helps them who help themselves," so I'm going to take it as Your divine will that I do just that.

And, Lord, if You can't help me, please don't help any of those other churches, either. Amen.

* * *

In an altogether different sanctuary across town, Pajan Mosby was staring at a stained glass window of a blond, red-robed angel helping two children across a swinging bridge. She wasn't really seeing it, though. The words of the sermon washed over her, while her mind wandered to subjects that had little to do with church.

She thought about Jimmy Powell's funeral, and his legacy of NASCAR memorabilia. How odd that a race car driver should turn up in town just when they urgently needed one. So ... was Camber Berkley an answer to prayer? Well, if so, it certainly wasn't her prayer. If they needed some professional driver to instruct their ministers in the fine points of racing, she didn't see why God couldn't have sent along a gentlemanly, older past champion like Bobby Allison or Terry Labonte. Or a woman race car driver. Or, at the very least, some short and homely driver, who could teach racing, and who would be otherwise easy to ignore.

She smiled, remembering an old saying of Jimmy's: *The Lord works in mischievous ways, His blunders to perform.*

He certainly had this time. He had sent Camber Berkley, who probably thought he was God's gift to women, and who was certainly more trouble than he was worth. He always looked so bewildered when his heretofore infallible charm failed to work on her. It made her want to laugh to see him trying the usual magic and falling flat on his face.

Chapter Eight
Blind Faith

Camber stood in the infield watching Fr. Frankie circle the track for his first laps. The sight made him remember the first time that he ever drove a race car. It was in a setting much like the one today. A small local track in southwest Virginia had allowed him to come and practice with a car he had bought from one of the track's past champions. It had been a sunny weekday morning in early spring, and the stands were empty. No college buddies had come along to watch Camber's first run on a speedway. The only soul in sight then was the grounds keeper on a John Deere tractor, mowing the large grass field that served as the parking lot. The champ who had sold him the car and his crew chief, who was his brother, were there to give Camber a few pointers to go with his purchase. Camber would learn that crew chiefs and team members were often relatives of the race car driver, at least in the old days, and the track champ had been in the sport a long time. *Things are different now,* Camber told himself. Except they weren't. When he raced Late Model Stock at local speedways his own crew chief was Brennan, the closest thing he had to a brother.

The Champ and his crew chief had watched from the infield as Camber circled the track, adding more gas each lap, as he got used to the feeling of the car and the track. More gas, more brake, turn harder every lap, until at last the car started speaking to him.

When he was instructing the ministers on how to take their first laps in the race car today, Camber had skipped the part about the car speaking to the driver. Even a bunch of guys with miracles as their stock in trade would have a hard time understanding that concept, much less believing it. He wouldn't accomplish anything by convincing them that he was crazy. As it was, they had already lost two participants. The Fundamentalist Baptist had decided that racing was a little more excitement than he could stand. The skinny blond Quaker guy caught flack from his "clearness committee" about the implication of gambling in the race. They had both sent their regrets via Paul Whitcomb, the Episcopalian minister, who had exchanged his jogging suit for more sensible attire today: jeans and a Hilton Head tee shirt.

"Everyone will take ten laps at a time," he told them. "And you'll be out there by yourself. I don't want you running into each other while you are still getting accustomed to racing."

His students nodded in solemn agreement. They didn't trust themselves at high speeds yet, much less each other.

Camber explained the practice procedure. "I will be watching you from on top of the concession stand here in the infield. I want you to work your speed up slowly, a little more each lap. Be smooth." His charges looked more serious when they arrived at the track this time. The van ride had—he smirked at the thought—*put the fear of God in them. Good.* Caution was good. For today's session the ministers had left their shorts and slip on-dress shoes at home. Instead, most of them had come outfitted in dark denim jeans and tightly-laced running shoes, for which Camber was thankful. *The more seriously they take this, the less chance there is that I'll have to scrape one of them off the Turn Four wall.*

Camber had never had a chance to sit down and talk to a Jeff Gordon or Dale Earnhardt about the concept of race cars talking to a driver, but then again he had never talked to them one-on-one about anything else, either. He only saw those guys when they happened to be racing the same track on the same weekend that he was. Normally he just got to say hello before a PR person redirected the star's attention to a waiting reporter or a sponsor's rep.

From the way that the elite Cup drivers described what the car was like in qualifying or how it changed during the course of a race, Camber knew that they had felt the same thing: that communication between man and machine. *"The car was really unreliable today,"* a driver would say; or *"This chassis had a great personality. We hate that it got wrecked like this."* Camber didn't think it was a mistake that a race car always got personified, as if it were a thinking member of the race team. *"The car didn't really like that last set of tires we put on,"* the driver might say.

He supposed that most people who watched racing on TV thought that these remarks were all just figures of speech, because they had never experienced the phenomenon of a car communicating with them. A car doesn't speak to just anyone. It runs silent, content to remain strictly a tool until someone with the gift of speed drives it close to its limit. *"The car and I worked well together."* Camber knew that it was when a car stopped doing exactly what you wanted it to do that your relationship and experience with that car really came into play. Communicating with a car always happened when you came close to the edge.

He decided that this concept was advanced racing information. He didn't need to discuss it with a bunch of one-shot racers.

"After you have driven your ten laps, someone will wave the checkered flag so you will know when to come in." Camber told them. "When you are learning new tracks, new cars, always come in take a break and think about what is going on. Climb out of the car and allow yourself to stop shaking and then come talk to me. I may have some useful information that will help you in your next run."

Camber was still thinking about communicating with the race car. He wondered if he could get any of these guys going fast enough so that they could experience that. He thought again about trying to explain it to them before they started, but again he thought better of it. Maybe later when they had a few laps under their belts. Besides, he only half-believed it himself. He supposed that Brennan, for instance, would explain away the phenomenon by invoking his expert knowledge of mechanical engineering: how the suspension on a race car loads up as the forces of cornering build at higher speeds. Yeah, but Brennan hadn't raced cars, either, had he? He wanted it to be all science and not art, because that would mean that he could do it as well as Camber, but Camber thought otherwise.

Deep down he knew that the driver-car connection was more than just a matter of physics. It was something else. Something—he'd never use the word aloud of course, but—it was mystical. The gas didn't always make the car speed up. The brakes didn't always slow the car down. And, often, turning the steering wheel does not turn the race car.

Camber thought that people who doubted this should listen to the radio on race day, and try to decipher what a driver is telling his crew chief about how he is getting the car to do what he wants it to. The driver's account of the man-car bond made it sound as if he were working with a person, perhaps even a fractious child. Drivers knew that when the car didn't do what you wanted it to, you had to get creative, and use some alternatives. You treat the car like a child. If a child doesn't go to bed when you ask him to, then you might order him to bed, and if he still won't go, you might pick him up and put him there bodily. In stock car racing, 'child psychology' could mean using the gas to turn the car, or using the steering wheel to slow it down.

"How fast should we go out there?" Paul Whitcomb asked.

Camber hesitated. His usual response to this question at the racing school was, "This is not about speed; it is about getting comfortable with the car, and getting the line right." That speech normally came right before his cliché line: "Here at the Racing school we hand out diplomas, not prize money or trophies." Camber realized that the racing school line of reasoning wasn't going to work in this situation. These ministers were getting more serious about winning this race as its lunacy faded into a chilling, but exciting reality. They each had their own motivation, some had shared more than others, but Camber realized that coaxing them to drive to win was not going to be a problem.

The group stood in respectful silence waiting for him to give them an answer, but he wasn't ready to give one. Holding up a finger, signaling for patience, he said, "Give me a second, guys." How fast should he let them go?

He began to do some calculations in his head: *I have nine of these fools. I only want them on the track one at a time, and I need to try to get every one of them in the car today twice for ten laps each time. Okay, that's 200 laps. Then factor in some time to refuel the car, check the tires, run people across the track to the flag stand, and add a little more time to get in and out of the car. Oh, and throw in a lunch break and some extra time for advice now and then … Jeez, we'll be here till midnight!*

Camber reckoned if he got the ministers running laps in twenty-odd seconds rather than in forty or sixty seconds, he could exponentially reduce the time required to carry out the exercise. Then he could use the time he'd saved in practice in order to do some damage control on this whole situation concerning his racing career. He could make some phone calls, calm Brennan down, try to put a positive spin on this experience before somebody e-mailed the story to Jayski and labeled him as a criminal. He had to be really careful of his reputation. The NFL had killers and they let druggies play pro baseball, but in NASCAR they expected you to behave like an altar boy. NASCAR once fined Dale Earnhardt Jr. for saying shit on national television. Ten thousand dollars. And here he was doing time in a local jail. *Incarcerated.* The watchdogs of racing were not going to be happy about that. If they found out, he'd be lucky to keep his hard card.

He had already spent some time trying to work out a positive spin on the situation. Something along the lines of, *"Yeah, I had a little traffic mishap in this little rural community, and I found out they were having a charity event at the local speedway to benefit one of the churches in town, so I volunteered to stay and give them a hand with it."*

But he'd have plenty of time back in his cell to worry about all that. Back to the lesson. Camber let out his mental clutch and connected his mouth to his brain. "How fast should you go? Right. Um, well, that is simple really. *As fast as you can.* Let me share with you something that somebody told me the first day that I got to drive a race car. This was an old Late Model Stock champ, and he said, 'Trust me, on your first day of driving, boy, your body is not going to let you drive that car fast enough to spin it out'."

"As fast as we can?" echoed William Bartlett. "Do you think that is a wise idea? Shouldn't you give have us start out slowly, and work up to increased speeds?"

"Mr. Bartlett I want everyone to progress at their own pace, but with all due respect, staying under a certain speed is not going to win this race." Camber said, hoping that he sounded more confident than he felt.

"Staying under a certain speed does keep cars on roads and out of funerals, though," said Rev. Scarberry.

Camber grinned. "Have a little faith, Reverend."

The others laughed, probably more out of nervousness than amusement, but at least it broke the tension. "Okay," said Camber. "Let's get you guys out on track, shall we? Reverend Bartlett, would you like to be our pace setter and drive first?"

Bartlett nodded, looking a bit apprehensive, but game. "I don't suppose they call us the First Methodist for nothing," he said. "One question, though, what about a helmet? Or a professional-looking fire suit, like the one you're wearing in those internet pictures."

Camber winced. He had been Googled. "I take it you found my web page?"

Bartlett nodded. "It was my wife's idea, really. When I mentioned your name, she went straight to Google, and I must say she seemed impressed. I believe it was the fire suit."

"I'm afraid there are several pictures of you floating around the garden club," said Paul Whitcomb, trying hard not to laugh.

Bill Bartlett nodded unhappily. "I hope you don't mind.

The ladies were all fussing about how handsome you are, and insisting that I must try and bring you by the church. We are having a potluck dinner in the church hall this week. It's not just for members of the congregation, you know. Anyone in town is welcome."

Even residents of the county jail? thought Camber.

Aloud he said, "So they're passing around pictures of me, huh? It's an occupational hazard for race car drivers."

"It certainly is for the clergy," said Fr. Frankie.

Rick Cunningham nodded. "We could tell you stories …"

Camber smiled. "Well, it would be a shame to meet these garden club ladies and spoil that wonderful fantasy they've got going. But if you'd like me to stop by the potluck dinner, I will." Whatever they were serving at the church event had to be an improvement over jail food. Besides, Camber figured someday he'd need all the fans he could get. In modern NASCAR image counted for at least as much as driving skill. "As for you guys, I'm sorry to disappoint your female admirers, but I'm afraid the fire suit and helmet that was left for us to use is not nearly as cool as the one I've got. Professional drivers get them custom-made, you know. But for safety reasons, you will need to use the ones we have."

Camber led the group over to the car, and pulled out a solid black jump suit with a wide white stripe across it. He handed the bulky garment to Bill Bartlett, who was first up to drive. "Here, slip this over your clothes for now. We will work on finding suits that will fit everyone before race time." The fire suits would be on loan from the local race car drivers. They would just have to hope that their sizes corresponded with those of the ministers. Camber thought that in the case of the portly Rev. Scarberry, it was almost past praying for.

There were no sponsors' logos or shiny finish on the loaner fire suit, which had been left by the owner of the race car. It was typical example of what any short track driver would wear. "Bill, here's your helmet, too," said Camber, handing him the heavy headgear.

He turned to the rest of the group. "Now I need some people to help out. Mr. Whitcomb, could you go up in the flag stand?

Once we get started, I want you to count ten laps, and then wave the checkered flag to signal the end of that driver's time on the track. Don't worry; you'll get your turn to drive. When we're halfway through practice, we will bring you down and put someone else up there in your place."

Camber pointed to the flag stand, a three-foot by five-foot platform about ten feet in the air, positioned right at the start finish line. It protruded about two feet out from the steel catch fence, far enough out so that the field of track-focused drivers would be able to see the flag man, but close enough to the fence so that if a piece of dangerous shrapnel came off in a wreck, the flag man could still duck back to safety.

Paul Whitcomb gave Camber a playful salute and clambered up the thin metal rung ladder that led from the outside of the catch fence to the top of the stand. The floor of the platform was diamond plate steel with standing room for one person and a metal folding chair. Two levels of black metal rails encircled the platform, covered by sheet metal painted to match the track's logo. The platform contained a switch to activate the yellow flashing caution lights around the track and the holders for the various flags that were waved during a race: green to start; yellow for caution; red to halt the race for wreck or debris; white for the penultimate lap; and checkered to signal the end.

Whitcomb inspected the flags and switches. "This thing is like an extra-tall pulpit!" he called out. "I may get the urge to preach up here."

"Then go have a lie down until it passes!" Fr. Frankie yelled up at him.

Camber turned back to the rest of the group. "Okay, Mr. Scarberry, I want you to work the stopwatch. You will note the times for each lap, write them down on a piece of paper, and hand them to me just as the car is coming in."

"Father, you're up next to drive. We will all switch around as necessary to get everyone in the driver's seat. Hopefully, we can get all this done before dinner time."

As Paul Whitcomb was admiring the view from the flag stand; Scarberry was trying to locate a pen and paper; and

Bartlett was struggling into the fire suit. Now that they were sorted out, Camber decided to go over the car one last time before he turned it loose.

He checked the tire pressure, and raised the hood to make sure all caps were on tight. Then he bent over the carburetor, twisting the throttle linkage while his hand primed the engine. Then he reached in the cockpit and threw the switches eliciting a thunderous roar. When he looked up, everyone was staring at him. Camber let the car idle to warm the motor. Hiding his face in the window. He leaned down toward the steering wheel and spoke softly. "In advance, I'm really sorry about all this," he said to the car. "I know these aren't going to be the fastest laps you ever turned here, but if you get through this amateur hour, I promise that when this is all over, I'll give you a good tune-up."

Just then a suited and helmeted Reverend Bartlett, looking like a robot from a 50's space opera, tapped Camber on the shoulder, motioning that he was ready to get strapped in. He appeared to be speaking, but because of the rumble of the car's engine, Camber could not hear a word he was saying. He nodded anyway, because he got the general idea.

Now Camber took a quick glance at the water temp gauge in the car: 160. *That's warm enough to get started*, he thought, as he flipped the ignition down to off. The sound died away, and peace was restored.

"Sorry, what did you say?" Camber said as he turned to Reverend Bartlett

"How do I look?" said Bartlett, mouthing the words as he bellowed.

Camber considered it. "Like an elephant ready to hang glide," he said. "Now let's get you out there."

Camber took off the steering wheel and placed it on the dash."In you go! Remember the way we practiced getting in."

Bartlett climbed in more gracefully this time than he had in the initial practice session, when he'd nearly ended up on his head. When he was settled into the driver's seat, Camber went to work on the seat belts. "Start with your left lap belt, then your left shoulder, then your crotch strap, right shoulder and last your right lap belt." With some initial fumbling, Bartlett followed the instructions and finally managed to get himself strapped in to Camber's satisfaction.

"Good, you're strapped in. Now just pull these tabs till you're nice and snug. We don't want you doing any squirming out there."

Reverend Bartlett did as instructed. "I'll be right back to put your window net up," Camber told him. "I'm going to check that everyone else is ready."

"All set up there?"He called up to Paul Whitcomb on the flag stand. Whitcomb's reply was a grin and a thumbs-up. Then he walked over to Andrew Scarberry to give him a few pointers on operating the stopwatch. Finally he checked to see that the track was clear and the gates were closed, before he headed back for a last minute chat with Bartlett, sitting in the race car, about midway down pit road.

"Ten laps, Reverend. Focus on your line. Go a little faster each lap. Look for the checkered flag from Whitcomb up there to tell you when to come in. Stopping right here will be fine."

Camber checked the steering wheel just to be sure it was indeed snapped into place. "Are you ready?"

The helmet nodded, and Camber fired the motor. Stepping back, he motioned Bartlett to the track. As he was turning to climb the stairs to the top of the small concession stand to see the first laps, he heard gears grinding together. In an instant he was back at the driver's window.

"*Use the clutch!*" Camber stabbed with his finger at the pedal all the way to the left.

Bartlett nodded, gave Camber an apologetic wave, and lurched forward toward the track. He almost stalled a few times, but finally did manage to get the race car rolling down pit lane. Camber, heading back to the platform on top of the concession stand, could hear Bartlett fumble through the gears as he brought the car up to speed. He just got settled as Bartlett eased the car toward the start finish line to begin his first lap.

Meanwhile, Whitcomb had gotten into the spirit of race day excitement, and was wildly waving the green flag. Camber sighed and shook his head. *Rookies.* They were acting like this was the Daytona 500, but Reverend Bartlett was going about 25 miles per hour. At that speed you could do a paper route. Oh, well, it was early yet. They were bound to get better.

Since there was no radio contact with the driver, all Camber could do from the infield was watch the slow-motion performance on the track, which put him in mind of the first day of a driver's education class in a high school parking lot.

What happened to all those instructions Camber had given them before they started? *Entry, Apex, Exit*—Camber saw none of these put to use as Rev. Bartlett meandered around the track in what—from above—looked like a large squiggly line. Luckily, he wasn't going fast enough to cause any concern, except maybe for the expenditure of daylight. From his vantage point in the infield, unable to communicate with the hapless driver, Camber concentrated on devising ways to speed up the class's learning curve. *He has got to be almost done,* he thought.

He leaned over the roof of the concession stand, and called down to Scarberry, who was hunched over the stopwatch. "What lap is he on?"

"Four!" Scarberry yelled back. He stood up and raised four fingers, in case his answer had been drowned out by the engine noise.

"Right." Camber had seen enough. With a determined scowl he climbed down from his observation perch, and started hunting around the infield parking area until he found what he was looking for: a stack of orange traffic cones.

"If they are going to drive like they're in Driver's Ed., then I'm going to teach it that way," he muttered to himself. As he returned to pit road with the cones tucked under his arm, he could hear the car slowing down as it made its approach onto pit road.

Andrew Scarberry hurried up to him waving the time sheet.

"Thanks," said Camber, wincing at the recorded times.

"When he stops the car, get him out. and gather everyone else around the car. I'll be right back."

Camber ran out on to the track with his stack of orange cones in one hand and in the other the large black Sharpie marker that he had found discarded at the concessions building.

On the first cone in large black letters Camber wrote, "***Brake!***" He placed that cone on the outside concrete wall, and walked several paces farther down the track to the point where he had instructed his pupils to start their turn into the corner. There he placed another cone on the wall, this one bearing the instruction "***Turn!!***"

At the middle of the corner, on the apron of the track just off the banking, he placed a third cone, and on this one he wrote the word wrote "***APEX!!!***" This was where the car should be the lowest in the turn. After the driver passed this cone, he should be letting the car slowly drift up the track until he was back up against the wall for the dash down the straightaway.

Staying down at the bottom of the track, Camber walked a few car lengths past the apex cone and placed a last cone on that corner, this one labeled "***GAS!!!!***"

I should write a book, thought Camber. *One Hundred Ways to Know You're Not Cut Out to Be a Race Car Driver. Number 57: You have to stop and ask directions to make it around the track.*

Moving more quickly now, Camber went to the other end of the track, repeating the same directions on four more cones. With the prompts in place, he jogged back to his clueless flock. They were crowded around Bill Bartlett, who was regaling his colleagues with an account of his white knuckled laps behind the wheel. He had the helmet tucked under his arm, and occasionally he would pause and grin for a photo taken by one of his colleagues.

"If any of these turn out, e-mail them to me, will you?"

When he saw a scowling Camber approaching the group, he waved at him and called out, "Wow, what a thrill that was! Never felt anything like it. How in the world do you do that?"

Camber summoned a wan smile. *I know,* he thought, *I find it hard to drive under the speed limit, too.* "Glad you like it, he said evenly.

"So how did I do?" Bill Bartlett asked, still grinning with excitement.

Camber sighed. "Well, you didn't break any land speed records, but you also didn't wreck the car or run over the rest of the class. So let's call it a fair beginning."

"For all we know, Bill might be the fastest minister ever to drive a race car," said Rev. Albright.

Camber shook his head. "No, there's a NASCAR driver named Morgan Shepherd who won his share of races back in the day. Now he competes in his own car, and says he's *Racing for Jesus*."

Why discourage them this early, though? Everybody had to start somewhere. He looked at their crestfallen expressions, and decided that the best thing to do would be to change to a more positive subject. "Listen up, guys," he said. "I didn't change anything, but I did put up some reminders out there in case you forget to put your brain in gear when you leave pit road. *Brake, Turn, Gas, Repeat!* Remember me telling you that? Now have you got it?"

From their shame-faced expressions, Camber could tell that in the excitement of the driving lesson, they had completely forgotten all the technical points he had covered in his initial lecture.

"Well, *mea culpas* all round on that one, I think," said Stephen Albright.

"But we will try to remember the instructions."

"The cones will help," said Scarberry. "We're used to working with notes, aren't we, fellas?"

"Good," said Camber. "Father Frankie, you're next up. Let's get you belted in."

A suited-up Fr. Frankie slithered gracefully into the driver's seat and was quick to get situated, but, in order to be able to get good contact with the pedals, he needed a pad behind his back.

Camber returned to the concession stand and saw three of the ministers pushing the race car with Fr. Frankie inside to a rolling start as if trying to get him back into the race after a pit stop. *These guys missed their calling,* thought Camber. *Maybe they were supposed to be pit crew members. I know they were never meant to be drivers.*

As the car looped around the half-mile track, Camber was slowly turning in circles following its progress. He thought he heard the faintest squealing of tires as the car picked up speed. Fr. Frankie seemed to be settling into a groove and slowly accelerating as he negotiated the turns and straight-aways, each time a little more smoothly.

Ah, now this is more like it! Camber smiled. He waved to get Scarberry's attention and motioned "What lap?" In response, Scarberry smiled and held up nine fingers.

Camber smiled back. *Now we are getting somewhere,* he thought.

Moments later Paul Whitcomb was waving the checkered flag. Camber noticed that his flagging skills had already improved. He had instinctively mastered the tight figure eight pattern used by professional flag men. Well, at least they were learning something.

"Romney Marsh! Head out there and get the helmet and fire suit. You're next up!" Camber called out as he came down from his observation perch.

Romney Marsh waved his thanks and hurried toward the pit stall.

Grinning broadly, Scarberry handed Camber Fr. Frankie's times. "He was almost twice as fast!" he said, pointing to the list of numbers.

Camber glanced at the numbers and shrugged. "Times don't mean much until you guys are scoring in the low 20's. I'm going back up on top of the concession stand. Would you send the flying father up there when he gets out of the car? Thanks."

The other would-be drivers were belting Romney Marsh in, as Fr. Frankie climbed the stairs to talk to Camber. He was leaning his forearms on the roof's guardrail, watching to see if his pupils had perfected the operation of the seat belts and the window net. They were neither fast nor graceful, but he thought that they were managing to get the job done.

"Good Run, Father," he said, as the priest came up beside him.

Fr. Frankie seemed a bit shaken from his ten laps. "Thank you, for saying so, but it's harder than it looks, isn't it? I was certainly motivated—the spirit was willing, but the talent may have been a bit wanting. I may have got it wrong, but I felt that this early on, the speed is the salient point of the exercise. The seat took some getting used to, after a saddle, but the real difference to me between this and point-to-point was that I was on me own out there."

"How do you mean?"

"Well, a horse is your partner, especially if you've worked with him for years. You know what each other is thinking, and you can act accordingly. It's a team effort. But that great hunk of metal out there is a blank slate. Totally unpredictable. It doesn't know what I want, and it won't take up the slack if I get meself in a bind. To my mind it's a cold sport. You're alone out there. But never mind. I mustn't knock the sport. What advice do you have for me then?"

"Next time you go out, I want you to unwind the turns earlier," said Camber. "You're holding the car down at the bottom of the race track too long. When you do that, you bind the car up and lose a lot of speed. Do you follow me?"

"I think so, yes. I'll bear it in mind."

"Good. After Marsh finishes his run, why don't you go up in the flag stand and relieve Whitcomb? Watch the next drivers carefully. I think you'll see what I mean, because some of them are bound to make that same mistake of staying too long at the bottom of the track."

"Right. I'll do that."

"Oh and Father, don't give up on that partnership so early. That car may surprise you. That team spirit you felt with the horse may come yet."

* * *

They had been practicing for hours. Camber was sure it was three o'clock by now, and the routine seemed to be going smoothly, just not *fast*. But finally they were down to the last one's turn to drive.

Agnes Hill-Radnor, who was climbing in the race car now,

was the last person to go, which meant that soon they would be able to start on the second set of ten laps. She had chosen to let everyone else go before her, saying that since she had very little experience with cars, she thought she might benefit from watching the others' performance.

"Are you nervous?" asked Stephen Albright, who had been quite apprehensive before his own run.

Agnes shook her head. "I believe in angels, remember? So, I have to think I'm protected. There'll be one in the passenger seat."

"Only there isn't a passenger seat," muttered Paul Whitcomb.

Gallantly, Scarberry and Whitcomb helped her into the driver's seat, and supervised the adjusting of the belts, and then she was off. She seemed to be taking to the Monte Carlo well, going smoothly through the gears as she exited the pit, and accelerating heavily down the back stretch.

Camber studied the car closely, momentarily forgetting that the car was being driven by a novice because of the competent way it left pit lane. He was soon reminded otherwise, however, when the driver was late to the brakes and failed to slow quickly enough for the turn. Camber's heart skipped a beat, and he remembered who was in the car: probably the rankest novice of the whole bunch.

Now she was drifting way up the track, but the banking helped the car turn, keeping it off the wall. Just as it was pointed in the right direction, Agnes hammered the throttle just as Camber had done in the van on their first spins around the track. *Uh oh.* By this time Camber was racing down the steps, and sprinting flat out toward pit road.

He cleared pit wall in one bound, and continued on to the inside wall without breaking stride. He was waving his arms frantically, but he was only in time to see the blue streak of a race car hurtle down the front stretch at full speed. As Camber peered at the back of the car streaking down the straightaway, he saw Agnes again begin to brake late. Panic must have set in about the time she passed the "Turn!" cone that Camber had placed on the outside wall.

Camber saw the rear tires lock up as the car slid sideways into the turn. He dropped his arms and held them to the sides of his head, but the headache was purely psychological. He knew what was coming in about … oh … two heartbeats. Agnes and the race car slid helplessly toward the wall, rotating another 180 degrees before slamming into the concrete barrier.

Camber closed his eyes. *This is all I need,* he thought. He knew the hit wasn't that bad, but any impact on a race car always seemed to take a lot of work to fix. An instant later he was running toward the wrecked car, which was resting on the banking in turn one. Agnes was still sitting in the car, looking dazed but, fortunately, quite calm. He had been dreading a display of hysterics, and it might still come, but so far she just looked bewildered.

He let down the window net and asked, "Are you okay?"

"I believe I am fine." Agnes replied. "I don't really know what went wrong." *You were too hard on the gas; you braked too late; you jerked the steering wheel; and you locked up the wheels.* Aloud Camber said, "I think you were driving a little over your head."

Now that he had reassured himself that Agnes was unhurt, Camber began surveying the damage. The others were on their way to join them. He waved to let them know Agnes was all right, then he went back to surveying the damage. "Got to fix that fender," he muttered. "The toe looks a little off, too. Yeah, it is definitely out of alignment. We may even need a new tie rod end."

"I thought you said we couldn't drive it hard enough to spin it out," said Agnes. She had left the driver's seat, and was now perched on the car window, not yet trusting her legs to support her after such an ordeal. "What happened on the first day you drove a race car?"

"I spun it out." Camber mumbled under his breath, "but I didn't hit the wall. I guess instinct took over."

By now everyone had reached the disabled car, and were bombarding Agnes with expressions of sympathy and concern.

"I'm fine," she murmured. "It's not like being in a real car wreck. Apparently, all the safety equipment really does make a difference."

When they had accepted Agnes's assurances that she was fine, they turned their attention to the car itself, crowding around the wreck, and surveying the damage with expressions of dismay.

Camber said, "Look, guys, these things happen. It's not a big deal, but we do need to call it a day. I think this is enough excitement for all of us at this point. But we do need to find a way to get this car repaired before next time."

Travis Prichard was examining the crumpled fender with the dexterity of an expert. "I work at Farley's Garage," he said. "Don't know if I would have the know-how to get it back together, but it looks pretty straightforward. I do know I have the tools, and the space to work on it. You're welcome to bring it my way."

Agnes Hill-Radnor smiled up at him and laid her hand on his arm. "Well, Travis, it would seem that you are an angel unawares."

"Thanks, Travis," said Camber. "That would be really helpful." He knew he would need a hand with the repair job. Fixing race cars is hard to do from a jail cell.

Chapter Nine
Dirty Nails

Agnes Hill Radnor thought she had handled the situation well enough. This afternoon she, who had never been in a wreck in her entire life, had crashed a stock car into a concrete wall at more than a hundred miles an hour, but she had not screamed or succumbed to hysterics, and she had brushed aside all offers of sympathy and assistance from the men, insisting that she was perfectly fine. Now she was at home, sitting on the teakwood bench in her garden, and holding a cup of herbal tea with two shaking hands. Finally the tears came.

It was peaceful in the garden. The azaleas were in bloom, and where the flagstone paths met in a circle, stood an angel birdbath, encircled by clumps of fragrant white peonies. She didn't suppose that the effeminate looking figure in the sculpted robe looked anything like an actual celestial being, but she hoped they would appreciate the gesture. The garden, a well-tended plot behind Agnes's trim Cape Cod home, sat on the edge of the hill, overlooking the Institute for the Study of Angels in the meadow below. The Institute, a glass and cedar structure looking more like a small contemporary home than research building, was Agnes' pride and joy, and she had spent most of the inheritance from her father on its construction. So far, she and the cleaning lady were its only employees, but at least the project was underway. And she hoped that perhaps angels had taken notice of the graceful building, and that they graced it with their presence. It was comforting to think you had angels for neighbors. That was why she took such pains with the garden, really. She had never been interested in plants, but she felt obligated to provide a beautiful setting for any celestial visitors who might drop by. Otherwise, as far as she was concerned, the work of tending the garden would have been more trouble than it was worth.

Agnes mostly lived in her head, which meant that for much of the time she was scarcely aware of her surroundings. She ate whatever happened to be in the refrigerator whenever she was hungry; she wore comfortable, but unfashionable, clothes; and her house was furnished with utilitarian pieces, with no regard for decoration. But nothing was too good for the angels. Their building was serene and simply furnished with Chinese elm temple altars for tables, graceful teak stools, bamboo plants and soothing fountains of falling water. Its room spaces were partitioned with hand-painted parchment screens. She didn't know why she thought of angels as having Oriental taste in décor, but somehow it felt right to her. It was peaceful.

"Couldn't you just get six cats, Agnes?" her mother had asked her, when she mentioned her plans for the institute. "Although, I don't suppose you have to put down litter boxes for angels, so that's in their favor."

Agnes was offended by that remark, but she did not show it. Long ago she had learned not to show much emotion in front of her parents. It never got you any sympathy, so what was the point? Almost anything that ever made her cry was deemed silly and trivial by her parents. She just retreated farther into her own thoughts, and shut out as much of the world as she could. Things didn't improve as she grew up, because her parents' indifference was matched by the scorn of her schoolmates, who had no use for a plain, shy girl who didn't seem to be good at anything except reading.

When Agnes took refuge in angels, her logic was somewhat unexpected. She did not think she was more virtuous or holy than other people, and she certainly wasn't beautiful. So it wasn't that she thought she was special at all. Quite the reverse. *Paradise Lost* and other works touching on the subject of angels stated that these beings felt themselves infinitely superior to the plodding, earthbound humans, so dim in intellect, so inferior in every way. It would be so impossible to impress an angel that Agnes decided her deficits would hardly matter to them. To a superior being of light and wisdom, she would hardly be less beautiful or brilliant than the best human on earth—they were all worms together, as far as angels were concerned. So if angels took it upon themselves to be kind to human beings, then they wouldn't think her inferior to any of the other sorry specimens under their care. She found that quite comforting. From an ethereal point of view Agnes was the equal of beauty queens, scientists, ballerinas, and famous singers—no less beautiful or graceful or intelligent.

She didn't even mind that you couldn't see them. It was more comforting to think of an angel as a kind, sympathetic creature, always hovering nearby, and too considerate to show off with a burst of blinding radiance.

She looked at a circle of sunlight on the flagstone path. "Hello," she said softly. "I wrecked the race car today. I guess you know that. And I was so afraid. I felt so clumsy and useless. The others didn't say anything, but I know they think I'm hopeless. But, to you, we're all hopeless, aren't we?" In the quiet garden the shaft of sunlight blurred into mist as Agnes Hill-Radnor began to cry.

* * *

Danny Simpkins backed the rollback wrecker up to the rollup door on the side of Farley's Garage. Since he was a new employee and a little slow on the uptake, Darrell Farley would send Danny out on errands, so that while he was gone Darrell himself could check his repair work for disastrous mistakes.

When Travis Prichard had phoned the shop to let Darrell know that the race car he had driven today needed fixing, Darrell put the call on speaker phone so that everyone in the garage could savor the moment. After a round of jokes about Travis's driving ability, despite his assurances that the wreck was none of his doing, Darrell told him that help was on the way, and he dispatched Danny Simpkins with the garage's white Ford 350 Rollback wrecker to pick up the damaged race car.

Although it was located in a postage-stamp sized town, Farley's Garage was a formidable operation with gadgets you'd expect to find only in more elaborate establishments. The side roll-up door was opened by a trigger cord laid across the pavement, much like the ones that used to activate the bell at full-service gas stations. This roll-up door opened up to the aisle between two rows of well-spaced vehicle lifts: Five lifts on the right side, the front side of the building facing the road, and one fewer on the left, leaving room for the office and changing room at the far side of the building.

Between the second and third lifts was a large black appliance: a waste-oil heater. Since he had such a large shop to heat, Farley liked the idea of saving money on fuel, and he didn't mind that the waste oil heater smoked up the building a little when it was first cranked up. A little smoke was a minor inconvenience in exchange for being able to burn all the oil that they drained out of the cars while doing the routine oil changes.

Some of the mechanics complained about the smell of burning oil, but Travis Prichard was not one of them. He was too busy. He was the only mechanic in the shop allowed by Farley to use two lifts, which allowed Travis to work on one car until he had pinpointed the problem, then to order the repair parts from the local auto parts store. While he waited for the parts to arrive, he could start work on the car on his second lift, without needing to waste time making sure the first car was sufficiently assembled to be moved. Ideally, by the time he had reached the point of ordering parts or waiting for customer approval on the second car, the parts for the first car would have arrived. This back and forth method of auto repair was much more cost and time efficient than the one car/ one lift method.

Darrell Farley himself had operated like this when all he had was two lifts in a little filling station garage. When prosperity allowed him to build this larger shop, he found it was easier just to keep one lift for himself, and to use the downtime between jobs to tend to the managerial duties of the shop: ordering supplies, paying bills, and calling customers to let them know their vehicles were ready. He was quite content to pass the workhorse duties on to Travis Prichard. Travis's second lift was the one he and Camber would use to repair the slightly crumpled Monte Carlo.

Camber jumped down from the passenger side of the wrecker, and walked around the truck to look at the damaged corner of the race car. Now that it was up on the bed of the rollback, he could inspect the damage from another angle. Danny Simpkins was disconnecting chains and preparing to raise the truck bed to unload the car. When he had finished inspecting the damage, Camber walked through the open door, and stood in the middle of the aisle surveying his new work environment. *Finally something civilized,* Camber thought. *This place is nice.* He noticed Travis standing nearby, organizing some tools on top his tool box. "I won't say what I was expecting," Camber told Travis, "but this is better, for sure."

Prichard smiled. "I'll introduce you to Darrell. I'm sure he will appreciate the kind words. It's his place. He built it a few years back. I told him I was going to let you use my second lift, so you can pull tools from my box if you need."

"I'm sure I will," Camber pointed back in the direction of the rollback. "I keep finding more things we'll have to do to get her back on track. I'm afraid the damage is more than we can take care of with a drill and some pop rivets. Er—There's nothing in that box of yours that might bite is there?"

Camber was looking at Prichard's black mechanic's toolbox. On racers' toolboxes, he had seen perfect airbrushed portrayals of Dale Earnhardt, Sr. and the occasional Virgin Mary surrounded by glowing light emanating all around, but the design on this toolbox was one Camber had never seen before. The scene was a beautiful garden; the Garden of Eden, Camber suspected. In the center of the picture was one fruiting tree, bordered by small flowering bushes, but the foreground was piled two and three deep with serpents, coiling over and through each other. The writhing snakes continued around the trunk of the tree, and dangled from its branches in a way that had made Camber mistake them for tangles of moss, before he had taken a closer look at this eerie but magnificent work of art.

"Oh, I wouldn't worry too much about that," Prichard said softly. "Now we'd better go help Danny off-load that car before he rips off the whole front."

Camber was not reassured by Travis Prichard's evasive answer, but he decided not to press the matter. He backed away from the toolbox and followed Prichard to the rollback.

They managed to unload the race car, but Camber's efforts to use the steering wheel to direct the car into position proved fruitless. The left front wheel was stuck a good twenty degrees to the right, while the right side pointed dead ahead. This imbalance rendered the car impossible to steer. Despite the combined efforts of Camber, Travis and Danny, pushing and pulling, it remained immobile. Finally, they decided to stick a floor jack under the front of the car and lift the whole front end off the ground. Camber steered the wheeled jack, while Travis and Danny slowly guided the race car from its windows. By the time they had the car positioned on the lift, all work in the shop had stopped, and the other mechanics had gathered around to examine the damaged Monte Carlo.

"What's this blueberry patch about?" said Darrell Farley, coming out of the office. *Blueberry patch* was Farley's favorite term for his mechanics in their blue coveralls all grouped together. He tried to break up blueberry patches whenever he could, because they meant that productivity was coming to a standstill. In order to make a profit in a big shop like this, he needed to keep a steady stream of cars going in and out as quickly as possible, which meant keeping socializing to a minimum.

"This is the wrecked race car I phoned about, Darrell," Prichard told him. "And let me introduce our new local celebrity racecar driving coach, Cameron Berkley."

Camber felt like correcting Travis Prichard on two points: One—he would hardly consider himself a celebrity, even if he did drive a race car now and then, and two, he was not local. He would be out of this bad dream as soon as someone removed that pesky ankle bracelet.

Ankle bracelet! Then he remembered.

Pajan Mosby, he thought. *She must be almost to the Speedway right now. I told her we would be there most of the day. She is going to have a fit when she sees I'm not there. Come to think of it, she is going to have an even bigger fit when I have to tell her that someone wrecked.* Summoning a wan smile, Camber shook hands with Darrell. "Pleased to meet you, sir. Great shop!"

Darrell Farley swelled with pride. "Thank you. Thank you, young man," he said. "Now what number did you say you drove?"

Here it comes, thought Camber. "Umm, well, actually, most recently I drove the 10, the 8 and the 62, but not in the Cup series." He needed to change the subject quickly or else he'd have to explain his complicated, and exceedingly minor, career in stock car racing. "Say, do you have a phone I could use? I've just remembered that I need to call my Paro ... er, my *ride* from the race track." He glanced around self-consciously to see if anyone had been listening closely enough to pick up on his slip. Apparently, they hadn't.

"Why don't you use the phone in the office. It will be less noisy in there," he said, motioning toward the far end of the shop. "Right through those doors." He turned back to the blueberry patch. "All right, y'all, I guess it is quittin' time, anyway," he said, because he couldn't resist the urge to inspect the racecar, either.

In Farley's office, Camber searched his jeans pockets for the tattered business card Pajan Mosby had given him when she had ordered him to call in and report the slightest change in plans. This detour to Farley's Garage was indeed a change in plans, and he hoped that in his absence she had not already issued a bench warrant for his capture. Bracing himself for the coming storm, he dialed the number marked "cell," and waited her to answer.

Before he could speak, Pajan's voice barked out of the receiver. "Darrell Farley, you were going to be my next phone call. That beltway brat has skipped out, and I wanted to warn you that he may come after his car. When I got the page I was right in the middle of—"

"I guess you already know where I am then." said Camber.

After a shocked silence, followed by what sounded like a

growl, Pajan said evenly, "Oh, it's *you*."

"Don't sound so happy to hear from me, I figured I just saved you the hassle of tracking me through the swamp with the bloodhounds."

"We don't have swamps, and don't flatter yourself," Pajan said. "After I got the page that you had left the track, it didn't take two phone calls to locate a pretty boy without an accent in this town."

"Right, then, I won't flatter myself" said Camber, now thoroughly confused as to whether he was being complimented or put down. "I just wanted to let you know there was some damage to the race car. Reverend Prichard and I are at Farley's garage figuring out what it's going to take to fix it. Don't worry, though. No one was hurt."

"A wreck? What happened?"

Now she was distracted from the legal implications of his temporary vanishing act. Good.

"It was just a spinout with a little damage," he told her. "The angel lady, Agnes Hill-Radner brushed the wall, that's all. Like I said, no one is the worse for wear."

Pajan sighed. "I told Jimmy when he made that silly will that this race wasn't a good idea. It's not the old days anymore. He didn't grow up in the days of litigation. Oh, he insisted that the estate could pay for tires and gas and any damage, but nowadays they put the name of everyone involved on lawsuits. Did he give a moment's thought to everyone that had to carry out his crazy plan? Oh, no. He said, 'What can they do to me? I'll be dead.' Just like a man."

That speech answered the second reason for Camber's phone call. He figured that he could fix the car without too much trouble. Many a time, out of necessity, he had been required to work on his own cars, but in this case he had been wondering who was going to pay for the new tie rod, or the A-arm, or the sheet metal and Bondo they would need to make the new fender.

Old Jimmy was quite a race fan, thought Camber. *I need to find an Angel investor like that until I can attract a big name sponsor. I hope crashing his funeral didn't saddle me with any bad karma in that department.* He ventured an interruption into Pajan's train of thought. "I'm sorry. I totally forgot about the ankle bracelet, I didn't realize that coming here was going to cause such a big problem. I was only trying to get a jump start on fixing the car."

"Well, there won't be any fixing tonight. I have got to get you back to your cell and show that the situation is under control. I'll have you report to Farley's garage for your service tomorrow morning. Just make sure you stay where you are."

Camber went back to the shop floor and looked over the car one more time, reviewing his mental list of what had to be done, and what parts needed to be bought or fabricated. By this time all the mechanics in the shop, including Travis, were locking their tool boxes and scrubbing up in preparation for leaving. Camber thanked Travis for the space and said he'd be back in the morning to tackle the repairs.

He walked outside in front of the shop, and sat on a wooden bench next to some planters by the road. As he turned to watch a passing car head into town, he realized that he was only a few blocks, not miles, away from the jail. It annoyed him to have to wait on Pajan, or on anyone for that matter, when he could accomplish the objective quicker and easier on his own. Fighting the urge to begin walking toward the jail, he leaned forward with his face in hands, closed his eyes, and took a couple of deep breaths.

Camber often thought that he was in a race against time, against his own age, to make it big in racing. In his late twenties, he certainly wasn't old, but in a sport where stars are being made out of 18 and 19-year olds, he knew his time was limited. Having to sit and wait for things to happen irritated Camber even more than setbacks like spinning off the road. Obstacles were to be dealt with and put aside until there were no more obstacles, and the end goal had been accomplished. As long as he was making progress or using his time productively, Camber felt a since of rightness with the world.

After half a dozen deep breaths, he opened his eyes. He had thought of something that would be a productive use of this waiting time; something that he could accomplish under his current constraints. He walked around to the back of Farley's garage where a fenced lot housed both the customer cars waiting to be worked on and the impounded cars from Farley's Towing Service.

As he had hoped, the gate was unlocked, since a few mechanics were still inside finishing up work. Now he was feeling that familiar and strangely comforting sense of racing against time. Now was his chance to inspect the damage to his own car, which had been towed here after the wreck. Also, if he had time before the guys locked the gate and before Pajan arrived, he desperately wanted to get at least a text message off to Brennan, telling him where he was.

He slipped down the row of cars until he found his own-not-so trusty ride. The sight of it made him wince. *I don't remember it looking that bad,* he thought. His recollections of the events surrounding the crash were hazy at best, due to the probable concussion. Now he began inspecting the car in earnest. Action movies make it look as if cars can fly, but reality had proved to Camber that automotive acrobatics do not come without a severe amount of damage. He was going need to get this fixed, or else he was going to be stuck in Judas Grove even after his sentence was served.

He got down on his knees beside the car and eased open the door furthest away from the building in order to avoid being seen. He wasn't sure if this constituted evidence tampering, or attempted escape, but he was pretty sure that anyone seeing him might take it the wrong way. He only wanted to find his cell phone. He remembered placing it in the cup holder, before he had spotted Tracy in his rear view mirror. It wasn't there now. It must have slid somewhere during the wreck. He groped for it beneath the seats.

"Bingo!" He muttered, feeling his hand close around the cell phone. Better hurry, though. Pajan must be almost here, he thought, as he waited for the phone to power up. Finally its screen flashed "*Welcome,*" and then went blank again.

Dead. He grabbed the car charger, still dangling from the cigarette lighter, and plugged in the phone. He made sure the red light started to blink, signaling it was receiving power.

Good. They didn't disconnect the battery, he thought, tucking the phone between the driver's seat and the center console in case anyone walked by. After looking around to make sure the coast was clear, he closed the door softly, and hurried back to the bench to wait.

He was rounding the corner just as Pajan 's car came into view. He slid into place on the bench with a smile of satisfaction.

He had made progress.

* * *

When Camber reached the jail, half a mile and one blistering lecture later, he discovered that he was no longer the only inmate. In the cell across the corridor, a small dark-haired man in jeans and a white tee shirt was doing push-ups.

Stoney, who had been eating a take-out chicken dinner at his desk, had not escorted him back to the cells. "It's unlocked," he said, between bites. "Go on back. If you need anything, lemme know."

"Thanks, man," said Camber, heading for the door to the holding cells. "I'll grab a shower later." But Stoney had forgotten to mention that he had company.

"Good evening," he said to his fellow inmate. Idly, Camber wondered what the guy was in for. He figured that if it had been for something momentous, like murder or bank robbery, Stoney would have mentioned it.

The new guy was a little chicken hawk with crinkly black hair, a genetic tan, a tiny pencil moustache, and a cocky demeanor suggesting that the only reason he didn't rule the world was because he didn't like the hours.

Before he took any notice of Camber, he finished a dozen more push-ups, muttering, "*Noventa y ocho … noventa y nueve … cien …*" After "cien," he wiped his forehead with the back of his hand, rolled back on his haunches, and looked up appraisingly at the newcomer. "Do ju work here, *Compa?*" His tone of voice made the question a preamble to the litany of complaints that would follow.

Camber shook his head. "I'm your neighbor," he said, pointing to the cell across the corridor. "Name's Camber Berkley. Reckless driving."

The response was a regal nod. "I myself am a political prisoner," said the man, pushing back a forelock of black curls to display a long gash in his scalp line.

"Jesus!" said Camber.

"Oh, you have heard of me? And, while I do not wish to insult your pronunciation skills in español, in fact it is more correct to pronounce my name *hay-soos*. Jesús Segovia. The last name is not so difficult," he added kindly.

"I was reacting to that gash on your head," said Camber, still eying the blood-encrusted wound. "Please tell me Stoney didn't do that to you."

"You refer to the *chota* in the other room? You are joking, right? Although it is true that he did insult me by claiming that at the time of arrest I was *ebrio.* Ha! It would take a lake full of that horse piss they serve at Jacks Or Better to make me in-e-bri-ated." He grinned happily at Camber. "You see? My English is perfect."

"Better than my Spanish," Camber conceded. "But what happened to your head?"

"This I am telling you. There was an altercation at this tavern, Jacks Or Better, and I am inflicting more damage on the other guy than I am receiving, and so I am charged with assault." With an eloquent shrug, he added, "Assault I do not deny. It was a matter of honor, and the *cabròn* had it coming."

Camber, threading his way through this narrative, thought for a moment and said, "So you got in a bar fight with some guy and he cut your scalp, and you—what did you do to him?"

"I rearranged his nose for him. With my right fist." He paused to show Camber the bruises on his knuckles. "The cabron is now in the hospital providing the local doctors with an amusing human jigsaw puzzle."

"Okay. So what did the guy do? Make fun of your name?"

"My name?" Jesús Segovia waved aside the suggestion. "Such things do not concern me. I am a man of great good humor and tolerance." He peered up at Camber. "Did I understand the *poli* to say that you are a race car driver?"

"Yes. — Not a famous one, though."

"Modesty is an admirable thing in a man. I myself am the soul of modesty. You will never hear me bragging about my amazing good looks or my keen intelligence. Still, it is good that you are a race car driver. You will be able to understand the source of my displeasure."

"You were fighting about racing?"

"I was defending the honor of my chosen NASCAR driver."

Camber nodded. "Juan Pablo Montoya." It was hardly even a guess. Montoya, a former winner of the Indianapolis 500, and originally from Colombia, was the only Hispanic driver currently in NASCAR, which gave him a built-in fan base of several million *aficionados.*

Jesús nodded. "And you are also a supporter of the estimable Montoya?"

Camber hesitated. Then, choosing discretion over honesty, he said, "Well, he's generally my second choice to win," carefully not adding that his first choice to win would be the other forty-two drivers. And the pace car.

"For me, he is the only choice," said Jesús. "A very great man, Montoya. Almost as talented as myself, though in a different field, of course. And so in the bar tonight, this *cabròn* from Mexico City, who is, for reasons beyond my comprehension, a supporter of the tiny vanilla Jeff Gordon, starts to make fun of Montoya's number."

Camber blinked. "Make fun of his *number?* Montoya … He drives the 42, right? But so what?"

"It was an unfortunate choice," said Jesús Segovia with a theatrical sigh. "But the team for which he drives knows nothing of Hispanic culture, and even Montoya himself, who is Colombian, was probably not aware of the significance, but in the D.F., that is Mexico City, *forty-two* has a meaning."

"What kind of meaning?"

Jesús Segovia took a deep breath. "Very well, I will tell you the long story, so that you will see how complete was my justification in rearranging the geography of the face of the cabròn. The story begins in 1905, in Mexico City. The *oficiales* raid a notorious nightclub, and arrest forty-two men, who are not dressed as men. They are—"

"In drag?"

"Just so. But, within a day, the authorities release prisoner number forty-two, saying that this one in women's clothes was really a woman. But at once the rumor goes around the city that this is a lie to cover up the fact that this forty-second man was a close relative of *el presidente,* Porfirio Diaz, and that the prisoner's prominence has protected him from prosecution."

Camber nodded. "So now in Mexican slang number forty-two means … a drag queen?"

"I told you it was unfortunate. We Montoya supporters do not speak of it in connection with NASCAR. But this *retrasado* in the bar: he is drunk; he is loud; and he will not shut up with his 42 jokes. So with my fist I apply to him a restrictor plate." He inclined his head in a restrained bow, indicating that he felt that the appropriate response from the police would have been a medal, rather than a jail cell. "So here I am, locked up in the *poli,* but Honor is served."

Camber gave an inward sigh of relief that he had been diplomatic in expressing his own opinion of Jesús's favorite driver. "So how long are you in for?"

"That is yet to be determined. Since I was not able to come up with bail money, I will be here for some little time, anyway."

"Yeah, me, too," said Camber. "So what do you do, when you're not sticking up for Montoya?"

The brown eyes sparkled. "You could say that I am in the car business."

"Good to know," said Camber, stifling a yawn. "Well, I'm going across the hall to turn in.

* * *

The next morning Camber was still rubbing his eyes and trying to wake up when Stoney dropped him off at Farley's Garage. The clock on the patrol car's dashboard read 8:00, but when Camber entered the garage, work was already going on at full tilt.

"Hey, guys, Camber is here!" Danny Simpkins shouted,

spotting him from across the shop. They had gotten acquainted when Camber rode from the track to Farley's with Danny in the wrecker. Some of the other mechanics waved, while others gave him a friendly nod, while they went on with their work.

Camber walked over to Travis Prichard, who was working on the rear axle of a van. From the look of it Camber figured that it belonged to a local plumbing contractor. Travis had put a drain pan under the rear differential and removed the differential cover, exposing its ring and pinion gears. The most likely problem in an over-loaded work van was excessive wear.

"Glad to see you made it back." said Prichard.

Camber stifled a yawn. "I don't know that I'm awake yet, but I'm here. If I'm at the track, four or five a.m., it isn't a problem, but just about anywhere else, it seems like getting up at seven is a stretch. Good thing I live right above the machine shop where I help out. Good thing I am buddies with the owner, come to think of it." said Camber. *That damn metal plate that passes for a bed in the jail probably has some thing to do with me getting up so early,* he thought.

Prichard nodded. "Machine shop, eh? So you know your way around a tool box, then. You seemed like you knew what you were doing around the car, but I still thought you might be one of those drivers who never worked on a car."

"Oh, I know the type," said Camber, thinking of Tracy. Once when he and Tracy were racing at a local track, the distributor wire had come off Tracy's car just before the race, and the engine wouldn't fire. Tracy had just cranked and cranked until the battery died. Then he went over and asked Camber to fix it for him, because the mechanic that Tracy's parents hired to work on his car had ducked out to the bathroom just before the start of the race.

"Guess I've never been fortunate enough to have the mechanics done for me by somebody else," he told Prichard.

Prichard smiled. "One thing I remember from my time racing down at the speedway was talking shop with all the other drivers. We'd discuss the parts on the car that kept breaking. There were always a lot of mechanical problems we had to solve. The guys who have never worked on a car themselves—what on earth do they talk about with each other? Their next hair appointment?"

Camber held the button on the lift to raise the race car into the air. When it was in place, he started digging tools out of the box with the Garden of Eden artwork. "If you don't mind my asking, Reverend Scarberry mentioned that you were from a snake handler church. Was he serious about that?"

"Well, his terminology leaves a lot to be desired, but that's the gist of it," said Prichard. "We are a Pentecostal sect, and we prefer the term *sign-followers.*"

"Sign followers," mused Camber, savoring the term. "I don't think there were any of them close to where I grew up." He paused long enough to cut the crumpled fender off the front of the race car with a reciprocating saw. "What does that mean exactly?"

"There are a number of signs that show that one is anointed in the Lord. Speaking in tongues. The gift of prophecy. Healing the sick. Protection from fire, and poison, and—yes—serpents. We don't say *snake,* either, because a snake can be any old harmless belly-crawler. A serpent is always poisonous. Where are you from?"

"Northern Virginia. Inside the Beltway. All our serpents are elected officials."

Travis laughed. "No, I don't guess there are many serpent handlers up there, unless you count lobbyists. Not that you'd know of, living in suburbia." He was scraping small piles of metal shavings from the axle housing. "Yeah, this is going to need a whole new gear set. Frank is going to be peeved about that, I bet."

The fender Camber had cut off lay discarded on the floor. The front tire was off, and now he was disassembling the front suspension. "Okay, but do you all really dance with snakes? Serpents, that is. I mean this toolbox art is kind of scary." Camber dropped a few more parts on to the floor. "I hope your parts guy can get us some ball joints and a tie rod for this sucker."

Prichard nodded. "Do we dance with serpents? Well, they

don't have any legs, you know."

Camber laughed. "Yeah, but you could carry them around while you did the dancing."

"That has been known to happen when someone is filled with the Holy Spirit. The serpent just coils around your neck or your arm, while you move," said Travis. "But of course, he can't hear the music. Snakes can sense vibrations, but they can't hear. So it's not like snake charming. They act the same whether music is playing or not." Travis paused while he counted the teeth on the ring gear so that he could order the correct ratio replacement. "You know, I'll bet our church service is not a whole lot different from the ones you went to growing up. Lots of singing and praising the Lord, a sermon, and some praying. I guess we do have some different ways of letting the Holy Spirit shine through."

"We never handled snakes," said Camber, as he opened a drawer to the tool box in search of the open-ended wrenches.

"Well, hardly anybody at our church does that, either. Only those who have been called to do it, and that's generally just one or two people. We wouldn't let just anybody try it, and certainly not anyone under voting age. But we do cite Biblical authority for speaking in tongues, testifying, and, yes, picking up a serpent or drinking poison, if we feel that the Holy Spirit is calling on us to do it."

"Remind me to stay away from the Kool-Ade if I stop by." Camber felt a chill down his spine.

"I told you: nobody is forced to do anything. It is like a calling. My wife wouldn't go near a serpent for anything in the world. I tell her that according to the Bible, if she believes in the Lord, she'll be safe, but she says she's afraid that the snake might be an atheist." He grinned to let Camber know he was joking. "It's only a small part of the service, and of our beliefs. It just gets the most publicity, unfortunately. We don't pass serpents around like the collection plate, if that's what you're thinking."

"But you have done it? Held the snake and drank poison?" Camber stopped working and looked at Travis, waiting for an answer.

"And I'm still alive and kicking. It is a nice feeling not having to be scared, knowing someone is watching over you."

I don't know; I thought it was kind of creepy having Jesús looking over at me this morning, Camber thought.

An hour later, when Travis announced that he was going to call in his parts order, Camber handed him the list of new parts the racecar was going to need, and took the opportunity to slip outside and grab his cell phone.

He unplugged his phone from the charger, pressed the power button and hurried back into the building. When the screen powered up this time, the battery indicator was on Full, and the screen flashed the message "15 New Voice Mails." Camber pressed okay. Then it said "8 New Text Messages," and again Camber hit okay. "1 New Reminder."

Oh crap, thought Camber, remembering what he had set a reminder for. *Brennan's bank meeting!*

He had promised to be there with Brennan to help him secure a loan for the production of the new molds for the cylinder heads. Since Camber didn't have any money to put into the venture, he was supposed to act as an expert witness on business and racing, and otherwise promise the money people that Brennan's new cylinder heads were going to be financial success.

In the last few weeks, Camber had drawn up some charts and figures to present at the meeting, but he had only half explained them to Brennan, telling him not to worry about the details, because he would be there to present them.

Camber equated the bank meeting with any other sponsorship presentation: *You give us all this money, and we will put it to good use, and make it give you back a lot of money.* In fact, Camber thought talking to the bankers was going to be a lot easier than a sponsorship pitch. In racing, a sponsoring company was taking a real leap of faith, because they wouldn't really have any recourse if the race team performed poorly. But in return for this loan, the bank would be able to get collateral against Brennan's equipment, or the business itself, or possibly even his personal car; basically, whatever they could get to secure their risk.

Oh, this situation was getting bad, thought Camber. He knew that because of this current legal trouble, his own season of racing was in jeopardy—and maybe even his whole career—but now his friendship and partnership with Brennan Morgan was also at risk. Several times in the past his crazy antics had been an annoyance to the steady and practical Brennan, but that had been mostly unintentional. Camber had never absolutely let him down on a promise.

Not showing up for this bank meeting would constitute a disaster for Brennan, who had been fretting over it for weeks now. His cylinder head production depended on a favorable outcome to this meeting. Brennan and Camber had mapped, measured, and tested those prototypes as much as they could. Now they needed to start putting rubber to the road on the project, and begin production, except that to do so would require an influx of capital that neither Camber, who was flat broke, or Brennan, whose credit was maxed out, could manage.

Camber knew that Brennan's machine shop was just barely surviving on the day-to-day work that it brought in: motor rebuilds, high-performance modifications like porting and polishing, and other custom work that people from around town needed done. The problem was that Brennan had some of his first commercial notes coming due, and he had planned on being able to start selling cylinder heads before he had to pay back those notes.

Brennan could lose everything.

Camber felt a pang of guilt for having been so selfish. He looked down at his phone, brimming with messages, probably all from the increasingly frantic Brennan. He wished he could reassure him, but he couldn't think of what message he could text that would make the situation any better. *Help I wrecked my car please send money?* Or *Sorry you are going to lose your business, but could you come get me out of jail?* With a helpless sigh, Camber powered off the phone to save the battery, shoved it into the pocket of his jeans, and went back to the race car.

Just as he was coming back, Travis walked out of the office. "Parts are on their way," he said. "We're in luck. Everything will be here after lunch."

Camber, still choked up with guilt over Brennan's situation, didn't trust himself to say anything. He nodded, returned to the car, and picked up the fender, pounding it violently. Hammering this one back into shape, instead of calmly fashioning a new fender out of flat sheet metal, would offer him an emotional outlet while he was waiting for the parts to arrive. It might even improve his frame of mind.

Travis and Camber kept working and making small talk. The day went quickly for Camber, as almost all days did when he was working on a race car. There were never enough hours to get everything done.

Camber had almost finished riveting the fender when Travis announced that he was going to order a sub from the local diner, so that they could keep working through lunch. Camber, who remembered a box of Pop Tarts that he kept in his truck for just such emergencies, said that he would be fine. At least Prichard had remembered lunch. Camber recalled several past occasions in which he had walked into a racing shop and as he worked, the hours had passed by like the old cinematic image of fast-forwarding hands on a clock.

By the end of the day Camber had put the car back together and was applying thin layers of Bondo to smooth out all the hammer marks on the fender.

"I think she's all set," he said to no one in particular. "I still have to align the front end, but I can do that at the track. We'll give her a coat of paint before the big race as well."

Before he left the shop, Camber took the cell phone out of his pocket, typed in a brief text message to Brennan, and clicked *Send.* He switched it off, walked back inside to the newly-repaired race car, and stashed it under the worn racing seat cover. As he said good night to Travis and Danny. He was thinking that on all fronts, he had done everything he could do today. He hoped it was enough.

Chapter Ten
What A Friend We Have in Jesús

In the Bren-mor Race Shop in Mooresville, Brennan Morgan scowled at the text message as if he wanted to hold his cell phone personally responsible for the absurdity of it.

Camber had finally checked in with a cryptic message, but although Brennan had been calling his cell phone all morning, his calls kept getting shunted straight to Camber's voice mail, so he really didn't know any more about Camber's whereabouts than he had before. He did know that Camber wasn't dead, but Tracy had already told him that much when he'd called earlier.

So he wasn't dead. As far as Brennan was concerned, the question now was whether he deserved to be. Or whether he was in his right mind, or suffering from a concussion, or drunk, or what. Considering the text message Camber had sent, any of those things seemed possible.

For the tenth time Brennan looked at the message. Camber was speaking in tongues again. Or, to be exact, he was using their old code system from the days when Camber raced Late Model Stock with Brennan as his crew chief. During a race a driver can communicate with his team on a radio frequency, but that conversation can be overheard by anybody who tunes in to that wavelength. Some strategic decisions, like whether to pit on a given lap or whether to take two new tires or four, should be kept secret from the other teams out there, so NASCAR drivers often used innocuous-sounding code words to convey their messages more privately.

In Late Model Stock races such subterfuges weren't strictly necessary, because the races were too short to require much in the way of tires or fuel stops, but Camber was an incurable Tom Sawyer, who reveled in all the trappings of adventure. He had managed to memorize most of the ten-codes used by police and rescue personnel, and he insisted on trying to communicate with Brennan by way of these codes.

"Ten-fifty-nine," he would say when he wanted to complain about another driver.

Brennan, who refused to waste a single brain cell on such a frivolous exercise, would pull the cheat sheet out of his pocket and consult the key: 10-59 reckless driver. Then he would bark back another ten code, as an exercise in sarcasm, because Camber refused to be discouraged by his lack of enthusiasm. "Ten-ninety-six," he would say. *Mental patient at large.* But try as he might, Brennan could never dissuade Camber from using his precious codes. Over the years Brennan had even managed to learn a dozen or so of the most popular ones, although he grudged the brain space.

The message that appeared now on his cell phone was a string of ten-codes and a two-word message. *Oh, now what?* Not only was Camber missing and unaccounted for, now he was back to playing James Bond with his cell phone. With a weary sigh, Brennan opened his desk drawer, and rummaged through its contents for his cheat sheet.

"10-50, 10-82, 10-20 Judas Grove, 10-33. 10-33."

Brennan studied the message. He knew the last one without having to consult the key. Ten-thirty-three. *Help me quick.* The fact that this one was repeated twice meant that the matter was especially urgent. It always was, thought Brennan with another sigh. Now what did those other three numbers mean?

He ran his finger down the list. Ten-fifty: traffic accident. That didn't come as a surprise. He had figured that much, especially after his conversation with Tracy. He didn't recognize ten-eighty-two. That wasn't one of the usual ones. He had been expecting something like ten-fifty-one: wrecker needed. He consulted the list again, running his finger along the columns. Ten eight-two: prisoner in custody. That couldn't be right. What was Camber doing, taking hostages?

He glanced again at the 10-code list. It couldn't be that much of an emergency if Camber was still jaunty enough to use his old spy routine. Brennan typed in his opinion of the crisis: 10-65 and then, relenting a bit, because, after all, he was worried, he added: 10-81? While he was waiting for a reply from Camber, he would go to MapQuest and determine the location of a town called Judas Grove.

* * *

Pajan Mosby had appeared in the jail corridor, ten minutes early and jangling her car keys.

In his cell Camber stifled a yawn, and reluctantly set down his mug of coffee on the metal bunk. "You know you don't have to drive me out to the track this morning," he said. "I could hitch a ride with Danny from Farley's Garage. He's going to deliver the race car to the track this morning." He tried to sound like someone who didn't want to be a nuisance, rather than like someone who wanted to finish his coffee and to avoid spending half an hour being treated like vermin by Pajan Mosby.

He must have given a less-than-stellar performance of humility, because Pajan glared him and said, "The condition for your work release states that you are to have regular contact with a member of the court to ensure satisfactory progress in your community service. I think of it as getting two things done at once. You can think of it as me doing you a favor by getting you out of regular meetings with a parole officer."

Camber shrugged. "Well, as long as you're doing me favors, could you get Stoney to release my driving bag?"

"What's a driving bag?"

"It contains my helmet, my driving shoes, and a fire suit. I think I'd better shake down the race car before I let anyone else get in it again. You know, to make sure that all the kinks are worked out from the repairs."

She thought it over for a few moments, but apparently she was unable to find a flaw in his request. "Fine," she said. "I'll ask Stoney to put the bag in my car. After he has searched it, of course. Shaking down the race car sounds like a good idea. If someone else is going to hit the wall, I'd just as soon it was you."

"Me, too," said Camber, and he meant it. Since he was used to wrecking cars on a speedway, and younger than any of the ministers, he thought he had a better chance of escaping injury if the car did crash.

Pajan turned to Jesús who was pacing his cell. "Good morning, Mr. Segovia," she said, still business-like, but with a few degrees more warmth in her voice.

Jesús acknowledged her greeting with a regal nod. "*Buenos dìas, Señorita,*" he said. "The day was not so *bueno* before, but now that you have come, there is more brightness here."

To Camber's amazement, his legal nanny smiled at this blatant piece of flattery. *Must be the Antonio Banderas accent,* he thought.

Still smiling, Pajan withdrew a business card from her briefcase, and handed it through the bars to Jesús. "I was informed that you were interested in posting bail. My name is Pajan Mosby, and I am a bail bondsmen. When you have your affairs in order, ask the deputy to give me a call."

Jesús took the business card. "Pa-han?" he said, sounding the "j" as an "h.," as the "j" in "Jesus" is pronounced in Spanish.

She laughed. "Well, that's better than 'pagan,' which is what I usually get. Actually, my name is pronounced pay-jan. It's a combination of Patricia and Janice; I was named after my grandmothers. And your name is pronounced Hay-soose?"

Camber contemplated his empty coffee cup, thinking he probably had time to ask Stoney for a refill. In fact, the way the chitchat was going between Pajan and her new best friend, he probably had time to grow the coffee beans.

"What a beautiful pronunciation you have," said Jesús. "To hear you read aloud from the works of Cervantes would be a symphony."

Pajan blushed. "Oh, I just had a couple of courses in college. But I won the Beginning Spanish award in high school."

"Of course, you did!" said Jesús. "But to return to this disagreeable business of my incarceration. Has the judge yet ruled on how much it will cost to finance my liberation?"

Pajan sighed sympathetically. She obviously regarded Jesús as an unfairly imprisoned puppy in a particularly foul dog pound. "Well ... Jesús ... Because you are a foreign national, the court considers you a considerable flight risk."

Jesús drew himself up, the personification of outraged honor. "Segovias do not *flight*," he said. "If I had flighted instead of choosing to do battle with that *ladròn* at Jack's Or Better, I would not be in this pretty pass."

"No, of course not," murmured Pajan. "You mustn't take the ruling personally. They simply go by a set formula of risk factors, and I'm afraid there is nothing we can do about it. I'm sorry I can't help you with that."

Jesús fixed her with his mournful brown eyes. "It is enough that I am no longer friendless."

"What am I, guacamole?" thought Camber. Aloud he said, "He got arrested for assault in a bar fight, you know."

Pajan turned to glare at him. "I am aware of the charges, thank you. At least he didn't terrorize innocent people at a funeral. Anyhow, I expect in Mr. Segovia's case, it was self-defense."

"You are so understanding," said Jesús with downcast eyes.

Pajan's smile was back. "Your bail was set at $50,000. You will have to come up with ten per cent of that amount .You must also produce someone here in town who can vouch for you, and then I can secure your release."

Jesús held up her business card. "This now becomes my new prayer card."

The spell was broken by muffled laughter from the opposite cell.

Pajan shot Camber a glance of pure cobra venom. She picked up her briefcase and headed for the door, "As for you,

Mr. Berkley," she said, "Be ready to leave in ten minutes. I have to leave some papers with the clerk."

"Don't forget my driving bag!" Camber called after her.

Jesús waited for Pajan to be out of earshot before turning to Camber with a dancing smile. " *¡Dios mio!* But she is a hot one."

Camber nodded. "Most dragons are," he said. "You know—breathing fire."

"A woman with spirit," said Jesús. "I think she likes me. The *machismo* is just too much for women to resist. Especially if all their lives they have had to make do with—" He waved vaguely in Camber's direction. "*Los gabardinos.*"

Camber shrugged. "Well, if whatever-you-said refers to me, she doesn't have to make do at all. I wouldn't touch her with a flamethrower."

"She would need a man of great fire to handle her, yes," said Jesús complacently.

"Well, I wouldn't say she was crazy about you," said Camber, "But at least she didn't look like she wanted to squash you like a cockroach, either. I guess that's a start."

"I will post the bail, and then she will be eating out of my hand. It is hard to work the magic from behind bars. But one embrace and she will feel my electricity"

"Or you'll feel hers," muttered Camber, thinking in terms of electric chairs. "So you're going to post bail, huh, Jesús ? I thought you didn't have any money."

"Not on my person at this time, this is true," Jesús conceded. "But it can be arranged, of course. My friend, in a place as provincial as this, it is possible that you do not know my family. I am Jesús Segovia. I am a *chilango*."

Seeing Camber's sardonic expression, he decided to forestall the smart remark, "A *chilango*, my friend, is one who comes from Mexico City. I am a Segovia de Ciudad Mexico. My father is most renowned in the ... *como se dice* ... drug business."

"Oh, boy," thought Camber, but he contrived not to look shocked. After all, this was a jail.

Serenely unconscious of self-incrimination, Jesús sailed on,

"But I tell you that I do not live off my father's money. I have a business of my own with my brother Jonas."

"Jonas?" said Camber, who had been expecting to hear Juan or José. "*Jonas?*"

Jesús lifted his shoulders in an eloquent shrug. "What can I tell you? We are a most singular family. The name was my father's choice. This is not so difficult to explain as my own middle name. So, as I am recounting to you, my brother Jonas and I are in the car business."

Camber stared. "The car business? Not racing?"

"No, I was telling you ... although I admire the estimable Señor Montoya, he and I work admirably in different professions. I have told you this. In the course of racing, now and again, regrettably, Sr. Montoya wrecks new cars. For me it is the other way around. In my business we process maybe two hundred cars per month. Not cheap junk. *Caro* ... Difficult-to-obtain cars. I procure them from many places all over the States, and I ship them back to Mexico City ..."

He's a car thief, thought Camber, but he willed himself to keep smiling and nodding. *He's a car thief for a south-of-the-border chop shop. No wonder he can afford bail It's probably part of his operating expenses.* On the other hand, he thought, it was nice to know somebody who might let him have a good car, cheap, because he had a feeling he was going to need one.

Just then Stoney walked down the hall carrying Camber's driving bag. "Breaking out the fire suit, huh, man?" He smiled. "You going to show them how it's done today, Camber?"

"Just a little shake down," said Camber. "Make sure everything is still safe. Thanks for getting my bag."

Stoney opened the cell, "No problem. I wish I could get time off to come watch. I'll walk you out front."

As they walked out through the sheriff's office, Camber nodded toward the bag in Stoney's hand. "So, did you search it?"

The deputy looked hurt. "'Course not, Camber! Pajan's trying to be tough and by-the-book, that's all. I didn't consider it at all necessary to do a search."

"Well, thanks, Stoney. I appreciate that."

"'Cause we already searched it when we brought you in."

* * *

As they headed out of town, Pajan drove past Farley's garage, which reminded her of past grievances, and she snapped, "I hope you have planned a safer day for the ministers than last time?"

Stung by the injustice of this remark, Camber took a deep breath, in lieu of shouting. "I didn't *plan* an unsafe day last time," he said. "I could hardly be expected to foresee that Agnes Hill-Radnor really would believe that she couldn't drive faster than her guardian angel can fly."

A brief smile flickered across Pajan's face. "Apparently, she can. You may have to be firm with her about knowing her limitations."

"I'll do that," said Camber. "Aside from a stringent safety lecture, I plan to assign them all practices, seat time, and a few more solo runs. We only have three more track days before the big race, and they still have a long way to go." Camber stared out the window, absently pulling his seat belt off his chest and letting it spring back tight again. "I don't know what else I can do."

"Well, remember that the judge will hold you personally responsible for the well-being of those ministers. And if he doesn't, I certainly will."

That did it. Bad food and trying to sleep on a metal bed had already frayed Camber's nerves, and now an early morning lecture from a woman who obviously used a broomstick as a suppository was way more than he was willing to put up with. Politeness, be damned. It certainly wasn't getting him anywhere. He braced himself for a shouting match, because he was ready to have one. But one blessing of being a race car driver is that you develop a reaction time measurable in nanoseconds. Before Camber could unleash a torrent of angry words, that command center in his head, the one that guided him through wrecks at 200 mph when he couldn't see past the hood of his own car, had analyzed the situation with cold and logical precision and cancelled the shouting match.

Camber stared at Pajan in silence for a few moments, until

she started to blush. "Why are you so upset about this?" he said quietly.

She tightened her hand on the steering wheel, still watching the road, without even a glance in his direction. "What do you mean?"

"I mean that you are totally bent out of shape about a little road accident that caused not one single injury and did no damage to anybody's property except mine, which by your own admission, you could care less about. So I have to wonder: what is it about me that has you choking with rage?"

She took a deep breath and drew herself up, making him think about broomsticks again. "Well, you are a lawbreaker," she said, "And I am an officer of the court."

"Don't give me that! My buddy Jesús back there in the jail gave somebody a nose job with a beer bottle, and you practically asked for his autograph. *Self-defense,* you said—oh, please! So don't give me that I-hate-criminals line, because it won't fly. No, it isn't lawbreakers in general who make you act like a crazed harpy—it's me. This is personal. So what is it?"

She was silent for so long that he thought she wasn't going to answer, but at last in the most subdued tones he had heard from her yet, she said, "It appears that I owe you an apology. I may have been overly harsh toward you."

"I don't want an apology," said Camber. "I want an explanation."

"I don't have to explain anything to you."

"Okay," said Camber, as they sped past the Church of the Crystal Path. "It would be more fun to guess, anyway." He studied her carefully for another few moments. "Now judging by your performance just now with that carjacking Casanova, I can only assume that either you are a sucker for flattery, or else you have a secret desire for some small-time hood to sweep you away from this town."

Pajan's one-word answer made Camber laugh. "You know they charged Tony Stewart $25,000 for saying that word on the air at the Brickyard in 2007," he told her. "So what's the deal? Did some local speedway hound break your heart, or do I look like the guy who stood you up for the senior prom, or what?"

"I didn't go to the prom," said Pajan quietly. "Our term papers were due the next week."

"Sounds like you didn't have much fun back then."

"No. I had expectations to live up to. That didn't leave much time for anything else."

"That still doesn't explain why you're furious with me. Look, I made a simple mistake on a winding road. I could have been killed, by the way, and I don't see you showing too much concern about that. So I end up in your little one-horse town, from a *car wreck*, and you act like I'm a terrorist. And then some petty car thief shows up, bragging about his daddy being a drug dealer, and he ends up in jail because he gets loaded in a bar one night and carves up some guy with a beer bottle. And do you treat him like pond scum? Oh, no! You practically offer to take him home and nurse him back to health."

"What are you talking about? What car thief? Mr. Segovia? He's not charged with that."

"No, he's too smart to get caught, I expect. Anyhow, he certainly put one over on you. *At least I am no longer friendless,*" said Camber in a reasonable imitation of Jesús' heartfelt tone.

"I don't see what he has to do with anything," said Pajan. She hit the brakes. They had come up behind an old pickup truck pulling a hay wagon well below the speed limit on this two-lane country road.

"Can't you pass him?" said Camber. The conversation had now become so awkward that both of them wanted nothing more than to get to the track as quickly as possible, so that they wouldn't have to say another word.

"No," said Pajan. "Believe me, if I could get around him, I would."

Camber grinned. "I don't suppose you'd consider letting me drive?"

"Nope."

"I *teach* race car driving."

"I know. It isn't that I don't trust you … to drive well, I

mean ... It just wouldn't look right. And besides ..."

"What?"

"Look, I know I've been pretty harsh around you. And the reason for it has nothing to do with you. You were right about that. So I'll make an effort to put aside those feelings, and be more civil toward you in future. Really. I'll try."

Camber laughed. "You sound like somebody who's about to eat bugs on a reality show."

"I didn't mean to hurt your feelings, Camber."

"No, don't worry about that. Actually it's pretty restful. Oh, I did wonder what it was that set you off, but, aside from that, I didn't really mind the cold shoulder."

Now she did turn to look at him. "Restful? What do you mean, *restful?*"

He shrugged. "I'm a race car driver, kid. And judging from the – er – personal items that girls ask me to sign, I must not be a bad-looking one, either. So it's really peaceful, not having to beat you off with a stick. I appreciate it."

"Oh, you don't have to worry about that, Mr. Berkley. I wouldn't touch you with a ten-foot pole. Your stunt at Jimmy's funeral has brought back some difficult memories for me. You'd have no way of knowing about it, and it's none of your business, anyway, but you certainly don't have to worry about me turning into one of your groupies. As far as I'm concerned a race car driver is just an overpaid trucker."

The double yellow line broke into dashes in the middle of the two-lane road, and Pajan floored her car and roared past the battered old pick-up truck.

They rode the rest of the way in silence.

Camber pulled his driving bag out of the trunk, and jumped back, because as soon as the trunk clicked shut, Pajan's car roared off, leaving him coughing in a swirl of exhaust.

The track was quiet. There wasn't a cloud in the sky, and the morning sun was still low on the horizon. Camber took a deep breath of cool morning air to clear his mind from the smoke of the last twenty minutes with Pajan. At least he would get to drive today, and that would make him feel better. On any other day at the track, he might as well be in an office cubicle, but, on days that he knew he would get to drive, the anticipation and excitement crackled in the air like lightning. Even if the car put him in the wall, at least he'd know why it happened. Pajan had just put him in the wall, and he had no idea why.

The repaired race car was still loaded on back of the wrecker, and Danny Simpkins was asleep in the cab, his head slumped against the driver's side window. On the dashboard a cup of convenience store coffee was fogging up a circle on the windshield. Camber rapped on the driver's side window, exactly where Danny Simpkins' head was resting, waking him with a jolt, and causing him to spill coffee all over the cab.

After a moment's disorientation, Danny smiled up at Camber, and let down the window. "Sorry, man, I must have nodded off." He looked around the deserted track. "Did someone drop you off?"

Camber rolled his eyes. "I rode here on a broom stick with the Wicked Witch of the West."

"Who, Pajan?" Danny laughed. "She can be a pistol all right, can't she? 'Course, I guess she's entitled. Anyhow, car's all set. I figured I'd wait for you before I set her down."

"Thanks for bringing it back to the track," said Camber. "I'll help you unload it. Then I'm going to set the toe, and shake it down for a couple of laps. By that time the saints should come marching in."

Danny's eyes widened. "Oh, man, can I help?"

Camber groaned inwardly. He had heard that tone before, and he knew that Danny would be less help than he needed and more of a distraction, but he didn't have the heart to turn him down. "Sure," he said, with more enthusiasm than he felt, "I could use an extra set of hands. I'd appreciate the help."

"Thanks, man!" said Danny happily. He climbed back in the wrecker, fired it up, and began to raise the hydraulic bed to unload the race car.

That was racing: trying to make it to the big time not only meant having to do without luxurious travel and hotels, and having to make do with baloney and cheese every day at the track—it also meant not turning away help from anybody. Camber couldn't count the number of times he heard someone say, "I know he can't do much, but we need warm bodies at this point."

When Camber was running his own team at a local track, there had been two brothers who showed up every week just to hang around the pits. They must have been right out of high school and working at a local gas station.

At the time Camber's team had consisted of just himself and Brennan, working on his first race car, a beat-up old Camaro. For the first few weeks Camber and Brennan had been so busy getting that old Camaro to run that they hadn't even noticed the two brothers in the pit area every week. It was only after Camber and Brennan's first win, a few weeks into the season, that Camber became aware of them.

That night after his victory, Camber had done a short burnout for the fans, and then climbed out of the car to wave the checked flag and collect the trophy. Brennan joined in the celebration, which ended with Camber and Brennan posing for pictures with the scantily-clad official Speedway Trophy Girl.

When the picture came out in the local paper the next morning, Camber was still giddy with excitement. There it was: the official record of his win. The trophy was wonderfully gaudy and huge: it must have been four-feet high. The photo showed Brennan and Camber on either side of the Trophy Girl, with one hand holding the trophy and the other around the girl's waist. But there were two other guys in the picture as well, standing in front of the Camaro, about a foot away to either side of Camber and Brennan, and grinning proudly.

"Who *are* those guys?" Camber asked Brennan, shoving the paper under his nose.

Brennan, who was trying to put the car back together after the tech inspection, ignored the question. "I don't see that it's really fair," he said. "You wreck the car, and I have to piece it back together again, but after you win they want to tear the whole goddamn thing apart to make sure we aren't cheating with some trick we weren't supposed to use."

"Yeah, well, that's NASCAR," said Camber. "It's their way

or the highway. But who are these two extra guys in the picture here?"

Brennan shrugged. "Oh, just a couple of fans. They started hanging around and asking questions while you were at the drivers meeting and I was trying to set the timing for the race. I asked if they could run and get us five gallons of gas to top off the car before the race. They have been around ever since."

Camber blinked. "Well … That's nice of them. But why would they want to help me?"

"Because you are racing a car, and they are not." said Brennan quietly. He was arranging the parts that they had brought home in cardboard boxes from the track the night before. "Anyway, they are two extra sets of hands, which can be a blessing if you need them."

Camber had set down his Pop Tart breakfast, so that he could help Brennan unload the old pick-up truck they had borrowed to haul the race car to the track. "Those guys—what are their names?"

Brennan looked back at Camber. "I don't have a clue."

* * *

"How are you going to set the toe? asked Danny. They had unloaded the car and found the flattest place on pit road. "The alignment machine is back at the shop."

Camber shrugged. "Ever use a set of toe plates?"

Danny shook his head.

"Didn't think so." Camber got two long pieces of 2"x2" metal box tubing he had taken from Farley's garage, and a tape measure from his driving bag. He handed one of the metal pieces to Danny. "I think these were used as wheel chocks at the shop," he said, "but they will do in the absence of real toe plates. In the lower echelons of racing, you have to learn to make do."

Danny was staring at the piece of scrap metal, trying to picture it as a piece of sophisticated racing equipment. "You can set the toe with this thing?"

"Yeah. Go hold that piece against the right front wheel," said Camber. "I will stay here and do the same on the left side."

When Danny had placed the metal tubing against the wheel, Camber did the same on the opposite side. The metal pieces extended a few inches past the front and back of the tire. "Hold it horizontally on the wheel, just a few inches off the ground." Camber said, as he extended the tape measure under the car.

"What are you doing now, man?" asked Danny.

"Now," said Camber, "I just have to measure the front and then the back of the metal pieces. They give us an easy place to take measures from, on the same plane as the tire. If the front and back measurements are the same, that means that the front tires are perfectly parallel. Any difference in the numbers means the tires are pointed either slightly towards each other, or slightly away. On a short track like this one, we want the tires towed out about 3/16 of an inch in order to help the car turn."

Danny looked at him doubtfully. "We always set cars dead-on in the shop."

"Of course, you do," said Camber. "Street cars spend most of their life going straight, so you need the adjustment to be perfectly straight in order to get good tire wear. But, see, a race car spends most of its time turning corners, and we know we're going to wear out some tires in a single day. We want the front of the tires to be pointed away from each other just enough to help in the turns, but not enough to bother the car in the straight-aways. Now grab me a couple of ¾-inch wrenches so I can adjust the tie rod."

When Danny came back from the truck with the wrenches, the hood to the race car was open, and Camber was rummaging around in the engine compartment.

"I thought you were going to adjust the tie rod."

"Yeah, I am."

"From under the hood? Isn't the tie rod underneath the car?"

"It's in the same place as in a regular suspension, but with the race car there isn't any extra stuff under the hood, like AC components or fuse boxes, so you can reach it from the top or the bottom."

Danny peered inside. "It does look kind of empty in there, compared to what I'm used to dealing with."

Camber was now leaning under the open hood, twisting the newly-installed tie rod with the pair of wrenches to get the desired number. "Oh, and, by the way, the worst thing you can do is have the race car towed *in*. That makes them hateful to drive."

"Speaking of driving ..." said Danny.

"Oh, yeah. Before the ministers get here, I'm going to find out what she can do."

Danny grinned. "This I gotta see!"

Chapter Eleven
Pure Air and Fire

"It's about time," Camber said to himself, pulling his firesuit over his shoulders. "It's not Lowe's Motor Speedway, and no one is going to offer me a ride if they see me out there, but, the way I feel right now, if I wasn't doing this, I might be trying to buy pills on a street corner. But there's nothing like *actual* speed to get your mind right."

The Monte Carlo was idling rough, trying to warm up, while Camber leaned back against the door and laced up his driving shoes. Danny, watching from a short distance away, looked on with dazed reverence. He was still in awe of the ingenuity of jackleg race car drivers, who knew tricks like how to set the toe on the race car using only scrap metal and a tape measure—no computer or laser in sight.

Camber had fired up the race car as quickly as he could to keep Danny from asking too many questions. The rumble of the engine made conversation impossible. When Danny tried to talk to him, Camber just kept pointing to his ear and shaking his head. Before Camber zipped and Velcro-ed up his fire suit, he reached under the seat where he had stashed his cell phone, and tucked it into a pocket of the suit.

As soon as Camber settled himself into the seat of the Monte Carlo, he went into auto pilot: fastening the belts, putting on his helmet, pushing the steering wheel into place, and then motioning for Danny to come and lift up the window net and latch it into position. Once the window net was secured, Camber went back through everything for a double check. Then he was off.

Camber left pit lane slowly, exactly as he had instructed his students to do, bringing the car up on the banking as he picked up speed. The first order of business was to make sure the car was safe, and that all the recent repairs had been done correctly, with nothing overlooked. As he looped the track, he kept the speed down, and swerved back and forth, feeling the steering wheel in his hands, telling him if anything was loose or if the tire was rubbing against the reconstructed fender. When he had determined that everything felt as it should, he accelerated hard, and then quickly hit the brakes. He did this several more times, still making sure nothing on the car was binding, rubbing, dragging, or loose.

Camber was looking for a feeling he thought of as "confidence." A race car driver needs confidence in his car, his crew, and himself in order to be able to work the magic on the track.

Camber tapped the steering wheel. "Want to dance?"

He drew the gear shift back into fourth and let his foot, which had been resting softly on the gas, push the pedal to the floor. As the car began to pick up speed, he nosed it in and out of the turns with expert precision. Now he was circling the track faster than any of his pupils had done it, but in this run there was not a single noise coming from the tires.

The silence reminded him of another racing tip to tell the group: Smooth car control means that you can push the limits before the car starts to complain.

Camber needed to reach that point today.

With each succeeding lap he pushed harder and faster, until he felt the first protest from the car. When he exited the turns, he could no longer keep the nose of the car pinned to the bottom of the race track. It would drift up three or four feet out of the groove. Camber smiled. The setup was nice and tight. *Good. For the ministers, that is, but I want to see what you can really do.*

He altered his approaches to the turns, making them a little wider, and pulling the car down the track faster, forcing it into a slide and thus aligning it to exit the turn in the correct groove.

Danny, who was watching open-mouthed from the infield, must have been thinking that the rear end of the car was about to get away from Camber. To an observer the car probably looked out of control, but, behind the wheel, Camber was in command. He felt like a scientist, carefully measuring inputs to an experiment, and adding variables one by one to see what would happen.

He realized that he was in the wrong groove; that is, the line he had chosen to follow around the track was putting too much strain on the motor. "Not enough horse power," he muttered. The car was sliding, scrubbing off too much speed, which in turn slowed the motor below the point of maximum horsepower. The gas pedal felt sluggish. Pushing it down further didn't seem to make any difference to the speed of the car, as if it was telling him, *"No, I don't like that either."*

He went back to his original line, but this time as he entered the corners, he allowed the left side tires to drop off the banking, thus transferring some of the car's weight and helping it to turn.

That was the right answer. He got back the response in the gas pedal, and now he was able to launch the car off the corners even more quickly. Now that Camber had determined what the car was capable of, he backed off the gas and let the car slow down by itself. Only then did he notice the audience lined up against the outside fence. His pupils had arrived for their practice session, and when they saw the Monte Carlo flying around the track, they stopped to watch. No one was willing to risk the alternative: to try to cross the track to the infield while a speeding car doing laps out there. Watching was better. When Camber finished his test run, they could open the track gate, and drive their own cars into the infield.

Camber eased the car back onto pit lane and shut down the engine. After he released his belts and let down the window net, he reached out of the window and set his helmet on the roof of the car. As he lifted himself out of the seat and onto the window ledge, he sighed and squinted up at the clear May morning sky, savoring the heat of the sun on his back. Its warm radiance mixed with the hot air rising from the car, putting him in mind of a horse that had just been exercised.

Across the infield, he could hear the ministers getting out of their cars, all talking excitedly, and then Danny's heavy footsteps trotting up pit lane. With weary satisfaction, he folded his arms on the roof and rested his head across his arms.

"Well, that certainly was an impressive display," said Bill Bartlett, hurrying up to the car. "Well done!"

Beside him, Stephen Albright, who felt a quotation coming on, drew himself up and intoned, *"He is pure air and fire. The dull elements of earth and water are not mixed in him."*

Romney Marsh nodded. "Shakespeare?"

Camber looked up. "Dale Earnhardt."

Fr. Frankie laughed. "It's from *Henry V.* Shakespeare has a Frenchman say those lines in praise of a grand horse, but I think the phrase might fit the Black Number Three well enough.—And, of course, your own grand self there, boyo. *Air and fire,* indeed."

"Seriously, though," said Rick Cunningham. "That performance was amazing."

"Thanks," said Camber. "I didn't know I had an audience."

"*Now* you're the guy in those internet pictures," said Bill Bartlett, looking at him appraisingly. "Er, I mean, you look like you do on the internet."

Camber raised his eyebrows. "If you mean that I am wearing my firesuit, that is very astute of you."

"It's more than the outfit," said Romney Marsh. "I don't know how to put it. I guess, there's an aura of authority about you that wasn't there before."

Camber nodded. "Firesuits are magic," he said, only half kidding.

"So what are we going to do today?" asked Paul Whitcomb, who had picked up the helmet and was examining it admiringly.

"Exactly what you just saw me do, lap after lap, until you can do it with your eyes closed." Camber replied.

"Well, that ought to pass the time until Judgment Day," said Travis Prichard, trying to suppress a grin.

Camber laughed. "I don't think it'll take you quite that long to get the hang of it, but we are burning daylight here, so let's get right to it. The next time we meet, I want you all to be ready to have multiple cars on the track, and from what I saw last time, we have a long way to go before you'll be ready to do that."

"Multiple cars on the track?" said Andrew Scarberry, looking noticeably pale. "You mean we'll be out there with *each other?*"

"It's going to come to that sooner or later," said Camber. "Those are the terms of the race." He looked around, mentally taking attendance. "Father Frankie, what do you equestrians do when you get thrown from a horse?"

"Limp. Swear. But the answer you were looking for is that you get right back on the brute. Don't give your fears a chance to fester. Would you be suggesting who you want going first?"

"I am," said Camber, searching the group for the lone woman, who was trying to make herself unobtrusive behind the bulk of her colleagues. "Hello, Agnes! How are you feeling?"

Agnes Hill-Radnor took a deep breath, and crept out from the shadow of Mt. Scarberry. "I'm still a little shaky," she admitted. "And seeing you zipping around out there at breakneck speed didn't help any, either."

"I've been at it a little longer than you have," said Camber, trying to sound encouraging.

"Agnes, if you think you're up to it, I want you to drive first. Since you wrecked last time, it is important for you to get back behind the wheel so that you don't lose your nerve."

She ventured a smile. "I was thinking that perhaps I had regained my common sense."

Camber nodded. "A race car driver needs nerve *and* common sense," he said. "Now before we start driving, I'll answer any questions concerning your feelings about driving, and what you think you learned the last time you drove. With all the excitement surrounding the wreck, we never got to do a proper debriefing."

He told them to get ready for practice, and excused himself to change out of the fire suit. Once inside the track bathroom, he checked his messages on his cell phone. Surely Brennan would have responded to his request for help by now.

Sure enough, there was a message from Brennan.

Camber retrieved the message and grinned. Brennan had responded with 10-codes, just like old times. 10-65. Brennan only used that one when he was really annoyed. *Juvenile problem*. That had been his standard response to any concern of Camber's that offended his workhorse sensibilities. Girl troubles? Money problems? Boredom. Brennan's reaction was always the same: 10-65.

Not this time, thought Camber. There was a second message, also from Brennan. Another 10-code. 10-55? He had received the message about the wreck, and he wanted to know if Camber had been drunk. Camber rolled his eyes. Brennan should know better. He was just being grouchy, asking that. He wondered how many cheap shots Brennan would need to relieve his frustration. From experience he had learned that the best course of action was to endure the jabs politely until Brennan tired of the joke. When that happened, Brennan would do everything in his power to help. But until then, he was going to be snippy about it. Camber sighed. Well, at least he had Brennan's attention.

Camber texted back, "10-10. Negative. And then, 10-12. Stand by." He would continue the conversation soon, but first he had to get practice started.

Ten minutes later he was back on top of the concession stand, watching Agnes being helped into the car by Rick Cunningham and Paul Whitcomb. They were getting close to firing the motor and starting this practice session. Much as he wished he could just talk to Brennan, he would have to continue their conversation by texting. But not yet.

Although he was fairly confident that the guys could manage themselves during the practice, he thought it would be prudent to have another little talk with Agnes, because of her wreck last time. Shoving his cell phone in his pocket, he ambled down to pit lane where Agnes had just finished strapping in, and stuck his head in the driver's side window.

Agnes Hill-Radnor was as pale as the white fire suit. She looked up at him with an expression approaching terror, and she was biting her lower lip, possibly to keep from crying. *Oh, boy.*

"Just take it easy," he told her. "Deep breaths. Panic isn't going to help matters one bit. You okay?"

"I don't know."

"Let's start slow and hit every stair on the way up, shall we? Jump too many stairs, and you are sure to come crashing down."

She frowned. "How will I know if I am going too fast?"

An interesting question, thought Camber. He decided against explaining it to her in too much detail, but, basically, when a driver is scared shitless, it's a sign that he has run out of talent, and his natural impulse, to slow down, is the correct one.

He said to Agnes, "We call it the pucker factor. Does that make sense?"

She nodded.

"But since that didn't seem to work for you last time, I will have the flag man hold out a yellow if I think you're going too fast. If you see that flag, slow down and work your way back up to speed again."

He did the usual a safety check of the cockpit, not leaving anything to Agnes this time. When he checked that the steering wheel was locked properly in place, he noticed a drawing stuck to the dash board.

As he took an extra tug on Agnes's belts to make sure they were tight enough and secure, he tapped the small pastel drawing which showed a vaguely human-shaped figure, wreathed in light. "What's this?" he asked.

Agnes blushed. "It's an angelic image to help me focus my concentration, and to strengthen my faith."

"Your guardian angel?"

"No. Just an image to focus on. You can't really depict an angel in two-dimensional form. This is to remind me that no matter how fast I go, no matter what happens, I am not alone."

"I'll buy that," said Camber, "It beats using St. Christopher's medals for hub caps. Just make sure you take your driving advice from me."

With that, Camber latched the window net, and nodded for her to fire the engine. As the car trundled down pit lane, he made his way over to the flag stand to explain his new yellow flag warning system to Fr. Frankie.

His cell phone was vibrating in his pocket, but he resisted the urge to check the message until he finished conferring with the flagman, and resumed his bird's-eye perch high atop the concession stand.

"So she's off again!" yelled Fr. Frankie, peering down the track, where Agnes was proceeding sedately.

"Yeah, but she's worried about going too fast. So we worked out a signal. If I think she's letting it get out of control, I'm going to wave my arms above my head, and I want you to display the yellow flag as a signal for her to slow down. Okay?"

"Good idea. Of course, if she keeps going at her current speed, I could just write it in the dust on her windshield as she goes by."

"Just be ready," said Camber. "She may get her nerve back any minute now. She's got a picture of an angel on the dashboard."

Fr. Frankie smiled. "She should let him drive."

"Yeah, well, keep an eye on me, in case I give you the signal. We'll test it once when I get up there."

When Camber was back in position on top of the concession stand, he demonstrated the "slow down" signal by waving his hands briskly above his head. Fr. Frankie responded with a grin and a thumbs-up to show that he would know when to wave a yellow flag. Camber nodded his approval, and settled back to watch Agnes take her practice laps. So far, so good. He eased the phone out of his pocket, and squinted at the new message.

"10-21." Brennan was asking for a call in person.

Quickly he typed back, "L8er, at track. 10-4 on my 20?"

He turned his attention back to the track. By listening to the RPMs of the engine, he could tell that Agnes was still driving much more conservatively this time. Up here on the roof, a light spring breeze brought the scent of race car with the crisp morning air. He sighed contentedly, listening to the soothing sound of a car circling the track: the steady build-up of engine roar, rising to a crescendo and then slowly fading away again. He glanced again at his messages. "10-4 JG, track? 10-21 when you can." Brennan had replied.

JG. *Judas Grove.* So at least Brennan knew where he was. *Good.* He would call him later.

He glanced up again. Agnes was still proceeding slowly around the track, but so far she was doing fine. Some of the others had come up the steps, and now they were grouped around Camber on the concession stand roof. After another signal from Camber, Fr. Frankie waved the checkered flag signaling the end of Agnes' run. As she pulled back into pit road, everyone applauded. She was going to be all right.

* * *

Brennan, who was keeping one eye on his phone while he printed out invoices for the shop, was now totally confused. So far he had deduced that the current problem was a typical Camber crisis, and that no amount of rational explanation on Camber's part would resolve the outlandish nature of the situation.

He sighed. Somehow Camber's escapades always landed him at a race track, and this one, Brennan realized, was no different. He thought of the time that Camber had taken a job to sell tools for an impact wrench manufacturer. Camber was supposed to travel to all the Home Depot store's grand openings in a ten-state region, ranging from Virginia to Texas. He hadn't really wanted to take the job, but after an agonizing discussion with Brennan about how he needed the money and just couldn't afford to run his own racing team any more, Camber had hit the road for the summer.

About a month into the deal, *two paychecks, if Brennan recalled correctly* Camber had called with a story about a man he met at the latest Grand Opening, who owned a local dirt track racing team. When Camber invited the man to try out his company's impact wrenches at their tire changing station, the guy promptly challenged Camber to a tire-changing competition on the spot.

He was so sure that he could change tires faster than Camber that if he lost, he said, he would let Camber drive his race car. Despite this tempting offer, Camber kept declining the challenge, reminding the man that he had not only racing experience, but also pit crew experience. Surely, he argued, such a competition would not be fair.

"But he still insisted on trying to take you on?" Brennan had asked, when he heard the tale over the phone.

"Well, yeah," said Camber. "And he was a lot older than me, too. I don't think he really took me all that seriously."

Brennan considered it. "Were you wearing ... you know, the *thing?*"

"Umm, yeah."

"That might explain it."

The "thing," which neither Brennan nor Camber could actually bring themselves to name, was the costume representing the tool company mascot: a furry lug nut. Someone in the marketing department had decided that they could get a lot of attention for the company's tool products if they dressed their field representative in costume as a furry lug nut. So, much to Brennan's delight, Camber became the large walking lug nut. The fact that the outfit was both heavy and uncomfortably hot was a minor quibble compared to its humiliation factor which, on a scale of one to ten, was about a thousand.

Brennan had fond memories of seeing his handsome, athletic, chick-magnet room-mate stumping around in a mountain of synthetic gray fur, looking like a gigantic dust bunny. He had wanted a poster-sized photo of the spectacle, but Camber had threatened to destroy not only the photos, but the camera, if Brennan attempted to capture the moment.

Brennan could certainly understand why the dirt track racer hadn't taken Camber seriously. The guy probably found it hard to believe that a large, furry lug nut with a beltway accent could beat him out in anything.

So the tire-changing challenge was on. The dirt track guy had indeed been a fast and competent tire-changer, but his skill did not approach that of the professionally trained and experienced Camber. It probably helped that the man had graciously allowed him to remove the furry lug nut suit for the competition.

Camber beat him with three seconds to spare, which in pit crew time is an eternity.

True to his word, the man had allowed Camber to drive his Late Model dirt car in a local race that Saturday night. When Camber called Brennan that night to announce his good fortune, he had been standing in the pits of Hog Chain Speedway, one of the hundreds of local dirt and asphalt speedways dotted across the country. Breathlessly, he assured Brennan that he would be racing the rest of the season for this low budget team, at Hog Chain Speedway.

"And will you have a furry lug nut firesuit?" Brennan asked sweetly.

The Hog Chain Speedway. Poor Camber. Those fly-by-night racing deals seemed to fall apart just as fast as they came together for him. After only four races the team owner lost his furniture business in a fire, forcing him to sell off all his racing equipment and disband the team. Brennan, who had been loyally planning to join Camber in this latest racing venture, had scarcely located Hog Chain on the map when Camber turned up, back in Virginia, crestfallen. And, once again, unemployed.

Brennan returned his attention to the Tennessee page of the road atlas where he had located Judas Grove, Tennessee. Now he had to find out where its nearest speedway was, and how on earth Camber had ended up there. And he was in jail. What was that all about?

Brennan could not resist deviating from their usual 10-code messaging system to type in his final comment on the situation: *Better an orange jumpsuit than a furry lug nut.*

* * *

Practice was progressing smoothly. Andrew Scarberry had taken over as flagman, and Fr. Frankie was waiting his turn to drive. Stephen Albright and Bill Bartlett had already completed their laps almost as sedately as Agnes had, with adequate times and free from mishaps, so Camber was beginning to breathe a little easier. He settled back in the old folding lawn chair on top of the concession stand, sipping a Coke and watching Travis Prichard circle the track, doing a reasonable approximation of an actual race car driver. Prichard was the best of them, at least so far, and other things being equal he ought to win the race. But things never were equal in racing. There was always mechanical failure, human errors, and a thousand other variables to alter the results of any competition.

Bill Bartlett, who had just completed his run, came up to the roof, pulled up a battered metal folding chair, and sat down next to Camber. "How'd I do?" he asked.

"You're getting there," said Camber. "Nothing Jeff Gordon needs to worry about, but you seemed to have pretty good control on the turns, which is good."

Bartlett smiled. "Well, we have a good teacher. I was telling Pajan at church Sunday that you might be an angel in disguise."

Camber winced. "I'll bet she got a good laugh out of that."

"As I recall, she said she was glad that you were being helpful. Why? Do you feel that she dislikes you?"

"I think she'd like to use my vertebrae for wind chimes."

Bartlett nodded. "And you didn't do anything to annoy her, I suppose?"

"Not that I know of. She was breathing fire from the first minute I met her."

"Well, then I'm sure you realize it isn't your fault."

"I hadn't really analyzed it. I just wish I knew why she hates me."

Bartlett mopped the sweat off his forehead with a crumpled tissue, and sighed. "Well, I suppose I could tell you. It isn't as if it were a confessional secret. You could find the story in back issues of the local newspaper, if you knew when to look."

"In the newspaper? A story about Pajan?"

"About her family." Bill Bartlett hesitated. "I could be wrong, of course. Maybe that old incident isn't the reason she dislikes you. Maybe you remind her of some college boyfriend or the villain in an old movie she once saw. Who knows?"

"I don't think so," said Camber. "Her reaction to me is much too strong to be based on casual resemblance. I haven't done a single thing to antagonize her, and sometimes she lets herself be almost human around me, and then something seems to click in her head and she goes back into dragon lady mode. Is it because I'm a race car driver? That occurred to me, but then she doesn't seem to oppose this race, so that didn't make sense."

"That's an interesting point. Yes, I suppose that the term racing can mean more than one thing, and the brain might compartmentalize them separately."

Camber was staring out at the track, where Travis Prichard was still in orbit and doing fine. "You're speaking in tongues, Bill," he said. "I didn't follow that at all."

"Sorry. Thinking out loud. It just occurred to me that it wasn't your job as a race car driver that upset her. It's the fact that you were racing out on the highway, and that you wrecked the car. Especially where you wrecked, I guess."

"The cemetery?"

"Yes. Her brother is buried there."

* * *

"One chef salad coming up," said Dinah. "Blue cheese dressing."

"Yeah, thanks," murmured Pajan, still staring at the same

page of a magazine she'd been looking at for the last three minutes. She was sitting in her usual booth at the diner, but she'd hardly said a word since she came in, and she'd barely managed a nod in response to Dinah's cheery hello.

"You *hate* blue cheesing dressing," said Dinah. "You've been staring off into space ever since you got here. You wanna tell me what's going on?"

Pajan shrugged. "Just a bad morning, I guess."

"Did you have one or give one?"

"Both, maybe," said Pajan. She stirred her iced tea, still staring off into space. Finally she murmured, "I shouldn't have come home for the summer. After classes ended I should have stayed in Knoxville, and found a job up there. I'm sure some judge would have been happy to have a law clerk for the summer. I wish I had done that."

Dinah studied her for a moment, and then with studied nonchalance, she said, "Well, maybe it's a good thing you didn't, what with Jimmy Powell dying so suddenly, and naming you as executor of his will. So you'd have had to be around anyhow, wouldn't you?"

"I guess so," said Pajan. "This race meant a lot to Jimmy, and I wouldn't want to let him down. I think he would be proud of it. His collection has all been catalogued, and notices have been sent to museums and people within the stock car racing community. And of course I contacted Sotheby's."

"The auction people in New York?" Dinah whistled softly. "I'll bet that was a memorable conversation."

Pajan laughed, "Once I explained to them that NASCAR was not a former president of Egypt, they coped pretty well. But there may not even have to be an auction. Several of the NASCAR museums have expressed an interest in the collection. I know Jimmy would like to see it all kept together."

"Wouldn't he love that? A little bronze plaque saying *The Jimmy Powell Memorial NASCAR Collection* in some fancy museum?"

"He might get his wish, then. We're still negotiating. And then there's the race itself to worry about, of course."

"So how *are* the driving lessons going? Is Reverend Bartlett any good?"

Pajan shook her head. "He didn't mention it Sunday. And I haven't stayed to watch them practice. I guess I ought to, but I can't seem to get away from him fast enough. Maybe I'll go back early today and observe."

"I'll bet he'd let you take a spin in that race car if you asked him nicely."

"Ask him nicely. Yeah, that'll happen. Dinah, I can't even make myself be civil to that race car driver I'm babysitting."

The waitress laughed. "I know exactly what you mean. Drop-dead gorgeous race car drivers get on my nerves, too. That Kasey Kahne had better not show his face around here."

Pajan managed a wan smile. "All right. Make fun of me. But the fact that he's good-looking is completely beside the point. I'm sure he's a legend in his own mind, but at least he has been well-behaved. I'll give him that. And I keep telling myself it isn't his fault he had a wreck. Well, it probably is his fault, but the law is supposed to be impersonal about doling out punishment, and, as far as he's concerned, I am the personification of the law for the next week or so. He's doing his community service without a word of complaint, so being civil to him shouldn't be a problem for me, but I cannot seem to make myself do it."

"Well, I'm not surprised," said Dinah softly. She reached under the counter for more sugar packets and filled the white ceramic container on the counter. "You know, Pajan, maybe you should talk to somebody about it. Somebody with a diploma on the wall, I mean. And, if you do, be sure to tell him exactly where the car landed."

"What do you mean?"

Dinah sighed. "You mean you haven't figured it out?"

"Figured what out?"

"I was at Jimmy Powell's funeral, too, remember? And when your race car driver did his spectacular swan dive off the highway, that car landed maybe twenty feet from where Logan is buried."

* * *

"I think Pajan was about twelve years old at the time," said Bill Bartlett. He was staring at the empty bleachers of the speedway as he spoke. "I had just come to town, straight out of seminary, to become the pastor of First Methodist, so I didn't know anybody very well then, but the Mosbys were in my congregation, so I was acquainted with them. And they were a nice family. Mosby was still an attorney in private practice back then. This was long before he became a judge. There were two children, Pajan, the oldest, and a little boy, Logan, who was about two years her junior. Their mother had died of cancer the year before, but the family seemed to be coping as well as could be expected. As far as I could tell, anyhow. The Mosbys aren't much on showing feelings."

"A look is worth a thousand words," muttered Camber, remembering the frosty glares that, as far as he was concerned, constituted Pajan's normal expression.

"You're thinking of Pajan, I suppose?" Bartlett nodded sympathetically. "It's pretty obvious that you two didn't hit it off. Things haven't been easy for her. I think the Mosbys had a housekeeper back then, but Pajan was still expected to look after her little brother when they came home and make breakfast for the family before she went off to school. Back then they lived in a brick ranch house just outside of town. On the same road that you were on when you had your wreck."

Something in Bartlett's voice sent chills down Camber's spine. Uh-oh, he thought.

Bill Bartlett paused for a moment, and then shivered a little, as if he were trying to throw off the pall of memory. "Anyhow, on that particular day in March, they got off the school bus, and started up the driveway to the house, and then little Logan decided to go across the road to the mailbox. He ran off before Pajan could stop him. It should have been fine. It was a quiet country road … most of the time. But on that particular day, a couple of guys were drag racing on that road." Bartlett broke off, looking embarrassed.

Cameron closed his eyes. "Go on," he said softly.

"They were racing side-by-side along that narrow two-lane road, and the house was situated just past a sharp curve, so they couldn't have seen him until the last second. He was dead before he hit the ground, poor child. And if anything could make it worse, Pajan, standing there in the yard, witnessed the whole thing. In fact, the men were caught and sent to prison because she was able to describe the cars."

Camber's eyes were following the orbit of the race car as Fr. Frankie flew around the track, but he was seeing another car and another road. "Well," he said at last, "I guess that would explain why she can't stand the sight of me. I brought back a lot of bad memories for her."

"Yes, she saw your speeding car on that very same road, and, as I told you, your car happened to land close to Logan's grave."

"I see," said Camber. "It couldn't have been much worse, could it? But if she's so dead set against racing, why is she helping with the Faster Pastor race in the first place?"

Bill Bartlett sighed. "You'd be amazed at how people compartmentalize their loves and hates," he said. "I had a parishioner once—a stubborn old fellow who insisted that all stringed instruments were of the devil."

"Never heard that one."

"Well, that superstition dates back centuries in some sects, but I'd have expected the fellow to be in Scarberry's church instead of mine. But the odd thing is: this old man who hated stringed instruments had an upright piano sitting in the middle of his parlor."

"A piano? Well—what did he think …"

"I believe he thought it was a percussion instrument. Apparently, he had never lifted the lid." Bartlett smiled. "My point is that in Pajan's mind the sport of stock car racing on a speedway is worlds away from the crime of reckless driving on a public road. She's right, of course. I think that childhood experience may have been what led her to become a lawyer."

"I'm sorry I reminded her of all that," said Camber. "But thanks for telling me. I kept wondering why she loathed me."

"It isn't you, Camber. She's seeing ghosts."

* * *

In the Judas Grove diner, Pajan Mosby was finishing her buffalo chicken salad, and still chatting with Dinah, who had tactfully switched to a less painful topic of conversation. They were discussing the relative merits of Knoxville shopping malls when her cell phone rang. Pajan glanced at the number on the caller I.D. "It's the jail," she said. "I wonder what they want. It had better not be Camber Berkley's great escape. Excuse me." She clicked on the phone. "Hello? Stoney? What's wrong?—Oh. Well, that's fine. I was afraid you were going to tell me ... well, never mind. I'm just over at Dinah's. Tell him I'll be there in a few minutes. Thanks."

Dinah, who had been clearing away the dishes, and making no pretense of not listening, said, "Something the matter with your race car boy?"

"No," said Pajan, "All is quiet on that front. This was business. Remember the guy I told you about? The one from Mexico who is in jail for a bar fight. Stoney says he's ready to make bail, so I have to go over there and get him out. Since he's a foreign national, he won't be allowed to leave town until his trial, so I need to make sure he understands that, and then arrange for him to have somewhere to go."

Dinah winked at her. "What does this guy look like? I might take him myself."

"No, you won't," said Pajan. "I'm trying to get him out of trouble, not find him new ways to get into it. I'll start by having a word with Father Spillane. I believe Mr. Segovia would be one of his flock."

Dinah's smile was full of mischief. "Father Frankie would be out at the speedway right now, wouldn't he?"

Pajan sighed. "I suppose he is. Well, it can't be helped. And I suppose I ought to keep a closer eye on the race preparations anyhow."

Dinah laughed. "I wish I could hang out at the speedway and call it working."

"I wish you could, too," said Pajan.

* * *

Half an hour later, Pajan was once again headed out of town on the road that led to the speedway. In the passenger seat a newly-liberated Jesús Segovia was peering through his Ray bans at the spring foliage of the countryside, with a smile suggesting that God had followed his specifications to the letter. It had only taken a few minutes of paperwork to secure his release from jail, and Pajan had assured Stoney that she was quite equal to the task of seeing Jesús settled in lodgings within the county to await his upcoming trial. Now they were off in search of Fr. Frankie to see what he would advise.

"It's a beautiful day, isn't it?" said Pajan in considerably more pleasant tones than she used when speaking to Camber.

Jesús's smile was exultant. "Even if it were the darkest, coldest day of winter it would be a day of radiant perfection," he said. "Again, I am a free man."

Pagan's smile flickered. "Well, you are and you aren't," she said. "I'm sorry to keep harping on this, but there are restrictions to your release. You cannot leave the county. You cannot break any laws, which means that you ought to stay away from beer joints and unsavory companions, just to be on the safe side. I hope that Father Frankie will keep an eye on you."

"Can you picture a priest, the resident of a parsonage, turning away someone named Jesus?"

Pajan laughed. "In theory, no. But he is awfully busy preparing for this race next week."

"But I can be an enormous help to him! I am such an expert on cars. He will be extremely fortunate to have me."

"Well, I hope we can convince him that you are a blessing in disguise."

"There is no disguise, however," said Jesús. "I am a blessing in plain view."

When they found Fr. Frankie, he seemed less sure that the recently-incarcerated *chilango* constituted an unalloyed blessing. He looked doubtfully at the beaming Jesús, and then at a worried-looking Pajan. "And you say this fellow cannot leave the county limits?"

"Yes, Father. It isn't because he's considered dangerous or anything. It's just that being a foreign national makes him an automatic flight risk, I guess. But he doesn't know anyone here in town, so I thought I'd bring him here. He needs someone local to vouch for him."

Fr. Frankie hesitated. "Well, I don't know … I could certainly use a chance to practice my Spanish. You know we've added a Sunday mass in Spanish now, and I'm finding the homily a bit of a challenge. But, you know, in addition to my regular duties, this race is keeping me awfully busy."

Jesús leaned close and murmured confidentially, "Father, I am very good with cars. You may need pit crew for this race. It is without doubt that God is on your side, but would it not be helpful also to have Jesús?"

Fr. Frankie ran a hand through his hair, currently grayer from track dust. "Well, that's an offer I daren't refuse," he said. "I suppose I can put him up in the rectory. Mrs. Mancini could use the practice in Christian fortitude."

Chapter Twelve
Serpents in Eden

Camber spoke hesitantly into the phone. "Listen, Brennan, you're not going to believe this."

His old room-mate said evenly, "Oh, knowing you, Camber, I think I will."

The chill in Brennan's voice told Camber that he'd be walking on eggs in this conversation, and he'd better start by showing some sincere concern for his old pal's predicament. "Look, before I go into the details of what happened out here, tell me: how did your meeting with the bank go?"

"I've spent the past week thinking up ways to kill you," said Brennan. "But, since you ask, suffice it to say that the meeting didn't go well at all. In fact, it was the Little Big Horn, and they were speaking Comanche."

"Sioux, I think you mean," murmured Camber.

"Thanks for the history lesson. Too bad you're not that good as a business major. You did all the charts, remember? Told me not to worry about it, because you'd handle that part of the presentation. The bank people were very concerned with my debt-to-equity ratio, and, thanks to your incomprehensible charts and figures, I couldn't even tell which way was up, so I was forced to stall them. I said that you were finalizing some production numbers, and that we would get back to them in two weeks. Didn't they teach you in business school to make sure that other people could present your business plan in case you couldn't be there?"

Camber closed his eyes, letting the calamity sink in. The worst part was that Brennan was absolutely right. He had made a mess of things. "I am truly sorry, Brennan. Really, I am," he said. "Look, as soon as I get out of this mess, I will take that meeting with you, and I'll be so brilliant that no bank will be able to say no to your plans. Only thing is, I can't leave here just yet."

"Why can't you? Just what the hell is going on, Camber? You have been totally off the radar for almost a week now. Texting your stupid ten codes, and not answering my calls."

Camber sighed. This is where it got tricky. "Well, see, I kind of got into a little wreck in a town called Judas Grove, Tennessee, not too far from my uncle's place at the lake. So now they are holding me hostage, and making me teach a bunch of local ministers how to drive race cars."

There was a long pause, which was probably Brennan waiting for a punch line to that outlandish tale. Finally he said, "Leaving aside for just a moment the fascinating concept of a town named after Judas … *Hostage?* You're a hostage? Tennessee is in the United States isn't it? How can they be holding you hostage, and why would anybody want you, or anybody else for that matter, to teach a group of ministers the fine points of stock car racing? Do you want me to call somebody on your behalf? The FBI? How about Amnesty International? I'm sure that would make a nice change for them. *Excuse me, sirs, but my friend is being forced to teach race car driving to clergymen in Tennessee.* – Are they subjecting you to any other forms of torture? Making you eat prime rib? Forcing you to date Swedish models?"

"No, and don't call the FBI, because I'm up to my ears in law enforcement as it is. Really. I'm serious, Brennan. I'm stuck in this town, because they sentenced me to do community service, and, since I don't have the money to pay the fine and court costs, I have to spend every night in jail. This is really getting to me. I haven't had a good night's sleep in days."

"I suppose they're refusing to put mints on your pillow."

"The bed is a metal shelf, Brennan."

"And I suppose you have a cell mate who calls you Honey-bun?"

"No. The only other in-mate is Jesús, and he's okay."

"When you wrecked the car, did you get a head injury?"

"I've had worse. Oh, you mean, because of Jesús? He's Mexican. I'm not making any of this up, Brennan. I swear it. They're even making me go to church."

"I'll put that on the human rights petition," said Brennan dryly." I'm sure the Dalai Lama will weep for you. But, assuming you haven't gotten a concussion and hallucinated all this, which seems pretty likely to me, why would anybody want you to teach ministers to race?"

"Because they are having this big race out here to determine who gets a multi-million dollar legacy. An old guy with a serious NASCAR collection recently died—"

"Did you land on him when you wrecked, by any chance?"

"Almost, but he was already dead. I crashed his funeral. Pay attention. The proceeds from the sale of his NASCAR memorabilia collection will go to the winner of a stock car race at the county speedway here. Only the local ministers can compete, though. And only one of them has ever raced before."

Brennan still didn't sound sympathetic, or even convinced. "As tempting as it is to digress into the improbabilities of that story," he said, "let's get back to your inability to leave town. I though you said that you just wrecked you car. So why did they *sentence* you to do anything?"

"See, what happened was ...While I was staying at the lake house, Tracy got a call from Flash, offering him the chance to relief drive last weekend at Charlotte. Only when the call came, I was the one who answered Tracy's cell phone. Flash was so out of it that he thought I was Tracy, so I said I would drive for him, and I left without telling Tracy about the call. Unfortunately, after I left, Flash called back, so Tracy found out about the offer, and he took off after me. You know his car is better than mine—"

Brennan snickered. There were skateboards better than Camber's car.

"... So it didn't take him too long to catch up to me, and he was furious. Let's just say he hasn't outgrown his anger problems."

"And you wrecked?"

"Well, I had a little help from Tracy, but, yeah, just as he was about to catch up with me, I went off the road on a steep hillside, and I sorta crashed this funeral in progress. Nobody was hurt, though."

"How fast were you going?"

"Well I'm not sure. The court said I was doing ninety, but I'm sure they were guessing. The road was about fifty feet higher than the land in the valley, so for most of the time I was literally flying. When they arrested me, they mentioned charges like speeding, reckless endangerment—"

"Flying too low?"

"Laugh it up," said Camber. "I could have been killed, you know. Listen, I can't talk much longer. They are waiting to take me to church with a bunch of snake handlers."

"A jury of your peers," said Brennan, but at least he sounded more cheerful now.

"Yeah, whatever. Listen, you know I didn't get paid anything for the driving I did in those last few races. I was just doing it for seat time, so I am kind of low on cash right now."

"You're broke Camber. What else is new? And it sounds like you're getting off easy with this crazy community service deal. I would have arrested you, too, if you had come at me doing ninety miles an hour, airborne."

"Thanks for the sympathy, man. Did I mention that I might have been killed?"

"Don't try to cheer me up. What is it going to take to get you back here in time for my meeting with the bank people? I have so many clearances and tolerance measurements in my head, that I couldn't possibly talk about margins and sale figures with any confidence. I was really counting on you to bail me out there."

"Funny you should use that term," said Camber.

"What term?"

"Bail. I'm having legal troubles myself, you know. Could you deposit $500 in my bank account? I told you I need to pay court costs. I'm sleeping in a jail cell, man. And then I need to start working on a way of getting out of here after the race. You know, fixing up my car, assuming it's salvageable, and making it back to Mooresville. I can charge the parts for my car to my credit card, but I already used it to pay my no-good lawyer, so there is no way I buy parts and pay court costs. I'd be way over my credit limit."

There was a long pause, which probably meant that Brennan was considering his options, and discarding a round of sarcastic remarks. "I don't really have a choice, do I?" he said at last. "I'll send you some money. Just don't let me down about this bank meeting. I'll deposit the money for you tomorrow, but I'm taking your signed Dale Earnhardt leather jacket, just so you know I'm serious."

"Thanks man," said Camber softly. You could always count on Brennan. Eventually. "Gotta go." he said, and clicked off the phone.

* * *

"I'm a little worried," said Camber.

A few minutes after six, just before the time when Stoney delivered the meals to the prisoners, Travis Prichard had turned up at the jail, and signed him out. It was an overcast spring evening, and a light rain turned the warm air into clouds of mist. Now they were headed out of town in Brother Prichard's pick-up truck, bound for the Wednesday evening church service in the converted laundromat that served as a sanctuary for the small, rural congregation.

"Worried about what?" said Travis.

"Dinner, among other things," said Camber. "When Stoney came to let me out, I reminded him that I hadn't eaten yet, and he said, *'You won't be needing any food where you're going.'* So I'm torn between anxiety over missing a meal and the thought that you guys might be practicing human sacrifice, in which case Stoney's mystery stew would be the least of my problems."

Travis Prichard laughed. "No, we aren't planning on serving you for communion. I believe Stoney was trying to do you a good turn by saying that. I take it you're not overly fond of the food they serve in the jail? People mostly aren't, I hear."

"Oh, you could probably kill sharks with the stuff," said Camber cheerfully, "but I suppose it's better than nothing, if you're starving. Which I usually am, after spending all day at the track."

"I figured that. I think Stoney decided you'd be better off keeping your appetite, because he knows that before services, we serve a big meal of home-cooked food. Fried chicken, cooked apples, pinto beans, homemade biscuits, ham, mashed potatoes—"

Camber brightened. "And gravy?"

"Oh, son, where I come from, gravy is a *beverage.* And we top all that off with a whole table full of desserts made by the ladies of the church. They've been baking chocolate cakes, brownies, and berry pies all day long."

"It sounds wonderful," said Camber. "Instead of a knife and fork, just bring me a shovel. But are you telling me that you eat all this *before* the church service?"

"That's right. Oh, I know there are some faiths that believe in fasting until after church, but we're different. Our worship service is a right strenuous process, and we feel the need to fortify ourselves before the undertaking."

Camber stopped watching the rain splash on the windshield, and turned to stare at his host. "Strenuous? Listening to a sermon may be tedious, but I wouldn't call it hard work."

Travis Prichard smiled. "Well, our congregation doesn't do much sitting still and listening. You'll see. Unfortunately, you may not get the full experience this evening. Brother Verrell, who runs our sound system is down with the flu, so we'll just have to do the best we can, but it'll put more of a damper on the services than this wet weather."

"Sound system?" said Camber. "I think I may be able to help

you there." He spent the rest of the drive telling Travis Prichard about his stint with the Back Stretch Boys back in middle school, and assuring him that he was quite equal to the task of managing a few amplifiers for a small church service.

Finally, as an afterthought, Camber asked, "You just want a microphone for the podium, and maybe one for the choir?"

"Well, no. We need separate amplifiers for the instruments. We have a Telecaster and a Firebird, and they need to be amped separately, of course, with a mike for each one. Have you ever worked with a Fender Twin Reverb?"

Camber was silent for a few moments, trying to think of a definition for "Telecaster" and "Firebird" that did not involve words like "Led Zeppelin" or "Brad Paisley." Of course, "Firebird" was also the name of a classical music composition by Igor Stravinsky. Which would be the more improbable thing to encounter in a backwoods church—Russian classical music or a legendary electric Gibson guitar? Camber, who thought that his knowledge of '70's music almost counted as archaeology, tried to picture the late Allen Collins, his broom straw hair streaming past his shoulders, playing *Free Bird* … in the sanctuary of a fundamentalist church in rural Tennessee. Now that would be a miracle.

He was still contemplating this cultural paradox, when Travis said, "Now, I play a Firebird, myself. Used to have a Strat—never managed to sound like Buddy Holly or Jimi Hendrix, but it was a fine instrument. Then I moved on to a Tele, along with about 95% of the musicians in Nashville. It sure does make a joyful noise unto the Lord."

Camber stared. "You ... play ... a ... Fender … Telecaster … electric … guitar … in … your … church?"

"Used to. Like I said, I got a Firebird."

"Now, that does surprise me, Travis," said Camber, treading carefully, so as not to say anything offensive. "I don't know exactly why it should. I guess it's because you didn't seem very happy about computers, or diagnostic machines for car repair, or cell phones. So I didn't think high tech music technology would be your thing."

Travis Prichard considered it. "We're not against modern

inventions *per se,"* he said at last. "But we do think there's a lot wrong with modern society—the rat race of hurrying and hustling, in order to buy material things. The emphasis on sex and flashy clothes. So we have a problem with most television shows, and with fancy devices like computers that just bring a lot of suspicious people and ideas right into your home. But anybody who has read about King David in the Old Testament knows that God Himself is partial to music. So, just as we switched from the horse and buggy to the automobile a long time back, we were willing to move forward in the realm of music."

"And you play hymns on electric guitars?" mused Camber. "Wow. I'm trying to imagine *Amazing Grace* …"

Prichard laughed. "I tell you what. You get that sound system working, and the grace will be more amazing than you can possibly imagine."

* * *

Stoney had been right to withhold the jailhouse "mystery stew," Camber decided. There was enough food on the table to feed a football team. The Sanctified Holiness Church of God held its pre-church dinner in the home of one of the anointed, a church member whose house was across the road from the laundromat building that was now used for the worship service. Travis had explained that the Wednesday evening meeting was in addition to the regular one on Sunday morning.

"We don't go as long tonight as we would on Sunday," Travis had assured him, and, just when Camber was thinking how nice it was that the service would last less than an hour, he had added, "We ought to have you back to the jail by midnight."

This last remark was mildly troubling, but Camber assumed it was one of Travis's deadpan witticisms, which he always delivered with a completely straight face, so he dismissed the alarm from his mind, and focused his attention on the buffet. After many days of Stoney's dubious cooking, he scarcely needed the encouragement, but still it was gratifying that so many of the church members treated him like a starving orphan and kept refilling his plate, saying, "Now, you just have to try this dish …"

There were about twenty-five people at the buffet supper, plus a dozen children, ranging in age from six to early teens. The stocky woman in blue who served him his third slice of carrot cake explained that during church meetings the babies and toddlers were kept in one of the homes by a different volunteer each time. That way the young mothers didn't have to miss the service.

The men all wore white dress shirts and dark trousers or work pants. Only Camber wore jeans, but, as he kept explaining, he really didn't have any choice in the matter, since all he had packed were casual clothes for his original weekend at his uncle's lake house. At least no one was wearing a necktie. Travis had explained to him that the group felt that neckties were "worldly," suggesting vanity and a preoccupation with appearances. Camber, who thought that a tie was an uncomfortable nuisance, hoped this point of view would catch on in the general population.

The women, who all wore cotton below-the-knee length dresses in a style that he thought of as "*Grapes of Wrath* dowdy," had long hair pinned up in buns, and their shiny faces were devoid of make-up. To Camber, who had never known a world without cosmetics and hair coloring, it was a little unsettling to see what women *really* looked like. They were kind, though, and they kept urging him to have another helping of meat or potatoes.

* * *

While the rest of the congregation was still eating supper and socializing, Travis Prichard slipped out the front door, and into the cool twilight of the front lawn, where a dozen vehicles, everything from rattletrap trucks to a new BMW, were parked, evidence that the evening service would be well-attended. He reached into the back of his pick-up to retrieve the small wooden box with the sliding plexiglass lid. As he lifted it out, the tilting box lurched and rattled ominously, which might have caused an unsuspecting person, or a less experienced one, to drop the box and run. To Travis Prichard that sound only served to bring back memories of his childhood in the old farmhouse out on Grinders Ridge.

He had been seven years old when they lived there. Daddy was still working at the sawmill then, but back in the fall he had got the call to preach, and now most of his time was spent praying and readying himself to do the Lord's work. Mama was pregnant with Amee Jo, and she tried hard not to show how worried she was about what they were going to do if Daddy lost his job, being away so much, and where the money would come from to see them through the winter, and—most of all—what would she do with four young'uns if her husband's peculiar notions about Scripture up and got him killed.

They'd argue about it late at night, when the children were supposed to be asleep, but the bedroom that Travis shared with Lee Roy was only a paper-thin wall away from his parents' bed, so it was hard not to overhear.

"Look at this verse, Joyce," his father would say. "Right here. Mark, chapter sixteen, eighteenth verse: *They shall take up serpents, and if they drink any deadly thing, it shall not hurt them ...* It's right there in the Bible, plain as day."

And then his mother's soft voice would answer, not arguing with the Word of God, no, but fretting over the consequences of tempting fate with such recklessness. "Well, I know you believe that the Lord will give you that power, hon. I'm just not sure that anybody explained that passage of the scripture to them serpents."

Daddy laughed then, like she knew he would, and then, in a graver tone she said, "It just don't seem right to me. Handling serpents is testing God."

"It's no such thing, Joyce. It's a sign for the believers to show that God watches over them that lives a righteous life."

"What if you's to die, Harmon? What if that snake was to bite you? Would you let them take you to a hospital?"

"No need for that. I trust in the Lord, and if it is His will that I be healed, then I'll get well. I have no need of worldly medicine. Faith is sufficient."

"What about me and the little ones, then? What will happen to us?"

"The Lord will provide. You must trust Him. As I do. That's why I will take up the serpent. To prove my trust in God."

After a while, when the fire burned low and it was too cold to sit up in bed any more, his parents' voices would become a soft slurring of sound, like watering running over a stony brook, and then Travis would snuggle deep under the blue star-patterned quilt his mother had made, and surrender himself to sleep. As he drifted off, letting go of his senses one by one, his last moment of consciousness would be of hearing two things: the wind tapping bare oak branches against the tin roof, and the answering rattle of the drowsy snake, coiled in its box under his bed.

* * *

The supper was winding down, and while the congregation was tidying up and putting away the food, Travis took Camber across the road to the church to get acquainted with the sound system. The sanctuary was a large bare room with two dozen metal folding chairs set up facing a foot-high platform, on which stood the pulpit, the electric guitars on stands, the sound system, and two foot-long wooden boxes. On the whitewashed cinderblock walls behind the platform, a hand-lettered sign read, *Sanctified Holiness Church of God of Signs Following.* Other posters quoted Bible verses pertaining to the signs, promising believers the power to withstand snake bites, poison, and fire. But Camber barely glanced at the artwork. He was staring at the two small boxes a few feet away from the sound system. They were simple home-made containers, painted black, and decorated on the side with a tin punch panel in the shape of a cross. Each sliding Plexiglass lid was fastened to its box with a small padlock, much to Camber's relief.

He clutched at Prichard's arm. "That's them, isn't it?"

Travis nodded. "That's them. But don't let it worry you. Those boxes are locked, and, even when the serpents are let out, we don't let them crawl around the room. Somebody will be holding him the whole time he's out."

Camber inched forward and peered into the nearest box, where a fat brown rattlesnake was curled up on a bed of cut grass. "Okay," he said, "I guess if that thing escapes during the service, I'll just run out the back door."

Travis smiled. "We don't have a back door."

Still staring at the snake, Camber said, "Where do you want one?"

* * *

They inspected the sound system and the amps that went with each of the electric guitars, while Travis kept assuring Camber that, since snakes were deaf, it would not matter to them how loud the music was. The next few minutes were occupied by the familiar technical chatter that made Camber feel most at home, even though the subject was guitar mechanics rather than cars.

"How do you like the Tele?' asked Camber, pointing to one of the electric guitars.

"Well, that's my old one," said Travis. "Brother Alton plays it now, but it's a great instrument. Teles are workhorse guitars. They're not the easiest to play because of the radius of the curvature of the fingerboard, but they're clear-sounding and nearly indestructible."

Camber nodded. "Yeah, Brad Paisley does amazing things with his. But if you switch a Tele to the neck pickup, it becomes a great blues and R&B axe, too. So, the Firebird is yours?"

"Yeah, but it's not a vintage one from the 'Sixties. Gibson started making them again in the 'Nineties, and I bought that one used in '98. It's got a chrome, dog-eared P-90 pickup in the bridge position and a Gibson *teaspoon* nickel vibrato arm."

Camber, who spoke fluent *Popular Mechanics*, actually knew what that meant. "What amps you got?" he asked, and the ensuing discussion would have sounded to a non-technical ear exactly like speaking in tongues.

A few minutes before the service began, Camber took his place on the low platform at the front of the simple sanctuary, next to the amps, just behind a small three legged table with a mason jar of water set on top of it. *That's handy,* thought Camber. *If it gets too hot in here, I can just take a sip.* He was less enthusiastic about the presence of the small wooden boxes a few feet away on the platform, knowing that if he peeked into one of the boxes, he would meet the unblinking stare of a coiled rattlesnake. He backed away and barricaded himself behind the sound system, resolving to dive for cover if anybody opened those boxes.

He had just finished tinkering with the guitar amps when the doors opened, and the congregation flowed into the hall, laughing and talking in happy anticipation of the evening service.

From his vantage point in the nest of machinery, Camber watched the parishioners, trying to discern some significant difference between them and the majority of the population, who did not indulge in such daring practices as serpent-handling. They were dressed in everyday clothes—the women wore no hats or fancy outfits, and none of the men wore ties, but informality in church was hardly a novelty anymore. One or two of the people he'd chatted with at the dinner nodded or waved to him, and then they settled in their chairs and waited for the service to begin. Camber returned his attention to the sound system.

Brother Travis quoted some scripture to get the meeting started, and then he made community announcements. It was all pretty standard church fare, Camber was thinking, but when they launched into the first hymn, he could tell the difference. Instead of the slow, sedate liturgical music normally associated with religious services, the Judas Grove Sign Followers made a joyful noise. The Firebird and the Tele kicked in, and the congregation followed along in a jaunty, syncopated sound that owed more to Chuck Berry than to Bach. People stood up and danced—not with each other, but alone in an expression of joy and rapture. A few minutes later, someone began to speak loudly, but not in a language Camber could understand. They might have been speaking in tongues, he thought, but since his knowledge of foreign languages was severely limited, it could have been practically any foreign language as far as he was concerned.

With a crowd of people gyrating in front of the platform, and the thrum of electric guitars resonating through the room like a giant heartbeat, the room temperature rose a couple of degrees in a matter of minutes. Camber wiped the sweat from his forehead, and twiddled the controls, trying to make sure that no shrieking feedback from the amplifiers interfered with the music. Both musicians were expert players. Camber thought he'd never heard anyone better. Odd that they would be content to use their talents in a little backwoods church instead of trying to make it in show business. He reached for the jar of water on the nearby table, but just then, the guitarists launched into a new song, and he had to adjust the sound again to accommodate them.

It was a long service. Occasionally someone would get up and walk out of the room, presumably to use the rest room, because a few minutes later they'd come back, ready to join in the service again. After the first hour or so, Camber decided it wasn't all that much different from church services in general, and he began to relax and enjoy the music. It was still hot in the room, and he was tempted to go outside and take a break, but he figured that if he did, the whole sound system would pick just that moment to go haywire, so he didn't want to risk it.

The mason jar of water was still tantalizingly close, but he still hadn't gotten around to grabbing it. He supposed it was there in case the preacher had a coughing fit, and he didn't like to help himself without permission. Still, it was pretty hot in the sanctuary. Race car drivers are used to high temperatures, of course because it gets over a hundred degrees in the cockpit during a race, but Camber tried to keep himself hydrated the rest of the time to make up for it.

Just as he leaned forward toward the water for the umpteenth time, Travis Prichard set down the Firebird, snatched up the Mason jar, and took a few gulps. Then he set it back on the table, and squatted beside one of the small wooden boxes, fumbling with the clear plastic lid.

Uh-oh, thought Camber, edging away from the platform, and making sure to keep the speaker was between him and the box.

When Travis Prichard stood up, he was holding a squirming three-foot rattlesnake in front of him, with his fingers encircling its neck, with his other hand cradling its swaying tail. As Camber watched in horror, Prichard allowed the serpent to coil around his upper arm, while he supported its head in his palm.

The crowd of worshippers fell back a respectful distance of three yards or so. *As well they might,* thought Camber. But no one screamed or fled the room. The minister himself seemed quite calm, as if he were holding his guitar instead of a poisonous snake. The worshippers formed a semi-circle around him and watched. After a few moments of concentrating on the snake, perhaps to make sure it was comfortably situated and not inclined to escape, Travis Prichard went back to preaching and exhorting the congregation to believe in the protection of the Lord. *Camber hoped that this protection extended to innocent bystanders.*

The rattlesnake, seeking a new vantage point from which to observe the proceedings, writhed up the minister's arm, and draped itself around his neck, so that its head and a quarter of its body curved upright above his left shoulder. Its beady eyes surveyed the room. It seemed to be observing the congregation with unblinking reptilian interest.

"Hamster for your thoughts," Camber muttered to himself.

After a few minutes an elderly man went up on the platform, opened the other wooden box, and took out a second rattler. He took his place at the front of the crowd, a few feet away from Travis, and began to pray in a loud, sonorous voice, as the snake curled around his arm and swayed gently as his body rocked in time to the music of Brother Alton on the Tele.

After a few minutes, the serpents went back to their respective boxes. They had shown exemplary behavior during their part in the service, frightening nobody, and making no attempts to strike. Camber was impressed, but not in the least inclined to get better acquainted with serpents, well-behaved or otherwise.

An hour or so later the service wound to a close. The two musicians unstrapped their guitars, the congregation headed for the cool night air in the parking lot, and Camber shut down the sound system.

"Well, that was amazing," he said to Travis Prichard. "You're a quite a guitar player."

Prichard, whose lined face and lank hair glistened with sweat, smiled. "Years of practice, son," he said. "Do you want another bite to eat before I take you back?"

"I'm still stuffed," said Camber, "But I wouldn't mind a swig of your water there."

He reached for the mason jar, but Travis Prichard's fingers closed over his wrist. "Let's go find you some water with ice in it. Not like that water … which has got strychnine in it."

Camber froze. "But—but I saw you drinking from that jar all through the service."

"I told you. We're Sign Followers. We believe the Lord protects us from harm. Not just serpents, but fire and poison—all kinds of dangers. Well, I guess we'd better get packed up." He lifted one of the wooden snake boxes and tucked it under his arm. "You want to get the other box, Camber?"

But Camber carried the Firebird.

Chapter Thirteen
Fanfare

"**Your** *starting line up for tonight's Mini Stock race will be ... Starting from the pole for the second time this year: Mike Huddleback. Starting second: Johnny Weeks. Starting third: Steve..."*

It was Saturday night at the races in Judas Grove, Tennessee.

Camber wished he had a rope to tie all the ministers' wrists together in a line, so that he wouldn't lose any of them among the crowds and the carnival-like distractions of the event. Camber had decided that the Saturday night race at the local speedway would provide the perfect opportunity for his little flock to see in action the men and women who raced there every weekend. They had spent more than a week practicing at this very speedway, but that would not prepare them for what they were about to see. Tonight the track was nothing like the peaceful, pastoral place that they experienced during practice, when they had the deserted track all to themselves. The speedway was now a hub of activity in a blare of noise, with people everywhere.

"Camber!" Romney Marsh tried to get his tour guide's attention over the uproar. "This place is amazing. It looks like there are more people here than at the state fair."

Camber nodded. "I don't know about that, but by the time the green flag drops on the feature race tonight, you'll know how lucky you are that we were all invited to watch from the VIP booth. If this place is like most short tracks I have been to, there won't be two empty seats next to each other in this whole grandstand."

A steady stream of cars, SUVs and pick-up trucks were inching along the track road and turning off to park in the large grass field behind the grandstand area. The line of vehicles backed up all the way on to the country highway, halting traffic in both directions. A Tennessee state trooper in a pressed uniform and white gloves was directing traffic. His patrol car was pulled on to the shoulder of the road, its blue lights flashing. Music and laughter spilled from open car windows, and people waved to each other as they crept along in the stream of traffic. Some of them called the trooper by name, and he grinned and gave them a jaunty salute as they rolled by.

In the daytime the track, set in a natural bowl among rolling hills, could not be seen from the highway, but at night the speedway lights made it easy to locate. It looked as if a UFO had landed between the fold of hills. The contours of the land would have made it possible for the track's owners to extend the grandstand all the way up the hillsides, like a baby Bristol Motor Speedway, if the expense and the attendance had warranted such an expansion, which it didn't. After dusk, the encircling hills cupped the light from the bright track lights so that it glowed in the hollow and continued in a V-shape all the way up to the night sky.

Inside the gates Camber felt like he was herding cats, trying to keep his little flock together in the swelling tide of fans surging past them on their way to the race track's other evening attractions: the multiple concession stands, the souvenir area, and the midway, where several portable carnival rides had been brought in so that families could make a gala night of going to the races. The air was filled with the greasy smell of deep fryers churning out batches of funnel cakes, corn dogs, French fries, and chicken fingers. Pink and blue balls of cotton candy dotted the crowd with sticky bouquets of spun sugar.

"Mini Stock Drivers, to your cars, please!" The PA announcer's voice squawked from horn-shaped speakers set atop the track fence.

The ministers, who were still in awe of all the raucous activity, craned to look every time a car in the pits reved up its engine. "This doesn't even feel like the same place." Reverend Bartlett said, pointing at the crowded infield. "The pits are packed. What are all those different cars?"

Despite the competing noise, Camber was trying to reply loudly enough for all of them to hear him, so that he wouldn't have to keep answering the same question over and over. He gathered them into a huddle, and said, "Several different classes of cars race on the same night, all leading up to the featured event, the premier class. At this track that feature division is called *Late Model Stock*."

"Is that what we'll be driving?" asked Paul Whitcomb, who had evidently used the dress code for the Masters in determining what to wear to a local stock car race. He was casually elegant in his tan Ashworth slacks and Greg Norman polo shirt, and spikeless Etonic golf shoes.

"No," said Camber, eying the outfit with raised eyebrows. "The cars you all will be racing are from the *Street Stock* class. Regular races here last from half an hour to an hour, so they will run several classes for a solid night of *en-ter-tain-ment* for everyone." Careful to keep a straight face, Camber nodded in the direction of a tattooed man in a white tank top, who was trying not to spill his overfull plastic cup of beer, as he plowed through their midst on his way back to his seat.

As Camber explained the fine points of local racing, a subject that had become second nature to him over the years, he was walking slowly backwards, in order to keep an eye on his charges, who had a tendency to wander away as new distractions appeared to tempt them. Sometimes delighted parishioners would come rushing up, eager to shake hands, perhaps just to make sure they were not hallucinating this sighting of their dignified pastor at a Saturday night stock car race.

As Camber led his flock across the space between the bottom of the grandstand and the track fence, they dutifully followed in his wake, but each one was taking notice of some different and captivating facet of the spectacle.

"Local tracks do not feature just one long race as they do in the NASCAR Cup series," he told them. "Each division represents a rung on the ladder of racing experience: skill needed in car control and racing prowess; more horsepower, and faster speeds. You work your way up to Cup." Actually, making it to the NASCAR Cup series was more like winning the lottery, but Camber needed to believe that perseverance and hard work would get you there. Brennan's comments on his childlike faith in this matter were scathing.

The loudspeaker erupted again. "Okay, folks! Unless you have had your head in the sand for the past month, you have heard of next week's main event. *The Jimmy Powell Memorial / Faster Pastor 100*. This race will be known as the spectacle that put Judas Grove, Tennessee on the map. A record purse for any race held at any short track, thanks to our beloved Jimmy Powell. Here's how it's going to go down!

"We have enlisted teams from our *Street Stock* division to donate the use of their cars to ten pastors from local churches right here in our community, and, folks, those ministers are here with us tonight! Later on we will have a drawing to see which minister will get what car. We have over twenty teams that compete here at the speedway in the *Street Stock* division, so the drawing will also determine which teams' cars will be selected. We're putting all the team's numbers in a hat, and one by one the ministers will draw a number. This will determine the pairings of ministers to cars for next week's race.

"Listen up folks I'm not making this stuff up. The late Jimmy Powell was a lifelong fan of racing, and you can tell that he put a lot of thought into this race. Here are some of his specific instructions. I'm gonna read 'em out here.

** Each team donating a race car will receive compensation in the amount of $6000.*

**Each clergyman participating in the race will receive $50,000 for their church.*

**The team whose car wins the race will receive a bonus of $25,000, and the winning pastor will take home all remaining net proceeds from the sale of the Jimmy Powell Racing Memorabilia Collection,* *which is to be auctioned to highest bidder.*

"When Mr. Powell wrote this will, he knew his collection was worth enough to make this race worthwhile, but I don't think he knew that the total value would be estimated at over two million dollars. This is amazing, people! This is a fortune. *Two … million …dollars.* Why, I've been afraid there'd be Cup drivers trying to get themselves ordained just so they can compete in this here race.

"Now this Faster Pastor race will be a must-see event. Come early if you want a grandstand seat. We will be selling hillside seating, as well, because we expect record crowds here at the speedway. We've had calls from a dozen different states, and there's some national media talking about coming in to cover the event. It'll be the Woodstock of NASCAR, folks. People who don't come to this race will have to lie and say they did."

Bill Bartlett put his hand on Camber's shoulder to get his attention, and leaned close to his ear in order to make himself heard. "We were asked by the track to deliver the invocation tonight as a group. Do you know where we will be doing that?"

"Most of the time, it is done standing on the track, right at the start finish line." said Camber, pointing in the direction of the flag stand. "They asked all of you to do it?"

"Yes. It's the only equitable way, really. They said they would give us a microphone to pass down the line so that each of us could say a blessing. They thought it would be a great way to promote our race, but they also asked us to say a special prayer for Baby Sarah Meyers. She is a local two-year old who needs a kidney transplant. They are taking up a collection in the stands to help cover some of the family's expenses," Bartlett explained

"We told them we would do anything at all to help," said Fr. Frankie. "We are not afraid to pass the collection plate, are we, boys?"

"If we're going to do the invocation, we had better make our way over there now," said Travis Prichard, the only one of the bunch with prior racing experience. "The invocation and the national anthem come right before the first race."

They followed Camber to the gate that led to the racing surface, where a security guard, posted to keep fans out of the pit area, checked to see that they all had on their VIP wrist bands, allowing them unrestricted access throughout the speedway. As Camber led them onto the track, he decided to take a break from chaperone duty, and turn over his flock to the PA announcer, who had left his booth and was making his way down to the Start-Finish line.

"They're all yours!" Camber told him, after the round of introductions and hand-shaking. "I think I'll walk a lap around the pits."

The man holding the microphone, who appeared to be in a state of chemically-induced excitement, stopped Camber before he could even get to pit wall.

"Oh, hey, don't leave now," he said. The announcer's syrupy voice sounded familiar. Camber suspected that he was a local radio DJ, because his rumbling baritone voice did not seem to match his scrawny body. "I was going to introduce you. Any time we get a big name driver in, it adds to the excitement of the evening, so we like to introduce him to the crowd."

"Sure, I'd be glad to," said Camber, who would have much preferred to poke around visiting the racing teams. He took his place beside Rev. Scarberry, idly wondering what the announcer meant by *big name driver*. He hoped no one would say anything about his driving that would put him in the awkward position of having either to correct a hyped-up version of his status in racing, or to falsely accept unearned adulation by letting a misconception go unchallenged.

His worst nightmare would be for the announcer to talk about the wreck that put him here in the first place. Then he'd feel like crawling under a hauler. The news that the national press was coming next week made him uneasy, too. NASCAR would take a dim view of an aspiring driver wrecking on a public road, and that might hurt his chances of ever getting a ride. No use worrying about it, though. He forced himself to think optimistically. Maybe tonight they would just ask him to give the command to start the engines for tonight's featured race. He could do that without thinking, and, considering the alternatives, it was the least embarrassing task he could think of.

The grandstand had filled quickly. Now the sun was dipping below the jagged ridge. Almost time. The announcer lined up the special guests facing the crowd: first, closest to Turn One, stood a man in a white firesuit, obviously one of tonight's competing drivers; then all the ministers in a row, and, finally, Camber himself on the Turn Four end of the line.

The announcer raised the microphone to his mouth. "Welcome race fans! What an action-packed night of racing we have for you tonight! Before we crank those engines, I have some special introductions to make. First off, I have here Bobby Meyers, our very own driver of the number 11 in the *Late Model* series. He'd like to say a few words on a subject close to his heart, so listen up."

The announcer passed the handheld microphone to the man in the white driver's suit, who squinted up at the lights and in a quavering voice began to speak ."I … I don't much speak in front of crowds," he said, "but I wanted to ask for everyone's help for the sake of my little niece Sarah. She needs a kidney. My brother's family is facing a huge challenge, and I just want to ask y'all for all the thoughts and prayers and support you can give us. Thank you." He lowered his head and handed back the microphone.

"You heard the man. A member of our racing family needs help, and I am sure some of us here today can help. Donation buckets have been placed at all of the concession stands, if you feel a calling in your heart to help. Now please stand and remove your hats as our own ten spiritual leaders of Judas Grove offer the benediction for tonight's race."

The ministers now seemed to grow in stature, suddenly comfortable and confident in their familiar duties, despite the unaccustomed setting. They had not prepared remarks, at least not on paper, but they seemed to be moved by the occasion, so that each one spoke from the heart.

Passing the microphone from hand to hand, they went down the line, each asking the Almighty for guidance and support, and giving thanks for the blessing of fellowship and for the joy of sport. They asked for protection for the drivers, the crews, the workers and the fans, safe travels back home for everyone, and for the strength to do the Lord's will and to accept His judgments.

Agnes Hill-Radnor, the only one of the group who was not really a minister, merely recited Psalm 91:11, "For He shall give His angels charge over thee, to keep thee in all thy ways," a sentiment that drew cheers and whistles from the delighted spectators.

Stephen Albright's solemn invocation suggested that he thought he had been called upon by Nero to bless the gladiators in the Roman Coliseum. Camber thought it was just as well that hardly anybody in the crowd knew the meaning of, "*Morituri te salutant.*" If anybody asked about him it, especially any drivers or pit crew, Camber resolved to plead ignorance.

Romney Marsh, the last to go, took a step forward as he was handed the microphone by Travis Prichard. "Hello," he said, beaming at the crowd, his white dress shirt and slacks almost outshining the sparkle of his hair gel. "My name is Romney Marsh, pastor of the Church of the Crystal Path. Instead of adding anything to the fine blessings already offered up by my colleagues here, I'd like to make an announcement. On behalf of all our churches, mine and those of my colleagues here with whom I will be racing next week, I would like to present a check for one thousand dollars to the family of Mr. Myers to start off the collection for that little girl who needs a kidney. And may God bless her."

The crowd erupted with cheers and applause, and Camber heard more cheers from the crews in the pits behind him. Since Bobby Meyers was a regular driver here, many of the pit crew people probably knew the family.

The announcer took the microphone again. "Well, talk about manna from heaven! A thousand dollars. This sure is a great start for Baby Sarah! Let's keep this love flowing, folks!" He led the crowd in another round of cheers, and then motioned for quiet. "Back to the introductions, folks. Now, I have the pleasure of introducing this young man at the end of this line of distinguished guests. He is professional NASCAR driver Cameron Berkley, and he has taken a break from rubbing fenders with the likes of Jeff Gordon and Dale Jr. to come to us special, to make sure we have a great race next week. This is the fellow who has been teaching our ministers how to drive a race car. Heaven help him."

That comment drew a big laugh from the crowd, and a few good-natured chuckles from the ministers themselves. The announcer went on, "Camber Berkley, folks. I'll let him say a few words to you. I'm sure he has a tremendous contribution to offer."

Contribution? thought Camber. What happened to: *Gentlemen start your engines?* Was the announcer referring to his coaching of the ministers for the Faster Pastor race, or was he expecting Camber to say something inspirational and life-changing, or—worse yet—was he angling for a donation to tonight's cause, something that, financially, Camber was ill-prepared to do. He looked down, as though contemplating some words of wisdom, while he frantically considered his options. The microphone was already in his hand; he didn't even remember receiving it. The crowd was hushed now, waiting expectantly for some grand gesture, which, thanks to Camber's split-second reaction time, he was able to give them.

"Thank you," he said, waving to the crowd. "This is really a great honor. What a beautiful track. What a beautiful town. What a worthy cause for Baby Sarah tonight." Camber pictured a curly-haired toddler lying in a hospital bed under white sheets, surrounded by anxious family, solemn doctors, and a wall of medical equipment. With those few careless words from the announcer, Camber now felt involved in the tragedy of a family he didn't even know. This was like a wreck happening before his eyes. He looked for the hole, the path through the wreckage. What could he possibly give this stricken child?

He took another deep breath and began, "I am indeed a NASCAR driver, and tonight I sure wish I was one of the famous ones so that I could afford to pick up the whole tab for this little girl's kidney operation, but I'm still way down the totem pole in racing, just trying to catch a break. But I've put in my share of time at a lot of local tracks along the way, so tonight I would like to offer to drive for one of the teams here, and, if I win the race, I will match the purse with a donation to help Sarah's family."

"WOW!" The announcer seized both the moment and the microphone. "Can I get an AMEN to that, people!"

"Hallelujah, amen!" shouted Bobby Meyers, throwing his hand in the air, while the crowd echoed his words.

"Well, right there's your ride!" yelled the announcer, throwing an arm around Camber, who was frozen in place, letting the calamity sink in. "Baby Sarah's uncle has just offered the number 11 car to our visiting NASCAR star. Folks, it looks like we have a race on our hands!"

The cheers rose again.

"Now hold on to your hats, race fans, because I have another exciting announcement. I was going to wait until the start of the *Late Model* race to introduce our other celebrity driver tonight, but now I feel like I have got to let the cat out of the bag, because I don't want any of you folks to miss this one. We have with us tonight Mr. Tracy Berkley-Brown, who is a part-time resident of our fair county, with a place over at the lake. Tracy is here tonight, fresh from Lowes Motor Speedway, where last weekend he drove in the Nationwide Race as the relief driver for his good buddy Flash Casone."

As he spoke, the announcer was clambering over the pit wall and walking toward a group of guys in fire suits. This was probably some horrible joke, thought Camber, but he searched the throng of crews and drivers for that familiar and much-loathed face that bore entirely too much resemblance to his own. Sure enough, there he was, the weasel, smirking like he owned the place. Tracy was decked out in a flashy black fire suit, emblazoned only with the required logos for the racing series, because he didn't have any sponsors, of course. Camber thought he should have his daddy's face embroidered on the firesuit, because that's who was financing his attempts at racing. That custom-made firesuit that probably cost more than some of the other drivers' cars.

Tracy was surrounded by a crowd of enthusiastic—one might even say 'fawning'—crew members. He bared his teeth in Camber's direction; from the grandstands, it probably looked like a smile.

The announcer had pushed his way through the racers straight to Tracy, leading the way with his trusty microphone, which he brandished like a battle flag. "Tracy Berkley-Brown, folks!" he thundered, inviting the crowd to indulge in another round of applause. "What a surprise, Tracy. You and Camber are first cousins, I think you told me. How about that, folks? Cousins in this race. NASCAR has the Busch brothers, the Labonte brothers, the Allisons. We've got cousins. Well, Tracy, I guess you heard the generous offer that Camber made just moments ago. So, what about it? You'll be competing in that same race. Are you willing to offer the same deal for Baby Sarah?"

Tracy is actually here, Camber kept telling himself. Things just kept getting worse. Maybe the concussion had finally kicked in and caused him to hallucinate, although, as monsters go, he'd much prefer giant hornets or komodo dragons to his smug and over-privileged cousin. He should be so lucky. He stood there baffled, trying to come up with some reason why Tracy would be at this race track on this night, other than as part of a cosmic scheme to make Camber's life even more miserable.

Tracy smirked at the announcer. With another regal wave to the cheering crowd, he leaned into the microphone and said, "I'm looking forward to this race tonight. I think this would count as the second race my cousin and I have had in this county. And I expect I'll win this time, too." He leered over at Camber, making no effort to mask the disdain in his voice. "As for matching the purse with a thousand dollar donation of my own … Why, sure. When I win this race tonight, it will be the least I can do. So, yeah, I will match the prize money with a donation for the kid. In cash."

The announcer whooped and pumped the air with his fist.

"That's the spirit!" he yelled, motioning for the crowd to roar even louder. Tracy acknowledged the adulation with the same complacent smirk.

Camber smiled through gritted teeth, and tried to look pleased at this new development.

The announcer was still enthralled by the almost-famous Tracy. "Why don't you tell us a little bit about the team you will be driving for tonight," he said.

Tracy launched into his practiced spiel. "Tonight I will be driving for Ernie Banes Racing. He ..."

Camber already knew the rest of this story. Tracy's dad had greased more than one palm to ensure Tracy's glacial rise though the ranks of stock car racing. Ernie Banes was a former Cup driver himself, now existing on the fringes of racing, taking pupils and competing in the odd event now and then, even occasionally in a Cup race ,when there was a chance of making the field due to a lack of well-funded competitors. Mostly he and his crew traveled the southeast racing circuit, competing at different tracks each week. Had Camber been paying attention when he arrived tonight, he would have noticed the sizable hauler parked in the pit area, much too grand a vehicle just for towing a local car from a Judas Grove garage to the local race track once a week. This vehicle was first class, as was most of the equipment that Ernie competed with. He drove a primary car himself, but he was known offer his back-up car to drivers who could pay large sums of money for the privilege of racing on a weekend. Having a back-up car was yet another extravagant rarity to the regular short track circuit.

Ernie tried to pick the tracks that had a bounty out for a regular driver, offering a special prize to anyone who could defeat the track's consistent winner. When one driver is unbeatable, it makes for a dull performance for the spectators, so many track promoters will offer extra prize money for anyone who wins a race and beats the driver with a bounty on his head. Ernie would travel to that track and compete, most of the time collecting the bounty. Collecting these bounties was Ernie's little hobby.

Camber knew that in the past Ernie Banes had received large sums of money from Tracy's doting dad to put Tracy in a Late Model car. He figured tonight's offer was Ernie's goodwill gesture in case Tracy ever wanted to drive Late Model on a regular basis again. Lord knows, he needed the practice.

The announcer was still beaming at Tracy. "That is just great that we have you here racing tonight. Now tell us how your weekend went in Charlotte."

Camber cringed. He had avoiding finding out how the racing opportunity had gone for Tracy. It hadn't been hard to stay uninformed, since he had lacked both internet and a sports page. You had to dig deeper than the glancing coverage of the races on the radio or TV if you wanted to follow a driver who had not made it to super stardom yet. Camber was always impressed when a fan came up to talk to him and actually knew where he finished, because that told him that the fan had done his homework.

Tracy's story droned on, while Camber thought about all the things he would need to do in the coming minutes.

"... So I have to say thanks to Flash for the opportunity," Tracy was saying, as Camber tuned back in. "And to let everybody know that he's doing just fine after that injury he sustained."

"Glad you got a shot at the big time," said the announcer, who was trying to clap and hold the microphone at the same time. "Now let's get to racing, Tracy. Get these racers fired up, boys!"

* * *

"Gentlemen Start Your Engines!"

The cars in the mini-stock class, lined up on the back stretch, began to fire up their motors. As the four-cylinder motors of assorted Pintos, Escorts, and Mustangs roared to life like a swarm of angry hornets, a track official ushered Camber and his charges off the track and into the upper area of the grandstand, to the VIP suite. It was a press box, whose lower end had been enclosed in glass, and instead of the metal bleachers of the grandstand, there were metal folding chairs, and a card table with bottled water and a few 2-liter bottles of Coke. Compared to the sumptuous suites of the major speedways, with their fireplaces, kitchenettes, and private bathrooms, this place it wasn't much, but because it was enclosed in glass, it muffled the noise to a level that made it possible to converse.

The relative quiet gave Camber a moment to reflect on what he had just done. After a few more lower echelon races, he would be driving in the main event—against "princess" Tracy. Although this was just a regular weekly race, the advertised purse was a thousand dollars for the winner. *Well, the offer of a donation to match that had sounded good to the crowd,* Camber told himself. *Just as long as I don't win, it won't be a problem. But I will be damned if I'll let Tracy win, either.* That's what worried him. Losing the race would be relatively easy. Making sure that both he and Tracy lost would be tricky.

Nobody was making much use of the seats provided for them in the suite. The ministers were pressed close to the glass overlooking the track, taking in all the sights and sounds of the race, and marveling to each other that in seven day's time, they would be the ones out there in fire suits, revving up the engines.

"Here comes those ground-pounding Street Stocks, folks!" roared the announcer's voice from the wall speakers inside the suite. "Listen to those V8's rumble!"

"Street Stock." Paul Whitcomb pointed to the track, with a worried frown. "Those are the actual cars that we're going to be driving next Saturday aren't they?"

"More like *this* week." Camber replied. "I'm not going to let you all out there without some good practice runs. Street Stocks are the last race before the feature. There's an intermission before the feature. That's when the drawing will be held to determine which car each of you will get."

"I hope I get the blue one," said Agnes, studying the colorful array of cars.

"I hope I get the fast one," said Fr. Frankie.

Rick Cunningham was listening to the announcer and watching the line of Monte Carlos, Camaros and Novas circle the track. "That's Luke Jensen!" he said. "I didn't know he raced. There he is in the 32. He's a member of my congregation ... Sits in the third row, always looks tired on Sunday mornings. Guess now I know why."

Camber, who was still brooding over his dilemma, was sitting in one of the chairs, paying no attention to the race. *Why hadn't some Street Stock driver offered up his car?* Winning one of their races only paid two hundred dollars. He might have some hope of matching that. Nope, it had to be a Late Model driver. It had to be the feature race, didn't it? The one with the thousand dollar purse. And of course Tracy had to be here, making the whole deal ten times worse, because now if he threw the race, he'd never hear the end of it. Camber rubbed his forehead, feeling the beginning of a headache that was probably a symptom of terminal stupidity.

Finally he roused himself out of his funk, and walked over to the window to do what he had come to do: instruct his charges in the fine points of stock car racing, by showing them a real life example of a race. Lap by lap, he gave them a running commentary of the action, fielding their questions, and pointing out bits of on-track strategy as the drivers maneuvered for position.

"You probably won't remember much of this in the heat of the moment next week," Camber told them, "but at least now you've seen it done, and you know what to expect."

"They make it look easy," said Bill Bartlett.

Camber smiled. "The first ten years are the hardest."

"It's just *us,*" Romney Marsh reminded them. "It's not like we're going to be racing the real thing."

"For which, thank heaven," said Stephen Albright.

"Travis is the real thing," said Rev. Scarberry. "Didn't you tell us you had raced before, years ago?"

"I wouldn't worry about that," said Camber. "I think the real advantage will be in who gets the best car. But on a race track anything can happen. A bad tire or any of a thousand other things can skew the outcome of a race. You can't really plan too much beyond doing your best as a driver."

"In other words," said Rick Cunningham, smiling, "It's in God's hands."

Chapter Fourteen
Born to Lose

When the Street Stock race ended, one of the track workers, a gawky kid in a Judas Grove High tee shirt, came to the door to remind them that it was nearly time for the drawing.

They made their way down the grandstand, back to the start-finish line, front and center, so that the crowd could watch the drawing take place. Camber left them there, and went over to the pits where the Late Model teams were checking tire pressure and making other last minute preparations before the race. He was careful to avoid a pre-race meeting with Tracy. Luckily, Bobby Meyers's team was pitted a dozen cars down from the Ernie Banes team. As Camber walked up to his soon-to-be chariot of fire, another thought crossed his mind: *What if I don't fit?*

The fact that Camber was taller than the average driver had caused problems in some of the other racing opportunities when he had been asked to drive on short notice. Seats were too small; pedals too close; and, with no time to be customized, the size discrepancy between him and the driver he was replacing had posed a real problem. This time, though, instead of a problem, he saw the size factor as an escape hatch. "I could respectfully bow out of the race in the name of safety," he told himself.

One look at Bobby Meyers close-up made Camber dismiss that idea with a heavy heart. Bobby looked like his day job might be bailing hay. Not only was he taller than Camber, he had the build of Jimmy Spencer, NASCAR's answer to the Pillsbury Doughboy. If there was a problem with this car, it would not be Camber's ability to fit into it.

"Mighty nice of you to do this for us Mr. Berkley." said Bobby Meyers. "I've got a helmet and a firesuit you can use."

"Thanks," said Camber, "but I brought my driving bag with me, so my gear is still here at the track from the last practice session. I'll get it and come right back."

Camber went to retrieve his gear, still planning his strategy not to win—a strange way to go into a race, he felt. With the size factor no longer an option, his revised plan to sabotage his performance was simple: citing his "professional" experience as an unfair advantage over the local racers, he would insist on forfeiting the car's fourth place qualifying position, posted earlier in the day by Bobby Meyers, and he would start "shotgun" on the field, that is: last.

Compared to Late Model races, Camber considered this a sprint race: it was only fifty laps. He could work his way up, pass twelve or fifteen cars, and end up with a respectable top five finish. For the sake of his ego, Camber hoped that he could pass Tracy late in the race. From previous encounters Camber was well aware that Tracy was capable of using his race car as a weapon if he could get a fender on you. For that reason, he did not want Tracy behind him for long. What the heck was Tracy doing here tonight, anyhow? Well, no matter why he had turned up, Camber decided that if he managed to finish ahead of Tracy, and place in the top five, his run would be considered a valiant effort and the track publicity people would have a great story for the local papers. The only flaw in this happy ending was that it would leave one sick little girl with two thousand dollars less in her medical fund. He felt bad about that.

Bobby Meyers leaned in the window while Camber was buckling in. "It sure is an honor to have you drive our car," he said. "I reckon you're an answer to prayer."

"I hope it'll help," muttered Camber, feeling like one of Travis Prichard's snakes.

"We have been working on the set-up as best we could," said Bobby, "but it still starts off loose and by the end of the race it is pretty tight. I think it burns up the right front. I don't guess you have to worry about wrecking cars, though, do you? A big NASCAR star like you. You could buy us five race cars if you wrecked this one."

Camber managed a weak a smile. Big NASCAR star, indeed. He couldn't even afford to buy them a new window net, much less a whole car. "The pleasure is all mine," he managed to say. He pulled on his helmet to hide his face.

He thought he might be able to afford to match the purse if he won— eventually—but paying for repairs to a late model race car right now was out of the question. It could easily cost five grand to repair even a modest wreck. It had been over a year since Camber had driven a Late Model race car, but, thanks to his financial straits, he had become very skilled at staying out of trouble and taking care of equipment. His first priority had just become *Not Wrecking*; then he would worry about saving face.

* * *

While Camber and the other drivers were getting ready to race, the announcer had assembled the ministers at the start finish line for the drawing to determine who got what car in next week's Faster Pastor race. The names and car numbers of each participating Street Stock team had been written on pieces of paper and deposited in a driver's helmet.

"Here we go, folks!" he boomed at the now-silent crowd. "Now that the Street Stock race is over—and congratulations to tonight's winner, Troy Sult in his number 17 Monte Carlo—the ministers here are drawing for the car and driver match-ups for their race next week. Overseeing the proceedings on behalf of the Jimmy Powell estate is Miss Pajan Mosby. She'll be holding the helmet here, containing the names of all the available Street Stock cars. You'll come up and draw one by one. Do you have anything you like to say first, Miss Mosby?"

Pajan smiled nervously into the bright lights, and stepped forward, cradling the helmet in both arms. She leaned into the microphone, "I'd just like to wish all our participants good luck and a safe and happy adventure in next week's race. I think Jimmy Powell would have been proud of all of you, and I'm glad that his memory will live on when one of you puts his legacy to good use for the betterment of the community."

Beside Pajan, armed with pen and paper to recording the pairings, stood a solemn Jesùs Segovia. Early in the evening he had arrived at the track with Fr. Frankie, but when he spotted Pajan talking to the announcer, he had excused himself, saying that Fr. Frankie was no doubt too busy to be bothered with a tagalong, and that he would keep Miss Mosby company for the evening.

At first Pajan had been startled to find herself saddled with a squire for the race, but he was so attentive and charming that she soon abandoned her cool civility and began to enjoy his company. When she remembered that Jesùs was an ardent NASCAR fan, as evidenced by his assault charge in defense of the honor of Juan Pablo Montoya, she relaxed enough to become positively chummy with him. They had chatted and shared cotton candy through the preliminary races, and, by the time of the drawing, Jesùs had appointed himself her assistant, now in charge of the official record-keeping for the Faster Pastor race.

"Is everybody ready for the drawing?" asked the announcer, surveying the nervous participants. "Who's going first?"

Tradition and gallantry dictated that Agnes Hill-Radnor would be the first to draw from the helmet. She closed her eyes, murmuring "I've never won anything," snatched a slip of paper, and handed it over to the announcer, who unfolded it and read out the name, "The number 11 for the lady. That's the '91 Lumina of Gabe Powers. What's that, ma'am?" He leaned down in order to hear Agnes's question. "Why, I don't know, hon. Hey, Gabe! Is he here? Oh, there you are. Gabe—what color is your car?—Blue?—It's the blue one, ma'am. Well, glad you like it. Who's next?"

After that they went in alphabetical order. Stephen Albright.

Bill Bartlett, who, much to his delight, drew the '86 Cutlass of Tony Moore, one of his parishioners. Rick Cunningham was next, then Romney Marsh. When Travis Prichard drew the number 15 car, he waved to its owner, an old acquaintance of his from his racing days.

When Fr, Frankie handed his slip of paper to the announcer, he gave a low whistle, and said, "Father, I think you hit the jackpot. You have just drawn the '85 Monte Carlo of Troy Sult. He was the winner of tonight's race."

When all the cars had been assigned, the spectators cheered the ministers again, and they headed back through the grandstand to watch the featured race from the VIP suite. Travis Prichard was waylaid by a worried-looking man whose wilting shirt and rumpled suit jacket suggested that he had come to the speedway straight from work.

"Even'n, Travis!" he said. "I just wanted to wish you luck next week in the race."

Travis Prichard shook the outstretched hand, but his tentative smile told the man that he didn't recognize him. "Thanks for your good wishes," he said.

The man smiled. "I'm Arnold Simpkins—Danny's dad. It's been a while since I was down at garage, I guess. But I remember that you used to do some racing, so I wondered if you could tell me how you think the drawing went."

Travis blinked. "How it went?"

"Well, I mean, some cars are better than others, right? And I thought you might know who's got a good chance. Not that I'm betting on it or anything. Just curious, as a church member."

Travis smiled. "Yes, there's a lot of plans riding on the outcome of this race. Well, I guess you know that Father Spillane got the car that won tonight, so that's good news for him. And I feel fortunate to have drawn Jake Bennett's 15, because he won the track championship last year. Mr. Whitcomb drew the car that finished second tonight. The others..." he shrugged. "Well, racing is a game of chance. A million different things can determine who wins and who doesn't."

Simpkins, nodded, "I understand that," he said. "So Rev.

Scarberry's car?"

"Well, like I said … there are no sure things in racing. But I wouldn't want to trade cars with him."

* * *

"You got a copy Mr. Berkley?"

The radio transmission seemed to come from inside Camber's head. He was circling the track on the pace laps with about twenty other late model race cars. "10-4," he said to the voice. "Call me Camber, though."

"Will do," said Bobby Meyers. Since he wouldn't be driving, he had agreed to spot for Camber in the Late Model race. Now he was sitting at the very top of the grandstand where he could get a good view of the entire track. A lot of the short tracks lacked a special stand or tower for spotters to do their job from. Not all divisions required radios, either, but Late Model did.

"Camber, this is a 50-lap feature," Bobby said into his radio. "Pull your belts tight, and keep the fenders on it, and you'll have a good chance of winning this thing."

Camber pushed the talk button on the steering wheel, "I'll do what I can." He didn't want to get the man's hopes up too high, knowing full well that he couldn't afford to win this race. He wanted to say that he didn't stand much of a chance on an unfamiliar track, but, of course, it wasn't an unfamiliar track to him. He had been there every day for a week now, and he'd done many practice runs. If the car was any good, and it seemed to be, he ought to be able to win easily—if only that he could afford to.

He warmed up the tires by weaving back and forth, and, by speeding up and slowing down, he brought the brakes up to optimum temperature. It was the same process of preparation that he had done with the Street Stock car when he tested it before the ministers' practice. Ahead of him he could see the bright orange and white 01, Tracy's ride for tonight. It was starting outside the third row, in the sixth position. *They got the color right at least,* thought Camber. Bright orange … the color of traffic cones, warning signs, and the Cup car of Tony Stewart— all indications of imminent danger. *Now all they need is to stencil CAUTION all around the car,* Camber thought, as he took an extra tug on his belts, pulling them just the slightest bit tighter. He took a deep breath and waited for the flag to drop.

"Get ready, get ready, Green! Green! GREEN!" Bobby Meyers was shouting into the radio, and in a heartbeat the field of shiny Late Model race cars made the jump to warp speed.

As they roared around the track, Camber settled in to a groove. and stuck to the plan. He was setting up cars, and passing them at the rate of one every couple of laps. Bobby Meyers would clear him on the radio every time he completed a pass, just to let him know that they were back single file again, and that he could use the whole width of the track.

* * *

High up in the grandstands, Pajan Mosby and Jesùs Segovia were eating snow cones and funnel cakes, and watching the Late Model race with the practiced eye of true connoisseurs of the sport.

"So, do you think he's any good?" asked Pajan, trying to sound casual.

"Who? Camber?" Jesùs shrugged. "It is too early to tell, but I do hope so. It is a fine thing he is doing—matching the prize money with his own contribution for an infirm child. A gesture of true nobility."

Pajan sniffed. "You could also call it showing off. And I'm sure he can spare it. NASCAR drivers aren't exactly hurting for money."

Jesùs was silent for a moment, watching the cars maneuvering for position around Turn Three. Then he said, "No doubt you are right, my friend. But something occurs to me. My parents back in Polanco, they send me a thousand dollars. And do I give this money to a sick child? No. I use the funds as they intended, to liberate myself from the jail. And Camber, he offers this sum to a child who is ill, whom he has never met. And yet … he stays in the jail. It makes me to think. You know?"

Pajan did not reply, but as she followed the action of the speeding cars on the track, she twisted her hands in her lap, and her expression was grave.

* * *

Now they were ten laps in. Camber had picked up several positions, easily passing the slower cars at the back of the pack. He could see Tracy's number on the score board: still in the sixth place. Coming up through the field with a good car is one of the most exhilarating feelings in all of racing. Despite the circumstances—that is, his dire need to lose this race—inside his helmet Camber was smiling.

There was smoke on the track up in the middle of the turn. Camber hit the brakes hard to slow the car to give himself time to assess the situation. Out of the corner of his eye, he saw the yellow glow of the caution light mounted on the fence.

The radio crackled, and Bobby said, "Car in the wall!"

Just as Camber was approaching the single car crash, the wrecked race car began a slow roll down the banking of the turn and right into the path of Camber's car. At racing speed, stopping completely was not an option. Instinctively, Camber hit the gas and dove for the apron of the track.

He held his breath, waiting to see if the race car rolling down the track was going to clip the back right corner of his car, but a split-second later he knew he had cleared it.

"Nice driving, Camber. No way you could have stopped for that one," said Bobby in his ear.

"Brakes are only for getting a good look at the wreck; the gas is what will get you through it," Camber replied. He wasn't sure if had coined that phrase himself, or if he was simply repeating something he had heard in many long nights of listening to racing stories from any old-timer who would who let him hang around.

The wrecked car that Camber dodged had been in fifth place. He crashed because Tracy had hit him in the left rear corner as they were heading into the turn, sending him back into the wall. *That's one way to make a pass,* thought Camber, shaking his head as far as his HANS device would let his helmet turn. The caution laps proceeded at the stately pace of a Sunday drive.

After the clean-up, the pack got the green flag, and they were back to racing.

Camber wasted no time returning to his rhythm of setting up cars for the pass, and then passing them carefully so as not to put a single dent in a piece of sheet metal.

Before long, Bobby reported, "Twenty laps to go. You're in eighth place."

"I can feel it getting tight, just like you said," Camber told him. He adjusted his line through the turn, again using the apron of the race track to help the car turn. He was right on the bumper of the car in front of him, and going down the straightaway he pulled to the inside and delayed his braking just long enough to enter the turn two-wide.

"Outside! Outside! Still there." yelled Bobby. He was telling Camber that he was still running two-wide with the other car, and, in order to avoid a collision, Camber would have to hold his car at the bottom of the race track through the turn, a difficult feat when the car's handling was tight. As soon as the left side tires of Camber's car hit the apron, he felt the weight transfer, and as he cleared the turn he beat his opponent back to the gas.

"Clear! All Clear," Bobby told him. "That's another spot. Keep pushing."

Sweat rolled off Camber's brow in the heat of the cockpit. Anyone who said this wasn't hard work was out of their mind.

Bobby was on again. "Caution! Spin in 4. It's behind you. Back it down."

Two cars had touched and spun coming out of turn four, forcing the flag man to wave the yellow flag to slow the cars down until the track was safe for racing again.

"Just what we needed Camber! This is going to be a five lap shoot-out. You are in third. The front two will be in reach.

You can get them. You can win!"

Camber did not respond. This was exactly the spot he didn't want to be in. Tracy had managed to bull his way into second place, which meant that, in order for them both to lose, Camber would have to get past Tracy and hold him off until the car in first place took the checkered flag.

The caution was a short one. There were no commercial breaks here and no pit stops. This was short track action, so the caution was just long enough to get the cars slowed down behind the pace car, and to allow the undamaged cars that had spun to get moving again in the right direction.

The caution gave Camber a chance to lift the visor on his helmet and wipe away the sweat pooled dangerously above his eyes. Then he checked his gauges to make sure that the car was mechanically in good shape.

The pace car ducked off the track, and, two cars in front of Camber, the first-place car led the field toward the green flag. Camber downshifted to second gear for the re-start, thinking that this was a lot closer to Tracy than he really wanted to be right now.

"GREEN! GREEN!" Bobby shouted into the radio.

The sudden acceleration pushed Camber back in the seat, but he quickly jerked the wheel to the outside and squeezed his car between Tracy and the outside wall, leaving only inches to spare on either side. His reflexes allowed him to avoid yet another disaster. Now he had landed in second place. Another possible factor in his success was that Tracy had not cleaned off his tires by swerving back and forth during the caution. Instead of lurching forward, Tracy's car was spinning its tires, making him a serious hazard for Camber. Tracy's sluggish car created a bottle neck behind him, but after he got up to speed, Camber found himself still running second.

"GET HIM, GET HIM" Bobby was jumping up and down in the stands.

Camber was now four car lengths away from first place. The car was almost begging him to drive it harder. The gap narrowed. Now he was relying on the remaining stick in the worn tires to stop the car from sliding violently into the wall. Taking quick glances in the rear view mirror, Camber could see Tracy— only one car length behind him.

Win and lose a thousand bucks or lose and never hear the end of it? It wasn't fun, anymore. The race couldn't end soon enough for Camber.

In the stands, Fr. Frankie nudged Travis Prichard. "What should I pray for?" he asked.

Without taking his eyes off the track, Travis replied, "Pray that Camber's tires hold out. Otherwise he's going into the wall."

"But no matter which one of them wins, the sick child gets the money, right?" Agnes said to Paul Whitcomb, shouting in his ear so that he could hear her above the roar of the crowd and the engines.

Whitcomb opened his mouth and closed it again. It was too noisy here for a measured discussion of the merits of charity versus the thrill of competition. In fact, he thought, taking a long look at Agnes, he doubted if there could ever be world enough and time to make her understand the concept. So he smiled encouragingly and pointed at the cars. Let her interpret that any way she wanted.

"That's our teacher out there," Stephen Albright was saying to the nearest dozen or so people in the crowd.

"LAST LAP!" Bobby yelled. "He's going to protect the bottom."

Camber was right behind the first place car, and its driver seemed determined not to let Camber underneath him in the turn. By now Tracy had made it back to Camber's bumper, and Camber felt the first jolt from behind as Tracy used Camber's car as a brake.

The first place driver had half of his car off the banking and onto the apron, a maneuver which slowed his car enough to force Camber to the outside, and into another hit from Tracy.

Now he was barreling down the back stretch and into the final turn side by side with the first place car, with Camber in the less desirable position on the outside of the turn. With only a few yards to go, Tracy forced the issue by bringing his car far to the inside in an attempt to dive under the first place car for the win.

Bobby keyed his mic to warn Camber. "THREE WIDE!!!"

Camber's car, protesting his hard braking, refused to turn, and began to slide up the track, dangerously close to the dirt and debris left there by a whole night of racing: a certain wreck. Camber responded by releasing the brake, letting the car coast through the center of the turn. It was the only way to keep the car on track.

Tracy, unable to hold such a low line through the turn, had slid up into the side of the first place car. Camber saw both of these cars now pushing up the track about to sandwich him against the outside wall.

Camber knew he had a split-second to make a choice: either get on the brakes and let the other two drivers see who would slide across the finish line first, or hit the gas hard and try to get out of the way. Forcing himself to look away from the battling race cars to his left, he directed his attention farther up the track, where the flag man was frantically waving the checkered flag.

Decisions had to be made in the space of a heartbeat, and much of what he did on the race track was a matter of instinct: his muscles responded to familiar stimuli without bothering to consult his brain. Now, instead of indulging in a cool analysis of the pros and cons of pulling ahead in a race he couldn't afford to win, his body reacted on automatic pilot. It knew there was only one thing to do, and without a thought, he did it. He hit the gas hard, just as he was passing the exact point where he had placed a cone for the ministers in practice.

He felt the engine grab for fuel as it surged ahead, and his car nosed past both Tracy and the poor sap stuck between them. The cars went across the finish line one, two, three, and it was over.

Camber had won.

Camber had won! Pajan realized she was hugging a prisoner-out-on-bond and squealing with joy. Immediately, reality sent her a wake-up call, and she took a step back, brushed the hair out of her eyes, and said primly, "Well, that was certainly an eventful race. I'm very pleased for him."

In the tradition of the true *hidalgo*, Jesús pretended not to have noticed her outburst. "Camber is indeed a talented driver," he said. "And he has won money for the sick child, so it is a double blessing."

Pajan nodded. "I'm glad about that. The Meyers are wonderful people, and they deserve all the help they can get."

"So perhaps they were sent an angel. But Camber—he does not drive in Cup racing?"

"No," said Pajan. "He's just one of the small-time wannabes."

"He is deserving of better things, then, and it is not his shame but that of the world if money and circumstance prevent him from succeeding."

Pajan looked doubtful. "Do you think he'd want us to congratulate him?"

Jesús Segovia smiled. "If we do, I think the honor will be ours."

Agnes Hill-Radner felt a cold shiver start in her arms, tingle up to her shoulders and settle in the back of her neck. Although she had never watched a stock car race before in her life, she found her hands squeezed tight with anticipation as Camber took the checkered flag, and for a moment she felt that she was all alone in complete silence while the world ticked on in slow motion. Then the crowd in front of her erupted in cheers, and she realized that some of the shouting she heard was a good deal nearer than that. Beside her, her fellow racing colleagues were going wild.

She found herself enveloped in a bear hug by Rick Cunningham, while a whooping Travis Prichard stood with the others to watch Camber take his slow victory lap around the half mile track.

"Did I just win?" said Camber over the radio.

"You did! You did, Camber. And I wanna thank you." In his headset Bobby Meyers close to tears. The emotion in his voice reminded Camber of the significance of the win.

"You have a great race car, Bobby," he said, "And I swear we had some extra help tonight. Thank you for the opportunity to drive."

"Praise the Lord! You don't even need to thank me, Camber. You were the answer to prayer. I'll see you in Victory Lane. I'm trying to get there now." Bobby was fighting his way from the top of the grandstand down toward the gate below the flag stand. A track official in a white firesuit motioned for the race winner to stop at the Start-Finish line, and Camber watched while the festivities came to him.

The moment he stopped at the designated spot, people from all directions descended on the race car. Camber leaned back, mentally bracing himself for the onslaught. First, he took off his helmet, and savored the cool feeling of fresh air blowing through his sweat-soaked hair. Then with a flick of his thumb he released the latch of the safety belts, and enjoyed the decompression of his chest and stomach as the belts sprang apart. He leaned his head back, hoping for a moment to think, to relax, and to figure out how he was going to live up to his word, but Bobby had already reached the car, and was pulling down the window net.

Bobby grabbed Camber's helmet to get it out of his way, and pulled off the steering wheel so that he could exit the car. "Amazing!" he said, thumping his hand on Camber's chest in congratulations.

Camber realized that the brief moment of peace he had been hoping for wasn't going to happen, and, with a shrug of resignation, he climbed out of the car to meet the cheering fans. First, he balanced on the car's door sill, pumping his fist in the air, in the time-honored stance of the winner. The crowd responded with still louder cheers, as if they didn't see this performance after every race, every week.

Then he hopped down off the car and was met immediately by the beaming announcer and his ever-present microphone.

"What a win!" he said, giving Camber a playful punch to the shoulder with his microphone fist. "You were driving with some amazing confidence out there. Like a true professional. So, tell us, Cameron, when did you know that you were going to win that race?"

Camber resolved to savor the win, and to postpone the nagging thoughts of the financial consequences. He chuckled into the microphone before giving his answer. "I would say coming off the last turn," he said. "Days like this don't come too often in racing, no matter what level you're on: coming from the back and making a final lap pass. This one is special, and I'm glad that this race was for a special cause. I would like to thank Bobby for letting me drive such a great race car, and to commend him and his crew on a job well done in preparing a car I could win with."

The announcer nodded happily. Winner's speeches in stock car racing were as ritualistic as a Japanese tea ceremony, and Camber had followed the formula. "Speaking of Bobby, let's get him in here for a word," he said.

Bobby Meyers stepped in between Camber and the announcer and slung an arm over Camber's shoulders, pulling him close. Camber felt like he was six again. Looking past the announcer, he saw that his flock of would-be drivers had grouped a few feet away and were beaming and waving, obviously waiting to congratulate him. Travis Prichard, who was in familiar territory, had taken it upon himself to lead the group of ministers down to the celebration. They joined the group of crew members, officials, and other fans who were taking pictures of Camber and Bobby and the car. Camber was glad to see them. It made the victory more meaningful to know that there were people around who cared that you had won.

The announcer thrust the microphone at the grinning car owner. "Bobby, you're obviously emotional about this momentous win. Tell us what it means to you."

Bobby Meyers wiped away a tear. "I just can't say enough about this young man. It was such an honor to have him drive our car. He made it look easy, and to my mind, that's a sign of true genius behind the wheel. I feel like he's an angel sent to our family and God willing, if my niece Sarah makes it through, this race is going to be a bed time story to be told for many years to come."

The announcer turned back to Camber. "And what do you say to that, Driver?"

Camber hesitated for only a moment. "I think every young kid dreams of using his super powers to help save a life," he said. "Tonight that dream came true for me." Then, because he couldn't resist the dig, he added, "I would also like to thank my cousin Tracy for not spinning me out, like he did to the rest of the field."

The announcer nodded. "It was so close we had to go to the electronic scoring to make sure. Your cousin Tracy finished in third. Tracy, come over here! Why don't you tell us about the race?"

Sure enough, Tracy was there at the edge of the crowd, looking uncomfortable, as he usually did when he wasn't the center of attention. Since Tracy was not known for displays of good sportsmanship, Camber had half expected him to have stormed off to the hauler to change. He wondered if Tracy had decided yet who to blame for his loss. Suddenly all eyes were on Tracy, and he had no choice but to hesitantly make his way through the ministers' disapproving glares, and up to the announcer's side.

"It was a hard race, a good race," he said into the microphone. "I thought I had a shot at the win, and so I took it. My dad always says it's not worth racing if you're not winning."

Camber breathed a sigh of relief. Thanks to the tea ceremony ritual of racing speeches, Tracy wasn't going to bad-mouth him. He was grateful for that.

"So, Tracy, Do you think the better man won?"

Uh-oh. That question was asking for trouble, but after a slight narrowing of his eyes, Tracy shrugged. "Well, I think the better man always wins. In the end." He sounded sincere enough, but his expression did not quite match his words.

Before the announcer could reply, Tracy went on, "I hope there aren't any hard feelings over this race. And just to show that I'm okay with how it went down, I would like to make that $1000 dollar donation that Camber pledged if he won. Right now. In cash."

From his fire suit Tracy pulled out a folded wad of slightly damp bills, and handed it to Bobby. He seemed oblivious to the deafening yells that greeted his magnanimous gesture. Even the ministers were smiling and clapping. Camber, who was speechless with shock, managed to shake Tracy's hand,

and to mutter, "I don't know what to say, man."

Tracy's smile wasn't reaching his eyes. "Oh, you will, Camber. You will." With a little wave to Camber and a nod to the still-cheering crowd, he turned on his heel, and headed in the direction of the parking lot, to be on his way back to the lake house.

After Tracy left, Camber had to pose for several rounds of pictures for the track, the local newspapers, and a legion of admiring race fans, who also clamored for autographs on the off chance that Camber would someday be famous. Or maybe because he was as famous as you got in Judas Grove, Tennessee. Then he posed for more pictures with the ministers, who were as thrilled with his victory as if they had won themselves.

"That was an inspiration to watch," Andrew Scarberry kept saying.

And Agnes asked him to sign a plastic soft drink cup. "As a memento," she said, blushing to the roots of her hair.

A beaming Jesús Segovia, looking like he had just found the Holy Grail in a Coke machine, shook Camber's hand over and over, and congratulated him in a torrent of English and Spanish. "We must talk!" he called out, as Fr. Frankie led him away to the car to begin the battle of race-exit traffic.

Despite his fatigue, Camber complied with all these requests with grace and enthusiasm. After all, it wasn't every day that people thought he was somebody. And with the weight of the donation lifted, he felt like he truly had won something.

Chapter Fifteen
Through Days of Preparation

The speedway floodlights winked out, leaving Camber in starlight. The Saturday night race night crowd was gone now, all the haulers had left the infield, and an eerie silence settled over the dark expanse of track. It was nearly midnight, and a chill wind shuffled the discarded Coke cups and candy wrappers across the deserted speedway. Camber shivered. The adrenaline from his victory had worn off now. He was standing alone in his fire suit, and at his feet were his driving bag and a two-foot trophy made of junk metal, but all he wanted now was sleep.

He looked back toward the dark stands, and saw a figure walking toward him. Surely not another autograph seeker at this hour?

It was Pajan. "I can take you back whenever you're ready," she said, stifling a yawn.

"Yeah, thanks," he said with a weary sigh. "I'd like to change clothes first. It won't take me long." He picked up his driving bag, and trudged off toward the now-deserted restroom.

Pajan called after him, "Congratulations. Nice race."

He shrugged and kept on walking.

Once inside the men's room Camber flipped on the lights, and balanced his driving bag on top of the plastic trash barrel. He unzipped it, and groped for his cell phone. Maybe tonight's win was smalltime and completely pointless, but at least he could share the victory with his best friend. After the past couple of weeks, it was nice to have something to celebrate, and he hadn't yet won enough races to take the experience in stride. Maybe he never would.

He pushed Brennan's number on SpeedDial, and while he waited for the connection to be made, he began to struggle out of his sweaty fire suit.

"What do you want?" Brennan did not sound amused, and for an instant Camber thought he might have interrupted Brennan on a Saturday night date. *Oh, wait. Not in this universe. He was probably watching* Modern Marvels *on the History Channel.*

"I have some good news for a change," said Camber.

"I hope it involves a lottery ticket."

"No. But I got to race tonight at the Judas Grove Speedway."

"Be still my heart," Brennan's voice could have frozen motor oil.

"And I won."

"How much did it pay?"

"Well, here's the thing ..." Hopping up and down on one leg and pulling at the cuff of the other leg, Camber decided to dodge the question. "You should have seen this race. Late Model Stock, owned by a local driver. And it was a charity race, to raise money for a little girl who needs an operation."

"So how did you end up in the driver's seat?"

"See, around here they think I'm a big deal in NASCAR." The sound on the other end of the phone might have been a sneeze, but it probably wasn't. "So when they introduced me, I offered to donate the prize money to the medical fund if I won, and the little girl's uncle lent me his car. Oh, and I sorta got carried away and offered to match the purse with a personal donation if I won. I didn't figure on winning, see. But it was a great race. I haven't had that much fun racing in a long time. You should have seen me make that last lap pass. It was genius. This was the kind of night that could make a career. I wish someone big had been here to see it."

There was a long pause on the other end of the cell phone, and then Brennan said, "The other racers on the track … Did they hear the announcement that you were going to make a personal donation if you won the race?"

"Yeah, we did it over the loud speaker."

"And the sick child's uncle is a fellow racer, a friend of theirs."

Camber finally realized what Brennan was getting at. "It was a hard-fought race," he insisted. "The other drivers didn't just pull over and wave me by, if that's what you are insinuating. And, of course, I had intended to lose, but you'll never guess who turned up unannounced and entered the race."

"Well, I know it wasn't Tony Stewart, because *you* won. So my second guess is your obnoxious cousin Tracy."

"Exactly. Only maybe we misjudged him."

"Really?"

"Yeah. I was thinking that, too. You know what a poodle he is about his racing career, and I just couldn't stand to let him beat me, so I passed him on the last lap and took the checkers. But, see, when I won, I thought I was going to have to use the money you said you'd put into my account to make the donation to the child's medical fund, but in the post race interview, the announcer interviewed Tracy and me together, asking us questions about the race. Tracy was all red in the face, and then the announcer asked him if he thought the best man had won. Do you know what Tracy's response was?"

"I'm beginning to think so."

"Well, it totally shocked me. He told the announcer that the better man always wins in the end. And then—you aren't going to believe this, but he whipped out his wallet, handed over a wad of hundred dollars bills, and announced that he was making the donation on my behalf, Brennan. Wasn't that great of him?"

There was such a long pause that Camber thought the connection had been broken, and then Brennan said quietly,

"Great of *him?*"

"Oh, I know we've said mean things about Tracy before, and, to tell you the truth, I figured he'd still be mad at me because I tried to beat him to Lowes Motor Speedway and take that driving job away from him, but maybe blood is thicker than water. I mean, a thousand bucks, Brennan! In cash. And he just handed it over like it was nothing. Can you believe that?"

Brennan sighed. "Yeah, Camber, I think I can. You see, I saw Tracy right before he left, and I gave him a thousand in cash to give to you. It was the money for your court costs."

The better man always wins … in the end.

* * *

Camber hadn't even opened his eyes yet, when he heard Stoney's soft whistling in the hall, his footsteps coming towards Cambers cell. Camber struggled awake from a deep sleep, his best sleep in days. He knew this because of the dreams he had during the night, the vivid life-like dreams he always experienced when he got good rest. Last night's dreams consisted of a smattering of activities and thoughts from throughout his day mixed with intense, imaginary situations. One dream still lingered in his mind, and he was reluctant to open his eyes for the fear that it would fade before he had time to consider it and decide what the dream might mean. He saw himself and Brennan and Pajan in Victory Lane, but they were at Lowe's Motor Speedway, not here at the little county track. He tried to recall other details, but they were eluded him. His last fading glimpse of the dream was a Cup race and he was pretty sure that he had won.

"I didn't expect to see you here after last night's win." Stoney's voice startled Camber so much that he opened his eyes. The last remnant of the dream was gone, so he shrugged it off, and got back to reality, which was: no ride, and a jail cell in Judas Grove.

"Well, Camber, I gotta hand it to you. That race of yours last night sure stood this town on its ear. If you wanna autograph some blank parking tickets, I think I might be able to sell them. I'd give you a cut, of course."

"Thanks, Stoney. I'll keep it in mind." Camber swung his feet off the bed, and leaned back against the cell wall.

"Well, that race was just a darn clinic on superior driving, is what it was. It got me to thinking how funny it is the way things work out, huh?" Stoney passed a mug of steaming coffee through the bars. "Just think—someone who can drive as good as you lands in our town right when we are having this Faster Pastor race and need some expert help. It can't be just a coincidence, can it?"

With the one eye that he could hold open, Camber eyed the deep blackness in the coffee mug, as if he expected an answer to float to the surface. He stifled a yawn. "Did you wake me up just to talk philosophy with me, Stoney?"

"Oh, no." Stoney was suddenly reminded of his reason for stirring Camber. "Ms. Julia Ryeland is here to see you. Did you have plans to go back to The Crystal Path worship service this morning?"

"God, no," said Camber, repressing a shudder. He searched back through the chaotic week. Normally, he didn't forget his promises.

"Well … Should I tell her that you are not available?" The way Stoney asked made Camber wince. He wasn't some huge rock star, and, if he ever did become famous, he hoped he wouldn't blow people off, no matter how busy he got.

"No, tell her I will be right out."

A few minutes later he found Julia Ryeland at the curb outside the courthouse, leaning against a three-year old Z06 Corvette—his favorite make of car. The 'Vette looked hot—freshly detailed, its gleaming lines extenuated by the sun from a perfect blue sky. The blue and black of the Corvette seemed handpicked to match what Julia was wearing. She was also looking freshly detailed in Camber's professional opinion. *This couldn't be a coincidence, could it?*

After an eternity of batting her mascara-ed eyelashes, Julia purred, "I was just on my way to church, and I thought I would check to see if you wanted to come along. Everyone would love to see you after your big win at the speedway last night."

"You were at the races last night?"

"Well, I actually read about it this morning in the paper." Julia nodded toward a newspaper machine, displaying a front page photo of Camber balanced on the window sill of his race car, pumping fist in the air.

That didn't seem like a good reason for going to church. In fact, it was probably asking to be struck by lightning, but he hated to pass up a chance to ride in the machine of his dreams. Maybe there was a solution. It would call for charm.

Sliding both hands into the back pocket of his jeans, Camber shrugged his shoulders, and tilted his head in his best aw shucks look. "I wish I could, Julia, but I only have a little bit of time. I have to be back here to meet with some people about the race next weekend. Thanks for stopping by and checking on me, though." Then as if it were an afterthought, he added. "Hey, do you think you could run me up to get some coffee and a doughnut?"

"Why, it would be my pleasure," Julia's drawl went two notches deeper and her eyes sparkled. "I know just the place."

During the short ride, the rumble of the Corvette's engine kept the conversation to a minimum, which was fine with Camber, who was enjoying the feel of the leather seat and the marvelous sensation of being connected to the road through the turns. Julia drove to a roadside truck stop café about ten miles north of town. They took their order of coffee and jelly doughnuts outside to a bench in a grassy area back from the road.

Camber had just bitten into his raspberry-filled doughnut, when Julia said, "I guess you haven't had much time to fool with your car have you?"

With a mouthful of doughnut, Camber could only respond by shaking his head, while he wondered if a sales pitch was coming soon. But he had guessed wrong. There was no sales pitch. In fact, there were no words. Instead, Julia reached out, gently wiped powered sugar from Camber's lips, and drew him in for a kiss.

Camber froze. He hadn't expected that, although he should

have. This wasn't the first time that attention on the track had got him attention off the track as well. Before he could move, he felt Julia's hand slide under his t-shirt and up his chest. The sensation felt great, but emotionally, he felt hollow.

This woman hardly knew him. As she caressed him, Camber contemplated the power he held in the situation. All he had to do was return her passion, play along, and she would probably give him anything he wanted: money to pay his court costs, endless sex, even a new car to ride back to Mooresville in. All because he looked good and knew how to drive a race car. It wasn't fair—and Brennan, to whom such things never happened, would be the first person to tell him so. Back when Camber was a teenager, older women would pinch his cheek and say half-jokingly, "He is going to be such a heartbreaker." This is what they meant. He could be if he wanted to. But he wouldn't have liked himself very much if he did.

Camber broke the kiss, and replaced it with a hearty, platonic hug, as if she was his maiden aunt. "Thank you Julia, for everything, but I gotta get back now."

As Julia drove off in the direction of The Church of the Crystal Path, Camber contemplated walking back in the court house, but the day was fine, and he needed some exercise. He decided that Stoney wouldn't mind if he were gone a little longer. He turned to take a Sunday stroll up Main Street, Judas Grove, with its neatly lined parking meters and its wide sidewalks shaded by century-old maples, with the brightly painted little shops on either side. Idle curiosity made him chose the direction away from Farleys garage, and as he walked, he let his mind wander. He passed the barber shop, which was closed; the florist's, which was closed; the Antique & Junque shop, which was closed. That was all right, though. Camber's thoughts were on racing, rather than shopping. Why couldn't he ever get a break as a driver? He was talented, hardworking, determined, and smart. It wasn't enough. He was wondering if racing was just a big shell game where the powers-that-be were moving the prize as soon as you made your selection. What was the secret ingredient to add to hard work and determination to make his career rise like a perfect soufflé instead of collapsing into a sticky mess? He pondered that question often, and this time he got no closer to an answer than ever, but he was pretty certain that jail time wasn't helping the situation. "Colorful pasts" had once been fashionable in NASCAR, but not in his lifetime.

Camber had walked all of two blocks when he came to the end of "downtown" Judas Grove. As he stood standing on the corner in front of the plate glass windows of the Main St. Diner *closed*, he happened to glance down the cross street, where, one block down, he saw a modest white steeple with some stained glass decorating below it. He decided to investigate. Behind a wrought iron fence enclosing a manicured lawn and a festive plot of geraniums, was a white sign that read "St. Jude's Catholic Church," and, in smaller letters underneath, "Fr. Francis Spillane."

As he walked up to the gothic-arched front doors, Camber could hear the sounds of the organ inside. One of the doors was ajar, and he slipped though quietly so as not to disturb the service.

Fr. Frankie, his red hair shining above the white vestments, so that he looked like a candle himself, was reading from the gospel, but he was stumbling through the words in Spanish, inflected by the lilt of his Irish brogue. The congregation was standing, and listening intently, with slightly bewildered expressions, as they tried to decode Fr. Frankie's Hibernian Spanish. The gospel was printed in the hymnal in English and Spanish so that those who were truly interested in the message could locate the printed version and follow along. Having worked his way through a long passage containing enough vowels to fund a Scrabble game, Fr. Frankie closed the lectern Bible and intoned, "*Palabra del Senor.*" Back on familiar ground, the relieved congregation responded with a heartfelt "*Gracias a Nuestro Señor,*" and then sat down.

As Camber prepared to slip into the last pew, which had only one occupant, he discovered that, appropriately enough, his set-mate for the service would be Jesus. Or rather, Jesús, his former neighbor from jail who, from the looks of it, had been ushering the morning service. As he sat down, Camber tapped

Jesús on the arm and smiled. Solemnly, Jesús nodded a greeting and handed him a program detailing the order of events of the 10 o'clock Spanish Mass.

Fr. Frankie had reached into his robes and pulled out the notes for his homily. Camber wondered if he was going to attempt this part of the service in Spanish as well, but then he noticed a middle-aged Hispanic man seated in the front row, who stood up and took his place beside the pulpit.

"Our reading today focused on choices," said Fr. Frankie, speaking in English. He paused to allow the man now standing beside him to translate his words into Spanish. "We are all faced with difficult choices in our lives, but God has granted us the free will to decide which path to take."

Camber remembered Fr. Frankie saying the congregation had a lot of families with young children, and today's audience certainly bore him out. Looking around, Camber saw that nearly a third of those third in attendance were children younger than ten. Most of the congregation seemed comprised of native Spanish speakers, but here and there he saw a family who had missed the earlier English mass, and were attending the 10 o'clock service instead. Apparently, the language difference presented only minor difficulties, because bi-lingual transcriptions were printed in the hymnals, and because by the time children had received first communion they knew by heart all the rituals and traditions of the service. The Homily, which Camber was listening to, was offered in both languages.

Jesús leaned over and offered to translate the rest of the service for Camber, but Camber signaled back that he could understand what was going on.

After mass Fr. Frankie was standing on the steps in front of the church, and Camber had intended to shake hands with him and to compliment him on the service, but he had to settle for a cordial wave, because he could not get within five feet of the priest, who was surrounded by a horde of wriggling children, plucking at his robes and yelling "*Padre! Padre!*" to get his attention. Fr. Frankie waved back and called out, "See you at the track."

A moment later, when Camber stopped to talk to Jesús, he was still watching Fr. Frankie, who had produced a plastic bag full of tiny Matchbox racecars, which he proceeded to hand out to each of the little hands reaching skyward.

"*El Padre es bueno, no?*" Jesus said smiling.

"Yes. Yes, he is," said Camber.

The Faster Pastor race was only days away, and the town of Judas Grove buzzed with activity as people made preparations for the historic race. Now the one motel in town had a "No Vacancy" sign in the window, and there was actually enough traffic on the sleepy little streets to warrant a stoplight, if they'd had one.

Since Camber did not have the money to pay his court costs and fine, he had resigned himself to staying in his current accommodations at least until the night of the race, which, fortunately, wasn't far off. Mentally, he had moved on to the next problem: arranging for the quickest way out of town when the race was over. Step one in that process was yet another call to the long-suffering Brennan.

"How are things in the slammer?" When he picked up the phone in Mooresville, Brennan was maliciously cheerful.

"Best diet I ever had," said Camber, hoping that an infusion of guilt would help his cause. "The food makes fasting a no-brainer. But it's almost over now. The race is Saturday night. And then I'll be free to leave—if I can."

"What do you mean *if you can?*" Brennan no longer sounded amused.

"My car is a total wreck, remember? And I don't have enough money to fix it. I was thinking about asking Mr. Farley, the garage owner here, to buy it for salvage."

"That ought to pay for a bus ticket," said Brennan evenly.

"God knows where a bus station even is around here." Camber wasn't going to be put off by sulking. He tried to sound casual. "But I guess what he'd give me for the car would cover the court costs and gas money if, say, *you* were to drive up here for the race and take me back to Mooresville."

"Yeah, I'm supposed to drop all the million things I have to do—like running a business—in order to drive to Tennessee and play chauffeur for you."

"Well, you're the one who gave my get-out-of-jail money to Tracy," said Camber. "And if that doesn't constitute funding terrorists, I don't know what does."

After this salvo, Camber could hear Brennan taking deep breaths. He imagined him exhaling flames. When he could trust himself to speak, Brennan said, "All right. Rather than debating whether insanity runs in your family, I will reluctantly agree to rescue you from Judas Grove. At least if I come up there, I can watch you so that you don't screw up anymore to further delay your return and our meeting with the bank executives."

"That's great, man!" said Camber. "You'll arrive in time for the race, won't you? I'd like to have somebody I can trust up here on the day of the race. With you here, I'm sure we could handle anything that came up, from mechanical troubles to the inspections process."

"*Having somebody you can trust,*" said Brennan. "I wish I knew what that was like."

* * *

When Camber arrived at the speedway for the last practice before race day, he found that the track, like the town, had become a swarm of activity. Not like Saturday night, when there had been a focus to the frenzy, but more like a busy ant hill where workers carried out many different tasks. Trucks were making deliveries to restock the concession supplies, while maintenance workers painted hand rails and walls. A sign crew with a boom truck was hanging new billboards around the track. No doubt the speedway owners were capitalizing on this unique opportunity to bring in some much-needed extra revenue. They only had today and tomorrow to prepare before race day.

Camber hoped that this last practice would go as well as the previous one. On Tuesday the prospective race car drivers got an up-close look at the car each would drive in the race. For the first time, they practiced in ten different cars instead of taking turns with one.

Even with the drivers practicing in ten different race cars, the day went smoothly. A representative from each team providing a minister's race car came to the speedway to deliver the car and to offer technical support. Camber was grateful for their expertise in familiarizing his fledgling drivers with their new cars.

The team representatives went over the fine points of the car for its new driver, and they made sure their seats and belts were a good fit, making whatever adjustments were necessary to accommodate the novice wheelmen.

In the driver's seat of her blue Lumina, Agnes Hill-Radnor looked bewildered. "But where's the ignition switch? It's supposed to be here." She tapped a forefinger on the blank space on the dashboard.

Gabe Powers, the car's owner-driver, smiled and pointed to the ignition switch. "They're not in the same place on every car," he told her. "But at least you didn't ask me for the key."

"Well, of course I didn't!" Agnes looked indignant. "I've been practicing for more than a week." She looked up into the blue eyes of the soft-spoken young man, and softened her tone. "I'm glad you're here, though. I'd be grateful for some help in getting accustomed to the new car."

Gabe Powers nodded. "It's likely to handle differently from the one you're used to. I'd be happy to stick around and make sure you're all right."

Agnes glanced at the Bible verse she had duct-taped to the dashboard. Psalm 91:11: *For He shall give His angels charge over thee, to keep thee in all thy ways.* She smiled up at Gabriel Powers, "I think you are an answer to prayer."

Camber knew that it would take some time for everyone to return to the comfort level they had achieved by the end of last week, when they climbed out of the familiar loaner race car for the last time. For that reason he instructed everyone to drive their first set of laps of the day at only 75% of their previous speed. They could work up from there as they grew accustomed to their new cars. In order to ride herd on his pupils, Camber decided to stand at the end of pit row and let out five cars at a time, thus keeping the traffic on track to a minimum, while still allowing everyone to get the feel of driving with other cars on the track.

In preparation for this first practice run, the representatives of each team checked both the cars and the drivers as they came in, sometimes making small adjustments before they pushed the cars back into line on pit road.

Camber was glad of the extra help, because now that all his charges were in their own race cars, he needed more people with expertise to make the practice go smoothly. Unfortunately for today's session, not all the team representatives had been able to make it, because most of them could not afford to take two days off from their day job in one week. Anticipating this, Camber had made a plea for additional help for the day's practice, and Fr. Frankie volunteered the services of Jesús Segovia. Travis Prichard offered Danny Simpkins, knowing that Danny's services wouldn't be missed much in Farley's Garage. It was a measure of Camber's desperation that he had even asked Pajan to stay and help.

Camber wasn't bashful about asking for help. He wouldn't bat an eyelash requesting what some people wouldn't dream of asking for. The way he saw the world, resources were around to be utilized, whether or not they were owned and controlled by him. He considered everything in his environment part of a connected web to accomplish goals. Today's goal was to get all the ministers comfortable with race procedures, such as lining up for the start and any restarts during the race. This practice was also a chance for them to spar with another car in close quarters at high speed. Before race day they needed to learn how to do that without panicking.

The safest way Camber could think to do this was for him to drive the loaner race car they all had practiced in, and take turns with each of the other ministers. They would follow him closely around the track for several laps, and then he would do the same to them. After they were comfortable with the routine, he would instruct them to spend a few laps taking turns passing each other. Camber thought that his smooth driving and previous track experience should provide enough of a safety margin to ensure that the cars would not make contact during race practice. An incident this close to race day would cost them hours in the garage repairing the damage before race day.

While Camber was contemplating the best way to conduct the day's exercises, Jesús Segovia, looking dapper in a white shirt and freshly pressed black jeans, sat down beside him on pit wall. "Will you be in need of my assistance today?"

"You said you had some experience around cars?" Instinctively, Camber looked at Jesús ' hands to judge how much "hands-on" experience he actually had.

"Experience. *Por supesto*."

"In that case, I could use you and Danny to warm up each race car, and give them a final safety check before you send them out on the track. I am going to be staying in a race car myself for most of today."

"I am honored to offer my services." With a solemn nod of farewell, Jesús ambled off to join Danny, who was burrowed under the hood of a race car, radiator cap off, checking to see if the water level needed topping up.

Camber called the ministers over to start practice. As he was explaining the order of activities he sensed the seriousness in the listeners. Just a week and a half ago these guys had looked like loafers ready to attack the food at a church picnic. Today Camber saw ten warriors, clad in fire suits, and holding helmets under their arms, like fighter pilots in flight gear, briefing for a mission.

A somber Agnes Hill-Radnor spoke up. "Camber, can we do the passing drill at full speed?"

Camber hesitated. "Let's say eighty percent. Slow enough so that the car doing the passing doesn't have to push it to get by. Let's save the real racing for Saturday night."

Their demeanor outside of the cars was not the only thing that impressed Camber. He was riding around the track in the pace car position with the ten minister drivers lined up two by two, as instructed. They circled the track at 35 miles per hour holding tight ranks, approximating the start of the actual race. Observing this in the rear view mirror, Camber decided that they were ready to put on a show.

* * *

Later that afternoon Fr. Frankie went off to make his hospital visits, and, with some misgivings, because it was Mrs. Mancini's day off, he left the rectory in the more-willing-than-able hands of his temporary house guest, Jesús Segovia. Jesús had assured Fr. Frankie that both his ingenuity and his English were equal to any situation that might arise during the priest's absence, and, as the final proof of his reliability, he recited Fr. Frankie's cell phone number from memory with fulsome promises to call immediately if anything happened.

After a long and relaxing coffee break in the rectory kitchen, Jesús managed to find a Brazilian soccer game on a satellite channel, and, although he was vacuuming the living room rug, as promised, he contrived to stay within sight of the television, so that he had been vacuuming the same square of carpet for ten consecutive minutes when the phone rang.

Eyes still on the screen, he kicked the power switch, and reached for the phone. "Good afternoon," he said in English. "By the grace of God and the genius of Alejandro Graham Bell, you have reached the parsonage of St Jude. The good father is not himself in residence at this time. May I assist you? This is Jesús speaking."

There was a sharp intake of breath on the other end of the phone, and then a quavering voice gasped, "*¡Díos mio!*"

Without missing a beat, Jesús slipped into Spanish, assuring the stunned caller that the telephone connection was not so long distance as he had apparently supposed. He had not reached the offices of heaven, but merely the ear of Jesús Segovia, a humble and pious *Chilango*, hailing from the same country as the caller himself.

Once the identity matter had been settled, the agitated caller held forth in a torrent of Mexican Spanish. "I am greatly troubled, *señor*. Still, I believe it is a sign, to call the church and be told that one is speaking to Him."

Jesús hesitated. "Confessions cannot be done by phone, my friend."

The man on the phone switched back to halting Spanglish, perhaps for greater privacy on his end. "No. I hear things. What I do? I do not sin. Is something I hear when I work. My job ... I work construction here in Judas Grove. This town—his name is not lucky. No, señor. And I hear a bad thing."

"What is it that you heard?"

One big *jefe*—I don't say the name—Today I hear him offer money to another man. He ask him to fix the race between the *padres*."

"That is a very serious charge, *mijo*." Jesús thought for a moment. "Unless, of course, some well-meaning benefactor is trying to arrange for Father Francis himself to be victorious for the honor of the Church. Then, perhaps, the matter is not so grave."

"No, *señor*. He insist that *Padre* Francisco is not to win. He wants fix race for another minister. This not right. I want to tell someone. But, me, I don't understand English good. I don't speak English good. And I think, 'I'm a poor migrant worker. Nobody believe me if I tell.'".

"Certainly I will believe you," said Jesús. "And you must tell me all that you know about this plan to fix the race. Surely God intended for you to do so when he put me here to answer this telephone."

The televised soccer game now forgotten, Jesús heard confession.

Chapter Sixteen
The Devil's Advocate

The sun beat down on the line of crew members waiting to sign in and receive their pit passes. The pit gates opened at noon, practice started at 1 p.m., and qualifying for all divisions took place at five, which was also the time that the main box office would open and begin allowing fans into the grandstand, all in anticipation of the 7 p.m. start of the first race of the night. "Hurry up and wait" could have been the slogan for NASCAR, and it only got worse the higher up you went in the racing divisions.

Brennan Morgan, who had just made the four-hour drive from Mooresville to Judas Grove, signed the slip of paper indemnifying the race track and its owners should a runaway tire strike him down, or should he be injured in any of the hundred other ways that harm could befall one at a race track. Thus dispensing with the legal formalities, he paid his twenty dollars, and received a wristband granting him access to the pit area, where he and Camber had agreed to meet.

Brennan scanned the unfamiliar surroundings in hopes of a Camber Berkley sighting, and then the look of the place registered in his brain. He found this little country speedway eerily similar to the last short track at which he and Camber had raced. He was even wearing the same shirt he had worn then. The mere thought of that night caused Brennan's ankle to throb. He fingered the small jagged hole in the tail of his shirt. The incident had happened more than a year ago, but he still swore that he could tell when it was about to rain by the numbness in his ankle. He often found it necessary to tell the ankle story at social gatherings and backyard barbeques, to let people know that working with Camber was not the happy privilege they seemed to think it was.

* * *

On the night of the Ankle Incident, Brennan and Camber had decided to travel to one of the big money races held at a track in the mountains of southwest Virginia

He was re-setting the timing of the engine after the qualifying laps. Advancing the timing was a trick that would squeeze a few extra horsepower out of the motor in the short term. The problem was you couldn't leave it adjusted that way for the entire race, or you would burn up the motor. Brennan, under the hood of Camber's late model Monte Carlo, had just reset the distributor to *32 degrees advanced*, a setting that he knew the motor could sustain safely throughout the race. The race car was pitted directly behind the 24-foot enclosed trailer that they had borrowed to pull the car to the track.

Camber, who had just finished setting the torque on the lug nuts, was in a hurry to get to the drivers' meeting, because he had posted a good time in qualifying, and he was slated to start in the third position. He didn't want to be sent to the back of the pack for being late, a penalty imposed by NASCAR when they realized that drivers would seize any excuse to avoid the drivers' meeting: a half hour of officials lecturing and berating them.

Brennan only needed to listen to the motor run one more time to make sure everything was right, so that he could push the car on to the starting grid while Camber was in the meeting.

Brennan noted that Camber's dash to the meeting had been delayed for showboating: he had stopped to sign his much-practiced autograph for the son of a fellow driver. If he had all that much time, he could certainly stay and make himself useful for another two minutes.

"Fire it up, just for a second Camber."

With a sigh of impatience, Camber reached through the drivers window and jerked the ignition switches, just as Brennan was saying, "Make sure it is out of ..."

Wham!

"Ge—eeear...."

When Camber threw both the start and ignition switches, the Late Model race car was still in first gear, and, since race cars lack street-style safety devices, the car immediately lunged forward, pinning Brennan between the back of the trailer and the front bumper of the Monte Carlo, with his foot lodged underneath the car.

An instant later the motor had stalled out, and through a wave of pain and alarm Brennan heard Camber yell, "Are you all right?"

His reply was in language unsuitable for backyard barbecues, so he usually glossed over that part of the story, and dwelt on the long, agonizing minutes before the pit crews of neighboring teams reached the car, jacked it up, and freed him.

After the mortifying experience of having other teams' pit crew members lift the car off his foot, he had been carted off in an ambulance to be x-rayed at the local hospital. Of course, he had missed the race, which Camber kept assuring him was all right, as if that had been his major concern. The accident had punctured the radiator and collapsed the duct work on the car, and Camber had finished outside the Top Ten, which Brennan was sorry about, but he felt that he had deserved more sympathy than he got.

Luckily, nothing was broken, but it took weeks for the swelling to go down and for him to be able to walk without crutches, and his ankle still throbbed every time it was going to rain.

"Look at it this way," Camber told him. "Your ankle wasn't broken, and you got a free barometer out of the deal."

* * *

As he stood there waiting for the official to open the chain link pit gate, Brennan felt a twinge in his bad ankle, reminding him that a single moment's inattention at a race track could be disastrous. He was still outside the gate, watching the crowd of crew members funnel past the official, when a sheriff's department cruiser pulled up to the sign, and stopped. Its lights were still flashing when a uniformed deputy got out and opened the back door of the cruiser. Camber emerged with a regal wave to the driver, as if he were the town's new mayor, chauffeured to the track by a trusty public servant.

Brennan sighed. No matter where Camber landed, he always seemed to come out on top. He thought that if you dropped Camber Berkley in some foreign country whose language he did not speak, with no money and no luggage, it would only take him about a week to be elected prom king, or whatever the local equivalent was. Well, at least, he wasn't too much of a jerk about it. He had the grace to fake humility about his extraordinary good fortune, anyhow.

After a few more royal waves to deluded local admirers and a couple of scribbled autographs for simpering village Valkyries, Camber caught sight of Brennan leaning against the fence, wearing his usual disapproving scowl and the torn racing shirt from the ankle incident. Today the Brennan guilt index was hovering around one hundred per cent.

"There you are!" Camber called out, threading his way through the crowd to reach him.

Brennan's grimace curved into a smile, and he had stretched out an arm for a handshake when Camber said, "It's about time you got here. Couldn't you make it any earlier?"

This was rich, coming from someone who had only arrived two minutes ago himself. Brennan stepped back and surveyed the conquering hero with raised eyebrows. "Where's your orange jump suit, Camber?"

Camber narrowed his eyes. "Maybe I should have worn my ripped-up clothes from the car wreck that put me here. Then we'd have matching outfits," he said, eying Brennan's "ankle incident" shirt.

"You want me to work on the ministers' cars, right? What did you expect me to wear? A choir robe?"

"Laugh it up, Brennan, but I need today to go smoothly if I want to have a future in racing and, might I add, in order to be able to set those bank people straight back in Mooresville."

Same old, same old. Camber thought everybody else in the world was a spear carrier in his personal opera. "Hey," said Brennan. "Out of genuine concern for a friend, I drove up here to help you, but I do reserve the right to laugh it up. Should I get used to seeing you getting out of the back of a police car?"

Camber gave him a martyred look as he scrawled his name on the speedway waiver. Brennan was entitled to a modicum of gloating, and Camber knew it. He was making the sardonic remarks to ease the tension he felt after the four-hour drive from Mooresville, and from his lingering anxiety over the disastrous bank meeting. As a peace offering, Brennan permitted himself a wary smile. As usual he was taking the high road: making a few sarcastic remarks in lieu of choking Lurch to death.

He decided to postpone further torment until later. Race day meant there was work to be done. "Okay, Camber, when do the saints go marching in?"

"What?"

"Your clergymen. What order do they practice in?"

"They don't. Today's practice is only for the other divisions. Over the past two weeks I gave the ministers all the practice they're going to get. I'm not going to risk having one of them put the car in the wall right before the big race."

"So who put you in charge of this race, anyhow?" They were walking across the track to the infield, wreathed in the smell of gasoline and the roar of 400 horsepower engines. It certainly felt like old times.

Camber smirked. "The judge, of course. He must know talent when he sees it."

"Yeah, I'll bet he also salts his cat litter and sells it to the tourists for grits. He sure saw you coming. So you're afraid to let your cherubs practice. What about qualifying? Are they allowed to do that, or does somebody get the poll by divine right?"

"Don't I wish, Brennan. Unfortunately, I don't have a choice about that. It is spelled out in the will. Just hope those holy rollers take it easy, or else you'll be doing some sheet metal work with a sledge hammer to get them ready to the take the green flag."

"Sounds like a typical day at the races with you. So how much time do we have left before they have to qualify?"

"Qualifying is at five. Do you think we can check all the cars over by then?"

"How many cars are we talking about?"

"Nine."

"Is that all? Most Southern communities have that many churches per block."

"Yeah, well, they invited everybody they could think of to participate, but these were the only nine ministers brave enough—or desperate enough—to try it. Two million dollars is a lot of money in a rural community."

"It's not exactly lunch money to us, either."

"Yeah, maybe I should have gotten myself ordained and entered the race."

Brennan smirked. "Poverty, chastity, and obedience. I'd pay two million dollars to see you try that."

"I'll bet you would. But can you get these cars checked over by five?"

"Shouldn't be a problem."

Camber had that greyhound-before-the-starting-bell look. Brennan knew what was coming next. Camber slapped him on the arm, and said, "Great! I knew I could count on you. Let me know if you need anything, or if you find anything unsafe about the cars. Now I have to go talk to a few people."

Brennan watched him lope off in search of people to schmooze with—local dignitaries, cruising reporters—anything to do besides actual work. Brennan was there to do that. He sighed. It was indeed like old times.

* * *

Camber made his way around the track, snaking in between the trucks and trailers pulling into their respective pit areas. As he walked past, teams unloaded equipment and set up the race cars on jack stands so that they could do the race day safety checks. One of the late model teams, whom Camber recognized from last week's race, was backing the repaired racecar off the trailer as he approached their pit stall. Since there were only two team members there, he offered to help them push the car into position. It was the natural thing for Camber to do at a race track: if someone needed help, he felt compelled to pitch in. He couldn't think of anyone in racing who operated any other way—kind of like Little League Baseball, he thought. When one team didn't have enough players to take the field, the opposing team would send a few over to help out. There were plenty of times when Camber had needed a spare part minutes before race time, and people had helped him out. Oh, and when he had needed help lifting his car off his injured crew chief—St. Brendan of the Sorrows with his torn racing shirt and his barometric ankle.

Camber found it hard to walk very far at all without having someone stop him to talk about his performance in last week's race, or to thank him for his help in raising the money for baby Sarah Meyers.

Camber made a special point to stop at Bobby's trailer to thank him for the loan of the race car last week, and to ask how his niece was doing. The 11 Late Model still bore traces of orange on the rear bumper where Tracy had tried to bulldoze his way past Camber in the final laps of last week's race. At this level of racing, there wasn't the budget or the manpower to get a fresh coat of paint or a complete set of decals in between races. Sure, in the Cup series there were always sponsors walking around the pits, and people taking pictures up close with the cars, making it necessary to have every square inch of the racecar manicured before the team arrived at the track.

Of course cars looked different from up in the stands than they did up close. In the past Camber had received many compliments from eager fans on how "pretty" his Street

Stock racecar had looked, but he knew that, if the admirers had come close to the car, they would be able to see the hasty body work that he and Brennan did between races that left the sheet metal looking like the surface of a golf ball.

Bobby greeted Camber with a welcoming smile. "There's the golden boy!" he called out.

"I was just wanted to see how things were going this week." Camber told him.

Bobby smiled. "You mean the race car? We figure if it can hold up to what you put it through last week, it can make it through anything. Now, if you mean little Sarah, my brother and his family are making final preparations for her surgery as we speak."

Practice for the other divisions was just starting up, and the roar of the engines ruled out long conversations. Camber shook Bobby's hand, and pressed on.

He decided that he needed to talk to some of the officials, such as the pace car driver and the flag man, just to make sure that the ministers were aware of all the race procedures. He also needed to see about plans for the inspection process.

The chief steward informed Camber that the usual county speedway racing procedures would be followed for the Faster Pastor event; that is, track officials would inspect the winning car to make sure that it conformed to all track rules for the Street Stock division. After the Victory Lane festivities, the winning car would be brought to the scales, weighed and inspected. This was another difference between local short tracks and the big leagues. At the short tracks, the inspection officials would normally just pick one thing at random to inspect, and it was considered a big deal if they made you pull apart your motor or transmission. At the Cup level, though, the officials didn't bat an eyelash at making you reduce your cars to a pile disjoined parts to certify your legality in a fifth-place finish. Money not only buys speed; it also buys red tape.

The thought of the impending inspection reminded him that Brennan probably could use some help. Thanks to Camber's patient instruction in auto mechanics, Brennan was good, but no one could accurately set the toe on a car while working alone. Camber looked at the time. Could really be three o'clock already?

They qualified in two hours.

* * *

It was almost time to begin. All nine cars were lined up at the end of pit road, waiting their turn on the track for the qualifying laps. With the sun getting low in the sky, Camber knew it was going to be hard for the drivers to see coming off turn four. For this reason, he had suggested that they all wear sunglasses. He was going to be holding his breath until all of his pupils had qualified. He wanted them to have the best chance of making it through in one piece. They had not practiced this late in the day, so the sun in their eyes would be a new experience for them. He wished he had thought of that. Well, it was too late to worry about it now.

Camber climbed up to his customary observation post on top of the infield concession stand, which was now doing a frantically thriving business in hot dogs and cold drinks. He was ready to see the results of his instruction.

The media must have had an idea that this might be the last time they saw all the cars in one piece. Several reporters were snapping pictures of the cars neatly lined up and ready to go. Camber looked up at the stands. So far, only a few dozen fans were seated in the grandstand. Some of the spectators were probably members of the various congregations or family members of the drivers, but mostly these were the diehards, the fanatics who craved both the excitement of racing and the drama of the details. They listened to scanners to try and hear what was going on between the drivers and spotters, and the kept their own accounting of qualifying times, writing down each lap time in their programs as the numbers flashed across the scoreboard. This way they could determine where their driver would be in the starting order before it was announced over the PA system. Other race fans would fill in later, because tonight's event guaranteed a packed house, but for now only the serious race fans were watching.

The track was ready. At the end of pit road a track official pointed to Paul Whitcomb in the first car and signaled for him to start the motor. Once it fired up, Whitcomb revved up the motor several times before the official motioned him on to the track for his one lap qualifying attempt. Camber let out a long breath when Whitcomb finished the lap, crossing the finish line as the checkered flag waved.

One down, eight to go, he thought.

Rev. Whitcomb was just pulling into the pits when the official sent Bill Bartlett onto the track. Was he wearing sunglasses? Camber had forgotten to look. Perhaps not, because although he completed his lap without incident, he had narrowly managed to avoid the wall coming out of turn four. Next was Travis Prichard, who showed his previous racing experience by besting the times of the previous two drivers by two tenths of a second. This was a closer field than Camber had expected. He wasn't sure who he'd bet on to win tonight.

Andrew Scarberry, who went after Prichard, seemed to be quick enough to beat his time, but, as he swung into turn three, the rear of the car slid sideways, fishtailing around the turn. The car slowed down considerably before Scarberry was able to get it pointed straight again. His time was shot, but at least he hadn't hit anything. Camber released the knuckles he had unconsciously started biting when he heard the squeal of tires sliding across pavement.

He took the concession stand steps two at a time and dashed over to the next car in line. Leaning into Stephen Albright's window, Camber said, "Take it easy out there! Remember there is no money for winning qualifying."

Albright looked grayer than usual, and he muttered, "*Ora pro nobis,*" which Camber hoped meant that he intended to drive carefully.

Camber held his breath for the duration of that lap, clinching his fist in triumphant relief as Albright crossed the finish line without incident.

Fr. Frankie went next. Camber had stayed on pit road to wish him luck. Fr. Frankie nodded solemnly, crossed himself three times, and then let the clutch out, spinning the tires as he roared onto the track.

Camber willed himself not to shout encouragement as the car sped past. It was a decent lap. His time was fast, but it was not the fastest. It might hold up for third. Rev. Cunningham ran his lap, and then a terrified-looking Agnes, and finally Romney Marsh, who had added his church's web site address to the other sponsor logos on his race car.

With the qualifying laps completed, Camber felt the thunderous beating of his heart subside. They were all still in one piece and ready to race. He went to get a copy of the starting order.

FASTER PASTOR RACE

Pos.	Driver	Time	Speed-MPH
1.	Travis Prichard	18.090	82.786
2.	Agnes Hill-Radnor	18.294	81.863
3.	Fr. Francis Spillane	18.346	81.631
4.	William Bartlett	18.360	81.569
5.	Paul Whitcomb	18.417	81.316
6.	Romney Marsh	18.452	81.162
7.	Stephen Albright	18.576	80.620
8.	Richard Cunningham	18.600	80.516
9.	Andrew Scarberry	19.481	76.875

Camber looked over the sheet. This was the order in which the drivers would have to lineup their cars for the start of the race.

* * *

Brennan Morgan was giving the race cars a thorough going-over, partly because he wasn't sure that Camber had devoted enough time to the task, but mostly because he was the sort of person who color-coded closets and alphabetized the spice rack. He had finished the cars for Scarberry, Bartlett, and Albright, and they had all seemed in satisfactory working order, but when he began to examine the motor of Travis Prichard's car, he found that a spark plug wire was loose.

He sighed. Trust Camber to miss the details. If Prichard had gone out to race with a loose spark plug wire, the vibrations of driving would have disconnected it completely after a few laps. With a disconnected spark plug wire, the spark plug doesn't get the signal or energy to fire and create a spark. Without the spark, that cylinder does not generate any power, and, in an eight-cylinder engine, that costs the motor one-eighth of its power—a guaranteed loss of the race.

In order to fix the problem, the driver would have to make a pit stop, which, in a 50-lap race, would also cost him the win. Brennan tightened the errant wire, and then decided to go back and check the spark plugs on all the competitors' cars.

He was sprawled under the hood of Pastor Cunningham's car, where he had just discovered another loose wire, when someone swatted him on the rump, and a feminine voice said, "So there you are!"

In his haste to disentangle himself from the engine, Brennan bumped his head on the hood, which did nothing to improve his current mood. He straightened up to find himself face to face with a dark-haired young woman best described as "Camber's type."

When she saw who he was—or rather, who he wasn't—her expression changed from white-faced shock to blushing embarrassment. "I'm sorry," she muttered. "I thought you were somebody else."

"So I gathered," said Brennan. "The guy you're looking for went walkabout, leaving me to pick up the pieces—as usual. I'm Brennan Morgan. I own a machine shop in Mooresville, and I'm Camber's best friend. Both those things are full-time jobs."

"I see." She didn't extend her hand. After you have swatted somebody's behind, a handshake was both too much and not enough. "I'm Pajan Mosby. I was Camber's court-appointed minder for the past two weeks, so my asking about him isn't idle curiosity. He's supposed to be here. It's one of the conditions of his sentence. Where did he go?"

Brennan realized that this wasn't just some stray girl that Camber had picked up to pass the time in *Hooterville.* Well, obviously she was, but she was also an officer of the local court, which meant that she had the power to put Camber back in the slammer if he misbehaved, which would make him to miss the bank meeting—again. "Oh, he's here," said Brennan, relenting into cordiality. "He just went off to talk to one of the officials, I think. But I have the cars are almost ready."

"I see," said Pajan. "Well, what about Jesus? Is he here?"

Brennan blinked. "Umm … He's everywhere, isn't He?"

She sighed. "Apparently not. Actually, he pronounces it Hay-soos. Jesús Segovia. He's also supposed to be here helping with the cars."

"Haven't seen him. Camber didn't introduce me to anybody before he took off, which is typical."

"Really? Is he that inconsiderate? Or is it arrogance? I certainly never made a dent in his self-esteem, and I gave it my best shot."

"I don't know," said Brennan. "It's probably thoughtlessness. He can be really single-minded when it comes to racing. And, as for self-esteem, that's supposed to be a good thing, isn't it? People go to a psychiatrist and get pills to feel as self-confident as he is."

Pajan shrugged. "Maybe they should go to plastic surgeons instead."

"Well, Camber should turn up soon, since the work is almost done. Good thing I spotted those loose spark plug wires, though."

"I hope you're planning to tell him about it."

"He's going to hear about it, all right. It's a long way back to Mooresville, and he'll be a captive audience." Brennan was watching her carefully. "You know, we're leaving tonight. As soon as the race is over."

"So I gathered," said Pajan.

Brennan tried not to show his relief. He had more experience than he wanted in dealing with Camber's Miss Right-Now's, but he still didn't find it easy to dash their hopes, no matter how diplomatically he managed to convey the message. He always dreaded the tears and the occasional tantrums that came when some hopeful pit lizard realized that her term had expired.

Serenely unconscious of this meeting of the minds, Camber ambled back onto pit road to see if Brennan needed any help putting the finishing touches on the set-ups for the race. He found Brennan and Pajan deep in conversation—that was disturbing. The only thing he could think of that those two could have in common was a curious lack of appreciation for his own irresistible self.

Jesús Segovia fell in step with him. "Are all of our holy drivers ready for the race tonight, my friend?"

"As ready as they'll ever be," said Camber. "I was just on my way to see how the car inspection is going. Come on, I'll introduce you to Brennan. He was my crew chief when I raced."

"What good fortune for him."

"Yeah. Tell him that."

Brennan had hardly finished shaking hands with Jesús before he turned on Camber, scowling. "Nice of you to drop by," he said. "I thought getting these cars ready to race was your responsibility."

"They *are* ready," said Camber.

"You think so? Lucky for you I was here. The spark plug wires were loose on half of them. I've spent the last twenty minutes fixing them. I could have used some help."

"The spark plug wires? But, Brennan, I checked everything after the last practice."

"Then it's a good thing you don't work for a bomb squad, because the motors you checked were defective. Those cars wouldn't have lasted half the race. I fixed them."

"I don't understand it," said Camber. "They were fine at practice."

Brennan and Pajan exchanged glances. "Well, it's fixed now," said Brennan. "Go give your drivers a pep talk. Talking is something you're good at."

When Camber walked away, Jesús smiled at Pajan. "My parents have arrived for the race. They are in the stands. Come and meet them."

Brennan slammed down the hood of Scarberry's race car. Alone again. As usual.

* * *

With only a few minutes left before his final check of the ministers' cars, Camber headed off to the rest room, hoping to get a few minutes of peace and quiet before the chaos of the race. He didn't want a call of nature to make him miss any of tonight's race. As he expected, the infield rest room was deserted. He knew that if he was gone for more than a few minutes, someone would panic and start looking for him. He had just entered the first stall and closed the door, when someone else came into the bathroom, and entered the adjoining stall.

"I need to talk to you."

Uh-oh, thought Camber. He didn't know why someone whose voice he didn't recognize would want to talk to him in a men's room, but none of the scenarios he came up with were good. "I'm busy," he said, truthfully.

"I know who you are. You're fixing the ministers' cars for the race tonight. Well, I want you to fix one or two of them real good."

"What do you mean?"

"Scarberry has to win tonight, see? And if he doesn't, you will have a problem."

"What's that supposed to mean?"

"Your 1980 Plymouth RoadRunner …" Camber thought he detected a snicker in the man's voice, "… is impounded behind Farley's Garage in town, and a little something has been added to it since you left it there. There is now a plastic bag of cocaine in the trunk of your car. So if you don't fix this race so that Scarberry wins, the local cops will be getting a phone call as soon as the race is over, tipping them off to your drug activities.'

"Am I supposed to believe this?"

The man laughed. "Well, let's see. Your trunk also contains

jumper cables, a scissor jack and spare tire obviously recently used (un-stowed), a few loose sockets, a Pringles can, some hero cards of yourself, and a few grubby articles of clothing."

"Okay, but ... Even if the police did find that stuff, it isn't mine. It was in the unguarded back lot of a repair shop. Anybody could have had access to that car. There'd be no proof, no fingerprints. You're trying to frame me, but they'd never convict me." He sounded more certain than he felt.

The man in the other stall sighed. "Sure, you might beat the rap—eventually. But that's not the point, is it? I hear you want to be a Cup driver someday. Given NASCAR's zero tolerance for drug use, I think that just being arrested on suspicion of cocaine possession would cost you any chance of ever getting into Cup.—Oh, and don't look over this partition or try to watch me walk out of here, because then I'll call the police immediately."

"Look, even if I tampered with the other cars, that doesn't guarantee that Scarberry will win. Anything can happen in a stock car race. A wreck. Tire trouble. Anything."

"Well, you'd just better hope it doesn't," said the man. "You'd better hurry up. It's almost time for the final inspections. So you don't have time to get to your car to remove the evidence, and you don't have time to mull over your options. In about two minutes, you either disable the cars of Prichard and Spillane, or you start planning for a much longer stay in jail. Your call."

Before Camber could reply, he heard the click of the stall door, then footsteps, and then the creak of the rest room door, closing behind the departing stranger.

Chapter Seventeen
Driving with the Devil

"I'd better check those spark plug wires one more time." Camber muttered, as he edged past Brennan toward the front of the line of cars.

"So now you're a worrywart," said Brennan. "I told you, I fixed them. But if you want to double check, you'd better hurry. They're about ready to introduce the drivers."

Brennan saw him lift the hood on Travis Prichard's car and disappear beneath it. He shook his head at this eleventh hour show of diligence, and went back to setting the air pressure on Scarberry's car, the last one in line.

The sky was dark now. All the other races had been run. The grandstands were packed, and the ministers had lined against the inside track wall, dressed in their borrowed fire suits. Brennan thought that, with the possible exception of the angel lady and the elderly gentleman whose native language was apparently Latin, they looked just like any other group of drivers at a rural county race track. Well, maybe they were a couple of years older than the average driver these days, he thought, but he couldn't have guessed they were all ministers. The sound of Pajan Mosby's voice on the microphone told him that the start of the race was only minutes away.

"A little over two weeks ago, many of us lost a dear friend.

Jimmy Powell was a gentle man and lively soul whose mere presence guaranteed a good time, especially if you were lucky enough to have grown up knowing him, benefiting from his teaching and his sense of wonder at the most ordinary things in this world. And he shared his love of racing." Pajan's words had quieted the unsettled crowd.

"Jimmy Powell is still trying to infuse us all with his love of racing. He devised a way to let his legacy live on, and to leave one last and lasting gift to the sport of racing and to his home town, Judas Grove. When that green flag waves to start the next race, Jimmy Powell's last wish will come true. I am sure that you would like to join me in saying, *Thank you Jimmy. We miss you, and I hope you have a good seat for tonight's race.*"

The chorus of raucous cheers from the grandstand gave Pajan time to wipe a tear from her eye. "There are many people to thank for toni ght's race," she went on, "the teams of the street stock division of Judas Grove Speedway, the speedway management; NASCAR driver Cameron Berkley, who coached our fledgling drivers ..."

Again she had to wait until the cheering stopped.

NASCAR driver, thought Brennan. *And I am Bishop Tutu.*

"Channels 4, 9 and 17 for being here tonight, as well as WJCW radio, but especially, for their courage and determination, we need to thank these eight men and one wonderful lady who are standing behind me." Pajan turned and swept an outstretched arm in the direction of the ministers as she made her way to Andrew Scarberry's side of the line.

"Before I introduce our brave new race car drivers, I would like to tell you exactly what prize they are racing for tonight. I'm proud to announce that just yesterday a deal was struck so that the entire *Jimmy Powell Racing Collection* can stay intact and it will henceforth be displayed in Charlotte, North Carolina's new Racing Hall of Fame. The Hall of Fame's payment for this unique collection of racing memorabilia came to 2.2 million dollars! Ladies and gentlemen, the winner of this race will receive a check larger than the purse of this year's Daytona 500."

This announcement brought a collective gasp from the

crowd, a breathless silence immediately followed by whistles and thunderous applause.

"Now let's introduce the drivers. Starting ninth, and representing the First Baptist Church, Pastor Andrew Scarberry of the First Baptist Church of Judas Grove." After Pajan's introduction she passed the microphone to Rev. Scarberry, so that he could let everyone know the cause that he was racing for.

"Thank you," said Scarberry, holding the mike too close. "I'm grateful for the opportunity to compete tonight. As many of you know, our church was placed on the Tennessee State Historical Society's list of historically significant buildings. I am racing to secure much-needed funding for a full restoration of the sanctuary and the exterior of our historic church." Scarberry handed the microphone back to Pajan, clambered over the inside wall, and made his way to his race car, where Brennan and Camber were waiting to buckle him in.

"Starting eighth: Rev. Richard Cunningham of the Presbyterian Church."

Rick Cunningham smiled up at the cheering crowd. "I wish I could see that many faces in my church on Sunday," he said. "If you did happen to come by Cumberland Presbyterian, you'd see that our sanctuary is badly in need of renovation. The red carpeting has faded to a lemonade pink, the woodwork needs painting and restoring, and our wonderful hundred-year old pipe organ is decades overdue for a tune-up. The parking lots needs paving, too. I know that doesn't sound like two million dollars worth of work, but, believe me, construction doesn't come cheap these days. You almost have to be a race car driver to afford it. So—wish me luck, people." With a cheery thumbs-up, Rick Cunningham tucked his helmet under his arm and ambled off in the direction of the race cars.

"In the seventh position, Stephen Albright of St. Paul's Lutheran Church."

Looking less frail than usual in the bulky firesuit, Stephen Albright blinked uncertainly at the sea of blurry faces beyond the spotlights. "*Ora pro nobis.* All prayers will be much appreciated," he stammered, eliciting a sympathetic ripple of laughter and a scattering of applause from the listeners. "Our church would like to establish a library. It has long been a dream of mine to have a collection of rare theological works, and perhaps some old manuscripts in the original Greek and Aramaic, for anyone interested in a scholarly study of Bible literature, but perhaps we could also include other sorts of books for the community in general. Books are a great blessing." When he finished speaking, he wandered over to the pit road wall, and Camber and Brennan, who helped him over it, escorted him to his car.

"Sixth, we have Dr. Romney Marsh of Church of the Crystal Path."

Watching from the infield, Brennan scowled. *Dude's an EdD,* he thought. *They're the only ones who use their title socially. PhDs and medical doctors have more class than that.*

Pajan had hardly finished the introduction, before the florid shepherd of the Crystal Path appropriated the microphone, and roared out a hearty "Praise the Lord" to the spectators. "Do y'all know what the word Gospel means?" he said, peering into the darkness. "Well, I'm here to tell you, folks. It means *good news.* And that's what the Crystal Path congregation is all about: sharing good news. So we'd like to receive some manna from heaven to enable us to spread that word more effectively so that many more of our friends and neighbors can join us in fellowship. Spreading the word, folks. That's what it's all about." He turned his back to the crowd so that they could see the large patch on the back of his firesuit spelling out in Day-Glo letters: www.CrystalPathChurch.com.

Pajan retrieved the microphone more forcefully than was strictly necessary. "Starting in fifth position tonight is the Rev. Paul Whitcomb of St. David's Episcopal."

Paul Whitcomb waved at the crowd. "Well, I can hardly believe I'm here tonight," he said. "If this isn't a leap of faith, I don't know what is. A few weeks ago, I thought NASCAR was a former president of Egypt, and now here I am in a firesuit, ready to go out there and race a stock car. St. David's is in need of a modern state-of-the-art kitchen in order to accommodate weddings and church functions, so I'm here to take the heat in hopes of getting out of our old kitchen. Thank you."

"Next up is Rev. William Bartlett of the Grace Methodist Church, who starts fourth."

Rev. Bartlett stretched out his arms and turned around slowly, modeling his white firesuit for the crowd. "It's me, don't you think?" When the laughter died down, he went on, "I suppose it's fitting that I've turned to an automotive resource to assist in our church fund-raising, because what Grace Methodist needs is a church bus. We have several active church groups—a senior citizens fellowship and a thriving youth group for our teenagers. We need some means of transporting them on trips, both for youth outings to places like Dollywood, and for senior trips, and also for some of our charitable work; for example, when we sent groups off to help with the clean-up in a community hit by a tornado. So, long story short—"

"Too late," said Pajan. "Rev. Bartlett needs a bus, folks. And right now he needs to go to his race car." She shook his hand. "Good luck, Bill. Next up 'tis himself, the driver in third position, Father Francis Spillane of St. Jude's Catholic Church."

Fr. Frankie got the lion's share of the cheers, and he waved to a contingent of familiar faces in the front row. "Many thanks for egging me on. I invited the bishop to come and watch me race tonight, but he was unable to make it. He did consider sending an exorcist, though. Now, why the devil am I doing this? He asked me that question as well, and I says to him, 'Well, your Excellency, there's a lot of good people in my parish who need a safe place to leave their children while they work, and I'd like to build a place that would take care of that need.' And it would be grand to offer evening classes for citizenship and GED and learning English, and whatever people need to be taught to make a better life. I learned to drive a race car in the hope of helping others to learn as well, and I hope they'll get the joy out of it that I did. It has been grand."

"Starting second: Agnes Hill-Radnor, founding director of the Institute for the Study of Angels. Here, Miss Hill-Radnor, take the microphone."

Haloed in the speedway lights, Agnes Hill-Radnor may have felt equal to the task of conversing with angels, but she looked decidedly uneasy in the presence of several hundred staring strangers. "I believe in angels," she said, in a hushed voice that was barely audible even with the microphone. "I think they are sent to watch over us and to keep us from harm. I'd like to think there'll be one with me tonight as I compete in this race. I've devoted my life to this institute, because I think that we should study the phenomenon of angels. I would like to be able to use my research to give the world the comforting news that we are not alone, that there is someone who watches over us in our time of need."

Agnes' voice died away, and in the grandstand there was silence, perhaps because people were wondering what to make of this unusual woman and her cause. Finally, someone in the crowd remembered his manners and began to applaud and others joined in with polite, but subdued, ovation. She was a poor, clueless little thing, but they wished her well out there. If she had to encounter a celestial being tonight, they hoped it wouldn't be the Angel of Death.

Pajan gave Agnes a reassuring smile as she stepped past her to introduce the last competitor. "And now … Starting in the pole position, having posted the fastest time in qualifying … Please welcome Brother Travis Prichard of the Sanctified Holiness Church of God."

In a hail of cheers and applause, Travis Prichard took the microphone with the same care he used to pick up rattlesnakes. He squared his shoulders and faced the audience with an uneasy smile. "Well, I'll tell you, folks, I'd just about rather drive this track blindfolded than stand up in front of this many people and make a speech, so I'll keep this short. My congregation needs a church, and, if it's the Lord's will here tonight, I aim to get them the means to do that."

* * *

As Camber was helping Fr. Frankie buckle in, he muttered, "I think I'm almost as nervous as you guys are. Be careful out there, Father."

The priest smiled up at him. "Well, the game was worth the candle, whichever way it goes. But I have faith in you as well as in Him, Camber. We are all in your hands, and I trust that if you need to make any adjustment on the car, for whatever reason, you would not put any of our lives in jeopardy. I take you for an honorable man."

Camber nodded. When he could trust himself to speak, he said, "Forgive me if this is too tight, Father." He cinched the belts down tight, squeezing the air from Fr. Frankie's chest. "It has to be adjusted like this. In case something did happen, I wouldn't want you bouncing around in there. Good luck." He put up the window net, and looked down the rows of car. Seeing that Brennan was taking care of Agnes, he moved up to wait for Travis.

When he had finished settling Travis behind the wheel, he saw Brennan give him a thumbs-up to let him know that all the drivers he had buckled in were ready to go. Camber nodded. It was zero hour.

He walked over to the window of the pace car and said to the track official behind the wheel, "I've done all I could do. They are all yours now. Keep your eye on the mirror; none of them has a radio."

"Will do," said the pace car driver. The yellow lights atop the pace car flashed on and off. The ministers fired their motors and, one by one, they rolled off pit lane.

The pace car, on loan from a Ford dealer in Johnson City, was a brand new Mustang GT, with *Judas Grove Speedway* printed on either side in vinyl, a light bar across the roof, and the dealership logo emblazoned on the hood.

Behind the pace car crept a string of nine automotive relics from a long-ago era, when racing was merely a second profession for an automobile after years of faithful street service. These cars were nothing like the born-and-bred racing machines of today with their tube frames and hand-built bodies. In the Street Stock division of small-time racing, the cars themselves were characters just as much as the people driving them.

One car length in front of her, the pole car driven by Travis Prichard began to swerve violently back and forth, reminding Agnes that she, too, needed to warm up her tires. She copied Prichard's see-saw maneuvers, remembering Camber's many lectures about its importance. The nine swerving cars looked like a streamer in the wind, rolling back and forth on the otherwise empty track. After a two-lap procession in single file, the flag man signaled that it was time for them to line up for the start of the race.

Agnes pulled up to her starting position on the outside of the front row, trying as best she could to keep right alongside Travis Prichard behind the pace car. He looked over and waved with his gloved hand, which she took to be a friendly gesture of encouragement. Hesitantly, she waved back. It was nice to have someone besides her guardian angel wishing her well tonight.

When all the cars behind her had taken their position two by two, ("Like Noah's ark!" Rick Cunningham had said), the crowd hushed to a reverent whisper. Despite the multitude in the stands, and her fellow drivers on the track, Agnes suddenly felt all alone. The only sound that penetrated her helmet was the thunderous rasp of her car's engine. She felt a lump in her throat as the pace car turned off its lights, signifying this was the last warm-up lap before the green flag. To keep from trembling, she went through her mental check list. A tug on the belts to make sure they were tight; a look across the gauges to make sure the oil and water temperatures were where they should be; put the engine into second gear for the start. When the cars reached the halfway point in the back stretch, her right leg began to shake.

Fr. Frankie was tucked up close behind Travis Prichard, determined not to be left in the dust during the first few seconds of the race. Matching the speed at such close range was difficult, and Fr. Frankie's Monte Carlo tapped the rear bumper of Travis Prichard's car. There was no damage, but the incident warranted a wave of apology from Fr. Frankie, which Travis barely saw in the limited field of vision obstructed by the roll bars in the rear window.

Starting in ninth place, Andrew Scarberry was the only car not rolling in two-by- two formation. As the last place competitor he was alone in the back row, which was not entirely a bad thing. This position gave him some extra space to swerve back and forth and prepare for the start. Before the race Camber had instructed him to stay back an extra car length, and to choose the faster of the two lanes at the start. Camber, who had started from the back of the pack and won in last Saturday's race, had told him that there were some aspects of starting at the back that a driver could use to his advantage. One of the main ones was the extra time and space you would have to avoid a wreck in front of you.

"There will usually be a wreck near the start of the race," Camber told him. "The only question is where. If you are starting shotgun, it stands to reason that the wreck will happen in front of you."

Camber's final words, "So be ready," still hung in Scarberry's mind. As the pace car made its final turn, he lowered the shield on his helmet, and his heavy breathing created a small patch of fog every time he exhaled. He contented himself with a silent prayer, so that he wouldn't fog up the visor even more.

Romney Marsh's shoulders were already sore from being squashed like a sardine and from the tension that made his whole body feel like piano wire. He was starting sixth: rows of cars in front of him, rows behind him, Paul Whitcomb to his inside, and a very daunting concrete wall to his outside. The noise around him was tremendous. He focused on the rear bumper of Rev. Bartlett's car, directly in front of him, and tried to ignore everything else. He hoped he wasn't sweating too much. There were sure to be interviews and photo sessions after the race, and he hated looking *shiny.*

As the pace car dove off the track to head down pit lane, Travis Prichard calmly pressed on the clutch and revved up the motor, sending black smoke to pour from the exhaust pipes and swirl from either side of the car. The Mustang pace car made a hard left turn down pit lane, leaving Travis with an unobstructed view of the race track and the flag stand. From behind the flag man's back came the green flag, and in a heartbeat Travis had jumped a full car length ahead of Agnes to his outside.

Fr. Frankie was shifting through the gears, only five or six feet behind Travis Prichard, leaving him side by side with Agnes. He made the shift to fourth gear and immediately had to begin braking for the first turn. The thundering herd of horsepower was now loosely packed behind him.

Travis Prichard had chosen the inside lane to make his advance, because Agnes' slow start had momentarily clogged the outside lane. Now Travis was on the back straightaway. Behind him still were four rows, proceeding two-by-two, with Travis now alone out front. Steven Albright's car drifted up in turns three and four, and bounced off Romney Marsh, leaving a black doughnut of tire rubber on his door panel.

With an utterance that bore no resemblance to prayer, Romney Marsh tried to keep going straight, but his natural reaction, which was to steer to the right, straped his whole right side across the concrete wall as he completed his first lap. On the next lap, Marsh expressed his displeasure with Albright's driving by maneuvering a few feet down the track and leaving a black rubber doughnut of his own on Albright's door. Each time this happened, the still-trailing Scarberry jolted, seeing the puff of smoke from the tire rubbing against sheet metal.

Checking out the action behind him, Travis Prichard could see that Fr. Frankie had cleared Agnes, and was lapping smoothly behind him. He was now letting the car drift up the track as it leaned hard on the right side tires coming off the turns, bringing the sheet metal within inches of the wall.

Although she was still in third, Agnes was stuck on the outside, silently chastising herself for forgetting to shift gears on the restart. Focusing on her mistake channeled her concentration and lessened her fear. She took it easy on the brakes, letting the car keep its momentum entering the corners, and allowing it to roll through the center of the turn. Now she was almost clear of Paul Whitcomb, whose front bumper she could barely see out her driver's side window in her peripheral vision.

Romney Marsh felt that he had just spent a few laps bouncing around on the inside of a pinball machine. On the entry to turn three he glanced over to see Albright's position on the track, and when he turned to look straight again, Rev. Bartlett's car had turned sideways, leaving him with only seconds to consider his options—which were non-existent, anyhow. With his arms and legs tensed, he pressed both feet on the brake pedal, and braced for the inevitable impact. There was a screeching of tires and a crunch of metal, all playing out in front of him in slow motion, as if he were watching an instant replay. He had hit Bartlett broadside, and both cars slid down the banking of turn four. Scarberry was somehow able to slip underneath the tangled cars, and Richard Cunningham narrowly missed them to the top side.

Seeing the yellow caution lights, Travis raised his arm in the air to warn Fr. Frankie that he was slowing down. Seconds later he came upon the wrecked cars, now resting on the inside of the track, and he led the remaining cars high through the turn. From behind pit wall the pace car emerged, and the track safety truck scooted out in the opposite direction from the traffic, heading directly to the wrecked cars.

It took a few seconds for Bill Bartlett to realize that he was all right. Several thoughts had flashed through his mind in the time between spotting Marsh's car, his tires locking, smoke trailing behind, and the actual impact to his driver side door. He figured he would wake up in a hospital bed, with weeks of recovery ahead of him. The world seemed to be a little hazy just now, but, otherwise, he was sure he'd had worse crashes in bumper cars when he had chaperoned the church youth to an amusement park. He had hardly moved around at all in the car. Once he figured out that he was okay, he reached up and re-fired the motor, pulling away to catch the now single-file line of cars. Nothing seemed amiss with the car. The blow had hit only sheet metal and roll cage. He was still a contender.

Seeing the crash, Camber and Brennan had sprung into action, collecting tools to try to get Romney Marsh back in the race. The safety truck slowly pushed Marsh's disabled car down pit lane toward Camber and Brennan. When the truck deposited the battered race car in front of them, Brennan went to work, hammering the crumpled hood with a sledge hammer, in an attempt to get it down far enough to enable Romney to see over it.

Camber took down the window net, and stuck his head in the car. "Stay ready!" he yelled at Marsh. "Caution laps don't count in these short races. If we can get you back out before they go green again, you will just start at the back."

Marsh nodded that he understood, and, without waiting for a further response from the driver, Camber took a reciprocating saw to the front bumper that was pushed down so far it was dragging the ground.

Brennan squatted down beside him to minimize the shouting. "There's no water anywhere!"

Camber nodded and smiled. That was a good sign. It meant that he radiator was intact, so that the patch job would be a quick fix to get him back on track. With the driver's visibility restored and no car parts dragging on the race track, he was ready to go back out. Camber put up the window net and motioned for Romney Marsh to head back onto the track with all deliberate speed.

As he prepared for the restart, Fr. Frankie looked up at the scoreboard. Lap 10. Forty laps to go. Okay, so far.

The cars were now single file on track: Travis Prichard, Fr. Spillane, Agnes Hill-Radnor, Paul Whitcomb, Stephen Albright, Andrew Scarberry, Rick Cunningham, Bill Bartlett, and finally Romney Marsh, whose car looked naked in front, having been relieved of its bumper, grill, and front fenders.

The crowd stood to watch the restart. The pace car peeled off the track, and Travis led the line of cars back up to full speed. After four laps, Agnes felt a spurt of courage and decided that Fr. Frankie was holding her back. Ever since the restart, she had been following him closely. Coming off turn four she pulled her car to the inside, and tried to get past him. She only made it up to his rear tires before she had to brake for the entry of turn one. In order to avoid a collision, she was forced to give up on her attempt to pass. She would have to make it up at least to the level of his door to ensure that he would see her underneath him in the turn.

On the next lap, she tried it again, this time closing the gap a little more, but the straightaway was not long enough to enable her to complete the maneuver, and again she fell in behind Fr. Frankie.

They had settled into the rhythm of racing now, and they were starting to try out their newly-learned driving skills. Andrew Scarberry pulled out of line, and tried to out-brake Stephen Albright going into the turn. He hadn't quite made it to Albright's door when Albright started coming down the track, arching his turn. A panicked Scarberry tried to avoid hitting him, but his car had too much momentum. The rear of Albright's car slid sideways after the impact, slowing dramatically as Albright managed to save it from going into the wall. Albright hit the gas once he was pointed in the right direction, but he wasn't soon enough to prevent a collision. Rick Cunningham slammed into him from behind, which actually helped him get the car back up to speed but, unfortunately, the crash bent Cunningham's car into a large chrome-and-steel V.

There was no caution.

Fr. Frankie saw that he was slowly losing ground to Travis Prichard. Trying to remain calm, he began to chant Camber's mantra: "Be smooth. Be smooth." Idly, he wondered how one would render that phrase in Latin, but before he could summon up the correct word, he heard the sound of a motor over his, and he shot a look to his left to see Agnes's hood creeping past him. He ran the high line through the turn, a position he had not yet taken in the race. Agnes flew past Fr. Frankie, successfully completing the pass as they swept by the flag stand for the twentieth time. A few laps later, the race leader Travis Prichard caught up with Romney Marsh's damaged car, to put him a lap down. Now that he was all alone, Romney Marsh was running the middle of the track, often drifting from side to side. Eying the wobbly disaster in front of him, Travis decided that he would just have to think a prayer, pick a side, and get by him fast. Seconds later, Travis was aiming low to pass on the inside, when Marsh made a sudden jerk to the left, forcing Travis to change directions. Fortunately his reflexes were still sharp, and he made the adjustment in time, passing Marsh easily on the outside.

Paul Whitcomb and Andrew Scarberry had been running nose to tail for several laps now, and the crowd was paying close attention, sensing a duel in the making. The flag man held out crossed flags, indicating that the race was at the half-way point: 25 laps to go.

Agnes, still in the second position, slowed to safely pass the disabled Marsh. When she had cleared him, she looked ahead just as Rick Cunningham cut off Travis Prichard, sending them both into the wall.

The move on Cunningham's part had been unintentional. He had been having a hard time seeing over the raised hood from his previous wreck, and he had not noticed Travis Prichard's car passing him to the outside. Agnes checked up in time, and, followed by Fr. Frankie and then the rest of the field, she safely navigated past the wrecked cars. The pace car pulled in front of the field directly ahead of Agnes, indicating she was now the new leader of the race.

Inside the stalled car, Travis Prichard lowered his window net to show that he was all right, so that the track safety truck could check to make sure that Cunningham had not been injured in the mishap. Cunningham's car got the worst of it, crossing Prichard's nose and smashing head on into the wall. Steam and fluids poured from its battered front end.

The track workers assisted an unsteady Cunningham from his car. Disoriented, he started to stagger toward the pits, when a track worker steered him back in the other direction, into a waiting ambulance. Finally regaining his bearings, he gave the anxious crowd a wave, and disappeared into the ambulance

Relieved to see that Cunningham was all right, Travis nursed his battered car back to the pits. His steering wheel had been damaged: it turned 45 degrees to the right while the car was going straight. The wreck must have knocked the front wheels out of alignment.

From his vantage point on pit road, Camber looked out at Cunningham's wrecked car, and knew right away that this crash would put him out of the race. Even if he could repair the damage quickly, he doubted that Cunningham would want to climb back in a race car anytime soon.

A few feet away, Brennan already had the hood up on Prichard's car, trying to determine how well he could get the toe adjusted, so that Prichard could continue. The caution would be a long one, because the track safety guys had to get Cunningham's car off the track, when it wouldn't even roll. Then they had to dry up all the spilled fluids with oil dry. All that time-consuming activity should give them enough time to get the adjustment close to perfect. All they had to do was loosen two bolts and start spinning the tie-rod until both wheels were pointed in roughly the same direction. Two good mechanics was all a team needed at a short track race 90% of the time.

"I wish I'd had help this good back when I was racing," said Travis.

"Thanks," said Camber. "You're good to go." He secured the hood and waved Prichard back on to the race track. Then he looked down the line of cars: Hill-Radner, Spillane, Whitcomb, Scarberry, Albright, Bartlett, and Prichard. Where was Marsh?

Camber turned and saw the disabled racer of Romney Marsh lumbering down pit road. He rushed to the window. "What's wrong?"

Romney Marsh pulled off his helmet. "Well, I'm a lap down anyhow," he said. "And after seeing Cunningham's car get turned into scrap metal, I just decided to pull in and watch the rest of the race from the safety of the pits."

Camber nodded. "No problem." At this point he just hoped at least one of them actually finished this race.

On this restart it was Agnes's turn to bring the shortened line of cars up to race speed. She had managed a comfortable lead in front of Fr. Frankie, and now she was content to settle into a grove to wind down the laps.

As the race resumed, Travis Prichard was using due caution to see if his car was still race worthy. He kept pace with Rev.

Bartlett easily enough, but he waited a few laps before setting him up to pass as they were going down the back stretch.

Scarberry was now running side by side with Whitcomb, trying to take over the third spot. Scarberry, who had the preferred inside line going into the turn, made the pass stick, pulling in front of Whitcomb.

Agnes held the lead. She had a totally clear race track in front of her, and at least three car lengths back to Fr. Frankie. It looked like smooth sailing, but suddenly, in the oscillating hum of the motor, she heard voices. "GGGEEETTT OOOUUUTTT. GGGEEETTT OOOUUUTTT NNNOOOWWW."

Get out? She glanced at the Bible verse taped to the dash board. It was the usual one: Psalm 91:11 *For He shall give His angels charge over thee to keep thee in all thy ways.* If you're going to put your trust in a guardian angel, then you'd better listen when he tries to tell you something. That's what faith was all about: trust and listening.

And she was in the lead, too. Oh, well ... With a sigh of resignation, Agnes waved her arm, as Camber had instructed her to do, signaling everyone behind that something was wrong, and that she was about to slow down. She stood on the brakes hard, and dropped the car off the banking onto the apron. She coasted into pit road not knowing what was wrong, but certain that something was.

Gabriel Powers, the owner of the car Agnes was driving, shook his head sorrowfully, as his seemingly perfect race car gave up the lead to come down pit road. That move cost him several thousand dollars of the owner's bonus, but he conquered his disappointment. At least she was all right. She had avoided a wreck. He could be thankful for that.

When Agnes pulled off the track, the crowd rumbled with confusion and dismay. Pajan turned to the track official beside her. "What's going on?"

The official shook his head. Nobody knew.

As Agnes steered toward the pit box, Camber and Gabe ran to her side. Even before they pulled down the window net, they saw that Agnes was frozen, wide-eyed with terror. Now she knew what the matter was.

"What is it? What's wrong with the car?" asked Gabe.

Barely moving, Agnes inclined her head toward the passenger side of the car.

"Is it the brakes?' asked Gabe. "The steering mechanism?"

Camber touched his arm. "Look on the passenger side floor."

Gabe poked in head farther into the driver's window so that he could see past Agnes's helmet. Then he saw it: in the hot floor of the car was a fat, coiled copperhead, glaring at them through yellow-slitted eyes. Camber's first thought was to reach in and pull Agnes out as fast as he could, but every time he reached in the car to release her seatbelts, the snake stiffened and raised its head, daring him to make another move. Agnes was wearing driving boots and a fire suit, but Camber was sure that a copperhead's fangs could easily penetrate either of those fabrics. Maybe they should leave Agnes where she was and focus on removing the serpent.

"Keep her calm," Camber told Gabe. "Just don't either of you move."

He grabbed the dry-erase board that was hung on the concession stand wall to display menu items. Wiping the board across the leg of his firesuit, he took the marker and wrote out a message in gigantic letters.

Out on the track, Travis was working his way back through the pack, having just passed Bill Bartlett. He had much more confidence in his car now. It seemed to be holding together just fine. As he came out onto the front straightaway, he saw Camber leaning over the inside wall, holding a white sign board, and pointing at his car. As he flashed by, the words registered on his brain for an instant before they went out of focus, but it took a moment for him to make sense of them. "PIT NOW! SNAKE!" Pit Now. A green flag pit stop would cost him the race and two million dollars. Was this some kind of stupid joke about his faith? A gimmick to ensure that one of the more orthodox religions got the money? Surely, Camber wouldn't do that. He treated all of them the same. Besides ... why had Agnes dropped out of the lead and pitted with a perfectly sound race car?

Snake.

Pit now.

Travis Prichard pulled into pit road.

Travis handed his helmet to Camber and slid out of his car window with practiced ease. "What's going on?"

"Over here," said Camber, ushering him to the passenger side window of Agnes Hill-Radnor's car. She was still behind the wheel, motionless, but through the helmet visor they could see tears glistening on her cheeks.

Travis gave Camber a puzzled look and then looked where Camber was pointing— down at the floorboards, where the copperhead was watching Agnes with its unblinking stare.

Travis closed his eyes and took a deep breath. After a few moments of silent prayer, he slowly reached in and grabbed the snake just below the head, while it was looking toward the still frozen driver. As soon as he had it, Gabe Powers loosened the belts and hauled the now sobbing Agnes from the car.

In Travis's grip the snake writhed and thrashed its tail. "What do you want me to do with it?" he shouted to Camber.

Brennan appeared with an empty tool box: its tools were now scattered over the ground behind the infield wall. "In here!"

Travis dropped the snake into the tool box and Brennan slammed the lid.

"How the devil did it get into her car?" Travis asked Camber.

Camber shrugged. "That'd be my guess." He didn't want to talk about the threat.

The race wasn't over yet. When Agnes had been led away by Gabe Powers, Camber turned his attention back to the still circling cars of Spillane, Scarberry, Whitcomb, Albright, and

Bartlett. He knew that the snake in Agnes's car, like the loose spark plug wires, were the work of whoever had threatened him before the race. He wondered if there were any other little surprises left in store. With both Travis and Agnes out of contention, it looked as if Scarberry just might pull it off, which would solve the problem of the threat toward him, but that didn't mean he was happy about it.

Camber had been silently cheering each time Scarberry made a pass, knowing that his success meant he was one step closer to having his life back. According to the scoreboard, this was lap 45. In a couple of minutes it would all be over.

Camber slipped away from pit lane, knowing there was nothing he could do for anyone now. Slowly, he climbed the ladder to watch the final laps from his usual vantage point on the roof of the concession stand.

Fr. Frankie was in the lead, but with each succeeding lap he had given up ground to Scarberry, so that now they ran nose to tail. Camber held his breath as Scarberry pulled to Fr. Frankie's inside. Side by side they went through the turns, trading the advantage back and forth like a tennis match. As the white flag signaled the last lap, the cars of Fr. Frankie and Andrew Scarberry were still running side by side.

Only seconds more to go. Camber closed his eyes, and tried to think of a prayer. He had intended to say something like, "Please let Scarberry win, so that the guy who fixed this race won't trash my life," but then he heard himself say, "Just give it to Fr. Frankie, Lord. He needs that day care center. I guess I can handle whatever comes next."

As he opened his eyes, Camber heard the roar of the crowd over the sound of the now coasting down motors.

It was over.

Chapter Eighteen
The Rising of the Moon

The race was over.

For the first time since he climbed behind the wheel tonight, Fr. Frankie allowed himself to look up at the crowd, haloed in the flickers of flash bulbs. He held a hand out the window, waving in acknowledgement and gratitude. Someone reached in and handed him the checkered flag, and he roared off again on the victory lap.

No other sport has such a formalized celebration by the winner. The victory lap around the track is a chance for the driver to slow down and to savor the meaning of the victory, and finally to notice the well-wishers celebrating with him. Fr. Frankie timed his silent prayer to last the length of that one lap before he pulled to a stop back at the start finish line. He did not indulge in a smoke-filled burnout, or in the sliding jaunt through the infield grass as Cup drivers often do. Excessive pride was a sin. Besides, Fr. Frankie figured that since he had made it this far, he wouldn't tempt fate by showing off in a borrowed car. This mechanical steed had served him well, and he had every intention of giving it back to its rightful owners in one piece.

Jesús Segovia was one of the first spectators to reach the car. Even better than his exuberant congratulations was the help he offered in exiting the car, because after the fifty-lap race Fr. Frankie discovered that his legs felt like rubber when he tried to put weight on them. When he was on solid ground again, Jesús handed him the small towel and a bottle of water that he'd had ready, knowing that the padre would need them, whether he finished first or last.

The track's security guard, trying to hold back the rest of the crowd, had opened the gate in the front stretch fence to admit a buxom Miss Judas Grove Speedway, resplendent in her stiletto heels, white shorts, and a halter top. She was teetering under the weight of a giant metal trophy topped by a little brass race car. Next came the onslaught of media to the side of the car, all talking at once, and trying to position Fr. Frankie with the car behind him for a photo op.

In Victory Lane Fr. Frankie's car was engulfed by a sea of celebrants on the front stretch. With a practiced eye for the best camera angles, Miss Judas Grove Speedway presented the trophy, deciding to forego the customary winner's kiss out of respect for a man of the cloth. Then Pajan came forward and presented Fr. Frankie with a four-foot cardboard check, representing the two million dollar prize money. Cameras flashed, recording the check presentation, the trophy presentation, the other drivers congratulating the winner, and various track and local dignitaries jockeying for a piece of the limelight. Fr. Frankie insisted on having Camber in some of the photos.

"I couldn't have done it without you!" he shouted over the din of the crowd.

Meanwhile, track officials had circled the race car in an effort to preserve the integrity of their post-race inspection. The assembled reporters did not take much time in getting their quotes and a few more photos so that they could meet their deadlines for the early edition (although, in the case of the *Judas Grove Tribune*, the deadline was Wednesday or so.) When the journalists finished, Fr. Frankie received handshakes, pats on the back, and even hugs from jubilant well-wishers.

In the roar of celebration, Fr. Frankie heard the low rumble of Travis Prichard's voice, and felt a heavy hand on his sore shoulder. "You won it fair and square, Francis. I guess we got the answer we were all wondering about." Travis spoke close to Fr. Frankie's ear in order to make himself heard.

Fr. Frankie smiled. "Camber proved to be an honest man, for which I thank heaven. You know, Travis, I believe I'm as grateful for that as I am for the gift of the victory. But now I'd hardly say I won the race entirely fair and square. Wasn't it you there pulling out of contention in order to save poor Agnes from the snake, and I thank heaven for the gift of that, as well. Somebody had to save her, and I wasn't fancying meself in the role of St. Patrick."

"The snake." Travis Prichard scowled. "I wish I knew who did that, and if that particular stunt was for my benefit. I have a little love offering for whoever it was that was trying to play God. It's shut up in a tool box on pit road, if he ever shows his face."

"Well, Jesús and I have a bit of an idea who was behind the mischief, but we haven't the proof. Sometimes divine retribution is a comforting thought, isn't it? Still and all, that was a brave and noble thing you did, Travis, and it shouldn't have cost you your hope of a new church. I know that your project will cost more than the fifty thousand participation money you're set to get." Fr. Frankie shook Travis' hand. "You know, in good conscience, two million dollars is more than we need to start our day care center. I was thinking that we could spare enough money to buy the materials to help you build that new church you were racing for. And, you know, half the construction workers in town are in my flock, so I'm thinking St. Jude's could lend a hand on the labor side, too, just to make sure you get your church."

"Now that is a blessing I can't refuse, Father." Travis said, smiling as the crowd began to envelop him.

"I think the others will be all right. They each get fifty thousand, which should put them well along toward their respective projects. Except perhaps for Agnes's angel institute."

Travis Prichard smiled. "Did you see her with Gabriel after I took the snake out of the car? It looked to me like she'd found her angel."

"I've also suggested to Pajan that as executrix of the estate she should allocate some of the money to cover Camber's court costs and fines. We couldn't have done this without him, and he deserves at least that much for his hard work."

Travis Prichard nodded. "Couldn't agree more."

"Padre! Padre!"

Fr. Frankie looked around to see three of his youngest parishioners pressed against the fence, swooping toy race cars through the air, and laughing.

"Muchas gracias, mis hijos!" He called out, giving them a wave.

"Congratulations Father," Camber said, appearing with Pajan Mosby at his side. "I was afraid your engine might have been hurt there at the end. I wasn't sure that you could hold off Scarberry."

Fr. Frankie winked. "One thing I learned from horse racing: you don't show your speed until the home stretch. Then you give it all hell, so to speak. I thank you for your patience and your faith, Camber. And not least for resisting a mighty temptation."

Camber froze. "You knew?"

Fr. Frankie smiled. He was leaning against a gold and wooden trophy almost as tall as he was. "Well, I knew that there was more being tested tonight than the mettle of the cars. So what is next for you?"

Before Camber could attempt an answer, Stoney Westcott in uniform and scowling emerged from the crowd, and gripped his elbow. "I waited as long as I could, Camber, but I'm going to have to arrest you. Someone called in an anonymous tip, and we found this bag of drugs in the trunk of your car."

To Brennan Morgan the scene in Victory Lane looked frozen, as if someone had pressed "pause" on some cosmic remote control. There was the uniformed deputy, mournfully holding up a small plastic bag of white powder, and facing him was Pajan Mosby, gaping in horror. Several of the onlookers mirrored her shocked stare, but, when Brennan looked over at Camber, he saw something that disturbed him even more. Camber showed no surprise at all. His face registered weariness, and a crumpled look of misery—but he didn't seem *surprised.*

Brennan barely had time to register these thoughts before the moment passed and everyone started talking at once.

Pajan got in the first response. Brennan's impression was that she usually did.

"What's this all about, Stoney?" she said, much more loudly than she needed to, considering that she was about six inches from his face. "Is this a joke? Are you accusing Camber of drug use? That's preposterous."

The deputy looked considerably more ill at ease than arresting officers did on television. "No joke." He indicated the plastic bag. "Sorry, Pajan. I hate it just as much as you do, but we did find this evidence in the trunk of Camber's car. Someone phoned in an anonymous tip a little while ago. Sheriff's on his way back from the lake."

"But this is absurd!" said Pajan. "I can vouch for him. I've spent the last two weeks monitoring him, and he's been a model prisoner. This is a frame-up. Camber, I'll defend you."

"I thought you didn't have your law degree yet," said Camber, in tones of one who is simply making an observation.

Fr. Frankie stepped out of the winners circle, and thrust his prize trophy at Brennan. "Excuse me, could you hold this for me, lad? Thanks."

As Brennan struggled to regain his balance without dropping the unwieldy hunk of brass-coated aluminum, he saw a smiling Fr. Frankie saunter up to the deputy with an outstretched hand. He seemed so nonchalant that Brennan wondered if the priest realized what was going on. "Could I see your wee bag of evidence there for a moment, Stoney? I'll give it right back to you, word of honor."

The young deputy appeared to be so befuddled by this request from one of the local authority figures that he handed over the bag without a murmur. "No funny business, though, Father Spillane," he said. "It's evidence .We've got him dead to rights with this."

"To be sure," said Fr. Frankie, as calmly as ever, peering at the contents of the little bag.

As Brennan peeked over the top of the little brass race car atop the trophy, he saw the priest open the plastic bag, thrust his finger into the white powder, and then place a bit of it on the tip of his tongue. A moment later he smiled up at the deputy, and said, "Well, this is a fine thing. I don't suppose you'd have a doughnut about your person, would you, Stoney? I only ask what with you being a *garda* and all."

Stoney blinked, confused by the unfamiliar word and the priest's jubilant attitude. He looked warily at the assortment of faces before him, trying to determine if the situation was a prank at his expense.

A still twinkling Fr. Frankie held out the bag to the deputy. "Here. You might try a bit of it for yourself, man. It would go a treat on doughnuts. Did you say you had any?"

Conscious of all eyes upon him, Stoney blushed to the hairline, but he inserted a tentative finger into the powder and brought it to his lips. "It's...tastes like ... well ... *powdered sugar?"*

Fr. Frankie nodded. "So it is."

The ripple of laughter from the crowd made Stoney blush again, but he maintained his dignity. "Well, but that doesn't prove anything. Big time drug dealers cut their narcotics with all sorts of household substances. Powdered sugar is one of them. Well known fact."

"Yes, but if there was cocaine in the mix, you'd feel a numbing sensation on your tongue."

Stoney's eyes narrowed suspiciously. "And how would you know that?"

Fr. Frankie shrugged. "This isn't my first parish, and there weren't any angels in my last one."

"That's still not proof. It needs to be tested."

"Test it then, man. Send it off to a lab straightaway. I think you'll find it's all powdered sugar. And I don't think you'll find Camber Berkley's fingerprints on that bag, either. That's what I think. I have the untrammeled faith of a blessed saint with four aces and a wild card."

"Amen," said Travis Prichard.

Stoney still looked doubtful. "But we got an anonymous tip. Fella said there were drugs in the trunk of Camber's car, and sure enough we found this bag."

"Well, there you have a real crime," said Pajan. "How would anybody know what was in his trunk? What you're saying is that somebody was breaking and entering into Camber's private property. He does have constitutional rights, you know, even if he is a prisoner. And, unless you had a warrant, I think you have some illegal search and seizure going on here, too, Stoney. Even if you had found the body of Jimmy Hoffa in Camber's trunk, you couldn't use the evidence in court. As it is, you found..." she sneered, "*Powdered sugar.*"

"The lab will tell us if it's plain powdered sugar or not," said Stoney, determined to defend his dignity in the face of overwhelming opposition.

"Well, if you want to detain Camber on the suspicion of possession of sucrose, I will help him draw up a lawsuit against the county for false arrest, harassment, and anything else I can think of. I'm sure he could use the money."

Behind the trophy, Brennan stirred uneasily. Pajan's hectoring tone was just making the cop more entrenched in his position, and more determined to make his case. Somebody who was not given to sarcasm and one-upmanship ought to defuse the situation before Camber ended up in even more trouble. As usual, that somebody would be him.

Brennan set down the trophy and stepped forward. "Excuse me, officer," he said in his meekest tones. "But do you have a field test kit for drugs?"

Stoney squinted in his direction.

"I'm Brennan Morgan, sir. I have friends on the police force back in Mooresville, and they said something about carrying kits in their squad cars to test for drugs. I just wondered if you happened to have one."

"Well ... yeah. We just got one in. I haven't had a chance to use it yet. We were supposed to go to a workshop over in Knoxville ..."

"Perhaps I could assist you?"

Only the excitement of victory and then the imminent threat of arrest could have made the assembly overlook the sleek gentleman in the white linen suit who had just approached them. His coppery tan and tennis-toned limbs gave no sign of advancing years, but he had probably been forty for the last two decades. It was his style as much as anything else that marked his generation: a certain overly-formal 1920's-stye elegance not fashionable with people who really were the age that he appeared to be. The same subtle cues marked his nationality—his English was too perfect, too carefully precise to belong to a native speaker.

Stoney scowled at the stranger. "Who are you?"

"Allow me to introduce my father, Stoney," said Jesús quickly. "You remember, I told you my parents were flying up to collect me."

"Juan Carlos Enrique Segovia, CEO of Segovia Pharmaceuticals," said Jesús's father, producing a crisp, white business card. "My PhD. is in biochemistry, from Stanford University. So, you see, I am fortunate to have experience in areas that are broadly related to the drug testing you were discussing. That is, I am engaged in the development of new antibiotics, but I would be happy to assist you in this small matter of chemistry. May I see the test kit?"

"I'll go get it," said Stoney.

Camber tapped Jesús on the arm. "I thought you said your father was a drug dealer."

Jesús smiled. "My family says that I have a puckish sense of humor. And may I also present to you my mother? She is a homemaker."

"How do you do?" said the regal looking woman, who, without being made-up or over-dressed for the occasion, still managed to look like a queen on her day off. She seemed to be composed entirely of precious metals, from the soft bronze sheen of her hair to the coppery glow of her tan, to the shining gold links of the necklace at her slender throat.

Camber's eyes widened. "You're ... not a homemaker, are you?" he said at last.

She had a silvery laugh. "Jesús is entirely too fond of saying so. It is his favorite joke, to make a play with English words. I am an architect, and I specialize in designing very large upscale houses, so, technically, I am indeed a home maker."

"And when you came here to get Jesús ..."

Her lips twitched into a carefully-subdued smile, and she nodded, "Gulfstream jet. Juan Carlos is very proud of his prowess as a pilot."

Camber blinked, still trying to readjust his assumptions. "You know, Jesús and I were in jail together for a day or two. And we all thought—"

"I'm sure you did. It is another of my son's little jokes. He says it is easier to judge someone's character if they think themselves superior to you. Most people are nice to the rich. But to the poor—not so much."

"There are a lot of people around here testing my character," muttered Camber. He turned back to Jesús. "I thought you were a car thief."

Jesús's eyes sparkled with mischief. "I know. It was most entertaining. And very kind of you not to hold it against me."

"So what do you really do? Anything?"

"Oh, yes. I told you the truth, essentially. I purchase damaged luxury cars, take them back home, and restore them. We do a good business in car sales, quite legal. That, too, is entertaining."

"So much for getting a line on a cheap car," said Camber.

Jesús shrugged. "I can give you a good price on a Maserati."

"But why did you stay in jail for even five minutes? I'll bet the Mexican ambassador would have come in person if you had called him."

"I'm sure he would. He has a daughter that … well, never mind. I had a little adventure, and I met people I would not have otherwise encountered. I enjoyed myself. And this race—I would not have missed it for anything. I am so happy that Father Frankie has won. By way of congratulations, I hope to persuade my wonderful mama to design a magnificent day care center for him."

Señora Segovia sighed and shook her head. "Only if you promise to behave for five minutes, Jesús. Let us talk to Father Francis, and see what can be done."

Stoney had returned with the drug testing kit, and he was insisting that he and Señor Segovia read the directions before testing the powder.

"But it is really quite uncomplicated," Señor Segovia said.

"You put the little stick into the substance, and it turns colors. See, there is a chart on your instructions."

Finally, when Stoney had read through the directions aloud—twice—he conceded that the directions really did seem foolproof, and with great ceremony, Juan Carlos Enrique Segovia inserted the testing stick into the white powder. While the little crowd of bystanders watched, they waited twice the recommended time for the result.

"Okay, it didn't turn blue," said Stoney, announcing the obvious.

"Then you're not pregnant," Brennan said—not quietly enough.

Stoney glared at him, but Señor Segovia laughed at the joke. "That, too, no doubt," he acknowledged. "But I think we may say conclusively that the substance in question does not contain narcotics. It is—to use the vernacular—powdered sugar."

"It was probably a prank, Stoney," said Fr. Frankie soothingly. "I'm sorry someone ruined your evening. But you are to be commended for your diligence."

"But why would—"

"Somebody broke into my car," said Camber.

"Don't push it," said Fr. Frankie, patting his arm. "No harm done. Your car is as good as ... well ... the poor thing could hardly be in any worse shape now, could it? I expect you could break into it with a toothpick."

Stoney looked wary, as if he suspected that something was being put over on him, although he couldn't pinpoint exactly what it was. Fortunately, in a rare burst of tact, Pajan salvaged his ego by expressing great interest in the testing kit, and the Segovias joined them in the discussion.

Grateful for the momentary distraction, Camber turned to Fr. Frankie. "But I don't understand. So some guy planted *fake* drugs in my car?"

"Oh, no," said Fr. Frankie, careful to keep his voice down. "He planted the genuine article right enough."

"Then what happened?"

The night before the Faster Pastor race … It was past midnight, and all had been quiet for hours in the little town of Judas Grove. Above the mountains, the full moon floated between wreaths of clouds, illuminating the otherwise dark streets and buildings.

"I don't see what good it does to wear dark clothing when the moon is blazing away like a spotlight up there," said Rick Cunningham. "And I'm not putting that grease stuff on my face, either. Y'all have been watching too many war movies."

"We'd just as soon not get caught in the act of breaking and entering," In the dim light of the parked van, only Travis Prichard's eyes were visible. The rest of him was shrouded in greasepaint and a hunter's camouflage outfit. "And keep your voice down, Cunningham. You'll set every dog in town to barking."

"It's not breaking and entering, surely?" said Bill Bartlett. "After all, Travis, you work here."

"But it's not my car we're breaking into."

"Breaking into is such a harsh and unforgiving term," said a voice in the darkness. "Let us rather think of it as restoring order to already-vandalized property, señores."

"Well, here's hoping the angels are on our side, boys, because I'd hate to explain this to the boys in khaki."

Rick Cunningham laughed. "If you wanted the angels on our side, Father, you should have brought Agnes along."

"Leave her to heaven," said Jesús. It was a line from hamlet, but he didn't think anyone would notice. They had other things on their minds.

The weedy back lot of Farley's Garage had a motion sensor light, but, fortunately, Darrell Farley's concern for the rusting hulks of derelict cars on his property did not extend to equipping the place with electronic alarms or guard dogs. No one had ever broken into the fenced-in lot before, or, if they had, whatever discarded parts they had taken were never missed.

At the moment, the ministerial commandos' chief concern was the disintegrating 1980 white Plymouth RoadRunner belonging to Camber Berkley.

"What is that you're humming, Father?"

"Oh. Sorry. Didn't realize it wasn't just going through my head. It's an old song about the Rising of 1798. Tonight's mission put it into my head." In a soft tenor, he began to sing a verse of the Irish ballad.

Up and tell me, Sean O'Farrell, where the gathering is to be.
In the old spot by the river, right well known to you and me.
One word more: for signal token, whistle up the marching tune,
With your pike upon your shoulder, at the rising of the moon.

"So these men are fishing?" asked Jesús.

"I'm sorry. Fishing? Oh. No, not that kind of pike, Jesús. It's a weapon, like a club. But the song is about a group of fellas who meet at moonrise to engage in covert operations, as they say in the war films."

"That's us," said Rick Cunningham. "So, what happened to them?"

How well they fought for poor old Ireland,
And full bitter was their fate.

Fr. Frankie was silent for a moment. Then he said, "Er, it all went off without a hitch."

"Never mind that," said Bill Bartlett. "Are we sure that the white car belongs to Camber?"

"I'm sure," said Travis Prichard. "I work here, remember?"

"Then couldn't you get the keys?"

"Not without going into the building, which is locked. And I didn't bargain for breaking into it."

"No, no," Jesús assured him. "That will not be required. It is a simple matter to pop the trunk of a car." He sighed. "With a car as old as this poor RoadRunner, just to scrape off the rust might do the trick."

"What if we don't find anything in the trunk?"

"My informant in the matter seemed quite truthful," said Jesús. "I think we must believe him."

"Let's get on with it, Bill. It's too late for what-ifs."

"Yeah," growled Bartlett. "The sooner we get out of here, the better."

Jesús led the way, making a great show of creeping from one derelict car to another, and keeping in the shadows as much as possible. With considerably less grace, his three co-conspirators followed. They crouched behind the trunk of the battered old RoadRunner. Fr. Frankie pulled a flashlight out of the pocket of his windbreaker, and directed the light at the locking mechanism of the trunk.

Jesús leaned in for a closer look. "Shine the light a little over to the side, Padre. The wreck that Camber had may have been a blessing. Just there, por favor—along the line of the closing of the trunk. Gracias. Yes. I thought so. We are lucky."

Travis Prichard peered at the circle of light. "He's right. Look! The wreck twisted the chassis just enough to leave a gap where the trunk should seal."

Jesús nodded. "... Leaving enough room for me to stick a long screwdriver up into the crack and jimmy the latch mechanism."

"Who's got the screwdriver?"

Several anxious minutes later, the trunk flipped open, and Fr. Frankie trained the flashlight on a clear plastic bag resting on top of the spare tire.

Bill Bartlett picked it up. "Is this it?"

"One way to find out," said Jesús. "If it burns when you put it on your tongue, it is drugs."

"You mean we should taste it?" said Fr. Frankie.

"I'll do it," said Travis Prichard. "After all, I'm accustomed to sipping poison in the worship service. I reckon this qualifies."

"A tiny taste will not harm you, my friend," said Jesús, handing the bag to Travis Prichard. "And it is best to make sure."

"I suppose we must," said Bill Bartlett. "For all we know Camber could carry a bag of detergent in his trunk."

"Well, I reckon he doesn't carry arsenic," said Travis, licking his finger and dabbing it into the powder. He touched his fingertip to his tongue, and spat on the ground. "It burns, all right! So that fellow man was telling you the truth, Jesús. Now what?"

"Now we get rid of it," said Fr. Frankie. "Camber cannot be incriminated if we destroy the evidence."

"But suppose the person who planted it comes back to make sure it's still there?"

"Well, that's where forethought comes in. I thought the informant might very well be telling the truth, so I took the precaution of bringing along a substitute." He reached into the pocket of his jacket and brought out another plastic bag, also filled with a white substance. "This bag is a bit larger, but if we fold it over, it should fool someone taking a quick glance."

"It looks the same." Bill Bartlett looked uneasy. "How did you know what to bring?"

"Well, I hedged my bets a bit. In my other pocket there's a bag of rosemary and another one of aspirin. I figured one of them would match the goods."

"And what is in this bag?"

"Powdered sugar. I think I saw it in a film once. It's nice to know they get some things right in the movies, isn't it?"

"We need to hurry," said Travis Prichard. "Just put the bag down there on top of the spare tire, Father, and let's get out of here, before a patrol car comes by."

"By all means, let us depart," said Jesús. "I have no wish to return to your local jail."

"Who's going to tell Camber about this?" asked Rick Cunningham.

Fr. Frankie settled the bag in the hub of the wheel, and stepped back, gazing up at the moon for a few moments. "Why don't we keep this to ourselves, boys?"

Bill Bartlett closed the trunk. "But what if they try to force him to fix the race? If Camber doesn't know that we've removed the threat, he might be tempted..."

They looked at each other.

Finally Rick Cunningham said, "Gentlemen, I think that's what they mean by free will."

"So you knew?" said Camber. "You knew that I had been told to fix the race, and you didn't tell me you had removed the threat. And you didn't try to prevent me from rigging the race? But what if I had?"

Fr. Frankie smiled. "We thought it was important to know the content of your character."

"Why would you want to know that?"

"Oh, not us. We thought it was important for *you* to know that."

"But who planted the drugs? Who wanted to fix the race? I never saw the guy who threatened me."

"We have an idea, but we can't prove it, so perhaps it's best not to ..." He broke off, staring at a figure who had staggered into the circle of light, cradling his right arm against his body.

As the boy stumbled and nearly fell, several people rushed over to him, but he shook them off, and lurched the last few steps toward Stoney Westcott. "I need to report a crime."

Stoney stared at the pale and sweating young man, who seemed a heartbeat away from collapse. "Call 911 for the ambulance," Stoney said to Pajan. He turned back to the tottering youth. "Have you been shot?"

"Naw. Snakebit. Thanks to my daddy!"

Juan Carlos Enrique Segovia leaned close to his son's ear and murmured, "Who is this man?"

"His name is Danny Simpkins," said Jesús. "He worked in the garage with Mr. Prichard, and he helped us with the cars. But his father owns a construction company that employs many laborers *mexicanos*—or Hispanic, anyway. I spoke to one of them on the phone, and so we were warned of the plot to tamper with the race."

Stoney blinked. "Snake bit?"

Danny rolled up his sleeve, revealing a bruised and swollen forearm with two ragged puncture marks just above the wrist. He had wrapped a dirty rag above the bite to act as a makeshift tourniquet. "Yeah, before the race somebody put a snake in Agnes Hill-Radnor's car," said Travis Prichard. "We were going to mention that, before you brought up this whole drug business, Stoney."

"Ambulance is on the way," said Pajan, pocketing her cell phone. "Danny, sit down here on the cooler. You look terrible."

Danny nodded. "So would you if you'd had to pry a copperhead off your arm. And that was a couple of hours ago. I figured it would stop hurting after a while." He glared accusingly at Travis. "It never seemed to bother you, getting snakebit!"

Travis sighed. "It can kill you, Danny, even if you're a believer, which you're not. Why did you do it? Did you want me to lose that bad?"

"It wasn't about you, Travis." Swaying a little, Danny sat down on the ice chest. He squeezed his arm, and winced. "My daddy made me. He's got bank loans coming due in his construction business, and he said he needed the two million dollars to stay afloat."

"But how—" Travis shook his head. "Oh, sure. Construction. If Scarberry had won the race, they'd have hired your dad to do all the work on the First Baptist Church renovation."

"But that was such a long shot, Danny," said Fr. Frankie. "You can't really fix the outcome of a stock car race. Anything can happen."

Danny nodded, dizzy with pain. "I tried to tell him that, but he wouldn't listen. He was awful desperate. He even planted drugs in Camber's car to force him to rig the race, but then he was afraid Camber wouldn't go through with it. Which he didn't. I told him I'd pull the spark plug wires, because that wouldn't get anybody hurt, but Daddy insisted on putting a snake in one of the cars for good measure. He made me do it, and the thing up and bit me!"

They could hear the distant wail of a siren coming up the road to the speedway.

"Where is your dad now, Danny?" asked Stoney.

"I called his cell and told him to meet me at the hospital. I reckon I gotta get this snake bite looked at."

"I'll go with you in the ambulance," said Stoney, motioning to the rescue squad driver. "Come on, Danny. We'll meet up with your dad at the hospital, and I'll take it from there."

Pajan was smiling at Camber. "I knew you didn't do it," she said, giving him a hug. "You know, for a race car driver, you're a pretty nice guy."

"Compared to that thing in the toolbox," muttered Brennan. In a louder voice, he remarked to no one in particular, "You know, we have to be getting back to Mooresville soon. We have that meeting with the bank people, you know."

Before Camber could reply, Juan Carlos Enrique Segovia appeared at his elbow. "You are a race car driver," he said. "I was most impressed with tonight's performance. My son was telling me that you instructed these courageous novices in the art of racing, and that you yourself race cars."

"When he can afford it," said Brennan.

"That brings me to what I wished to discuss. An opportunity of sponsorship. You may have heard that I am CEO of a company. You know, the NASCAR Nationwide Series holds a race in Mexico City, and my son mentioned to me that it might be a good thing for Segovia Pharmaceuticals to sponsor a race car ... Perhaps we could discuss this."

"Mooresville!" wailed Brennan. "Bank meeting!"

"Yeah, Brennan. I'm coming. This won't take long, I promise."

Camber and Señor Segovia turned and walked toward the track, happily discussing cars and business opportunities.

Pajan called after them. "Camber! I thought before you go—"

Camber looked back. "Yeah. Yeah. Don't go. I'll be back in a minute."

With a weary sigh, Brennan sat down beside the trophy.

Fr. Frankie smiled and patted his shoulder. "Never fear, lad. He'll be back. After all, you're his crew chief, aren't you? Have a bit of faith. He won't let you down." He tried to pick up the trophy, but it was nearly as tall as he was, so he deferred the honor to Jesús, who hoisted it easily and escorted

Fr. Frankie away, while Señora Segovia asked about his plans for the day care center.

Brennan and Pajan watched them go, and then turned back to the dark track, where Sr. Segovia and Camber were rounding turn two, still in an animated discussion of racing matters.

Pajan sighed. "Is it always like this with him?'

"Pretty much," said Brennan. "Cars come first, last, and always."

"How do you stand it?"

Brennan shrugged. "Are there any drinks in that cooler? You might as well sit down. It'll be a while." After all, she was a pretty girl, and Brennan figured that he had plenty of time before Camber finished talking business and decided to come back. They rummaged in the melting ice for cans of soda.

"What's that you were saying about a bank meeting?" asked Pajan.

"Oh, it's a business venture that Camber and I are embarking on. Let me tell you about my cylinder heads. But first ..." He smiled happily. "Say, did Camber ever tell you about the time he had to dress as a furry lug nut?"

THE END

Adam Edwards

Race car driver Adam Edwards has driven in the ARCA/RE-MAX national racing series, managed and spotted for a NASCAR Nationwide Series race team, and worked as a race car driving instructor at the Fast Track School of Racing. In 2006 Adam was a contestant on Jeff Hammond's *Ultimate Pit Warrior* reality TV show. A member of the Screen Actors Guild, Adam has appeared regularly in national television commercials with NASCAR Cup drivers, such as Tony Stewart, and Dale Earnhardt, Jr.

A 2002 graduate of Virginia Tech, Adam received his MBA from the university in 2007. He currently works as Administrator of a Long Term Care and Rehabilitation Center in Virginia.

A native of Falls Church City, VA, Adam was always interested in racing and auto mechanics. As a Virginia Tech student, he founded E Squared Racing, assembling a crew of college friends to form a team in the NASCAR Weekly Racing Series Pure Stock Division. After graduation, Adam continued racing, winning Rookie of the Year, and finishing second in championship points at a local speedway. In 2002 Adam worked for the DeWALT division of the Black and Decker Corporation, running show car and fan events at NASCAR Cup races, on job sites, and in front of Lowes and Home Depot stores. He raced his own NASCAR Late Model Truck in a 22-race season, finishing fifth in Championship points, the top owner-driver team.

Moving to Mooresville NC in 2003, Adam began training

with Nextel Cup drivers and crews at Lowes Motor Speedway, learning and drafting with world class drivers. He spent evenings at a state-of-the-art pit crew training facility, honing his skills as a tire changer and carrier and fueler—essential skills later, when he worked on pit crews in the ARCA, Craftsman Trucks, and Busch racing series. In 2004, as general manager of the Busch 16 team of Wayne Day in Goodlettsville, TN, Adam spotted at most of the tracks on the Busch Series Schedule from Bristol to Talladega, while furthering his driving career by competing in the Top Late model division at west Tennessee's Highland Rim Speedway.

As a 2005 spokesperson for the Nation Pit Crew Championship sponsored by Tyson Food, Inc., Adam crisscrossed the country promoting the event, appearing on TV, radio, and in person with NASCAR personalities Larry McReynolds and Jeff Hammond.

In December 2005 Adam tested an ARCA car at Daytona International Speedway for former NASCAR Cup driver and ARCA champion Andy Hillenburg, who hired Adam as an instructor at his Fast Track High Performance Driving School. Adam completed thousands of laps in Cup, Busch, and ARCA style race cars at large super speedways and at local short tracks, working both with novice professional drivers and fan-experience customers. In 2007 he raced in the ARCA/REMAX Series for the team of Andy Belmont Racing.

In the spring of 2006 Adam advised New York Times best-selling author Sharyn McCrumb on her NASCAR novel ***Once Around the Track***. The author and the aspiring race car driver presented programs at area cultural centers, combining their expertise on stock car racing. The partnership worked so well that they collaborated on ***Faster Pastor***.

Sharyn McCrumb

Sharyn McCrumb is an award-winning Southern writer, best known for her Appalachian "Ballad" novels, set in the North Carolina/Tennessee mountains, including the New York Times Best Sellers *She Walks These Hills* and *The Rosewood Casket.*

Her novel *St. Dale,* The Canterbury Tales in a NASCAR setting, in which ordinary people on a pilgrimage in honor of racing legend Dale Earnhardt find a miracle, won a 2006 Library of Virginia Award as well as the AWA Book of the Year Award.

McCrumb, who has been named a "Virginia Woman of History" in 2008 for Achievement in Literature, was a guest author at the National Festival of the Book in Washington, D.C. sponsored by the White House in 2006.

Her other best-selling novels include *The Ballad of Frankie Silver,* the story of the first woman hanged for murder in the state of North Carolina; and *The Songcatcher,* a genealogy in music, tracing the author's family from 18th century Scotland to the present by following a Scots Ballad through the generations. *Ghost Riders,* an account of the Civil War in the mountains of western North Carolina, won the Wilma Dykeman Award for Literature given by the East Tennessee Historical Society and the Audie Award for Best Recorded Book.

McCrumb's other honors include: AWA Outstanding Contribution to Appalachian Literature Award; the Chaffin Award for Southern Literature; the Plattner Award for Short Story; and AWA's Best Appalachian Novel. A graduate of UNC-Chapel Hill, with an M.A. in English from Virginia Tech, McCrumb was the first writer-in-residence at King College in Tennessee. In 2005 she was honored as the Writer of the Year at Emory & Henry College.

Her novels, studied in universities throughout the world, have been translated into ten languages, including German, Dutch, Japanese, and Italian. She has lectured on her work at Oxford University, the University of Bonn-Germany, and at the Smithsonian Institution; taught a writers workshop in Paris, and served as writer-in-residence at King College in Tennessee.

A film of her novel *The Rosewood Casket* is currently in production, directed by British Academy Award nominee Roberto Schaefer.

Her most recent novels is *The Devil Amongst the Lawyers* (Thomas Dunne Books 2010).

Sharyn McCrumb lives and writes near Roanoke, Virginia.

Ingalls Publishing Group, Inc
PO Box 2500
Banner Elk, NC 28604

For the Best in Award-Winning Regional
and National Fiction:
www.ingallspublishinggroup.com

Editorial office:
editor@ingallspublishinggroup.com

Ingalls Publishing Group Books are distributed through Atlas Books. Book stores served by Atlas, Follett, Ingram, and other wholesalers may order IPG Books through their regular channels. However, we are happy to serve libraries, schools and organizations directly, and to offer discounts on book cost and shipping.

Sales office:
bookkeeper@ingallspublishinggroup.com
Phone: 828-898-3801
Fax: 828-898-4930

Atlas Books
30 Amberwood Parkway
Ashland, OH 44805
Phone: 800-Booklog
Fax: 419-281-6883
Email: order@atlasbooks.com